ONE MAN

25th Anniversary Edition

Kerry Johnson

Published by
HARPAZO Publishing, Inc.
10 Pinckney Colony Road, Victoria Building 200
Bluffton, SC 29909

www.HarpazoPublishing.com
www.SeizeTheCulture.com

ONE MAN

First printing: July 1999
First digital publication: March 2011

ISBN 978-1629672564

Cover Art design by Juan Acosta,
www.Behance.net/Juan_Acosta_Art

v25-0617

Acknowledgments

First, thanks must go to my parents, ROBERT H. and ANNE L. LANG. Thank you for staying committed to each other and to the children you made. You gave me an ideal childhood and a message. Next, I need to thank my children, LIZA and LAMAR, for their patience, a costly gift from the very young. Also, my stepchildren, CB and Claire, who maintain an encouraging attitude regarding my curious nocturnal writing habit. Special gratitude goes out to the entire HORN family; REBEKA, for her loving hands and tender heart to my kids while I was upstairs, writing this book, ZARA, for formatting it, GENE and DIANE for cheering me all the long way to publication. Thanks to WILLIE DAVIS, LORETTA DOYLE, JANICE MALAFRONTE, MARGOT H. ROWLAND and JAMES K. WILSON for your insights, also DR. JOHN GRAY, GAYLIC MA, and all the folks who helped with research. TIFFANY JACKSON for sharing her grammatical expertise. GEORGE G. TRASK for his advice. BEVERLY CONEY HEIRICH for blessing me with timely encouragement and expert editing. A lifetime of gratitude to my husband, BARRY L. JOHNSON, for introducing me to *the issues,* for walking *the walk*, and for affording me the common riches of a wife and mother. Eternal thanks to God for creating women equal, but different from men, and for reconciliation through His Son, JESUS CHRIST.

To every committed father
the real-life heroes of their sons and daughters

"See, I will send you the prophet Elijah before the great and dreadful day of the Lord comes. He will turn the hearts of the fathers to their children, and the hearts of the children to their fathers; or else I will come and strike the land with a curse."

Malachi 4:5 (NIV)

Part One

Childhood

Chapter 1

Ruth sat at her kitchenette table, chatting with her good friend over a cup of tea, as her first grandchild was being conceived. Other than that, the day passed as one of no particular consequence.

Earlier, as in ten-thousand days before, the yellow bus had labored down the winding, country road at its usual speed of 40 miles per hour. Then, running out of pavement, it continued on dirt for several minutes before stopping amidst the quiet frenzy of flashing lights. The hinges of the door shrieked as they were forced, ungreased, to swing open one more time. A tall black boy, close to manhood, stepped lightly to the ground, a worn backpack swung behind one shoulder. The pale palm of his hand flashed as he turned and waved to a girl, still aboard.

He walked along a dirt driveway past his grandmother's house in long, graceful strides that indicated only a moderate measure of attitude. A lanky, Lab-type mongrel appeared from beneath the listing porch and slid his head under the boy's right hand. The two fell into step.

"What's happening, Boog?" the boy asked, patting the head.

In truth, the backyard of his grandmother's house was the front yard of his house; a long, white double-wide with red shutters, mounted on a series of cinder block pilings. It was embellished with a modest deck leading up to the front door, and encircled by recently trimmed hedges. His mama insisted on keeping it looking fresh and clean inside and out. The inside never concerned him. That was his mama's realm. But outside work fell to "the man of the house," when the weight of him was barely enough to budge a lawn mower. Now that Abe had moved out, there was Big Mama's yard to keep up with, as well. Joab liked to picture his own home in his mind, the one that he would own someday. The details of the house were always obscured by a yard that proclaimed sweet neglect.

Joab took the deck stairs three at a time, unlocked the door, and stepped into the dark, cool quiet of home. He dumped his backpack on the dining room table, switched on the TV and hit the fridge.

After a large helping of last night's beef stew, microwaved to perfection, Joab clicked on the TV, rotating between VH1, BET, and ESPN. On the sports channel, an Italian-looking commentator enthused over the recent history of football while running the highlights. Alone in the house, Joab thundered expletives over this tackle or that awesome catch. Ah, here were clips of his current favorite team, the New York Giants. And here was the great Lawrence Taylor mashing some poor slob into the ground. Joab figured Lawrence Taylor was just about his favorite football star ever. He wondered if the man had happened to have been in Savannah, Georgia around April of 1973. It was a game Joab began playing when he was just a skinny kid. Since his mother would not disclose to him anything about his father, other than, "he was big and fine looking," theoretically, his father could be just about any African American close to his mother's age. And since his father was entirely theoretical, Joab could, kind of, pick whomever he wanted. This week it was definitely the great Lawrence Taylor.

At 5:30, Joab spread his homework out across the dining room table and changed the channel to MTV because it was only mildly distracting and his mother couldn't abide it. When Ruth walked in at 6:12, it appeared as though he'd been pouring over school assignments for hours.

"How can you think with that noise on?" Ruth asked, cutting the power after hanging her keys on the rack beside the door.

"Can I have the car tonight?"

"How did you do on the math test?"

"I don't know. She hasn't graded them yet. I think I did fine. Can I?"

"Sure." Ruth said, and bent over to give her son a kiss on the cheek. "I already asked Edna if she could give me a lift."

"Thanks, Mama."

"What time's it start?"

"Probably around eight. Depends on when JV finishes up. I've got to be there in an hour."

Ruth was relieved the football season was over and he was into basketball again. After a broken leg in his sophomore year, Ruth would never again be truly able to enjoy his football games. Basketball was a different story. It was fast and exciting and infinitely less dangerous than that clashing of bodies on the football field. Then, too, basketball was played indoors, safely beyond the reach of thirsty no-see-ums. Ruth figured she'd donated gallons of blood to the cursed creatures since Joab first put on his Pee-Wee uniform back in fifth grade. It was a true test of love and pride to willingly offer your flesh to swarming gnats in order to holler for your boy.

Over the years, Ruth had prepared and delivered thousands of hot dogs from the concession stand, sold many hundreds of booster club tickets, driven untold miles in team buses, and had even been known to change a tire or two. Teachers and coaches alike knew they could always count on Ruth Johnson in a pinch.

Through it all, Ruth remained covertly untouched by the fires of genuine fanhood. She could have lived quite happily in a universe void of athletic events, were it not for her son. Early on, Ruth had recognized the invaluable worth of sports in a fatherless home. The experience, for Joab, had been worth every hot dog, every mile, every gnat bite. His role models, for the most part, were athletes. He had formed rich relationships with two coaches, in particular, who had taken a special interest in the boy. More than once, Ruth was thankful for access to male perspective on a current crisis.

And now he is seventeen. With most of high school behind him, Ruth relaxed a bit into the notion that the worst of adolescence had been weathered.

"God is faithful," she often repeated when the thought crossed her mind again.

✦ ✦ ✦

Ruth's estimation of tip-off time was right on as usual. When she and Edna walked into the white brightness of halogen light, the varsity boys were already warming up to the violent notes of heavy metal played over two pairs of speakers left sizzling by the preceding decade of hightop warriors.

On their way to the "faithful parent" section of over-crowded bleachers, the two ladies passed the freshman section and the upperclassmen section where an attractive young woman shot up a hand and shouted an enthusiastic "Hello, Ms. Johnson!" Ruth ignited a warm smile and nodded. By the time they had settled in and made appropriate greetings to their fellow booster club members, the guest team had been introduced and the home starters were making their entrance.

". . . playing forward and measuring six feet, five inches," sputtered the speakers, "a junior at St Paul's Academy, Joab Johnson."

Ruth was always amused at Joab's larger-than-life introduction as she knew that the boy stood only a hair over six-four. He touched hands with the opposing coach and jogged center court.

Joab's mind raced over the last time his team met the Cougars on the planks. His own team, the Tidal Waves, had been at an immediate disadvantage as they were, on that occasion, the visiting team. He remembered watching the first string hold the score to a spread of three. The lead switched hands three times per quarter, until the last, when the Cougars pulled ahead and kept on going. There was little hope for a victory when his coach pulled the starters long enough to let the second and third strings have a taste of real, high-pressure court time.

Joab made himself a silent pledge while waiting for the tip-off. *Tonight, the outcome will be much different. Tonight the Tidal Waves will dominate.*

Glen tipped it his way and the game exploded. He heard a smack as the soles of his own Adidas slammed the court under the weight of a young man who had just sunk a deft, reverse layup and scored the first points.

The voices of the home fans rose in common crescendo and, as though on command, Joab's body responded with a wash of adrenaline.

Ha! This is shaping up to be a hell-of-a-game! he thought, *And tonight I am first string. Tonight I can win the victory! Well, anyway, me - and my teammates.*

On this night, Joab could not miss. Comfortable on his home court, with the boys he'd grown up with, fingertips thoughtlessly sensing the perfect measure of touch or spin to drop the orange ball through the rope lace beneath the hole. Joab was alive with the consummate balance of challenge and confidence. His body did not fail him; after so many years of practice it was made to obey the desire of his heart. There was not the faintest awareness that moments like these were finite, not the most fleeting consideration that his body might someday peak and then embark upon the slow decline of adulthood. The game, the night, belonged to the Tidal Waves and the Tidal Waves belonged to Joab.

At the sound of the buzzer, Ruth took a note of the final score and made her way down to the court in the flow of people. After the teams had observed the hollow formality of the "good game" handshake, Joab sought out his mother to offer the sweaty hug.

"I sure enjoyed that one, son," she spoke into his ear as she patted the back arched down over her. "Have a good time. Don't be too late."

"I won't."

"Don't forget to wear your seat belts."

"We won't," came the assurance over his shoulder. He was headed for the shower.

Several parents offered compliments or congratulations as Ruth and Edna made their way to the exit. Edna's son had graduated last year, but she still enjoyed a good game and was glad to accompany Ruth almost anywhere. They were near the door when Anita caught up with them.

"Hey, Ms. Johnson. He played a super game, huh?" She said.

"He sure did. That was one to remember."

"I don't think he missed but one shot," she gushed.

Ruth recollected at least three but did not correct Nita's misconception.

"I reckon a celebration's in order," Ruth teased.

The girl smiled and shrugged.

"Well, y'all have a fine time, but don't be too late, now."

"I'll get him in on time," the girl promised and then rejoined a circle of female acquaintances passing the time until their boyfriends appeared, freshly showered amidst sweet and spicy smelling lotions.

When Joab appeared, Anita unfastened a gold chain from around her neck and placed it around his. Once he heard the tiny snap of the clasp, he kissed her lips before her hands had a chance to fall. This was a ritual they had observed ever since Ruth had given him the cross for his birthday his freshman year.

"Great game!" She exalted.

"Yeah," he agreed with a sheepish smile, picking up his blue and white Tidal Waves bag with his right hand and swinging his left over her shoulder. She slipped her thumb into the outside loop of his jeans, sensitive to the motion of his hips as they fell into step.

"Where we goin'?" She asked.

"Where do you want to go?

"I don't care. It's up to you."

"A few guys are going over to Stan's house."

"Okay." It never really mattered to her where they were. Wherever he was, the company was excellent.

"I thought we might take the long way."

Her face flushed warm at his insinuation. Nor could he look her in the eye when he said it. The two had stepped beyond the threshold of virginity, together, not four months earlier. The intimacy of naked flesh on flesh had yet to become an act trivialized by talk.

Their decision had been slow and inevitable. Joab and Anita had been born three months apart. They had been baptized in the same church. When Ruth moved back home after college, Joab had discovered Anita Twedell living less than a mile away. First grade found them in the same class, and they had started dating in the sixth grade, when Joab had prevailed upon his Uncle Lyndon to take them to the county fair. Joab had had a crush on Anita from as far back as he could remember such things. Anita had always been, for him, the definitive expression of femaleness and the longer they remained together, the more convinced he was that his first impression had been an accurate one.

Near the end of Joab and Anita's sixth grade year, one of their classmates found himself on the losing side of a gang war. Half the families in the school turned out for the funeral. Shootings had yet to become commonplace. Ruth was not close to the boy's mother, but she felt drawn to express her solidarity. There is a maternal sisterhood, an understanding between women struggling to raise up children in a dangerous world. Ruth heard this sister's anguished wailing in the marrow of her being. She felt this sister's hopes and aspirations descending into the damp red earth that day and it made her blood chill in her veins. As Ruth watched the rest of the woman's clan huddle around, the message was clear: Ruth only had one son. She would not lose him to the impulsive trigger finger of an impassioned teenager. The following September, under fierce protest from Joab, Ruth broke into her life's savings and enrolled him in a private school. Once Joab realized that his mother would not be dissuaded, he started looking around for a compromise. Mother and son finally agreed upon "St. Paul Catholic School."

Ruth agreed because the school was not too big, almost one-third of the students were black, all of them were well-mannered, and over ninety-four percent of its graduates went on to college. Joab agreed because it was only five blocks from East Savannah High. Joab could still ride the public school bus with Anita, run over to his new school, and be on time for the first bell. It was three months before the bus driver realized that Joab was the only kid he'd seen in years who wore a tie to school every day. By the time a disgruntled preadolescent tattled, the bus driver had already decided Joab made no trouble and was welcome to ride on his bus with his little sweetheart any time.

The great breakthrough of Joab and Anita's romance came upon the heels of "the great tampon incident." While waiting for the bus one afternoon in their eighth-grade year, Anita dropped her purse spilling most of its contents. In horror, she watched as four tampons rolled out over the curb. Ever quick on the draw, Joab retrieved them and handed them discreetly to her before any of their peers even noticed her purse had fallen. Anita watched in grateful amazement as a boy actually touched the most confidential and vulgar symbol of the mysterious differences between men and women.

"I can't believe you picked up my tampons," she finally stammered for lack of anything else to say.

"Sarah and Maybell have been using them as long as I can remember . . . and deodorant, and toilet paper, and toothpaste..."

From that day forward, they could talk about anything. And by the time they had grown through the awkwardness of adolescence they had discovered in each other a shared path around the insecurities that plagued their peers. Joab had his teammates and Anita her girlfriends, but in the evening when the phone lines between their houses hummed, they would often smugly pity the friends who searched fruitlessly for what they owned in each other.

Aware of his beginnings, and having been informed of his mother's abortion through the malicious gossip of a second cousin, Joab's convictions kept pace with the growth and strength of his body. By junior high he had become quietly, but fiercely, pro-life. Anita understood. She understood why Joab never pushed for sex in an increasingly promiscuous teen culture where MTV and VH1 flooded every home with a deluge of sensual imagery, twenty-four hours a day, seven days a week, from adolescence through adulthood. As a result, Anita felt safely sheltered, knowing Joab would protect her even from himself.

Even so, by seventeen, the conclusion dawned with fearsome power that the most sacred altar on which to offer their innocence was each other. One morning at school Anita shored up her resolve and went to visit the school clinic. She complained of irregular periods with terrible cramping. The nurse was quick to take the bait. Arrangements were made for the Planned Parenthood shuttle to take her to a doctor's appointment and return her to school in time to make the bus home. The first three months of The Pill were provided, free of charge, by Planned Parenthood and a continuous prescription was secured. Anita counted out the first thirty days before surprising Joab with her news.

Tonight, Ruth's blue Impala came to a stop at the end of a dirt road beside a river bluff. Joab almost giggled as he reached in the glove box and popped the trunk. Then he disappeared around back. When he reappeared he was holding a rolled up sleeping bag as though it was Eve's very apple. For her part, Anita was astonished and thrilled by the sheer premeditation of it all. In electric silence, they spread the thick bedding.

The two sat in rapt silence as their eyes adjusted to the nocturnal beauty of the Lowcountry. A faint sulfury scent informed them that the tide was low. Joab's chosen site was a place where the earth had given into the sea, surrendering a piece of herself, leaving roots exposed in a cliff that descended to a shallow estuary. Stretching away were ribbons of brackish water winding through tender shoots of marsh grass. Having been seduced to the deep by an irresistible moon, receding waters left jagged edges of oyster shells exposed in their beds of silky black. In need of only a sliver to be whole, the silver sphere was already high, making a shimmering, white path wherever it touched water, as though including the young lovers in its invitation beyond the horizon.

All around them the robust sounds of amphibian lust barked and bellowed from damp places close to the earth. Crickets sang while lizards and skinks waited quietly for opportunity. Silence between Nita and Joab was often as full as conversation. Tonight they were well aware of the resplendence of creation. Tonight they were the center of it.

And why not? Who more than young lovers have a right to the breadth and reaches of God's astonishing artistry? And the wealth of this moment would have been bitterly bankrupt were half of this couple made to endure such beauty without the other.

Joab's arms slipped strong around Nita's shoulders. He kissed her heavily.

"I love you, Nita," came his breathless words, "I love you and I need you and I belong to you. Whatever you want, Nita."

She slowly unbuttoned his shirt. He unbuttoned hers with thick, inexperienced fingers. Anita made a mental note to take two pills as soon as she got back to her purse in the car. Yesterday's had slipped her mind. A mosquito buzzed close to her left ear. She mused inwardly at the idea of explaining a bug bite on her left boob to her mother.

"I want you, Joab. I want you," she whispered honestly . . .

Around 2:30 AM, Ruth woke from a light sleep to the sound of a key in the front lock.

"Joab?" she called past her open bedroom door.

"I'm home," came the answer in the dark. His tone had an unusual edge.

"What's wrong?"

"Aw, some son-of-a... some jerk stole Nita's purse out of the car! And if I ever find him, I'll have the whole football team tear him apart."

"I'm sorry, Son. Did they break my window?"

"No-o-o. I forgot to lock the car. Night."

"Did you lock the front door?"

"Yeah."

"Night," Ruth heard the running water as Joab brushed his teeth. Then she settled into a deep sleep.

The wedding was small. With child-like simplicity, the couple had conceded that this was not the ideal circumstance under which to wed, but they had always assumed that they would marry each other - someday. The baby just put them on a slightly faster track.

Joab had chosen his Uncle Jethro to be his best man. Anita had hoped that her father would come to give her away, but when his invitation returned to her own mailbox, address unknown, it was decided that her mother would have that honor. Both Lucinda Twedell (or Miss Lucy as Anita's mother was called) and Ruth tried to overcome their reservations. Still, both mothers appeared a bit subdued as Joab and Anita exchanged their vows with a bright confidence.

Inwardly, Ruth was struggling not to resent her new daughter-in-law. Surely, Anita had known how Joab felt about abortion. Over and over again she willed down the idea that Anita had trapped her son on purpose. But the thought continued to resurrect itself. It would usually slip in on the tail of Ruth's silent lamentations over Joab's future.

She had so hoped to see him fly, like a bird thrown into the sky by her own hand. But now, with the weight of a wife and child... The world should just be beginning to burst open for him, his horizons spreading beyond east and west. How many times had Ruth sat quietly and imagined how different his college experience would be from her own? And she, vicariously and with greater joy, would watch as the scope of his personality expanded with each new experience. The dances and parties he could attend had been out of reach for a single mother working to close the gap between a scholarship and babysitters. How she had hoped he would have found a woman who would be an asset to him, a helpmate in a competitive world. And it wasn't that she didn't like Anita. Anita was nice enough. It was just that Joab had never tasted anything else. How could he know? How could he *know*? She was an average girl, pretty and sweet, with her life's ambition having been met this day and possessing none beyond becoming Mrs. Joab Johnson. And in this one thing she had won. With no hope of college, there was little doubt that Joab would be the best prospect for a husband ever likely to cross her path. Ruth had to give her credit for her choice of men. *But had she cheated to get him? There it was again!* That thought, that one thought was malignancy in her soul and would choke her relationship with the daughter of her son's choosing. This day, God had blessed her with a second child and had given her the promise of a grandbaby to love. And how long? How long had she dreamed of a daughter? How long had her arms ached to cradle an infant?

"Sweet Jesus," her silent prayer went out from the fellowship hall of the little country church where she and all her kin and her son had been baptized, "You know my heart. Help me not to hate her for clipping his wings so young. Help me to love her with your love, the steadfast love that always overcomes and never fails, that the blessings you are pouring down upon this woman, this day, will not be wasted on a bitter heart."

Jethrow invited the bride to dance. Soon Joab had his hand extended to Ruth. Her forehead rested squarely in the center of his chest. She looked up at him, tall and handsome in his black tux. He rolled his shoulders down putting his ear close to her lips.

"Where is Mama's treasure?" She asked the childhood question.

"Right here on this dance floor," came his answer.

"I love you, son."

"I know, Mama." Then Anita was in Joab's arms and Jethrow held his favorite sister until he was sure the lump in her throat had dissolved.

By the time Ruth found her chair, few people were left sitting. One of Joab's buddies had offered to spin CD's on Ruth's stereo. One old, slow, song was all he could tolerate before the throbbing syllables of <u>Boys II Men</u> shook the walls.

Ruth watched as her boss and his wife (the only white folks at the wedding) attempted hip-hop. Ruth couldn't help laughing at them. It was a laughter she afforded herself because she genuinely loved Charlie and Susan Keylar.

A week after graduating from Furman, Ruth had sat across the giant desk from Charles R. Keylar again. By that time, he had quit the large firm and gone out on his own.

"Do you remember me?" Ruth had asked.

"Yes," Charlie had answered the question honestly. In fact, Ruth's case had been one of the reasons he had decided to strike out on his own. He didn't like being told what cases he could and couldn't take.

"I graduated from college last week."

"Congratulations!"

"Here are my transcripts." She slid the papers across the expanse of the desk. "I graduated eleventh in my class. . . I majored in English with a minor in Pre Law."

"Impressive." He scanned the papers.

"I'm completely computer literate and I would very much like to work for you. . . if you're looking for a secretary or something."

"I'm sorry. I just don't need anyone else at the moment." Charlie saw Ruth's face drop. His heart went out to her for the second time. Obviously she had been a good student who was not afraid of work, but he was struggling to meet payroll as it was. He and his pretty little wife had just made the decision to put his house on the market. It was time for a smaller one, just until his practice took root. And chances were good that his wife would deliver a healthy child, their first, in two short months.

"You know you won't have to worry about maternity leaves or anything like that, Mr. Keylar."

That sounded practical. He started building his case for her employment. She spoke perfect English and presented herself well. A little shy, perhaps, but he felt certain that would change as she gained more confidence in her field. He tried to recollect any black secretaries in other private firms. The only ones he could think of were government employees. Somewhere in Charlie Keylar's liberal, yuppie soul the thought appealed to him. His current secretary, an old and faithful warhorse, had balked at every piece of new technology he brought into the office. Technology was clearly poised to revolutionize business. To keep up, he was going to need someone with computer sense.

"I'll tell you what," he had said finally, "We'll try you for three months. At the end of that time, I'll either let you go or we'll start talking about benefits and that kind of thing. I don't know where I'll put you yet, but I'm sure there'll be plenty for you to do."

"Oh, thank you, Mr. Keylar!" She had practically jumped out of the chair. She reached across and shook his hand. "When can I start?"

"Monday, 7:30."

"Yes, sir. See you then." She had said, shaking his hand again.

As she had turned to go he had asked, "I think I remember you having a son?" Her face had become still brighter.

"Joab. He's a fine boy. Very healthy. Never gets sick. He starts first grade in the fall. My Mama'll take care of him until I get home from work every day."

"I look forward to meeting him. Susan and I will be expecting our first this August."

"Congratulations, sir."

"Thank you. Thank you."

"See you Monday!"

Charlie Keylar had always been a soft-hearted attorney, a luxury few attorneys can afford, given the real and pressing issues of sky-rocketing taxes, employee benefits, and office space rental, not to mention malpractice insurance. As it turned out, Charlie Keylar was a good enough lawyer, but he had a real gift for investment. So when Charlie settled a lucrative case, he simply parlayed part of the proceeds into something even more lucrative. One day, Ruth approached him about investing a portion of her paychecks. Through the years, he had done well for her. Ruth would never be a wealthy woman. But she owned her mobile home outright and had a hefty nest egg the size of which would have shocked most of her peers.

Over the years, if anyone ever tried to take advantage of Ruth, in the way some people will when they think you're poor and without recourse, Ruth would write a stiff letter under Charlie's letterhead, he would sign it, and satisfaction was on its way.

After Ruth had been working for Charlie for three years, he sent her to night school to become a certified paralegal. The move saved him the expense and aggravation of hiring an associate and elevated Ruth to second in command. For her part, Ruth was conscientious, a quick learner and had great people sense. She afforded her employer peace of mind when he was away. Besides all that, Ruth babysat during the delivery of Susan and Charlie's third child, an emergency C-section at three in the morning. Charlie never questioned Ruth when she required "sick days" to nurse her son or to attend one of his special events. During the long years of hoping for children, Charlie had developed a life philosophy: he would always work to live, not live to work. He would maintain the same priorities for his employees as well. Throughout the years, Charlie and Ruth developed a working relationship based on real affection grounded in mutual respect.

Charlie was now covered in sweat. His tie loose and the first button of his collar popped. Susan laughed as she tried to keep pace with him. She still looked like the All-American-Darling Ruth had first seen in the picture on Charlie's desk. Ruth was glad they were having a good time. Few deserved to dance at this wedding more than Charles R. Keylar, Esquire and his cute little wife.

Joab and Anita danced, too. They danced until they were breathless and their skin was glistening. At four months, Anita's tiny passenger was barely noticeable under her frilly white gown. Besides the Keylars, the bride and groom appeared to be the only ones at the wedding unimpressed by the invisible shotgun.

A cousin from St. Pete, Florida could not make the wedding, but offered his apartment to Joab and Anita for their honeymoon. He would be visiting relatives in Chicago that week, and had no need of it. They drove down in a pre-owned, red, Chrysler LeBaron convertible: Ruth's wedding gift. The apartment was small and run down, but it was private and close to the beach. Cousin Ned, with delightfully iniquitous foresight, knew that they would not be able to purchase alcohol, legally, and had a bottle of pink champagne waiting in the fridge. Anita could be talked into only a half a glass, to toast her new husband, after which she swore not to touch another drop until after the safe arrival of their baby.

The couple emerged only one time in the first three days, weak-kneed and swollen-lipped, driven by a second hunger which would not be deferred indefinitely. They stocked provisions and locked themselves in once more.

Within the walls of Cousin Ned's one-bedroom apartment, for that one week, was the delicious sense that the horses had already escaped from the barn. There was no longer any need for caution or reserve. Nor was there any.

By the fifth day, however, neither husband nor wife would admit to a specific soreness. Anita jumped at Joab's suggestion to "do Disney." They enjoyed the Magic Kingdom that day and danced in the teen clubs of Pleasure Island that night, feeling quite grown up.

Late afternoon, the following day, they packed the car and walked the flat white beach one last time, before heading their topless sedan north. The wind licked furiously at their backs, while Joab spoke of ambitions and Anita made plans; two children, oblivious that they were driving headlong into adulthood. The sun set. Anita put her head back and took a long look at the stars. When had she ever felt so free?

Joab's eyes darted from the road to the smooth arch of Nita's neck and the angles of her silhouette in the moonlight. He had to pull his eyes back to the road. She was so beautiful. He felt a new possessiveness. *This is my woman.* The words formed in his mind. *My woman . . . for always.* An unexpected uneasiness stirred from someplace within him, then it was still.

"MY WOMAN!" He shouted out loud to the wind. Anita laughed joyously.

Trying to integrate Anita's possessions into Joab's bedroom was a more stressful experience than either of them would have imagined. Negotiations went on for hours. When they were over, Joab's clothes were in the guest room closet, his bed was covered in lace, and his shaving equipment had been squeezed out of the medicine cabinet to reside, henceforth, on the back of the toilet.

Sensing some tension when she walked in from work, Ruth invited herself over to Edna's for a cup of tea. Sometimes Ruth missed Big Mama so badly, she ached. It had been over three years now since her mother's fatal stroke. Tears still surfaced with every thought of the beloved woman. She needed Big Mama's wisdom. She wanted to know how to help the young ones make it. At thirty-four, she herself had never been married, had never lived with a man, had neither pursued men nor allowed herself to be pursued. Remorse for her role in the death of her second child combined with the resulting infertility left Ruth with the conviction that she would ever remain single. God had blessed her with an extraordinary son. This seemed to her an extravagant source of joy from a good and gracious God.

Jethro could always be counted on for sensible advice, but he was so busy with his young family and building a business to support them. He was a good man and a fine father. Ruth was proud of him. He had started out working for a subcontractor in Charleston. But after Hurricane Hugo tore the old city to pieces, Jethro went out on his own and his construction company was growing year after year. Ruth hated to call him for anything but a true crisis. Annie was no help. She had a worse track record with men than Mama. And even now she was going through another breakup with a man she had moved in with less than six months earlier.

Ruth stayed at Edna's as late as she could, but there was nothing she could do about the thin walls when she finally returned home. For several years, she had felt an inward tug to be more active in church ministries, but had decided that Joab was her primary mission field. That night, Ruth decided this was her season to get busy in the church.

For his part, Joab was a little surprised at himself for letting this moving thing bother him so. Although he had been raised pretty much with his aunts and uncles, once Mama moved back home from Furman, he had always enjoyed the luxury of his own room and expected that his own things would be left alone. Now, all of *his* things belonged to Anita, too. And it looked like she was always gonna be moving them around or cleaning them or something. He supposed *her* things belonged to him, only he really didn't have any interest in doing anything with them except just leaving them alone.

The week after "the children" moved in, school started again. After several discussions, Joab and Nita decided against a transfer. Joab knew that he would stand little chance of being chosen captain of the basketball team in a school five times the size of St. Paul's. Anita had no intention of entering a more conservative school in her less conservative condition. Ruth, who had offered to pay Anita's tuition at St. Paul's, was relieved. The added respectability of driving a car to school figured into the equation in no small way. Not to mention a flashy, red convertible.

Ruth was pleased, for Anita's sake, that the social stigma of teen pregnancy had dissipated since Joab's birth. What she had *not* expected was for it to *raise* social status. In fact, it had given Joab status, too. Among her peers, Anita's belly inspired daydreams of frilly baby booties and cozy lullabies. No less than three pairs of hands clamored for a touch when Nita announced, "the baby's kicking," in study hall.

"I might just let someone give me a baby, too," declared one of Anita's classmates. Nita was on the cutting edge of a trend.

At St. Paul's, things were a bit different. Joab presented a peculiar dilemma for the faculty. In a Catholic context they could not condone his knocking-up his girlfriend. On the other hand, he deserved great deference because he had chosen the harder path and preserved the sanctity of life. Most of them simply avoided any direct reference to his domestic situation, publicly. But the sincerity of their efforts to make his wife feel welcome on school grounds was hard to miss. At the start of football season, Father Philip, or Father Coach, as he was affectionately called, invited Joab into his office for a conference.

"I just wanted to congratulate you on your marriage, Joab," he said. "Although I have never been married myself, I know more about life than you might think. My door is always open for you - anytime . . . I just wanted you to know that."

"Thank you, Father." Joab responded, not knowing exactly what to say when faced with the sudden void of formality.

"Good. You can go."

"Thank you, Father," he repeated. It really was strange.

Even the nuns, who had always seemed so dried up and humorless to him, warmed when they saw Anita approach and could not let her pass without asking, "How are you feeling today, Mrs. Johnson?" Anita melted at her title.

Initially, Joab's teammates apportioned him new respect. This was curious, too. They treated him as though he had become an adult over the summer, as if the gold band on his left hand transported him to his mid-twenties without going through the convention of finishing his late-teens. The potency issue was not wasted on his peers, either. The strength of his virility was as undeniable as his wife's (wife's?!) ripening form. But in the aggressive confines of the locker room, it wasn't long before the hands that patted him on the back began sowing seeds of discontent. Joab increasingly found himself sandwiched between fellow jocks comparing the sexual aptitudes of this piece of tail or that. The completeness of his satisfaction rendered their tauntings impenetrable. Anita had been his woman and his best friend as long as he could remember. The thought of any one of these guys having her was repugnant. Exclusive rights had always been in his plan. And now the cosmic blueprint of all the perfection that was her had miraculously united with all that was him, in a mega-microscopic zipping up of magical proteins within the dark, warm, secret places of her body. Belly-to-belly in the darkness of night, he could feel their son's strength growing. Although he could never put it quite into words, he considered himself mighty fortunate to have tripped and splashed into Anita Twedell's gene pool.

In the fall, Ruth and Anita sacrificed themselves to the gnats, side by side, on the football field bleachers, migrating lower and lower with Anita's ever-increasing girth. Both women were silently delighted when it was over and relieved that Joab's only injuries had been two broken fingers. On to basketball—indoors.

✦ ✦ ✦

Christmas passed with great joy and anticipation. Anita joined the sub-culture of holiday festivities as though she had been born into the family.

Some ladies from Ruth's church organized a surprise baby shower and set it for December 27th. When Ruth's blue Impala came to a stop outside the fellowship hall, she produced a small, wrapped box from the depths of her purse.

"I didn't want to give you my gift in front of a lot of people," she confessed. "My father gave this to my mother for her 19th birthday. My mother gave it to me for giving her her first grandchild. And now it's time to give it to you."

"I can't accept this," Anita stammered when she saw the ring.

"But it doesn't belong to me anymore, Child." Ruth replied.

Anita put it on and hugged her mother-in-law.

Even in the hollow absence of Big Mama, Ruth's siblings customarily exerted great effort in returning to their childhood home for Christmas. Various spouses and lovers came and went. Some, like Jethro's wife, stayed. Lyndon and Abe returned only when the Navy would permit. Still, with each passing year, increasing numbers of cousins filled the beds and swung from the tire on the great oak. The Johnsons returned as though driven by the same stirrings that move particular creatures to yearly migrations. As though the nurturing spirit of Big Mama remained within its walls, her modest home endured as a safe haven for any wounded by the jagged edges of life. In between occupants, the task of keeping the place up had naturally fallen to Ruth and Joab. If it needed a major repair, Jethro would send one or two of his men down to fix the problem. This year, Big Mama's house had been empty for over five months. Anita and Joab had considered moving in. But then, Annie announced that she would be staying on after the holidays.

Chapter 2

Lucinda Ruth Johnson was born one month after her father's eighteenth birthday.

Some weeks earlier, at the subtle suggestion of their Child Birth Instructor, Anita had made the noble decision to forgo pain preventative measures and afford her baby a natural delivery. Good thing, too, because as it turned out, Anita's labor progressed so rapidly, the medical team would not have had time to administer a spinal block, anyway.

Moments after they whisked Anita off in a wheelchair, Joab greeted the soon-to-be grannies in the lobby and escorted them to the maternity wing waiting room. Their praying and his fretting were soon interrupted by a nurse who presented Joab with a head-to-toe suit of blue, paper scrubs. Once dressed to the nurse's satisfaction, she led Joab to the operating room where Anita had already been prepped for the birth. The sound of the baby's heartbeat filled the space while a steady ribbon of graff paper recorded pictures of Anita's contractions. Activity seemed to increase with the length and intensity of them. This made the audible drop in heart rate all the more alarming. Assurances that the drop was completely within normal boundaries did little to calm the amateur parents.

Joab held his wife's hand and tried to reach beyond his nerves to his coaching instructions - he drew a blank.

"Okay. Here comes another contraction. Don't push yet," said the obstetrician.

"Okay. Here comes another contraction. Don't push yet," said Joab. He squeezed Anita's hand for lack of anything else to do.

"You're breaking my fingers," Anita said tensely when her abdomen relaxed. The minutes that followed dragged as though time, itself, stopped to leer at the spectacle of the agony of natural childbirth.

"Okay, Dahlin', here comes another one," said the doctor.

"Okay, Baby, here comes another one," said Joab.

"I can't. I can't. I can't." Anita stated in a parched voice.

"Yes you can," the doctor replied confidently. "This time I want you to push. I want you to push into the pain."

"Oh, no. Oh, no." she whispered as a new contraction gathered force.

"Push, Baby, push!" Joab cheered.

Anita drew breath, then turned purple as her body focused every cell on the searing pain. A sound escaped from somewhere deep within; somewhere that preexisted language.

Who came up with this system, anyway? his mind screamed as all his wife's will converged in the act of pushing his offspring into the bright coolness of halogen light.

Outraged, the infant's first breath produced a hardy protest.

Euforia swept over Anita like a mighty ocean wave.

And women are the weaker *sex?* Joab thought.

"It's a girl," the doctor announced.

Joab was not aware that his mouth was hanging open.

Even after witnessing the bizarre metamorphosis of Anita's body and studying birthing techniques, Joab was not prepared for the pure physical violence (never mind the bloody mess) of childbirth.

"Would the father like to cut the cord?" the doctor asked.

Joab took the surgical scissors only to discover that his hands were shaking. With a quick snip, he managed to sever the physical tie between his wife and his daughter and hand the scissors back.

Relief engulfed his body which seemed to be at the center of a medical dance he had not rehearsed. The doctor handed the baby to a nurse. This one passed-off to that one. That one cleaned it. *Ah, much better!* This one weighed it. That one poked the heel of its foot. This one watched it and took notes.

They wrapped its tiny body, hatted its fuzzy head and handed it to Joab who released Nita's throbbing fingers and laid the soft bundle in the crook of her arm.

Anita cried. Joab cried with her. Then she laughed. Joab laughed with her. The squishy infant made soft squishy sounds.

By and by, Joab came strutting through the waiting room door with the treasured bundle. Surgical mask still covering his mouth, Ruth could not see his face, but she knew he was beaming by the wrinkles at the corners of his eyes.

"A girl?" Ruth asked.

Joab nodded proudly.

"Ah, isn't she something." Ms. Lucy crooned as though Joab had just entered with the moon and stars wrapped in pink flannel.

"Lucinda," Joab almost sang, "she's finally here. Little Lucinda Ruth. Isn't she beautiful?"

All agreed. Joab handed the little one to his mama. Ruth looked down into the tiny, puffy face and recognized the one she had seen in her imagination, before Joab was born.

"How's Anita?" she asked.

"Just fine. She did great. She's *The Woman*. We're gonna go back and *teach* that Lamaze class next time! Pushed her right out. Like a pro! Only they won't let me back in there. We have to wait for her to come out to recovery."

"She's just like me," Ms. Lucy boasted, "I never had no trouble with birthin' neither."

Joab came and stood behind his mother so they could both stare down at the tiny, new face.

"You know she maxed out her APGAR's."

"Her what?" Ruth asked.

"Her APGAR's. It's a test they give them to see that everything's working right. She maxed them out. Didn't you?" He asked in a googoo voice. Ruth gathered her resolve and handed the infant over to her other grandma.

"Thank you, Jesus," Ruth half whispered. "Thank you, Sweet Jesus."

"Nita did the pushing," Joab stated.

"And Jesus made both of them come out all right." His mother's answer was immediate and retreated not one inch.

Joab thought of a response but decided not to challenge the moment. He just rolled his eyes as usual.

"Let's go find recovery," he suggested, "I want to be there when they roll Nita in."

Anita looked exhausted but well-satisfied.

"Can I hold her?" she asked her mother through dry lips.

"Certainly," the older woman answered, gently setting the soft bundle in the crook of her arm.

Joab was the only one embarrassed when Anita offered the infant a breast.

"Can't she wait on the milk?" He asked, and was promptly scolded by two grandmothers who would, henceforth, contend that Lucinda should have whatever she wanted whenever she wanted it.

Ruth looked down at Big Mama's sapphire ring as Anita's hand cradled the child's head. Ruth remembered the resentful young woman she had been during the delivery of her own baby. What a contrast Anita was to that memory. Ruth's heart ran over with thanksgiving that Anita did not have to go through such an ordeal without a mate, and that her grandchild would know the love of her father. She caught the tear with a finger before it escaped down her cheek.

There is very little, in the way of human experience, that can prepare the childless for the complete upheaval which accompanies the introduction of an infant into the home. Anita took to the nocturnal demands of motherhood as though this was her primary calling in life. Joab struggled to perform with no such calling.

The new parents had arranged to take the first week off from school. Ruth had considered asking Charlie for a few days but had decided it would be better to let the children work this out, on their own. Joab did his take-home assignments during Cinda's short naps. Nita seemed most happy with her chin resting on her arms, admiring over the edge of the cradle, the miniature perfection of the child her body had produced.

Father Coach agreed to let Joab play basketball over his break on the promise that his assignments would be complete when he returned. Joab was disappointed when Anita would not take the baby to the game. He was kind of looking forward to showing her off.

"Too many germs. She's not going out for at least two weeks." Anita announced. The schedule was *not* open to discussion.

In all of his eighteen years, Joab had never really considered how fast news travels. He wasn't even out of the car when the first congratulations came. By the time he got into the gym, he had collected three. Two nuns contributed two more at the door and he lost count by the time he made it to the locker room which had an "It's a girl" sign taped to the back wall. Even the other team congratulated him! For the remainder of his senior year, Joab would be known as, "Dada".

Anita had very little of her homework done when she returned to school the following week, and she didn't care. Annie, who had found a job waiting tables, offered to take care of Cinda during the day. Anita was more apprehensive than she let on. Annie had never had any children. But Anita had no money for daycare, and few options. She supposed she should be thankful, but it was extremely difficult to leave her eight-day-old with another woman. She was distracted at school and by the time she got home, her breasts were sore and engorged.

The following day, she asked Joab for the car and rushed home during lunch to feed the baby. It wasn't long before she wasn't returning to school after lunch, at all. By April, when the baby suffered her first ear infection, Anita found the excuse she'd been looking for. She dropped out, completely.

"You're not even gonna graduate!" Joab exploded when she informed him of her decision. "How are you ever going to get into college?"

"I wouldn't have gotten into college on my grades anyway! Even if I could go."

"You could have gotten in somewhere."

"Yeah, just when am I supposed to go? It's stupid for me to keep going when I'm failing anyway and our daughter needs me home. When she's a little older, I'll put her in daycare and get a job."

"Oh, yeah, and who's gonna hire you without a diploma?"

"And who's gonna know? Hell, half the people who *do* graduate can't even read! At least I can read."

"Nita, this is a mistake. I know it. It's a big mistake. And what are you gonna tell our mothers?

"I'll tell them we decided that Cinda needs me home for now, and that I'll get a job in the fall when you go to college, and that I'll get my diploma after you graduate and *you* have a job. It makes a lot of sense." Nita finished the presentation of her argument by kissing her husband on the lips and unbuttoning his pants. Very persuasive.

"We have forty-five minutes before your mother gets home," she observed.

Cinda began to wail.

"Let her cry," Joab pleaded.

"Just let me check and make sure she's okay. The Tylenol's probably worn off."

"She's okay. She's okay," Joab assured.

Anita entered their cluttered bedroom and returned with the baby.

"She doesn't feel hot, but her ear might still be hurting," Anita said. "Ah, Sweet Thing, I wish I could make it feel better," she crooned to the child.

Joab zipped up his pants.

Joab's graduation party wasn't the celebration Ruth had always hoped it would be. A friend of Annie's was hired to bring his giant pig cooker. He arrived at 7:00AM to start the process. Annie and Miss Lucy kept the barbecue sauce and potato chips flowing while Ruth boiled up the Silver Queen corn inside and the peanuts outside. Anita's big brother, Nicholas, (not known for being the first to lend a hand) volunteered to monitor the keg.

Of the sixty-plus kids who came, most were from St. Paul's. Northern intellectuals would have been shocked to discover the authentic interracial camaraderie among the graduates. Religion and sports had produced the common ground upon which blacks and whites now came together to celebrate a common accomplishment. Anita invited only five girl friends from East Savannah High. A dozen students crashed, anyway. They would make no trouble. St Paul's entire football team was here and Anita's big brother was guarding the keg. Three years after Nickolas's graduation from East Savannah, his reputation as a badass was still very much intact.

Joab and Anita had the best time they could remember since their honeymoon. At three and a half months old, Cinda was rounding out to be a perfect picture of a cherub. After deliberating over Cinda's outfit for weeks, the frilly pink dress with matching bonnet and booties had the desired effect. Anita's friends clamored to hold the breathing babydoll. Anita could feel their envy. She had a husband and a baby and could stay home and watch MTV all day long, *and* she had a red convertible. Anita could hardly conceal her smugness as she collected the crying child from an acquaintance, soothed her into gurgles, and strolled over to her handsome, young husband, (who had just graduated valedictorian over all those spoiled white boys) exacting from him one public display of affection.

From his circle of friends, Joab watched his wife and daughter approach with no less self-satisfaction. Except for a subtle bow at the belly, Anita had recovered her sumptuous form. His eyes watched with pride the excessively generous breasts of a nursing mother, the lanky length of leg which enabled her to move as though she never hurried anywhere but took pleasure in the going. The narrow hips ending in the high, tight roundness of a bottom that swelled more to the back than to the sides. Her eyes were large, almond shaped and black. Over the left nostril of a small, wide nose a tiny sapphire gleamed. A gift from Joab. His answer to her question: Do you think body piercing is sexy? Her lips were wide, a constant bait for kissing. She was wearing a sleeveless, purple, jersey dress. Her hair was plaited with gold and purple beads encircling her head just above the shoulder. *My woman.* His third beer almost gave him leave to pound his chest as she approached. *My daughter.* He gave his girls kisses and then held his woman's waist as he reentered his conversation.

✦ ✦ ✦

The following August, Ruth helped finish packing the orange U-haul behind the little red car, and kissed her children and her grandbaby good-bye. Then she turned to face the empty doublewide. Boog pushed his head up under her hand as though to commiserate. She patted him and entered the house. There was a bare spot in the kitchen where the high chair had been, and an equally empty place where the playpen wasn't.

"Well, Lord, I guess it's just you and me, now," she said out loud. "Please give them safe travel to Durham and surround them with your angels."

Then she went to her night table for her Bible.

Later that evening, she decided she'd better make herself eat something. When a jar of Gerber's strained peas rolled out of the pantry, Ruth just let herself have a good hearty cry. She was still crying when Annie let herself in toting a bottle of wine. Ruth hadn't had a drink in over a decade, but there were times when she had to concede; alcohol had its place. Edna arrived with her own bottle not ten minutes later.

Joab kind of wished he could have put the top down, but the baby didn't like the wind and Anita was convinced that it gave her ear infections. Still, there was a feeling of keen liberation as Joab's family drove out from under the protective wing of his mother. When Cinda fell asleep in her car seat, Anita climbed over to the front, snuggled up to her husband

and stuck her tongue deep into his ear. The car behind them saw the U-haul fishtail.

"Shit! Nita, you want to get us killed?" Joab shouted a whisper.

His wife just smiled and shrugged her shoulders.

"Do it again," he said.

"We can make the bed squeak as loud as we want," she whispered in his ear. "We can go naked for days, months, years . . . or until the baby turns one."

Chapter 3

Once within the city limits of Durham, Joab pulled his family into the parking lot of an inexpensive, but tidy, hotel. It had a pool and was owned and operated by a gracious, middle-Eastern Indian family. Joab signed over several of the two thousand dollars worth of travelers checks his mother had given him. It was a loan; startup money for a new life, and it was more money than Joab had ever seen in one place before.

His girls, worn out from the drive, still could not resist a dip before nap time. Cinda laughed and sputtered as her father bounced her gently in the water. Anita swam up behind him and put her arms around his neck kissing his shoulders. After a long nap, Joab treated his family to a non fast-food dinner. Just before the sun went down, they drove to Duke University, just to look.

A fresh excitement washed over Joab as he walked with his family down the long, main quadrangle of Duke's west campus. Gray stone buildings, with Gothic flourish and pointed arches reached skyward as they strolled by. The Johnson's stopped to linger before the statue of James B. Duke. Then, reverently toured the ornate chapel behind it. The Clock Tower rose above one end of the quadrangle with giant masses of hospital buildings spreading out over the other. Joab drank in the stoic grandeur while Anita felt vaguely oppressed and handed him the squirming baby.

The following morning, they were off to the University's housing office for some advice on cheap, off-campus places to live.

Late in the afternoon, on their second day of house hunting, the Johnson's Le Baron turned off a rural highway into a trailer park. The sign outside read "Shady Oaks," though there were neither oaks nor shade anywhere near the trailers. The place looked, in fact, like a great farmers field dotted evenly with gray singlewides like so many giant bales of hay drying in the sun. They came to a stop outside the only doublewide on the place. It was marked "office." James (Bubba) Finkley must have heard the car drive up, 'cause he was standing outside before Nita could get the baby out of her safety seat.

"Hey," he called, scooping out the vowel sound. "I'm Jimmy Finkley. I run this place here. Most folks just call me, Bubba."

"Hey, Mr. Bubba," Joab said, extending a hand. "My name is Joab and this is my wife, Anita, and our daughter, Cinda. I'll be attending the university this year and we were looking for a place to live."

Bubba nodded to Anita. "Well, ya come to the right place. Daddy and me just finished expandin' the park here, and we got two more brand new mobile homes for rent. Never been lived in. One's furnished. One's not. My daddy owns the place," Bubba stated with obvious pride. "He got too old for farming, so I decided to start a new bidness. Doin' real good, too. I got plans to open up yonder field to doublewides in a few years."

"Wow, your daddy must be glad to have a son like you." Joab decided to put fish on Bubba's pole.

"Yeah," Bubba hitched his pants. "I kinda got a knack for land developin'."

"Looks like," Joab affirmed, noting the missing molar on the upper right. Joab pegged Bubba as the quintessential redneck right down to the grease in his hair and the dirt under his nails. *Only seven or eight more years of beers and he'll have a respectable girth.* Joab observed silently.

"Do you work on cars?" Joab ventured that the question would not be taken as an insult.

"Yeah." Bubba answered. "And I do all the maintenance on the place here myself. I'm pretty mechanical."

Cinda began to squirm. "Think we might be able to look at that new trailer?" Nita asked.

"Sure. Sure. The furnished or unfurnished?"

"Furnished."

"Great. I'll get the key, and we can drive on down."

Ol' Bubba knew he had Anita the moment he opened the door. He could tell the newness of the place appealed to her.

The trailer had few windows, and the ones it did have were small. It had no landscaping save free standing concrete steps to the front door. The furniture was cheaply constructed of laminated pressboard, but the curtains were homey. The kitchen had no disposal and no dishwasher. It wasn't exactly loaded up with frills. However, the master bathroom was equipped with an extravagant, giant, red bathtub that could easily fit two. It had mirrored walls on two sides. Joab and Nita exchanged a sideways glance.

"I make sure all my trailers come with a good size tub. Folks really like them," Bubba said, winking at Joab. He knew the boy was close.

"And, look. Here in the closet is a hook-up for a washer and dryer for you." Bubba opened the closet door to show them. "You know you ain't gonna do much better than $315.00 a month for a brand new trailer. Especially in a nice country-type neighborhood like this," he went on. "And next week, Shady Oaks will be crawling with college students looking for cheap housin'."

When J. (Bubba) Finkley turned to show them the other two bedrooms, Joab looked to Nita for a signal. She nodded a vigorous "yes."

"I think we'll take it, Uh, Mr. - - Bubba." Joab said.

"Great. Let's head to my office for the paperwork."

"Can I just stay here?" Nita asked.

"Sure," Joab smiled.

"Are the people here nice?" Anita asked hopefully. "Are there any children?"

"Oh, yeah, nice folks," their new landlord assured. "Plenty of kids."

"Course, now, the furniture will cost you an extra $45.00 a month." Anita heard him say as the two men headed down the front stairs.

When Joab returned 30 minutes later, Anita had decided which room would be Cinda's and which room Joab could have for a study. It took them less than two hours to unpack the U-Haul. Joab found the drop-off place for the trailer and picked up a pizza on the way back. After the baby had been put to sleep in her own room, Joab and Anita drew all the curtains in the house and christened the tub.

The next day, Anita made notes of all the household things they would be buying as soon as they could find the K-Mart. They had received a set of towels for a wedding gift and Nita had managed to pick up kitchen items at garage sales here and there, but Anita's list was long: sheets, cleaners, an iron and ironing board, a broom and a mop, groceries, salt, pepper, and on and on. By the following evening, Joab had less than $450.00 of the original two grand left.

"We're gonna have to find you a job, fast," he told his wife who hated the thought of it.

The next morning, Cinda woke at her usual time of 5:00AM. Nita sleepwalked to her room, changed her diaper and placed her beside her husband in the middle of their double bed. Then Anita crawled in for a feeding/snuggling session. This was her favorite time of day. Awash in contentment, her last conscious thought was a wish that things could always stay like this; warm and secure with Cinda safe and dependent between her mommy and daddy.

Joab rolled over and curled his body around his baby girl. He forced his eyelids up and looked at his wife. She was smiling in her sleep. He knew her heart was in the house with Cinda. He wished there was a way. He still could not get over his luck at having been accepted to Duke, (his first choice) and receiving an academic scholarship that would cover three quarters of the cost. He had been offered full scholarships to lesser schools, but Ruth had insisted on Duke assuring him she could come up with the rest of tuition and book money. Still, someone had to pick up the household expenses. He loathed the idea of daycare for his daughter. His heart sank at the thought. The only consolation was that there would be other children someday, and perhaps by then, they could do it right and Anita could stay home with the second one.

Joab threw the covers off, tucking them around his girls again. His mind was racing over details of jobs and classes as he drove to the closest Quick Stop for some doughnuts and the local paper.

By the time Anita found her way to the kitchen, Joab was dressed and showered, the coffee was stale, Joab had circled every possible job in the want ads, and he had been pouring over his college course catalog for an hour.

"Mornin', Babe," He said. "I got the paper."

Anita placed Cinda in her high chair, dumped a small mound of Apple Jacks on the tray and poured herself a cup of coffee (heavy on the sugar and milk).

"I circled some jobs you might be interested in," he continued. "I've been trying to decide what courses to take. I wish I knew what I want to major in. Business, I guess. Law maybe. But they offer some really incredible black history and literature courses. Man, it's tough to decide. But what can you do with history and lit? Not a damn thing but teach. Who the hell wants to teach?"

Nita shrugged her shoulders and looked down at the open paper. "A fry cook at McDonald's?" she asked incredulously.

"I circled every realistic possibility. Baby, we need some kind of cash flow, now. We'll just need to take what you can get to start with. Once we've got some kind of paycheck coming, you can keep looking until you find something decent."

"Great," Nita rolled her eyes.

In one move, Cinda cleared the Apple Jacks from her tray and began to fuss for more.

"Cinda! Don't do that. You eat them. You don't throw them," Nita scolded. She took a doughnut from the box and ripped it into tiny pieces for the baby.

"I think I'd better register for classes today before they get all full. I'll probably be back by 2:00. Be ready to go and we can fill out the paperwork at the phone company and then go take you job hunting. I'll pick up lunch someplace." Circles of cereal crunched under foot as he came around the table to kiss his wife. "See ya later."

"Yeah," she said.

After kissing the baby, he was out the door.

✦ ✦ ✦

The first call Joab made on their new phone was to Ruth for another five hundred dollars. He was astounded at how quickly money seemed to evaporate and how many expenses he never knew were out there. There were deposits on everything from electricity to checking accounts! At Anita's new job as a cook/server at the food court in the new mall, she had to pay Chick Quick for her uniform before she ever made her first nickel. Joab was sure she didn't pay cost either. Although it only paid minimum wage, Joab and Anita decided to take it because it was a national chain and could afford to offer insurance after the first month. The mall ran its own daycare for employees. It was relatively reasonable. But even they required the bill to be paid a month in advance.

Joab enrolled mostly in business classes, but could not resist a course in African-American Literature. He also decided to take an intro to computers. St. Paul's had never quite been able to fit them into the budget. His mother had tried to give him some lessons at her office, but the time slot couldn't compete with sports. In college, laptops appeared to be standard equipment for students and faculty alike. He figured he'd better play catch-up, quick.

Once classes started, the most difficult piece of the domestic puzzle was scheduling the car. As the new employee, Anita was at the mercy of everyone else's preferences. Twice, within the first week, Joab and Anita had a miscommunication resulting in hours of waiting around for each other. Joab was not quite sure that the second time had not been retaliatory. Then too, it was clear that the baby had to be weaned. Anita knew it was time. At six months, Cinda was ready. But Anita couldn't help resenting the synthetic deadline.

Faced with Nita's struggles to adjust, Joab sensed wisdom in keeping his enthusiasm to himself. His business courses were going to be a grind, but he was crazy about computers. Like a quasi Chris Columbus, Joab felt the adventurous urge to sail over the edge of the earth and free fall into cyberspace. It really was a whole new world. Also, the director of the African-American Studies Department for the University just happened to be his Afro-Am Lit. professor. George Gibbons was awesome! Joab wanted Anita to meet him, and he couldn't wait to immerse himself in the reading. This, too, was a whole new world.

By the third week, the responsibility for supper had fallen to Joab. If Anita worked the day shift, she was simply wiped out. If she worked the evening shift, Joab had to pick her and Cinda up between classes and get her to the mall by 2:30 so she could drop off Cinda and be on the job by 3:00. Then, after his class, Joab would pick the baby up, stop at the grocery store, fix supper, straighten the kitchen, get Cinda ready for bed, pick up Anita at 9:30, return home and fall into bed. He found the best time to study was between 2:00 and 5:00 in the morning, when the baby was asleep. On weekends, he often managed to find study time when Nita and the baby went to the laundromat.

✦ ✦ ✦

Early in October, Joab and Nita were awakened around midnight by shrill cries. When they rushed to the baby, they discovered a green liquid oozing out of her right ear. Joab pulled on a pair of jeans and grabbed the keys.

"I'll go start the car," he told Anita over his shoulder.

A cool rain was falling.

"Better wrap her up. It's raining," he shouted before closing the door. As he was unlocking the car, he found that someone had slit the top and there was a gaping hole in the dash where the stereo had been.

"Son of a bitch!" He cursed as he started the engine.

Anita was too panicked about the baby to comment on the car. She strapped the shrieking child into her safety seat, climbed in the back with her, and shielded her from leaking water with her back. Joab drove to the emergency room holding a baby blanket over the slit in the roof.

Anita paced the waiting room with Cinda while Joab filled out the paperwork. Finally they were shown to a room. An ancient doctor examined both ears with calm indifference to the screaming. Then he held a stethoscope to her chest and did some pressing on the tummy.

"A little girl?" he asked at last.

Joab and Anita nodded.

"About six months old?"

Two more nods.

"Were you aware of the ear infection?"

"No," Anita answered. "I don't think she had a fever. I don't remember checking after work. Babe, did she feel hot to you? Did she eat any supper?" His wife was babbling.

"No. She didn't eat much," Joab responded.

"Well, you should have known something was wrong when she didn't eat. She always eats. She's a good eater."

Joab sensed an attack. "She doesn't always eat. Who knows what they've fed her at daycare? Sometimes they give her a snack or something before I pick her up. I guess I should have checked for a fever or something. I don't know."

"Damn right, you should have checked," Anita snapped.

"Now hold on." the doctor interjected. Sometimes there is no fever. It only feels like a low grade fever now. In any case, her eardrum has ruptured from the pressure."

Anita started to cry.

"What is the mother's name?" the Doctor asked Joab.

"My wife's name is Anita."

"Anita." the old man nodded, "Can you hold this under the baby's arm until it beeps?" He asked Joab indicating a digital thermometer. Joab leaned over his daughter on the table and held the instrument in place. He did his best to comfort the child in a soft voice. She looked into the eyes, above her face, and quieted.

"Anita," the old man put his arm around the young woman, "This is not good, but it's not really all that bad. I'll give her some Tempora for the pain and start her on antibiotics and—"

"Is she gonna be deaf in one ear?" Anita begged.

"No-o-o-o-o. At this age the ear drum will generally just grow back together."

Anita turned into the little man and rested her head on his shoulder. "Oh, thank God," she cried. He patted her back softly.

The ride home was tense but dry. Thankfully, both the baby and the clouds appeared to have spent all their rain drops. Quiet settled as Joab and Anita drove across town in search of an all-night drug store. By the time they reached their front door, it was four-thirty.

"Joab, I think we need to put the crib in our bedroom for a few days."

These were the first words his wife had spoken to him since they left the hospital. He could tell from the way she had spoken them, that this was not an issue open for discussion. He moved the crib.

"I'm calling in sick today and tomorrow if I need to. Saturday and Sunday, you'll be home." His wife stated.

It was hard to sell the Le Baron, not because of what it was, but because of what it represented to Joab and Anita. It was their honeymoon ride. It was the wind in their hair and the envy of their peers. It was fun and sexy and very cool. It was traded for a used, powder blue Ford Escort, good gas mileage, very practical.

Ruth had agreed they would not be able to get their money out of the Chrysler with a hole in the roof. She paid to have it fixed. Joab prevailed upon Bubba to pick up a cheap stereo from Wal-Mart and installed it for $65.00. After they sold the convertible, bought the Ford and paid Ruth back, there was $700.00 left over.

The yard behind Mr. Finkley Sr.'s house was somewhere between an automotive hospital and an automotive graveyard. On an impulse, Joab made ol' Bubba an offer on a somewhat dilapidated Japanese motorcycle. J. Finkley, being the "bidness man" that he was, jumped at Joab's offer but not before Joab had extracted a promise that he would keep the thing running so long as Joab paid for parts.

Anita had lost a first and a second cousin on motorcycles. She was afraid of them and afraid for Joab. But she could not argue. They needed a second mode of transportation and this was all they could afford. She ultimately resolved herself to the "bad bike" on Joab's word that he would always wear a helmet and would sell the wretched thing as soon as they could afford a second car.

Joab loved the machine from the first time his jeans pockets met the narrow seat. It was like having the convertible, only better, freer. When Joab was astride his bike, blasting through the countryside, he could forget the pressures of home and school and pretend to be something less than the adult he'd become. It was his secret; his place. Since Anita refused to ride, it became the place he went to escape even her.

After the first week, Anita had to admit life was easier with two vehicles. Cinda remained prone to ear infections. Antibiotic prescriptions, deductibles and uncovered medical expenses began eating up dollars. Joab found himself calling Ruth for the short fall 'most every other month. He knew he'd need a part-time job. He hoped his family could make it to the end of first semester finals.

By Christmas break, finals were over and Joab had done well. Ruth sent "the kids" money to come home. Joab used it to keep the electricity turned on. When he told his wife they could not afford to go home, she wept. When he told his mama, she wept, too.

The day after finals were complete, Joab took a job as a night monitor for a security system company. He blessed his luck for having found it. Home Guard was perfect. He was on four nights from 9:00PM to 6:00 AM. There were a few maintenance type responsibilities that could be done in an hour. Then his time was his own to study, or sleep, except in the rare instances when there was an emergency or a break in. In that case, all he had to do was relay a message to the police department, fire department or hospital.

Two days before Christmas, Joab got his first paycheck: $127.43. It was Anita's day off, so she made arrangements to leave the baby with their neighbor, Tiesha, while she and Joab hurried off to Toys R Us. The place was packed with parents in a spending frenzy.

Joab and Nita didn't know it at the time, but this was their Christmas. This one trip to the famed Big Daddy of toy stores was it. What fun it was, too! After so many months of counting pennies, what jubilance to break the constraints of practicality and freely spend on purely frivolous items. Damn the electric bills, the phone bills, the insurance bills, the rent! Time to buy their kid some Christmas. But beyond this, the sweetest treat, by far, was anticipation.

If asked, both Johnsons could still recall the moment they had discovered *the truth about Santa*. That first bitter step from the sheltered warmth of childhood into the stark wilderness of reality; an unenchanted place with no magic to transform what *is* into *what should be*. Both Johnsons were astonished to discover, tonight, *the real truth* about Santa. He was standing right there in the fourth aisle of Toys R Us. He'd traded in his white beard for Anita's cornrows and his red suit for Joab's jeans and sweater. His mind dancing with delight over his Good Girl list of one.

By and by the young Johnson-Clauses found themselves on the doll aisle.

"Her first baby doll," Nita reflected, a faraway look in her eye. "I remember my first baby doll."

"You probably still have your first baby doll somewhere in our room," Joab teased.

"She was white. Her name was Veronica"

"White, really?"

"Well, did you ever have a black G.I. Joe?"

"Yeah," Joab recollected. "But they didn't come out until I was seven or eight."

"Look at all these pretty black babies," Anita marveled.

"Well, we can't adopt them all. Pick one." Joab yielded this decision to his wife.

Anita carefully considered the candidates one by one, offering a rejection analysis as she went, "Her body's too hard, not cuddly enough. This one has a funny face. This one's too big for Cinda. It would take up the whole crib. This one looks too old. This one cries. Ooo! Who could put up with that?... Oh-h-h-h, look at this one," her voice softened. "It's perfect. And look, you fill it up with warm water and it feels like a real baby."

"Great," Joab was running out of patience, "We'll take her. Now, where is the talking telephone section? I think she'd like a phone of her own."

"And a sandbox. She needs a sandbox."

"A sand box? . . . for a girl?" Joab was amazed.

"Sure. All kids love sandboxes."

"Then let's save it for the spring and I'll build her one. A big one."

"Let's don't forget the stocking stuffers!" Anita was positively giddy.

"Oh, and the candy canes!" Joab said, grabbing a box full. "And look at this! They have all kinds of 'em. You don't have to get only peppermint anymore."

By the time the Johnsons rolled their overstuffed cart out into the parking lot, *both* of them were giddy. The stress of the preceding months lifted and the tension vanished. They were remembering Christmas Past and so many of their memories were overlapping.

"Do you remember Big Mama's nativity?" Joab asked.

"Yeah." Anita laughed. "It was like she had one piece left from about 15 different nativity sets and none of them matched."

"They were all different sizes. One of the camels was the size of a dinosaur." Joab continued.

"My favorite piece was . . ."

". . the donkey with the bobbing head." Joab cut her off.

"And all three kings...

"... were black," they said together laughing.

"I wonder what she did with all the white ones," Nita puzzled.

"Somewhere there are two nativity sets with all white kings."

"Big Mama was a piece of work."

"Yeah, she was," Joab nodded, catching his breath. "I'm glad you knew her."

"I am, too," Nita said.

"Where should we hide all the stuff?" Nita asked, as they pulled up in front of their trailer.

"How 'bout the closet of my study. She never crawls in there." Joab suggested.

"Good idea," Nita whispered.

The couple moved the goods from the back of the car to the closet in the silence of co-conspirators. When the last package was in, Joab caught his wife's wrist, spun her around and gave her a premarital type kiss.

"C'mon," he urged.

"Joab, I should pick up Cinda. It's late and I hate to take advantage of Tiesha."

"Why? She takes advantage of you. And she's got three kids. We only have one. Besides, we've never done it in the living room before!"

Anita just giggled, taking care not to kick over the Christmas tree stand as her husband lowered her to the floor.

Anita returned from Tiesha's trailer with a sleepy daughter and two six packs of Budweiser. Tiesha always seemed to have a stocked fridge and since Joab and Anita were still two years out from legal, Tiesha let them buy it through her.

By the time Anita had changed the baby and placed her in the crib, Joab was in the living room, working on his second beer. All the lights were off except for the tiny, multi-colored bulbs flashing from their synthetic tree. He held a silver can out to his wife. She took it and nestled down on the sofa, under her husband's arm. In rich silence, they watched the lights blink on and off, on and off.

"Nita, I should go ahead and declare a major soon," Joab broke the long silence, "I can do business, but I hate it. But the things I love are not practical. Man, there's a world of Black literature out there I never knew about. And I love to study history, any history. It doesn't really repeat itself, it's just that people can't seem to learn from the preceding generations and every one of them makes the same mistakes over and over again. The dynamics change with the passing of the years, but the basic human flaws are the same. It's cool as hell to study. It's human nature, and human nature stays the same.

Shakespeare understood it. That's what makes his plays so timeless. One of the guys at school says that there's a Shakespeare Festival here every spring. I've never seen a play. Wanna go?"

"Sure! After you build the sandbox."

"Anita, what should I do? I mean, I should probably major in business right? Maybe I should try some law courses."

"Whatever you decide," Anita rolled around and kissed his mouth.

"But what can you do with history? Nothing! Starve. Hell, I can starve us without a college degree."

Anita was at a loss. She did not know how to counsel him, but she knew he was struggling and she *did* know how to comfort him. She went to the kitchen for his third beer, placed it in his hand and began undressing - slowly. December 23rd turned out to be a big night for the Johnson's living room.

The following day, Anita was scheduled to work a double shift in order to meet the nutritional needs of the bustling masses of last-minute shoppers. Joab would not work until 9:00PM, so he was free to spend a little special time with his baby girl. Around noon, there was a knock at the door. Ruth appeared wearing a Santa hat and shaking jingle bells.

"Mama!" Joab exclaimed, engulfing the small woman in an embrace and practically lifting her off the steps into the house.

"Merry Christmas, Son!" She said.

"Why didn't you tell me you were coming?"

"'Cause it would have ruined the surprise. Where's my little girl?"

"She's in her high chair. We were just finishing lunch."

Ruth peeked around the kitchen corner. "Where's Granny's girl?" she asked, "Great day! She's gotten so big!"

Ruth removed the tray from the high chair and lifted the toddler out. She held the child up to her face, and the dimpled hands reached for her earrings.

"Watch out, Mama. The kid loves jewelry," Joab cautioned.

"Anita tells me she's an old pro at walking. Oh, I can't believe it," she mused, placing the child on her fleshy little feet. "My, look at her go! Did Anita have to work on Christmas Eve?"

"All day. *I* go in at 9:00. Anita will be so glad to see you! I can't believe you drove all this way by yourself."

"I've always driven by myself. Besides, I have the car phone for emergencies."

Joab unpacked Ruth's car while she played on the floor with the baby. Later, while Cinda took a nap, they had a long talk over hot tea. Joab was amazed at how smart his mother had become since he had become a parent only eleven months earlier.

It was a special blessing to Ruth to have a few hours of Joab all to herself. She had been anxious for a chance to look him in the eye while he told her how fine he was doing.

These opportunities will become rare indeed, she thought to herself while savoring the outpouring of all that was on her son's mind. Just as she had always dreamed, the stimulation of college was expanding the borders of his consciousness like the Big Bang was to have expanded the very borders of the universe. It was as though the extreme compression of the narrowness of his experience combusted when met by the spark of diversity and knowledge.

"What do you think about political science? Or Afro-American Studies?"

Before Ruth had a chance to answer, Joab continued enthusiastically.

" . . . or history? I'm trying to be practical. But it seems that all the things I am drawn to are impractical. Business. I can do accounting well enough, and I understand economics and all that, but they just bore me to death. I need to think about a good living for my family but . . . ." Joab finally ran out of words.

"Have you been in to talk with an advisor?" Ruth asked.

"Yeah. All she said was that I really have at least another semester before I need to make a choice. But I really don't have any time to waste. I need to get that degree and get to work so Nita can get back home where she's happy."

"You're putting yourself under a lot of pressure for your first year, Son. Why don't you just take some courses that interest you, and pick as many brains as you can when it comes to practical application in the real world? There are millions of career choices out there that you'll never find in a book. And you have more time than you think you do."

"No I don't, Mama. I have less time than I think I do."

Ruth enjoyed fixing supper and fussing over her son and grand-daughter. Anita recognized the Blue Impala and before her own car rolled to a stop, she was up the stairs and through the door.

"Mama!" She cried, hugging the older woman.

"Ms. Lucy wanted to come in the worst way, but she just had to stay home and keep the Christmas fires burning for your big brother. I had to promise her I'd take lots of pictures. She sent along gifts for y'all, though."

Anita turned, still in her coat, to view the tree. All around the base of it, and spilling out to the whole corner of the room, were gifts. Anita squealed like a child and danced with delight.

Ten minutes after his wife got home, Joab was out the door on the way to his job. Ruth and Nita stayed up till 4:00 in the morning wrapping gifts, sipping tea and running their mouths like a river at flood stage.

When Joab fell into bed at 6:40, Cinda was already finished with her first bottle and was snuggled in beside Nita. By 8:00 neither Cinda nor her mother could be kept in the bed, and Ruth could be heard puttering in the kitchen.

"Merry Christmas, Daddy," Anita whispered in her husband's ear, then she placed the wiggling Cinda on his stomach. "D-a-a-a-a-a-d-d-y, let's go see if Santa Claus has been here," Anita coaxed.

Joab rubbed the grit in his eyes. "Okay. Okay," he said. Then he focused on the chocolate cherub straddling his abdomen while jumping up and down. "Cinda! Did Santa Claus come!? Have you been a good girl!?!" He asked.

"Of course she's been good. She's been great! She's been perfect! C'mon, c'mon, c'mon!" Anita answered impatiently. Like her daughter, she too, was jumping up and down.

"Go get Grandma," he said, stumbling to the bathroom.

Joab entered the living room amid the mini-lightning storms of flash photography. Ruth handed out coffee and then the trio of adults circled around the hallowed child at the base of the tree, taking turns behind the camera. By the fifth gift, Cinda was showing signs of sensory overload and flash shadows were floating on her vision with barely any time to dissipate.

It was hard to say who, among this group of four, was having the better time. Cinda, as the pole on which the earth spins, would be the most obvious candidate. Yet her mother, well-pleased with her choice of a spouse, rich with the gifts of motherhood, safe from the winter cold in her own cozy home, was a woman most satisfied. A rare female, indeed. Then there was Joab, presiding over his women, three generations of them, as the singular male presence. As such, his opinion was respected, his direction was heeded, and this morning, as provider of Christmas, he was the undisputed king of his humble domain. But it was only Ruth who possessed the wisdom to savor the sweetness of this moment in the knowledge of how infrequent they would become amid the business of the months and years ahead.

Ruth watched with a long smile as Cinda rode the pink, bouncing pony she had bought the child. Then her attention turned to Joab as he unwrapped his gift.

"Oh, Mama!" he whispered in awe, "How? This is too much."

"Mr. Keylar was upgrading his, and so he offered this one to me at a very good price."

Joab pulled his refurbished IBM laptop computer out of the box as though it were priceless china.

"Oh, Mom, do you know how much easier this will make my classes – my life?"

"Yes, Son," she answered honestly. "I'm very familiar with this one if you ever need help with it."

Joab lifted the screen and his fingers began the quiet clicking which would accompany much of his life henceforth.

"Wow," he said. Then he said it again, and again. Ruth turned her attention, still smiling, to Anita. The younger woman lifted the lid from an exquisite nativity set.

"Oh, Mama, it's so pretty," Anita said.

"No home should be without the Baby Jesus at Christmas," Ruth softly commented.

"But it only has one black king," Joab observed and they all had a good laugh on Big Mama.

After the gifts had been opened and the wrapping paper collected in the trash can, Ruth put the turkey she'd gotten up at 5:00 to prepare, in the oven. Then she dressed herself and her granddaughter and set off to find a Baptist church in which to celebrate the birthday of "the greatest Christmas present of all time" with her "brothers and sisters in the Lord." Joab and Anita declined her invitation but could not withhold Cinda from being shown off in the red velvet and white frills Grandma had provided for the occasion.

At 4:00, they all sat down at the kitchenette table and enjoyed a lavish feast. At 8:40, Joab reluctantly departed for work with a full tummy and heavy eyelids. It had been as fine a Christmas as he could recall.

The second semester fell into a fairly predictable routine. Cinda was still prone to ear infections which were generally followed by a call to Ruth for a little help with prescription expenses. But outside of that, Joab's paycheck turned out to be the margin that enabled the Johnsons to keep hanging on. This gave Joab some degree of satisfaction. Anita, however, had a hard time hiding her contempt for her job and the public she served. She referred to her manager as "that son of a bitch" and the mall shoppers as "the assholes with credit cards."

On the nights when Joab worked and Anita didn't, she generally took Cinda on a walk that ended up at Tiesha's house. Both women would sit in the kitchen drinking beers, talking a streak, and watching their children play through the window.

Tiesha was about six years older than Anita and as such, Anita looked up to her. She was currently between boyfriends but had prevailed upon Anita, more than once, to watch her brood of three while she went out seeking "some adult company." She was a third-generation welfare mom who knew how to work the system to get what she and her children deserved. She knew her rights.

The way Tiesha talked about sex made Anita's eyes drop to the floor and her face flush.

"Tiesha!" Anita would exclaim, "I can't believe you just said that!"

"Well, Honey, it's true." the woman would respond with a limp wristed gesture.

Anita was drawn to Tiesha the way folks are drawn to soap operas and for the same reasons. Anita had been raised in the flat, sandy woods of the rural skirting of Savannah. Tiesha had been raised in the inner city of Atlanta. Her life had been fast and action-packed from the start. She even had a pale scar on her left forearm where the bullet from a drive-by had grazed her. Anita's life began to seem dull and backward by comparison.

"You've never had no man but your husband?" Tiesha would ask with mock disbelief. Anita would giggle and stare at the floor.

"Well, don't tell me you never thought of another man with all them good-lookers who come shopping to the mall!"

"Tiesha!" Anita would respond with equal disbelief at the implication.

"Well, Honey, the first man I had was a member of my big brother's gang when I was 12. Only it was more like he had me. He was 19. I liked it. I mean as long as I was gonna get it anyway, may as well have fun, am I right? I don't mind telling you he was good-looking. And hung!"

"Tiesha!" Anita exclaimed, hoping her companion would continue.

"Well, Honey, it's true. I drunk from the sweet water of that well more times than I can count. Cassandra was born when I was 16. Ah, her Daddy was a good man and good to me. He loved me. He never hurt me. He still loves me."

"Well why didn't y'all get married?" The question seemed obvious enough to Anita.

"Married?" Tiesha repeated incredulously. "Married! Well, chil', he wanted me to. Begged me to, but he didn't have no job, no REAL job, and my benefits would have been cut if I was married. I moved out into my own place two months after Cassandra was born. Her Daddy lived with me for a while."

"How'd you get here?"

"My little sister moved out this way and talked me into getting my kids out of the city. She moved back but I stayed. I got two sons. They ain't gonna wind up dead from no gang wars. I miss my Mama, though. She'll never leave 'lanta."

"I miss my Mama, too." Anita agreed.

It was spring. The days were trying to stretch out and offer some welcome light at the end of a workday. Still, today, the sun was setting fast. The first and second Buds were urging Anita to sit and talk through a third. No. She had to get Cinda fed and bedded. They had work in the morning.

She bid Tiesha good night.

"You want to go to The Club with me Friday night?"

"Who'll watch the kids?" Anita was almost sarcastic.

"If you split the bill with me, I know one we could afford."

"Sorry, Tiesh, I still can't afford it."

"Well, maybe I'll babysit so you and Joab can get a little wild some night."

"Yeah, if we could get past the door."

Anita went out into the cooling evening, and gathered up her toddler.

"Stay, Mama!" the child insisted.

"Time to head for home, baby," Anita told her. "Night y'all." she hollered at the other children over the protest of the screaming one on her hip.

"No. Stay, Mama!" Cinda insisted.

Anita's mind was running ahead to tomorrow morning. Daylight would come too soon and all would be rushed. How she hated work. She hated the silly polyester uniform. She hated her bosses. She hated smelling like rancid frying oil at the end of the day. She hated the grease slick on her face. She hated obeying people who didn't even say, "please." Most of all, she hated being away from her Cinda and exposing her, day after day, to the germs of other children whose moms could not afford to miss work on account of a runny nose. And she hated leaving Joab in bed. She missed him. They never saw each other anymore. They had no time. The school year seemed endless. Anita wondered how she could do this for *three more years.*

Chapter 4

Domestic pressures mounted, tension upon tension, and culminated in finals week. Some days before, Joab had announced that he would not be picking Cinda up from daycare after class on the nights that Nita worked. It entailed switching cars, as Cinda could not ride the bike, and returning to pick up Nita and the bike at the end of her shift. With finals only days away, the study time for Joab was critical.

Anita didn't like the idea of Cinda staying one minute extra when her father was in the home, but she kept it to herself in tight-lipped resentment. Joab sensed it but figured he'd let sleeping dogs lie until after his battery of testing.

Friday night, Anita walked in the door after a double shift with a sick daughter.

"Have you seen the Children's Tylenol?" she asked Joab, without any greeting.

"No, Babe, last I saw it was in the medicine cabinet. Fever?" He asked looking up from his books.

"Yes. Fever. 101.2 when I picked her up," Anita said in a tone which implied it was his fault.

"What can I do?" Joab offered.

"Find the Tylenol and bring her a bottle of juice. I'm going to take her temperature again."

When Joab entered the baby's room moments later, the electronic thermometer was beeping at 101.7. Nita shot a glance at Joab and began changing the diaper.

"Joab, come look at this," she said.

Nita rolled the child to her tummy and lifted her shirt to expose a half dozen bumps rising with tiny clear bubbles in the center.

"Shit! I'll bet it's chicken pox," Nita spat.

Joab went for the family medical dictionary. He returned, reading out loud.

"Signs and symptoms: fever and weakness and a red itchy rash which quickly develop into spots that fill with a clear fluid and rupture. Generally appearing on the face, scalp, chest, and back but can occur on arms and legs as well. The rash continues the outbreak for 1-5 days. In children, chicken pox is a mild disease though it is more serious in adults, bla, bla, bla, (Joab skipped down) . . . . Seldom lasts for more than two weeks. Keep skin clean by frequent bathing. Cool compresses may relieve itch, also antihistamines. Consult a doctor."

"It was that damned Marilyn Franks," Anita declared, "She brought her little brat in with them. They shouldn't have let her in. I'm gonna give that damn daycare manager a piece of my mind!"

"Well, it says here that once you get them you're not likely to get them again. It's probably good for her to get them over with while she's young."

"Right! This week while you're buried in the fucking books and I'm scheduled to work another double tomorrow! This is a hell of a week to *get them over with!*" Anita sputtered. Joab knew he would not be able to say anything right. He decided it might be best to withhold ammunition and keep quiet. Cinda started to cry.

"I can't find the Tylenol. It's not in the medicine cabinet," Joab quietly admitted.

"Well, here, you hold the baby, and I'll find it." The unspoken tag line was: *Why do I have to do everything around here?*

Joab jiggled, rocked and crooned, but the child's crying became more and more shrill. The elusive elixir remained hidden even from the woman of the house and within moments Joab's bike was blasting through the dark, North Carolina countryside on a Tylenol quest.

His emotions swam as he pushed the old bike up to sixty mph. He was greatly concerned for what his baby girl was going through, but he felt sure the medication would make her more comfortable and the illness would run its course and be gone. *And just what is Anita's problem? It's not my fault the kid is sick. I have to study. I'm busting my balls to make a future for her. Anita's not the only one working. I'm working AND taking a full course load.* Righteous indignation rose with the thought.

How could he explain to Anita that there are no excuses in college? Each professor handles class as though it is the only one the student is taking, or at least, the only one worthy of study. No slack. No excuses. Joab's mind detoured to raced over facts, and precepts that he'd been studying. The cool, damp wind felt exhilarating as it smacked at his face. He roared into it. Crammed data was spinning in his brain like the spokes of his bike.

The motorcycle maxed out at seventy-eight when he realized he'd passed the Revco. Joab was slowing when he noticed the blue flashing lights behind him.

Oh, shit, he said to himself pulling over under a dim lamp post. "Evening, Sir," he said as the officer approached.

"License and registration," came the standard response.

Joab flipped out his wallet and handed the information to an immense black cop.

"Did you realize you were going sixty-six in a fifty-five?"

He only clocked me at sixty-six. Thank God. Joab thought. "Well, Sir. I was on my way to the drug store for some Tylenol for my kid."

"Which drug store?" Joab should have anticipated that question.

"Uh, Revco."

"You passed it."

"I know. I was just looking for a place to turn around when I saw your lights."

He took out his ticket book. His massive hands were poised with a pen.

"Girl or boy?" he asked.

"What?"

"Is your kid a girl or a boy?"

"A little girl," Joab pulled a Wal-Mart photo from his open wallet and showed it proudly to the officer. "That was last Christmas. She's sixteen months now."

"Ah, she must have a pretty mama," The officer commented, handing the picture, the license and the registration back to Joab.

Joab nodded, "And chicken pox, I think."

"Yeah. Fever, little bumps that kind of look like fire ant bites?"

"Yeah," Joab answered, amazed at this man's knowledge.

"My daughter got them last year. Try not to let her scratch or she'll scar that pretty face."

"Thanks," Joab was sincerely grateful for the advice.

"You might want to pick up some Benadryl, too. Helps with the itching but it makes them cranky sometimes." The cop turned to go.

"You're not gonna give me a ticket?" Joab asked, astonished.

"Not this time."

Joab could not make out his eyes in the dim light, but he did catch the white flash of a smile.

"But I'll be checking to make sure you slow down. That little girl's counting on you."

"Yes, Sir."

✦ ✦ ✦

Both Nita and Cinda were worn out when Joab got home. The Tylenol worked like magic and within 20 minutes the fever had busted and the child was sleeping soundly.

"You comin' to bed any time soon?" Nita asked, after brushing her teeth.

"I don't think so, Babe," Joab answered.

"Well, I guess I'll sleep in Cinda's room tonight."

"I'll come give you a kiss when I go to bed."

" 'kay."

"Nita?"

She turned, expecting him to say something, but he didn't know what to say. He just knew he didn't want her to go to bed angry with him.

"Thanks for being such a good Mama and for working so hard." There they were, the right words. He didn't know where they had come from, but Nita gave him the first real kiss he'd had for days.

"You're welcome," she said and went to Cinda's room.

Joab turned back to his studies, currently, Comparative Politics. It would be his first of two finals scheduled for Monday. Thankfully, it was not comprehensive and he would only be tested on the material given since mid-terms. Mostly, this consisted of global political pressures and power shifts leading up to, and resulting from, the Second World War. It was a course he rather enjoyed. Joab found it fascinating to track the ascent of political leaders, how they used circumstances to their advantage and what made people want to follow them. Clearly humanity, for the most part, was an astoundingly poor judge of character.

Joab was sound asleep, head resting on his books, when Anita woke him the next morning. She was almost dressed for work, but wanted Joab to take her so he would have the car in case Cinda needed to get to the doctor's in a hurry. Joab groaned inwardly at the loss of so much study time.

Cinda was cranky and miserable. Her sleep was restless, and her fever tended to rise a full hour before she was scheduled for the next dose of medication. Joab spent most of the day with her in the rocking chair. She was the only person in the world who could tolerate his singing. In fact, today, it was the only thing that seemed to comfort her. Joab knew few songs right through except for church songs. Today, Cinda happily endured more than fifty choruses of "Amazing Grace."

Joab must have rocked for miles staring down at the soft curves of her face, the wispy crescents of her eyes in slumber, the dimples marking the joints above her fleshy little fingers, the tight, shiny curls of her hair, the hushed, rhythmic sound of her breath. Each time he attempted to place the sleeping toddler in her crib, she would wake and cling to him and he would sit rocking for one more round of Big Mama's favorite hymn.

By the time Anita called to be picked up, the muscles in Joab's neck and shoulders were knotted for having held his little one most of the day. He had gotten virtually no studying done. But, his baby girl was feeling better, and he was satisfied with his choice of investment that day. Still, his wife was a welcomed sight. Cinda slept between her parents that Saturday night and all three slept soundly.

Thankfully, the following day was Anita's day off. Joab spent it at the University library. He spent almost all of his free time there until, one by one, his exams were behind him.

It was Thursday afternoon when he walked out of the stark order of the classroom into the bright warmth of a Southern spring day. He felt like a man sprung from prison. He wanted to celebrate. He wanted to find his wife and drink a case of Colt 45. He wanted to take her on a bike ride. He wanted to hug his baby girl.

On his way home, his mind projected his likely scores. He could only recall three or four answers he hadn't been sure of. *I did well,* he thought with satisfaction.

He drove straight to the mall and went to the food court.

"Hey, Sweet Thing," he said approaching the counter of Chick Quick.

"Hey, yourself," she responded, trying not to look pleased.

"When do you get out of here?"

"Twenty minutes."

"Can I take you out for a drink?"

"At three o'clock?! You could try, but I doubt they'll sell you anything."

"Well, then, how about a ride on my Bad Bike?"

"Where's your daughter gonna sit?"

"Right where she is. Just for a half hour."

"Now, Joab Johnson! You ain't laid eyes on your chil' for 'most a week and you're gonna leave her in daycare! She's been sick, remember?"

"Yes, I remember. I've been home with her while you've been here."

"And where have you been while I've been home with her?"

"What the hell kind of a question is that? Look, Nita, I just finished up. I think I did well, and I just wanted to . . . never mind. I'll go get Cinda and meet you at the car."

Anita knew she had made a bad mistake as she watched her husband stride away. She knew he'd been studying near-constantly. In her heart she knew, but there was this one little voice in her head which reminded her he'd never had to study this hard before. *Did he really need to be away from her all those hours?* Here she was, almost single-handedly supporting the family and nursing a sick child while he was spending more and more time gone. The bitter bile of resentment filled the pit of her stomach. So powerful was it that she had to remind herself to settle down. Her period was due in two days and Joab just might be falling victim to her hormones.

When she saw him with Cinda in the parking lot, she knew she should have swallowed her fear and gone for a ride on that damned bike. *Well, too late now.* When Joab saw Nita approach, he stopped making his baby girl giggle and strapped her into her safety seat.

"I'll ride behind you." were the only words he spoke before Nita started the car.

As she drove, she watched him in the rear view mirror. His head was covered by a black helmet and he wore dark aviator glasses. Leaning into the wind, he looked very handsome and exciting. She, on the other hand, smelled like rancid cooking oil. His lanky body was undergoing the thickening of full manhood. His neck was wider, his chest was wider, his arms more powerful. She thought about the tight ripples of his stomach. Then she thought about the layer of fat on her belly that had never quite toned up since Cinda's birth. Teen trends in fashion dictated half shirts from which the plane from hip bone to hip bone could be prominently displayed by all the young girls—all except her. Even if she could afford one of those skimpy little shirts, child-bearing appeared to have fixed her tummy for good.

They're probably showing off their skinny little bellies and pierced little innies all over campus, too, Nita conjectured resentfully. She made a mental note to be seen more on campus next semester.

"Cow, Mama! Mama, cow!" Cinda observed from her car seat as a pasture swept by. "Cow say woof-woof," Nita answered, engaging in their game.

"No woof-woof. Cow go Moo-moo," the child corrected.

"No," Anita insisted with mock finality, "Cow goes woof-woof."

"No-o-o-o." Cinda became a bundle of giggles. "Doggie woof-woof. Cow Moo-oo-oo-oo."

Anita cracked her first smile in days.

Cinda's bout with the chicken pox turned out to be more average than severe with only two bumps breaking out on her face. Anita had put Band-Aids over those and felt sure there would be no scars. Most of the other boo-boos were healing nicely and looked like little more than a few bad mosquito bites. Anita took another look in her rear view mirror and was surprised to realize how badly she wanted her husband in spite of feeling like a worn rag. He was handsome, and he was exciting and he was hers. Her conscience pricked her as she remembered his angry departure in the mall. On impulse, Anita pulled over at a Piggly Wiggly.

"You pick up the steaks. I'll see if Tiesha's got any six-packs for sale and I'll meet you at home," she hollered through the window when Joab pulled up beside the Ford.

Joab had been home for a half an hour when Anita finally walked in the door.

"That woman sure can run her mouth," Joab commented, taking two sixes of Budweiser from his wife and giving her a dry kiss. He didn't like the woman. Her children were foul-mouthed and unkept. He didn't like his daughter spending so much time in their company and he was uneasy about his wife spending so much time with their mother.

Well, someday, I'll move my family to a really nice neighborhood, he thought.

"At least she keeps the beer cold," Nita offered.

✦ ✦ ✦

Joab got a second job working construction that summer. It was no skill and all back, but they needed extra men and the pay was a full two dollars over minimum wage. Anita decided that this would be as good a time as any to switch jobs. A Piggly Wiggly had just gone up in a new strip mall not far from Shady Oaks. Anita applied because the want ad said they offered a group health plan. They hired Anita as a check-out clerk. Then, all she had to do was find a suitable daycare for Cinda. Anita finally settled on "Miss Tilly's Country Care for Kids." Miss Tilly was a thick-to-heavy white woman on the far side of middle age. She operated her "Country Care for Kids" out of the rundown farmhouse she'd lived in since she was, herself, a kid. A chain link fence encircled a full half acre of her back yard. Inside the fence was a fairly new swing set and a reasonably well kept collection of outdoor toys. Miss Tilly only took a dozen kids a year as "she didn't need *no mo' money* and she couldn't handle *no mo' chillun.*" Miss Tilly was not a woman one might call *eat up with personality,* but it was clear that she had a tender heart for children, and Anita could find no hint of color preference in her. Cinda was one of four African American children in this year's dozen.

Still, as Nita drove away that first day, she was nearly paralyzed by fear and misgiving. Cinda screamed and clung to her when it was time to go.

"Don't worry, Anita," Miss Tilly assured as she uncurled the child's fingers from around the collar of her mama's Piggly Wiggly uniform, "She'll settle right down. But, now, you gotta go. And once you're out the door, don't ever come back, or you'll be learnin' her to holler louder next time."

Anita kissed the hysterical Cinda and closed the front door. She stood beside it for a long time, listening to Cinda crying, "Mama! Mama!" Cinda didn't *settle right down* and Anita stood outside that door crying with her daughter for ten long minutes, wanting to scoop up her child in her arms and hold her until she quieted, then take her home and never leave her with anybody else ever again. But she had to work, and she was afraid to disobey Miss Tilly's orders. At last, Cinda's sobs gave way to a sporadic intake of breath. Nita found a window and peeked in. Cinda was sitting on the floor, playing with another little girl. Nita looked at her watch. She was already late for work and it took fifteen minutes to get there from here. She got in the car.

What do I really know about Miss Tilly, anyway? Anita's mind was racing faster than the car. The words of solemn news casters came to her as she recalled every horror story she'd ever heard about daycare centers. *So Marilyn Franks recommended Miss Tilly's. So what? I never liked Marilyn anyway. What a lousy deal to leave your kid with a stranger when they're little and can't tell you when something's wrong.* Anita thought . "This sucks!" She said out loud, "This just sucks."The day was already eighty-nine degrees. Anita slid the air conditioning lever over to Max/Cool before she remembered it had started blowing hot yesterday. She hoped the problem was something cheap, otherwise there was no telling how long they'd be doing without A/C.

✦ ✦ ✦

The summer passed at a frenzied pace. Joab and Anita tried to schedule days off together but those remained rare, and both were usually too tired to do much more than sleep in and watch TV anyway. They did manage to take Cinda to the zoo one Sunday. Then Joab took them on a tour of the campus on another day, and Nita packed a picnic lunch. But soon school was just around the corner and those were the only two highlights of the summer. One night, Joab asked Anita how many days off she could schedule in a row.

"Four max. Why?" She asked.

"Well, classes start on August 23rd and I was thinking it might be good to go home for a few days."

"Really, Joab!?" Anita jumped out of her chair and gave her husband a hug around the neck.

"You see how many straight days you can get off." Joab said, hugging her back, "and I'll just quit construction a few days early."

"What about your night job?"

"I'm sure I can get the time."

"Oh, I can't wait!" Anita squealed. "Can I call Mama?"

"Not until we're sure of the time off," Joab ordered.

The trip home was long and exhausting without air conditioning, but it was well worth it. Cinda's time had to be fairly divided between the two grand-mama's who took turns hanging on the child's every word and showering the toddler with toys and treats. Anita spent her time mostly with her mother, venting her frustration and finding the most sympathetic of shoulders.

"Only three more years," her mother repeated time and again.

Joab came to the conclusion that his mother had immersed herself in church activities to the extent that she had hardly any free time left. She caught him up on the trials and adventures of his aunts and uncles and other kin in great detail. Joab's family had a huge shrimp dinner at Miss Lucy's the first night, turkey at Ruth's the second night and the third night, they went out with several old school friends while Miss Lucy babysat.

Nicholas said he knew of a few bars where "his brothers" might forget to proof a few underage drinkers. In fact, he knew quite a few - all real rough. And in every one of them, Nicholas seemed to know half the people there and he apparently had a lot to talk to them about because he could barely sit at the table for five minutes without excusing himself to talk to a bro.

"Nicholas!" the bouncer at the door would say. (Everyone called him "Nicholas," never "Nick" or "Nicky." Only Anita and Miss Lucy were allowed to call him "Nicky.") "Hey, man, how's it goin', man?"

"This is my sister and her husband and some of my friends," Nicholas would announce, nodding to their party. "Ya got any tables?"

"Sure, man," came the response - every time.

As kids, Nicholas never really had much time for his only sibling or her little boyfriend. He was four years older than

Anita and preferred to spend his time with "his brothers." Later, in high school, his size and strength made him a football legend at East Savannah High where he earned the nickname, "Freight Train" as a fullback. He had also been notorious for causing injuries on the field. A distinction he had earned. Miss Lucy would always remember his high school years as a living hell. His Mama had worshiped him as a child, made excuses for him as an adolescent and endured him as a young man. By his senior year, even his coaches could not control him and he was kicked off the team for bad grades and a bad attitude halfway through his senior year season. No one knew how he managed to graduate.

Joab had always assumed that he liked Nicholas. He had always looked up to him the way younger boys look up to older boys. There was a time when Joab thought everything Nicholas did was cool. Joab had even tried to walk and talk like him, but no one could outdo Nicholas, especially when it came to talking trash with the brothers. Joab watched him tonight through the smoke and dim light of the club. He was leaning against a wall, smoking a cigarette and having an animated conversation with two male acquaintances. There was a lot of bobbing and nodding and back slapping. Every now and again, laughter would erupt. Finally, all three disappeared into the men's bathroom. In a moment, Nicholas took his seat at the table.

"So, Nicholas, where you working these days?" Joab asked.

"Ah, I just quit my job with Smitty's Construction. That Smitty is just a white man who gets his kicks out of ordering niggers around all day. Not this nigger. Not for what he calls a paycheck. I ain't never gonna work for no white man again."

Easy to say when you're still living with Mama, Joab thought with a contempt that surprised him. Nicholas never kept jobs for long.

"Hey, Neet, did I tell ya that I'm moving to Atlanta?" He asked, turning to his sister.

"No, Nicky!"

He took a full pull off his long neck and sat back, elbow resting on the back of the chair. "Course, Mama don't want me to go. But I can't stick around and take care of her my whole life, man."

Yeah, right, Joab thought sarcastically.

"Y'all remember Jojo Minks from my class?" Nicholas continued. Joab remembered him. Joab remembered him as a scurvy drug addict. "Well, he's doing real good in Atlanta. Says he could get me a job if I want to come up."

"Cool, man, doing what?" Joab asked.

"Bouncer at a really uptown club. Man, beats the hell out of working. Maybe even pick myself up a rich bitch."

Everyone at the table laughed and bobbed their heads as they imagined the perks of Nicholas' possible job. With that, he reached into his pocket and peeled the top fifty off of what looked like a wad of them. He placed it on the table and told Joab to order another round.

"I'll be back," he added. "I see a friend I need to talk to."

Joab wasn't sure Anita could hold another Peppermint Schnapps, but figured it wouldn't hurt her to get good and ripped. After all, they were on vacation.

At barely 11:30PM, Joab accompanied his wife to the parking lot where she retched to the soles of her feet. Then he said their good-byes and poured her into their little Ford and drove her to his mother's, head hanging out the window, where she was sick most of the night and all the last day of their vacation.

The busyness of the Johnson's lives found a pattern and settled into a routine by the second month of Joab's sophomore year. Anita worked mostly day shifts, except when someone quit or too many people called in sick at once. She didn't like this job much more than her last one but she did concede that it was good not to go home smelling like a week-old bag of fries.

Joab took a full course load and continued to work the graveyard shifts Tuesday through Friday nights. Since Anita was required to work at least one weekend day, usually

Sunday, Saturday's became almost sacred. Both Joab and Anita came to live for them.

Still, four nights a week, Anita and Cinda had just enough time to kiss Daddy "hello" and "good-bye" before he was back from class and off to work again.

Anita found herself spending more and more time with Tiesha. Often, Anita would watch Tiesha's kids while her friend went *hunting males.* Sometimes, the kids wound up spending the night. Once, Tiesha didn't come home until five minutes after Anita was supposed to have been at work.

"Girl!" Tiesha would say the next day, "You need to get out once in a while. Working all the time makes ya old. You need to come dancin'. You like dancin'? Whoooo! What am I asking? Who doesn't like dancin'. I could get you an ID from a friend of mine who looks just like you. Hell, I could have my brother make you one! Wouldn't be no trouble.``

Anita would just smile and shake her head. But each time Tiesha would ask, Anita got a little closer to a "yes."

Towards the end of his fall semester finals, Joab broke a date with his girls.

"I'm sorry, Nita, I'm not feeling good about this test. I just gotta study," he said, knowing he would draw fire. "I'll take you and Cinda to the movies next weekend, after finals. What is it? <u>Beauty and the Beast</u> should still be playing. Right?"

"Oh, that's okay, Baby," she said in a tone thick as honey, "I guess I'll be going out with Tiesha, tonight night, instead.

"Oh? Where are you going?" He asked.

"I don't know. Some place where you can dance, I guess."

"And how are ya planning on getting in? A bathroom window? Ya can't buy an O'Doul's in this town without an ID."

"Tiesha's got a friend who looks like me. I can borrow her's."

"Oh." There was a pause while Joab grasped at other available obstacles. "And how am I supposed to get any studying done with Cinda tearing through everything?"

"I'll just leave her at Tiesha's house with the babysitter."

"Do we know this babysitter?"

"Yes. We know this babysitter. She's very responsible. Joab, I don't think you trust me."

"Trust you? I trust you. I don't trust *Tiesha*."

"Then come with us."

"Right. During finals week."

"Well, anyway, you don't have to trust Tiesha, she's not your wife."

"Now there's the definition of hell on earth. I just wish you could wait until I could take you. We'll go out next week."

"You've had two and a half years to take me out." (Words straight out of Tiesha's mouth.)

"Fifteen dollars for the babysitter, ten bucks for drinks for you, ten bucks for drinks for me and it's $35.00 before you know it, and it's just too damned expensive."

"Well, it's my money, too! And it's time I had one night where I didn't change diapers or check groceries, or fold laundry or watch Disney's latest two-hour cartoon which I'll see 693 more times on video anyway!"

"Well, I didn't know it was so important to you."

"Well it damn-well is."

"Well, I just wish you could have waited until after finals week."

"Well, I can't."

"Fine."

"Fine. (pause) I think I'll take Cinda out for a walk," Nita announced as she gathered up the child and then left her husband smoldering in his study.

She's going over to tell Tiesha to get the ID. That woman will pick Nita up looking like trash, she won't even leave until after 10:00, and she never comes home before 2:00. God knows how her car makes it home without killing someone, Joab thought. Then he got a chill up his spine as he realized that most of those words were his mother's. He stared at the screen of his laptop without seeing it. He continued to smolder but changed the direction of the thought flow.

Doesn't Nita understand that I'm trying to make a future for her and Cinda? Doesn't she know I'd like to go out too? Hell, we just can't afford it. Ya can't have three drinks for ten bucks. Where does she get off spending that kind of money? She could have waited until next week.

When Nita and Cinda got back from their walk, Anita came and closed the door to Joab's study.

"I know how important school is," she said pointedly. "Me and Cinda wouldn't want to disturb you."

At dinner time, Anita served him tomato soup and cheese toast in his study.

"I thought you might want to eat in here with your books," she said, putting down the plate.

"No," he said. "I'd like to eat with you and my daughter."

"We've already eaten," Nita responded and left the room. Joab could feel the blood rushing to his face. The word "bitch" wrote itself in his brain.

By 9:00 Joab could feel his wife primping for a night out. After years of sharing a bathroom, he knew well the particular angle of her wrist as she applied lip liner. *Red. She'd pick red to fill them in.* Then, exactly five strokes of the brush to apply color to the swell of each cheek. How many mornings had he lay in their bed, half awake, watching her get ready for work. He had already realized that he might as well go with her, for all the studying he would get done, but he would not. It was the principle of the thing. They could not afford to spend the money and he had an exam in Modern International Politics tomorrow. He needed to study - whether he could concentrate or not. If he failed, it would be *all her fault.* If she wanted to be selfish and unreasonable, that was just fine. *Women! Once they decide to do something, you may as well just get out of the way.* He did wonder what she would wear.

"Tiesha's here!" She called from the living room.

He checked his watch. *See there? 10:20 p.m.*

"Study hard," she hollered from the front door.

He had to know what she was wearing.

"Wait!" He shouted jumping out of his chair, "I need to kiss my baby good-bye."

Whoa! Anita looked flammable. She wore tight jeans, low red heels, and a half red sweater with a neck cut wide enough to slip off one shoulder when she danced. He was right, her lips were as red as her sweater. He thought of her dancing, of the fluid way she moved her hips and shoulders and those long legs, and in his mind he could see himself taking her by the hand and laying her on the bed and tasting that red lipstick. . . but he was angry with her. Instead he kissed Cinda on the cheek.

"Daddy loves you," he told the child, "Have a good time. Tell the babysitter to call here if there is a problem," he told Anita.

Tiesha, patient and amiable as usual, leaned on the horn. No kiss. Anita was gone. Joab returned to his studies in a funk. Soon, he was fuming. He loathed the idea of her dancing with anyone else . . . of anyone else *watching* her dance.

It was 3:05 a.m. when they returned. Anita, light-headed and lead-footed, changed Cinda's diaper and laid the sleeping child in her crib. Joab stayed in the study until he heard her finish brushing her teeth. That was always the last thing she did before she got into bed. Then he shut down his computer and went to brush his teeth. He could smell the smoke in her hair as he climbed in beside her. Silence.

"So, did you have a good time?" He asked finally.

"Yes. I did," she lied. She had, in fact, done little dancing. She felt shy and awkward without Joab and stayed close to Tiesha's side. The older woman proved a valuable back-up for men who were not willing to accept the explanation that she really was married and really just wanted an evening out with her girl friend.

"Did you get much studying done?" she asked.

"Yes. I did," he lied. He had done nothing but imagine men hitting on his beautiful wife.

"Good," she said.

"Good," he said.

She rolled over with her back to him. The image of Anita in her red sweater and red lipstick practically glowed in the dark as he lay there. He longed to roll her over and feel her lips and legs and all in between. She longed to snuggle down under his arm, cheek resting on his chest, legs intertwined under the covers. It was over an hour before either of them fell asleep.

Chapter 5

It was only after the last exam was taken that Joab could close the books long enough to look at the calendar and grasp the nearness of Christmas (only eight more shopping days) and the passing of the year. Nita pulled out Christmas decorations the day after Thanksgiving and had been in a delirium ever since. Daily, she pressed Joab about plans for a visit to Georgia. Joab could feel the strong pull of his own homing instinct, but a look at their household bills left him little realistic hope of a southward migration. Still, Anita pressed.

"I miss my Mama, Joab," she was almost crying. "At least you got to see yours last year. This will be the second year in a row I haven't seen Mama for Christmas."

Joab knew she missed her mama. Truth was, he missed his, too. And Anita had been working so hard.

"Okay, Babe, I can't go with you, but if the Pig'll give you the time off, you tell Miss Lucy to expect you and her granddaughter for Christmas. I'll pay Bubba for the work he did on the alternator and tell him to go ahead and fix the brakes. That will be our Christmas present to each other and gas home will be my gift to you."

Now, Anita did start crying .

"What's wrong now?" Joab asked not understanding how, after relenting, he could have failed to fix the problem.

"I don't want to spend Christmas without you. I can't ever remember a Christmas without you," she sobbed.

"I'll tell you what – we'll do a Christmas with Cinda, together, before you go. Then on Christmas day, I'll work a double at Home Guard. It will let the other people spend the day with their families and I'll get paid time and a half."

Anita continued to cry for another ten minutes. Then she blew her nose and called her mother.

The following Tuesday was Anita's day off. She and Joab enjoyed a big lunch at the local Red Lobster and made the annual trip to Toys R Us. On the 21st, they had a quiet family Christmas. Cinda, two months shy of two years old, was oblivious to the dictates of a calendar, but had a firm grasp of "presents for me." Her big gift was a miniature toddler kitchen like the one at Miss Tilly's. After her initial delight, she squatted down and swung open the oven door for a closer inspection of her appliance. Next, she walked around her domestic domain and did the same to her fridge. Santa had also furnished her with dishes, knives and forks, plastic food to cook, and plenty of baby bottles for her growing family of dolls. The roots of her femaleness went to the core of her being and it was astounding to consider how much of her personhood was fed by them. Joab and Anita marveled in rapt adoration as their daughter busied herself about the business of domestic responsibility. She was nesting! And it didn't matter to her that she had stored the plates in what was supposed to be the refrigerator or that she set the forks, one by one, in the oven. This was *her* kitchen. These were *her* dishes. These were *her* babies. *Oops! Where were the babies?* She ran in short-legged strides to her room and dragged them by various limbs into the living room, placing two each in her parent's laps, then handing them bottles.

"Baby hungry," she announced. "Feed baby," she ordered. The parents obeyed. These were, after all, their grand-children (all girls).

✦ ✦ ✦

It was cold and drizzling the morning of the twenty-second when Joab loaded luggage and gifts and finally, his family, into the little Ford. He strapped Cinda safely into her car seat.

"Dubby, Dada," she said. This was Cinda's signature phrase for, "I love you, Daddy."

"Where's Daddy's treasure? Right there in your car seat!" He answered for her with tickle fingers to the tender spot just below her neck. The child responded with a splashing of giggles that consumed her entire body. Joab looked at the graduated pearls that were her teeth and wondered how it could be that she had a full set already. He asked Anita, one more time, if she was sure of the directions. Anita had tears in her eyes as she nodded, yes. She could not talk except to say she loved Joab and would call as soon as they got in. She had thought about wishing him a Merry Christmas but the words seemed trite and wholly inappropriate under the circumstances.

All at once, Joab was anxious for the safety of his women. He would have prayed if he had had any faith in God - but he did not. *Faith was for the feeble-minded who did not trust in themselves.* Still, somewhere within, his soul was comforted in knowing that two grand moms and half their church were praying for safe travel for his girls. He kissed them both, locked the doors, and watched his car turn right at the dirt entrance to Shady Oaks, then disappear over the hill.

For a long moment, he stood watching the place where the car had disappeared. He felt as though everything inside his skin had been replaced by thin air. Then he returned to the warmth of the trailer where Big Bird was demonstrating the difference between up and down. Joab fell back on the sofa and began channel surfing, but found nothing of interest. He clicked off the tube and sat staring at Cinda's miniature kitchen. For the first time in his life, Joab was aware of being alone.

This week, it wasn't difficult to pick up all the overtime Joab wanted. His coworkers had a million last minute holiday preparations to attend to, and since Joab's Christmas had come and gone, he was glad for the opportunity to be paid for killing time. He would be taking a course in African-American Literature next semester and decided to do some reading ahead. He had blitzed through Alex Haley's *Autobiography of*

Malcolm X, Alice Walker's *The Color of Purple*, and Toni Morrison's *Beloved*.

Joab worked his usual shift on the 22nd, fourteen hours on the 23rd, and on the 24th, Joab worked from nine to five and took a four hour break before going back for his usual shift of 9:00PM to 6:00 AM. He finished his McDonald's dinner on the way home, and had just settled in on the sofa for a nap when he thought he heard a knock on the door.

Suddenly, Tiesha was in the room.

"Merry Christmas, neighbor," she smiled, "Now, don't get up. I just thought I'd come by to deliver your Christmas gift."

Joab couldn't imagine why she'd include him on her Christmas list. He swung his feet to the floor and sat up. Tiesha was holding a case of Budweiser.

"Oh, thanks, Tiesh," he said, genuinely touched. He reached into his pocket for some cash. "How much was it?"

"Now, Joab, I told ya it was a Christmas present. I don't want no money!" She squatted down in front of the fridge and began placing the red and white cans on the bottom shelf. When she got to the last two she handed one to Joab. "Mind if I share one with you?"

"No," Joab answered, feeling a tightening in his stomach. "C'mon in and sit down," he asked, not seeing any way to avoid the invitation.

He chose a chair. Tiesha leaned back in the corner of the sofa.

"So, you ready for Christmas?" he asked.

"Oh, yeah. I did all my shopping the week after Thanksgiving. Yeah, I'm looking forward to watching the kids open their gifts. They're most a pain in the ass year round, but I love having 'em at Christmas."

Joab considered anew what a gift Tiesha had for crassness.

"Yeah, we celebrated Cinda's Christmas early, so Nita could go home."

"But, now, Honey, you know it ain't the same. Anita's such a child her own se'f. I guess it was more important for her to see her own Mama than for your baby to see her daddy on Christmas. I just hate the thought of you being all alone on Christmas mornin'."

"Well, it was my idea to send the girls home," Joab lied, "and I'll be working all day Christmas anyway. Um, I have to be back at work in an hour and a half and I really need a nap, so . . ."

"You know, I respect a man who works as hard for his family as you do. And going to school, too!" Tiesha rose, "Ya know, I'll bet you could use a nice back rub."

"No. I could use a nice nap."

Tiesha walked behind the chair and began rubbing the base of his neck.

"Would you like a little company?" She asked, "I could use a nap, too."

 The implication was clear and nauseating.

"No . . . No thank you," was all he could think of to say.

"Joab, now don't tell me you never thought what it would be like to sleep with a grown-up woman." He *had* thought about what it would be like, but he hadn't ever thought about the woman being Tiesha. She leaned down close to his ear and whispered so he could feel her breath and smell the rank scent of a two-decade, pack-a-day habit . . . "I could teach you such things. I could make you feel so good. I know how to please men." Joab could feel behind him the collective shadows of many, many men. "Anita would never know," Tiesha pressed, "Just a little bump on a cold day."

The possibility flashed across his imagination. He was becoming aware of the lack of variety in his experience. *What was there to be taught? . . . What was there to be caught?* He wondered if her hands felt him shudder as he considered the variety of diseases to which she might be host. Nope. If he ever were to cheat on Anita, it would not be with Tiesha.

"Tiesha," he said firmly, "I really do need some sleep. Thank you for the beer."

"Eat shit," she said on her way out the door, "You owe me 12 bucks."

"And Merry Christmas to you, too."

✦ ✦ ✦

When Anita returned from her Christmas visit home, Joab could tell she had something on her mind. But she was holding back and would not respond to his inquiries. He didn't like it, but he couldn't make her spill it. Anyway, if he knew her at all, she would not be able to keep it inside long.

He was right. It was a couple of days before the start of spring semester. Anita had worked until five and Joab had enjoyed a whole delicious day with his daughter. They had spent it outside, building a large sandbox. Actually, Bubba deserved most of the credit for the sandbox. It was his tools that built it, his design, his nails, and his borrowed truck that hauled and dumped the sand. Joab was not much of a carpenter, but he had bought the lumber and nailed it together, and both he and Cinda had enjoyed the process and the bright, cool, winter day immensely. As evening approached, Joab decided to surprise his wife and start dinner, chicken and rice. It was one of two meals he knew how to cook.

When Anita walked in the door she drew breath and announced, "Somethin' smells good!"

Cinda, who had been busy in her kitchen, cracked a giant smile and went rushing to her mother to embrace her leg (the most accessible hug) and repeat "Mama" six times, fast.

"Mommy, play," the child begged, taking her mother by the hand and leading her to her miniature kitchen.

"I was just gonna ask you the same thing," Joab smiled, giving her a kiss and a beer.

"Mama's tired," Nita answered, "Very nice, Baby," she said, not paying any attention to what Cinda was showing her. "Mama's tired," Nita repeated, "I'll be back in a minute. I'm going to change."

The dinner turned out to be one of Joab's best efforts. He served it with satisfaction while his girls ate. It had proven a rare thing for all three of them to sit down to a meal at once. Joab took the tray off of Cinda's high chair and pulled it right up to the table. She was good company even if she was still a messy eater.

When the meal was over, Joab offered to do the dishes while Anita put the baby to bed.

"You put her down," Anita offered, though it was clearly the more desirable of the two jobs. "I get to do it all the time."

As she cleared the table she could hear the beginning of Joab's version of *The Three Billy Goats Gruff*. Joab was a dramatic teller of children's stories. She smiled when she heard his voice strain to a high register to sound like the "Littlest Billy Goat Gruff." Cinda was smiling, too, but she was waiting for the trip-trap part, which was her favorite. Anita covered a sponge with dish soap and turned on the hot water. The sound of the water drowned out Joab's story and her mind started going over the sales pitch. She figured she'd found as good a time as any to reopen "the stay-at-home-mom debate" again.

"Who's that trip-trapping over MY bridge!?!" she heard her husband's voice bellowing over the sound of the running water. She giggled. She really was happiest in the home. Surely he could see his way to keeping her there, especially while Cinda was so young.

When Joab emerged from Cinda's darkened room, Nita was stretched out on the sofa. It looked close enough to an invitation to Joab. He lay down beside her. It wasn't a very wide sofa. He had to press in. He kissed her neck. It was right there and it smelled so sweet and felt so soft and warm on his lips. Then, he kissed it again.

"Joab, what if the baby wakes up?"

Joab jumped up, took Nita's hand and began leading her to the bedroom. She pulled away and sat back down on the sofa.

"Joab, I want to talk to you about something."

"Now?" he asked, almost whining.

Nita hesitated. "No, not now," she said and ran, beating him into the bedroom.

Later, in the dark, Nita knew she only had a short window of time between euphoria and sleep.

"Joab?"

"Hmmm?"

"I know how we can fix it so I can stay home with Cinda."

"Miss Lucy win the lottery?"

"No. But she agrees with me."

"Agrees with you about what?"

"Agrees with me that my place is here with Cinda."

"So do I. Just give me two more years."

"Two more years is forever. I was talking to Tiesha, and I know how we can do it, now."

"Tiesha's an ignorant pig."

"Yeah? Well if she's so ignorant, how is it that *she* gets to stay home and raise her kids and I —" her voice was raised.

"She doesn't stay home and raise her kids," he interrupted in a similar tone, "She passes them off to people like you, five nights a week, so she can go out and get laid."

"She does not!" Anita was shouting.

"She does too!" Joab shouted back.

"Fine. And I get up six days a week to bust my ass to pay some redneck, white woman to raise *my* kid! I suppose that makes me a walking-talking genius. Do you know that after I get done paying Miss Tilly, my time is worth less than $3.75 an hour? Hell, I can make more than that sitting at home. Tiesha does."

"Yeah, and she's on welfare."

"Yeah, well what's so wrong with that? The government's been taking plenty of money out of my paychecks for two fucking years now. The way I see it, I deserve to get some of it back!"

"No wife of mine is going on welfare."

"Great! So I bust my ass every day so your pride won't get hurt. Well, I've had enough!" Anita was screaming without restraint now. "I'm sick of it! I'm staying home with my baby whether you like it or not!"

When Anita finished her sentence, she discovered that Cinda was screaming too.

"Good going, Anita," Joab threw off the covers, flipped on the light and pulled on his jeans.

In a moment, she could hear her husband soothing their daughter from her room. He was singing "Amazing Grace." She could tell from the rhythm that he was rocking her. Anita got up to make herself a hot chocolate. It was clear there would be no sleep any time soon. Maybe she would be able to draw out a bit of the venom when Joab was done with the baby. She hadn't meant to lose her temper. She, herself, hadn't known the extent of her frustration.

In the near darkness of the nursery, Joab's mind was a million miles away from the words he sang. His daughter had quieted on his shoulder. He could feel her breathing slow and deepen. He stopped singing and kept rocking. Cinda's body relaxed and a foot twitched. He knew she must have fallen back to sleep. He kept rocking. Anger and resentment found its way to his jaw and he absently ground his back molars.

His thoughts raged. He had done nothing when she dropped out of high school. That had been a mistake. He knew that now. He had known it then, but he didn't have the balls to put up a fight. Now she wanted him to accept welfare. He could not. Her words had been open rebellion. She would do it *whether he liked it or not.* What recourse did he have? What could he do if she would not even listen to him?

He did not know how long he rocked. Gently, he set Cinda in her crib. There were two cups of hot chocolate on the kitchen table. Joab felt sick. He needed some fresh air. He pulled on a sweater and his hiking boots and grabbed his jacket.

"Where are you going?" There was panic in Anita's voice.

"I . . . I . . . I need to think about this," he said.

"Don't go, Joab. I didn't mean to lose my temper," her mind searched for an emotional Band-Aid. There wasn't one.

"No. I . . . I need to think about this." He pulled his keys out of the key drawer. A moment later the sound of his bike faded into the night.

Joab didn't know where he was going. The cold night air felt good on his face. He decided to head west on a country road he knew. He hoped his path wouldn't cross with a raccoon or a deer. He just needed enough road to think. Two of her phrases kept running through his mind: "I'm sick of it" and "whether you like it or not." He hadn't known she was sick of it. *What is she sick of? Is she sick of me or work or just not being home with Cinda?* He honestly didn't know . . . . *And if she is dead-set on doing something whether I like it or not, what recourse do I have? What could anyone do with that?* About three miles later, the word, "divorce" popped to the surface of his consciousness like a cork in the sea. *There it was. That's what it came down to. That's what it would always come down to when half of a partnership said, "Whether you like it or not." Two choices: accept or walk . . . Walk?* The image of Cinda sleeping on his shoulder flew into his mind. *How could I ever walk?* His heart sank. *Accept. That's the only choice she's left me. I guess I accept.* He had made his decision. But his disappointment in his wife was too deep to grapple with right now. He drove to Sammy's house. Sammy Yu was surprised to see him.

✦ ✦ ✦

Joab knew that Anita had to be at work by 8:30 the next morning. He returned home at 8:00. When the front door closed behind him, Anita sat up on the sofa, startled. Joab could tell from her eyes that she'd been crying.

"Don't you have work in a half an hour?" He asked.

She checked her watch. "Oh, yeah."

"You're gonna quit soon, anyway. What the hell."

"Ya want me to fix you some breakfast?"

"I'm not hungry. The baby still sleeping?"

Anita nodded. "So did you do any thinking?"

"Yeah." He was hanging up his jacket.

"Well, what'd ya think about?"

"I don't want to talk about it right now."

"I do. I won't be able to work if we don't talk. I've been up all night."

"Well, what's there to talk about? You're going to quit work and go on welfare whether I like it or not. Right?"

"Cinda deserves to be raised by her mother."

"Fine."

"But . . ." Anita could not bring herself to finish the sentence.

"But?"

"But, Tiesha says in order to qualify, we have to file for legal separation."

Joab let out one sarcastic laugh and shook his head in resignation. "Whatever you want, Nita."

"Only on paper. Nothing will really change. We won't even have to tell our mothers. Just get one of your college friends to lend you their address and tell the welfare people that you moved out and nothing will change except that I'll get to stay home with Cinda."

"Yeah, and we'll have to lie to my friends, our family, and the government."

"So we beat the system. So what? Who's the fool? We deserve it, man. How many decades did our people work in this country as slaves?"

Joab shook his head. The words were coming out of his wife's mouth, but he knew the whole lecture came straight from Tiesha. She'd probably gotten it from her brother who got it from his mother and God only knew where she'd gotten it from.

Anita took another tack, "Why can't you do this one thing for our daughter? Joab, Cinda needs me."

"It doesn't look like I have much of a choice, does it?" Joab went to the bathroom and closed the door.

On her way to work, Anita went over the conflict of the past 24 hours. She knew she had won the victory but she was not quite sure how high the price had been. She finally decided that Joab would see the wisdom of her decision once everything was in place. Anyway, she knew how to make it up to him once she had time to fuss over him instead of squandering away her life in a grocery store for pennies an hour.

When Anita hurried past her manager's office to punch in, he got up from his desk and asked her if everything was all right.

"It's not like you to be so late?"

She told him that Cinda had been playing with the lights in the car and that she had to get a jump.

"Well, next time, please give a call when you're gonna be this late," he asked.

"Sure," she said. *Two more weeks, max,* she thought. *Then, I'm out of here.*

♦ ♦ ♦

Second semester of Joab's sophomore year began. Now that a good number of his required courses were out of the way, he had more opportunity to take courses that simply appealed to him. His transcripts were shaping up to look like a political science major with a lot of history and literature credits. He had known for some time that it would be hard to find a practical application for his education without law school. He had been procrastinating on telling Anita because he knew how endless another three years would sound to her.

The couple of times that he had sought her advice on picking a major, she was of little help. She didn't really understand how science could be something other than chemistry or physics. How could politics be a science? She had gotten flustered, made jokes, and changed the subject. Joab had figured he was on his own.

Well, maybe law school won't seem so bad if she can stay at home, he mused.

♦ ♦ ♦

Two weeks later, Joab signed the separation papers. Tiesha found them a cheap attorney who would make it legal for $125.00. He worked out of a tiny, rundown office on the border where the bad side of town met the old side of town. As Joab sat in a worn leather chair across from the lawyer, his wife beside him, his daughter on his lap, a terrible misgiving screamed from within. But like a voice trapped in the nowhereness of a nightmare, it had no sound. He looked over at his wife's face wondering if she knew how hard this was for him. He knew she felt his eyes on her, but she would not turn her face to meet them. Her square jaw was set, and she was looking straight ahead at the attorney. She had made up her mind two weeks ago and forbidden any dissent in her household. Whole nights of debate and misgiving lay unresolved in his heart. As the lawyer droned on in passionless monotone, Joab imagined what his mother might think.

The humble and mighty Ruth found it a great source of pride that she had never taken one penny from the government. She had never said it, straight out, but Joab always sensed that it was a source of intimidation to his Aunt Annie who often seemed like the younger of the two women. One Christmas, when Joab was somewhere around his early teens, he remembered over-hearing the sisters argue.

Annie had been lamenting her latest breakup. Joab knew now Aunt Annie must have been drinking or she would never have raised her voice to his mother.

"What you gonna do with men?" Annie had asked Ruth. Joab was kind of hoping his aunt would get an answer, as his Mama had had nothing to do with them as long as he could remember. "They ain't one of 'em who's not a liar and a cheat," she went on, "They'll lie to ya soon as they look at ya. They'll tell ya anything you want to hear, take what they need and go. Well, I say, the hell with ya! Go on then. Go. And I give up a good job to move out there with that man, too."

Ruth broke in at this point to caution her sister about her language.

Annie was on a roll. "I mean it, Ruthie," she continued, "They can all burn for all I care. Making me have to go on government money till I can get on my feet."

"Now, Annie," his Mama interrupted with her calm, even voice. "There are plenty of good jobs around here. But you just gotta stay in one place long enough to build something."

"Yeah, like flippin' burgers."

"Now, you know that's not true."

"That's easy for you to say. You who got the college scholarship and found you a good job straight away! You've always had all the luck."

Joab remembered wondering why his aunt had raised her voice so.

"It's not a matter of luck," his Mama's voice had been just as soft as ever.

Now Mama's gonna give it to her, Joab had thought. *She'll tell Aunt Annie how hard she's had to work. About the hundreds of nights I spent in a sleeping bag on Mr. Keylar's office floor so Mama could get documents finished on-time, and how she deserves everything she's got.*

"God's been faithful to me and Joab," Mama answered quietly.

God! Joab had thought. *God? And who's hands would go numb after spending whole weekends at the typewriter? Whose ears were wired with Dictaphone tapes for days on end?* Joab would have said something, too, if he wouldn't have gotten in trouble for eavesdropping.

Joab stared at the floor. He knew he loved Anita less today than he could ever remember. Anita didn't know it yet, but a bitter seed had begun to send down tiny roots in her husband's heart. In truth, Anita had not the wisdom or perspective to even understand the issue. He stared at the imitation Persian carpet under his boots and wondered how she could make him do this. *How could she be such a profound disappointment? Why couldn't she just show a little guts and hang on for a few tough years?* He had always thought of his wife as a fine choice for a teammate. He had always been sure he could count on her to fight with him and beside him and guard his flank and build something strong and good and better than they had had - for Cinda. *Instead, she was wimping out and turning him into a failure before he could even make it to the playing field.* He felt his respect for her draining away. *Well, she could make him do it, but she could not make him like it.* The bitter root hit a growth spurt.

The attorney finished his dull explanation of the legal implications of formal separation. Then he rose and extended a hand to Joab. Joab did not look him in the eye as he delivered the first weak handshake of his life.

Chapter 6

It wasn't long before the first entitlement check came and Anita's goal was met. She quit work, without notice, and set about the business of being a full-time mom. Her first project was Cinda's room. She cruised used furniture stores and perused the classified section of the newspaper (people saved their yard sales for warm weather) until she found a cheap single bed for her toddler. The crib was disassembled and stored in the closet of Joab's study. Then Anita kept looking until she found a child's linen set complete with sheets and matching curtains, Winnie-the-Pooh, a miraculous find from the Salvation Army! One day Joab came home and found his wife painting Cinda's room a pale lavender. Cinda was also painted a pale lavender.

The next project was a thorough spring cleaning of the entire trailer. The whole project took less than four days. It was only a single wide, after all. Then Anita turned her attention to the car. Windex cut through two years of lollipop fingerprints on the windows and Bubba's borrowed Shop Vac sucked up two years of crumbs and dirt from the floor. Anita found countless pieces of Happy Meal toys and petrified hamburger pieces in the crack of the back seat. In her cleaning frenzy, she unsnapped the upholstery of the child safety seat, washed it and hosed down the remainder. Joab refused to let her near his motorcycle.

"You'd probably get the spark plug wet or something," he fussed. "It runs. Leave it alone."

In less than two weeks, Anita ran out of cleaning projects, except for the laundry which was as relentless as the tide.

She dusted off one of her three cookbooks and decided to try some new recipes, only to discover that the French must have a bigger grocery budget than she. Still, she tried to prepare a nice meal each day for supper. And each day, Anita delighted in singing a song to her daughter before nap time and sharing in her small victories and little milestones.

But no matter how many impossible spots she got out of her family's laundry, no matter how many curtains she hung, floors she vacuumed, toilets she cleaned, or windows she washed; no matter how much make-up she applied, perfume she wore, or even how skimpy the nightie, she sensed that she had lost a piece of her husband's soul. And Anita began to fear that she would never be able to possess that part of him again.

As the months passed, Joab and Sammy Yu became friends. It was a strange alliance really, one built upon Joab's need and Sammy's availability more than anything. They found themselves drawn to the same classes and running into each other several times a day. For the first time in his life, Joab had a problem for which he could not seek his mother's advice. Sammy was a good listener.

On Tuesdays and Thursdays, Joab and Sammy shared the last class of the day. It wasn't long before Sammy let Joab in on the whereabouts of a nearby bar, notorious for not proofing its clientele. Soon they fell into the habit of stopping by for a beer before heading home. Joab lamented the hard-headedness of wives and Sammy the unpredictability of women in the 90s.

"They just got us by the balls," they would finally agree before parting.

It wasn't long before Anita caught a pattern and inquired as to Joab's tardiness.

"Sammy and I went out for a beer," he answered honestly.

"Oh," Anita said. Joab could hear disapproval in her tone.

"Well, you and Tiesha have been known to down a few cold ones in the afternoons. Hell, half the days I come home you're sitting over in her kitchen watching soap operas and drinking."

"That's not true!" Anita snapped. "Twice. Twice you've come home and I was at Tiesha's!"

"It's been more than that."

"Bullshit." There was a moment of silence while both took aim. Anita was the first to fire: "And I wouldn't go to Tiesha's house if you were ever around."

"I'm around just as much as I used to be around, only you're around all the time and it just *seems* like I'm not around."

"Yeah, right. Only now you spend half the day drinking with Sammy at the . . . at the . . . at . . ."

" . . . the Pig's Foot Inn." Joab helped her out. "And we have one beer, ONE BEER!"

" . . . wherever you go. Did it ever cross your mind to invite me?"

Bull's eye! *Good question.* Joab thought. *No. It never had crossed his mind to invite his wife. He went there to talk about her. Why would he invite her?* "I didn't think you'd be able to find a babysitter." *Weak argument. Very weak. Too late. She'd already read his mind.*

"Right. When Tiesha owes me for about a million hours of babysitting. Maybe you never thought to invite me because you're not drinking with Sammy."

"Now, hold on!" Joab's face flushed warm with the implication. "You know, woman," he said. "You're just a jealous and spiteful woman! . . . and if you don't trust me then there's nothing I can do about it and it's just your problem!"

"Well, what am I supposed to think when you only have a few hours at home before you have to work and you'd rather spend them in a bar?"

"You can think whatever your jealous little mind wants to think!" Joab became aware that Cinda was pulling at his jeans. "What? What? What?" he asked, looking down at her upturned face.

"Dubby, Daddy," she said.

"I love you, too," Joab answered. *End of conversation.*

The Joab Johnsons shared an unusually quiet dinner. Then Joab went to work where he had plenty of quiet time to let the outrage of groundless accusation settle in.

✦ ✦ ✦

Overnight, it seemed, Cinda's confidence in her verbal skills strengthened until she became a perfect little chatterbox. Then, the diaper began to be an issue. Curiously for her, it just didn't feel as comfy as it used to. One day, upon returning home from a particularly hard day of classes, Joab was greeted at the door by an enthusiastic Cinda.

"Daddy! Daddy! I go poo-poo in the potty! Come see!" She spouted, taking his finger.

"Hey, Honey," Nita called from the kitchen. Somewhere along the way they had stopped observing the kissing-at-the-door ritual. "You better go see," Nita continued, "She's been saving it half the day."

Joab allowed himself to be pulled to the bathroom where an average, normal, child-sized bowel movement lay unimpressively at the bottom of the toilet bowl.

"Wow!" Joab shouted at a decibel level which startled even Cinda. "Did you do that all by yourself?" The child threw out her chest, tilted her head up, and beamed at her daddy. Joab scooped her up and tossed her almost to the ceiling. "What a big girl you are!" He said, catching her in his strong hands.

The child squealed with laughter and then remembered something of grave importance. "Wait, Daddy. Wait, Daddy. I have to flush now," she informed him with intense urgency.

Joab lowered her gently to the ground and Cinda's plump, soft hand pulled the mystical silver lever. Both peeked over the white rim to watch the little turd dance in a circle before sliding gracefully down the drain.

"Bye-bye, poo-poo," they said in unison.

The triumph in the bathroom was much the topic of conversation over dinner. Anita, delighted not to have missed this delicate rite of passage and embellished it with all the encouragement she could muster. Still, the child's joy was incomplete until her father could participate in it. Anita had never really noticed how much of a Daddy's girl her daughter was.

I change her diapers. I wipe her nose. I feed her and kiss her boo-boos. He spends all day with his books and four nights a week at his job, and he can still walk in here anytime and get all the glory, Anita mused in mild resentment. But her mind kept going. *Why not? I'm the one who has to discipline her all day long. I'm the one who has to spank her when she sasses me or won't mind. No wonder he can show up every once in a while and be the hero.*

Her husband was leaning toward her, whispering at her.

"What?" she asked.

"How long do we have to keep this up?"

"Huh?" Anita didn't have a clue.

"How long do we have to keep giving her poo-poos the big send-off?"

"Long as it takes, I guess."

"We need to put the lid on it before she starts dating."

Anita rolled her eyes and shook her head. "Put a lid on it?" she asked.

For all their arguing, Joab continued to grab an occasional beer with Sammy to which Anita responded by increasing her time with Tiesha. It was a stand-off which was rapidly turning into a vicious cycle. The more time Joab spent on campus complaining about his wife, the more time Anita spent with Tiesha complaining about her husband. Of course, Tiesha was not known for her peacemaking skills. Secretly smarting over Joab's rejection of her holiday proposition, Tiesha enjoyed stoking the fires of division until Joab was in an immediate state of tension whenever he set foot in his house.

Meanwhile, Sammy Yu was busy with an intrigue of his own.

"Joab?" He asked one day, "What do you think of Lesa?"

"Lesa?" Joab asked at a loss.

"Lesa. Lesa Shemasaki from Inter Pol II?"

Joab went through the class in his mind. *Oh, Le-e-e-e-sa,* he thought, "Is she the Chinese one with the long hair?" He asked.

"Chinese?!! No. She's Japanese. Lesa Chinese? With a name like Shemasaki?" Sammy grumbled.

"Well, what's the difference?" Koreans, Chinese, Japanese, they all looked the same to Joab.

Sammy mumbled something in Cantonese. "Joab, you're such a jackass sometimes. If my parents ever knew I was even thinking of dating a Japanese girl they'd cut me off."

"Really? Why?" Joab was surprised.

"You know, your ignorance of Eastern history is astounding. Americans have such a Western mindset. You know Oriental cultures were around for thousands of years before the first European even thought of brushing his teeth! Much less you Africans. Sometimes I'm convinced you're still barbarians. See? You probably take that as a compliment."

"Yeah? Well at least we *had* teeth 'cause we knew enough to drink milk." Joab was pretty proud of himself for pulling that one out of his hat. He loved to yank Sammy's chain. Still, his buddy's super-charged brain was close to spinning out of control. Joab figured he'd better reel Sammy in before he lapsed back into the peculiar dissonance of Cantonese again.

"So you've discovered you lack humility and you've chosen the famed Lesa S. to administer the required attitude adjustment."

"Thanks for the confidence, Man." Sammy's response was in English. *Good sign.*

"Sammy, that woman's convinced you could bottle her urine and sell it for perfume."

"Well . . . Maybe you could," Sammy offered.

"Right. And maybe she chews on men instead of tobacco."

"Well, I'm inviting her to have a beer with us after class on Thursday."

"A beer with *us*?" Joab repeated.

"I figure it's relaxed and non-threatening."

"It is for me," Joab answered.

"Does marriage turn all guys into wusses, or just you?"

"Kiss my ass, Yu," Joab said.

"C'mon, Joab. She seems very nice in class. What have I got to lose?"

How about your balls? Joab thought but decided to keep his mouth shut. *Sammy must be one of those guys who has all book smarts and no common sense,* he concluded.

He knew who Lesa was. Lesa was beautiful, exotic and wholesome all at once. She had a thin face with high rounded cheekbones and a softly curving jaw line. In fact, everything about her was thin—no, delicate. She never embellished her face with make-up, except for her full, almost-round lips over which she kept a clear and shiny gloss, making them appear always wet. Her dark eyes, like her intellect, could be piercing and unforgiving. They were clearly Asian but were wider than one might expect and could be curved into sparkling crescents if you could make her laugh, which was rare. Shining in black waves to her waist, Lesa let her glorious hair grow at a time when most girls were hacking theirs off to look more like men. She had manicured nails at the end of long fingers, a long waist and narrow hips. Her near-mulatto colored skin was even and smooth with never a blemish. She had the confidence of a good brain, a quick wit, loads of looks and limitless credit. There were few heterosexual males who hadn't considered the possibility and fewer still who hadn't quickly dismissed it. It would either take an overabundance of testosterone, a deficit of brains, or both to think one might have a chance with Lesa Shemasaki. Most guys opted to protect their ego. Joab agreed with most guys. Anyway, what was he concerned about? *Let Yu gamble with his own nuts,* Joab mused, *I'm married . . . well maybe not technically, but still.*

Sure enough, Lesa Shemasaki accompanied Joab and Sammy to *The Pig's Foot* the following Thursday. Joab was astonished. She appeared to be genuinely interested in Sammy. She even laughed at a couple of his jokes. Joab was impressed.

Later that evening, Anita was her usual, chilly self, so Joab accompanied Cinda to her sandbox for an hour's play before dinner. Then he left for work.

Around 11:00 it began to rain, and Joab remembered he'd left his wallet on the edge of the sand box. It kept on getting in the way when he sat down near Cinda, so he had taken it out and forgotten it. He didn't like the idea of waking Anita, but he decided to send her out for it anyway.

The phone rang ten times before Joab decided that he might have the wrong number and tried again. This time, paying attention to the numbers. No answer. An adrenaline rush swept over him as he pictured his child in an emergency room. He stared at the phone. Anita would call at her first chance. He wondered if cell phones had become standard equipment in ambulances. Then another thought hit him. He looked up Tiesha's number and punched the buttons.

"Hello," a sleepy voice answered but it wasn't Tiesha's.

"Hi. Is Tiesha there?"

"No, I'm the babysitter. Can I take a message?" came the response.

"How many kids you watching?"

"None of your business," Joab could tell she was about to hang up.

"No, wait. This is Joab Johnson. Does Cinda happen to be there?"

"Oh, hey, Mr. Johnson. This is Karen. Yeah, she's asleep on the sofa. That's her favorite place. You just missed your wife. Is there a problem?"

"No. No problem. Thank you. I guess I'll catch Nita later."

"'kay. Bye."

"Bye." Joab hung up. He was aware of his pulse.

The next morning, Joab rolled close to his wife and smelled her hair - smoke. He stared at her for a long time before deciding to let her sleep as usual. They'd have plenty of time for a fight over the weekend. Joab took a shower and started two cups of coffee running through the coffee-maker. In spite of his best efforts at silence, Cinda always heard him knocking around the kitchen and padded in to exchange a morning kiss for a warm bottle of chocolate milk.

This morning, she was wearing fuzzy pink pajamas with white plastic feet built into them. Joab heard Cinda scuffling along the linoleum before he turned to see her dragging a "baby" with one hand and offering him last night's empty bottle with the other.

"Mornin', Dada." she said, releasing the baby and wiping her eye with the back of a hand.

"Morning, Baby Girl," he said, scooping her up. This was the only reasonable response to a fuzzy, pink cherub fresh from slumber.

"Caw-caw miwk," she reminded.

"Where's my kiss?" he asked, to which the soft, pink center of her lips puckered and pressed to the freshly shaven flesh of his left cheek.

"Smooth," she commented, putting a warm, little hand to his face.

He put her down, grabbed a clean bottle, filled it with the perfect measure of two percent milk and Hershey's chocolate syrup, zapped it for exactly forty-five seconds, screwed the nipple on, shook it five times and presented it to the child.

"Gank you. Dubby, Daddy," she said before placing the nipple in her mouth, grabbing the wrist of her baby and shuffling towards the place where her mother slept. Her disposable night-time diaper crinkled with each step. Joab watched as she heaved the doll up onto the bed then placed a foot on the bottom shelf of his night table to climb on up. Her determination and ingenuity in dealing with a world designed for beings two and three times her size always amazed him. He watched her settle herself and her baby doll neatly under the covers as Anita rolled over to embrace them both.

His wallet had left a wet spot on the top of his dresser where he had placed it when he had gotten home just before dawn. He wrestled the soggy thing into his back pocket, zipped up his jacket, snapped on his helmet, grabbed the backpack with his books and computer, and locked the door on his way out.

Anita knew that Joab knew she'd been going out at night while he was at work. The babysitter had mentioned that she just missed Joab's call the night before. *So, okay, he knew.* She wondered how *he* liked it when *she* went out without telling him. Anita spent all day trying to come up with a good response when Joab called her on it. She wanted something cute and snappy and flip, like the lines in action-adventure movies, when the cool, sexy woman gets the last word, and no one can say anything because there's nothing left to say.

She went over and over it in her mind, each time justifying her nights out with his afternoons out, and each time becoming more convinced that he deserved a bit of his own medicine. In her imagination that day, she brought him to full repentance at least twenty times. The scene always ended with his contrite appeal for forgiveness, which she benevolently granted.

At 4:20 p.m., Joab walked in the door. Anita checked her watch and concluded that he must have come straight home. She took a measured gamble and decided to get in the first jab.

"You're home early," she said.

Cinda heard the door close and came running over from her kitchen.

"Hey, Baby Girl!" He said, kissing Cinda. "You were home early, too," he answered. "Say about 3:00 or 4:00 a.m. last night."

"It was 2:45, but we didn't leave home until after 10:30."

"Tell me, what kind of scum is out between 11:00 and 3:00, around here. I mean besides Tiesha."

"Very nice people. People our age who still act like they can have a little fun. People who enjoy themselves once in a while."

"Did you enjoy yourself?"

"Yes!" Anita said. "I did, and I'll do it again if I want."

"Fine," Joab said, seating himself on the sofa and picking up the newspaper. "I'll babysit for you on Saturday." He started to read. "That way, at least you won't be pissing away all our money on babysitters. I don't get to spend enough time with the baby, anyway."

This wasn't going at all the way she'd planned. Anita's blood was beginning to simmer. "It ain't your money! It's my money! Who's name is on the check, anyway? My name. Mine. And I can spend it anyway I want!"

"Fine," Joab answered, not looking up from the paper.

"Oh, yeah," she said, remembering her script. "And it's fine for you to stay out drinking after class with God-knows-who, but it ain't okay for me to have a little fun with my girlfriend."

"Isn't," Joab corrected, because he knew it would send her right over the edge. "'Isn't', okay. Not 'ain't.'"

"I'll talk anyway I damn well please, Mr. Big-Man-on-Campus-College-Man! Don't you tell me how to talk! Who the hell do you think you are? You can't tell me what to do."

"Anita," he said calmly, looking up from his paper, "I stopped trying to tell you what to do months ago. But I would ask that you watch your language in front of Cinda or she'll wind up sounding like all the fine company you keep at 4:00 in the morning."

"Fuck you!" She spat.

"Very nice, Anita," Joab said, going to the closet for Cinda's coat. "I think we'll just go for a ride until you get a hold of your temper. Come here, Baby," he said to Cinda who had been sitting on the kitchen floor watching her parents in bewilderment.

"Don't you take her out of this house, Joab," Anita warned. Joab just zipped up Cinda's coat, tied the hood around her face, and grabbed the car keys from the key drawer. "Don't you take her out of this house or I'll take her so far away from you, you'll have to book a flight to see her."

"Don't threaten me, Anita," he said in a measured voice, and was gone.

Anita stood there cursing at the closed door until all her venom was spent. Then she dropped down on the sofa and cried. She had let her temper get the better of her again. She regretted it. She wondered why her plan had not worked and where her prepared dialogue had gone wrong. It tore her apart to sit home while he was out with his buddies. She wondered how he could be so indifferent while she went out with hers. He wasn't even curious, let alone jealous. The chilling answer emerged: *Maybe he's not in love with me anymore. Maybe he just doesn't care. Oh, God, how could that be? He's always loved me.* Anita had presumed she had been born with his devotion like one is born to wealth or power or fame. It was her right, her portion in this life, and along with it came the ability to make their life together come out *her way*. The possibility of another woman became real in her mind. Suddenly she felt panicked and far from her mother.

Anita picked up the phone but replaced the receiver, not yet ready to admit trouble to the folks back home. It would have surprised her to know that Ruth had already sensed discord at Christmas and had been praying to Jesus for their marriage ever since.

Joab was not gone long. Anita knew he would not miss work. She had a fine-smelling meal simmering on the stove when they walked in, and she had resolved never again to lose her temper. She meant to apply sugar instead of vinegar to her domestic situation from now on.

"I'm sorry, Joab," she said before he got the door closed behind him. "I don't know why God gave me such a bad temper. It always makes me say things I don't mean." She unzipped his coat, slipping her arms around his waist and resting her cheek against his chest she said, "I'm sorry. I'm sorry."

"It's okay," he said, putting his arms around her shoulders. But in his mind her threat remained. He knew now that it was in her to take his daughter from him. She had given that much away. He had already begun to see her more as a dangerous opponent than as a teammate, with the prize being Cinda. In the future, he would be somewhat guarded with Anita. Never again fully trusting.

He unzipped Cinda's coat and hung it up. Anita went to the kitchen.

"You still have a little time to eat," she said, "Cinda, come let Mommy wash your hands."

Anita washed and dried the child's hands and placed her in her high chair at the table. Joab set his plate and the child's down. He decided he'd better throw some water on this fire, too, before it consumed their family.

"Anita, really," he started after she sat with her own plate, "It's just Sammy and I and we both mostly just like to sit and complain about class and have a brain break after school. It's no big deal."

"I know. I know," she answered. "I know you're working very hard. It's just that I need some adult company, too. Why can't I meet you out sometime? I'm your wife."

"I'd love for you to come," he lied. "I just thought you'd be bored talking about political science."

"How could I be bored when I'm with you? It's time you helped me understand what you're doing at school. I want to know."

They kissed at the door for the first time in months. Then Joab went to work.

On Saturday, Joab took his girls out for pizza and a matinee. It was the most relaxed family time any of them could remember in a long, long while.

The following Tuesday, Anita met her husband, Sammy, and Lesa at *The Pig's Foot* after class. Joab warned Sammy, and Sammy told Lesa. Anita was late as usual, and the three were half way through their first beer when she walked in. Given the limited nature of her fashion choices, Anita had decided on her red sweater with the low v-neck, her tight jeans and her red pumps. She was immediately aware that she was the only woman in heels.

Joab rose and accepted a bright, red kiss. "Hey, Babe, he said.

"Hey," she answered.

"I don't think you've met Sammy," Joab continued, pulling out her chair.

"Once, I think," Joab knew Anita was mistaken and had Sammy confused with another Chinese classmate from his freshman year. Sammy rose and took Anita's hand graciously.

As Anita sat, she noticed a lambskin coat draped on the back of an empty chair and a third, half empty beer sitting on the table.

"Oh, Sammy's girlfriend is in the bathroom," Joab said.

"She's not my girlfriend, yet," Sammy corrected with a smile.

"So, did you have any trouble finding the place?" Joab asked.

"Nope. It was right where you said it would be."

"Good," Joab said, rising, "Let me go get you a beer."

"Okay," Anita watched him walk away.

"So, Anita, how's the baby?" Sammy asked.

"Oh, she's fine." Anita nodded, with her eyes on the tabletop.

"Joab talks about her all the time. She must be pretty special."

"Yeah."

Sammy groped for more conversation. He started to ask her if she worked but remembered the welfare conflict before the words formed.

"How old is she?" Sammy already knew Cinda's age, her birthday, the latest additions to her vocabulary, and every gory detail of her delivery into the world.

"Two last January" Anita's eyes wandered to a woman emerging from what must be the ladies' bathroom. At first, Anita could only see her thin figure and the long, shining hair. She was wearing a sand-colored, loose-collared, turtleneck sweater and high-waisted cotton khakis with a thin black belt and thick, black masculine-looking shoes. She walked with a smooth confidence right over to their table.

"Oh," Sammy said, rising, "This is Lesa. Lesa Shemasaki, this is Anita, Joab's wife.

"Hi," Lesa said, rolling her eyes at Sammy, "I can handle my own chair, thank you. Don't you hate it when they do that?" The question was directed to Anita who liked when they did that. "It's like, I think I can sit down by myself."

"Somebody's gotta show these poor women from the Left Coast what manners are." Sammy teased.

"So, Anita . . . Anita, right?" Lesa started.

Anita nodded.

"I've always wondered what Joab's wife would be like," she said, pulling her hair into a ponytail and flinging it over the back of her chair.

At once, Anita felt much the object of curiosity, not at all comfortable. She was relieved when Joab appeared with her beer.

"Do you share your husband's passion for politics?"

"No. That's kind of his thing," Anita answered, playing with an earring.

"Oh, that's right. You probably have your hands full with the baby."

"You could say that," Anita smiled and looked at Joab.

"I'll tell you, that kid, you have to run to keep up with her, these days," Joab jumped in.

"I couldn't imagine having a kid right now," Lesa said.

"I couldn't imagine *not* having one." Anita was not sure she liked this woman.

"So, you stay home and take care of your child? That would drive me crazy. "

"I like it. Our daughter is a lot of fun. I like watching her grow. Besides, Joab and I have plans for me to go back to school someday after he's out."

"Yeah. But that will be, what? Five more years before you're out of law school, Joab?" Lesa asked.

"Law school?" Anita did not think to conceal her surprise.

Sammy sensed some friction. "How about that test in Post-WWII reconstruction?" He interjected, "I can never figure where her tests are coming from."

"Is that Ms. Peters?" Lesa asked. The men nodded. "I had her last year. Why can't she ever ask a question that she's covered in class? Her tests come out of nowhere."

The conversation was off and running. For the next forty-five minutes, Anita had very little to say and very little opportunity to say it. She had no idea what they were talking about and no association with common acquaintances. She inched her chair over to Joab and almost hid behind him, smiling and looking interested while Lesa directed the flow of conversation.

After the second round, all four left together. Anita noticed the soft fleece lining of Lesa's coat as Sammy struggled not to help her with it. She wondered if those big studs in her ears could actually be real diamonds. Outside, Anita had lucked into a parking space right next to Joab's bike.

"See ya at home, Babe," Anita said and made a point to kiss her husband as he stepped over his bike. "I've got to stop for some milk. Can you get Cinda from Tiesha's?"

"Oh!" Lesa exclaimed suddenly animated. "Too bad you guys came separately! I'll bet you have more fun on that bike! I've never been on one. My father hates them. Anita, you wouldn't mind if I talked your husband into a little ride one day."

It was a statement, not a question. But Anita answered silently, anyway. *You're damn straight I'd mind.* "Nice meeting you, Lesa," Anita said, stepping into her tired looking Ford.

"Nice meeting you, too, Anita," Sammy offered, hands in his pockets, waiting for Lesa to finish swooning over Joab's dilapidated bike so they could go. Anita waited for her husband to pull out and then followed.

By the time Anita had gotten back in the car with the milk, she had definitely decided that she did not like Lesa. She'd also decided she'd better keep it to herself, though she didn't know why.

Joab and Cinda were already home when Anita arrived. She gave her daughter a hug and began dinner preparations. Joab had no trouble reading her silence.

"So," Joab started. "Was our little club as exciting as you'd imagined? Wild place, huh?"

"It was nice. I enjoyed it," Anita figured her lie was white. "I just wish you'd told me you were planning on law school. I mean, I think I have a right to know little things like that."

"Well, I hadn't really made up my mind, for sure," Joab knew his lie wasn't white, but it just might save him some grief.

"That's not the way Sammy made it sound," Anita said, opening a can of green beans.

"Well, what does *he* know?" Joab asked rhetorically.

"More than me," Anita answered.

"Look, Anita," Joab fished out a pair of knives and forks from a drawer and set them down on the table. "I was hoping you would have a nice time this afternoon. Let's not argue."

Anita knew Joab was right. The advantage had shifted, and Anita could not let her jealousy or her temper keep her from a second invitation. She had to keep her head and use it if she was ever going to close the widening gap between herself and her husband.

"Hey, Joab!" She said suddenly, "How about you take me dancing Saturday night?"

"I don't know, Anita. I have a big test on Monday."

Anita contained the urge to snub him back and gave him a back hug instead. "Please," she pleaded, planting a succession of kisses between his shoulder blades. Then she let the palms of her hands slide over the tight ripples of his stomach, down inside the top of his jeans. He fought the impulse to double over at the tickle.

"I'm thinking about it," he said. The lid on the bean pot began to clatter and sputter.

"Remind me to finish convincing you later," Anita said on her way to the stove.

"I won't forget," Joab said. He didn't.

Chapter 7

Joab let Anita run the baby to Tiesha's. It was 10:30 Saturday night when they got to *Don's Place*. This establishment had the distinction of being Tiesha's favorite dive. Joab knew it must have pained Tiesha to think of them going without her, but someone had to stay home with the kids, and Lord knew, it was her turn.

It was obvious that Don, whoever he was, was no carpenter. His place consisted of an old double wide, furnished with more than one pool table and with half of one wall cut out to allow access to a dance floor/bar that was little more than a large cinder block wall around a cement slab and covered by a tin roof. The sound system consisted of a pair of cheap CD players, and a soundboard predating the industrial revolution. All this was hooked up to a half dozen huge speakers and presided over by a DJ with a passion for hip-hop and decibels. The only white person in the place was a giant Hell's Angel-type bouncing at the front door. The place was dark and full of smoke - all kinds. And no waitress ever came running when a member of the clientele accidentally spilled a beer. Spilled beers were encouraged to remain where they fell, adding to the ambiance. The room had a plywood bar down one end and was ringed by tables and chairs. Few of them matched. Don's Place was a study in function over form. But the open space in the center of the room was already alive with the rhythmic pulse of bodies, even though the action never hit full stride until after twelve.

The Johnsons moved around the edge of the dance floor until they found an empty table. Joab did not miss the sapphire stud in his wife's nose which he considered racy and provocative. He held a chair for her, then placed his coat on another.

"Bud?" he asked.

Anita smiled and nodded, then turned her attention to the dance floor after Joab disappeared in the direction of the bar. When he returned, there was a medium-tall man standing in front of his wife with one foot on Joab's chair. Joab handed Anita her long neck and turned to the man.

"Oh, Joab. This is Elvin G. He's a friend of Tiesha's," Anita hollered over the blare of *Two Live Crew*.

"This your chair, man?" Elvin G. shouted, taking his boot off of it.

Joab nodded, fighting an impulse to wipe off the spot with a napkin - if he could have found a napkin. He sat down. With that, Elvin pulled up a chair of his own and sat on it backwards, beside Joab.

"Yeah, I'm sorry Tiesha got stuck with babies, man. I could do with a piece of that bitch. Tiesha's alright, man."

Joab wasn't catching all of Mr. G's words. He didn't mind. It wasn't long before Joab concluded that ol' Elvin wasn't exactly substance-free. He began to babble.

". . . Yeah, man, I always liked Tiesha. She knows how to have a good time, man. But you gotta watch your stash when she's around, man. You know what I mean?"

Joab and Anita nodded and pulled a full gulp from their brown bottles.

Elvin G. motioned for Joab to lean in. Joab rocked his chair closer to his companion.

". . . Hey, man, you all want to buy anything?" He whispered loudly into Joab's ear. "I got some really good stuff. I mean, good, man. Real good."

"Thanks, man," Joab responded. "We just came here for the music. I think I'm gonna dance with my wife now."

"I hear ya, man," Elvin nodded his approval with a slow smile, "Anita, man, she's one fine looking bitch."

Joab grabbed Anita's hand and yanked her out of her seat.

"Man, Anita! Doesn't Tiesha know of any places on earth that aren't toilets?"

"Sure," Anita answered, "plenty of them. But they won't serve us. They'll sell us a beer in here 'cause the police don't give a shit what goes on as long as nobody gets shot."

"That's comforting."

"C'mon. Let's dance."

Joab didn't know when it happened, but somewhere along the way, his wife had become a much less inhibited dancer. He watched with amused satisfaction as she jumped aboard the "Soul Train" in her mind and let her body respond to the music in a succession of alternating abdominal contractions and releases which were reminiscent of only one thing he knew of. She stared steadily into his eyes as she moved closer and closer until her belly was almost touching his, then Anita slipped her thumbs in his belt loops and pulled his hips forward until they met hers. Joab placed the palms of his hands firmly against the small of her back and they danced as though the intention was to squeeze out even the air between them. Joab became aware of a more rapid intake of smoky air, and he was not entirely sure it was due to the physical exertion of dance.

When "The King of Gangsta Rap" mixed in a new tune, Joab decided he'd better sit down for a while.

"Let's head for the table," he said, taking Anita's hand and pulling her behind him through the crowd. A big guy in even bigger jeans danced into Anita, almost knocking her down.

"Man, watch out!" Joab shouted, putting his arm around his wife.

"You watch out," the guy responded, "You ran into me."

"I didn't run into you. You ran into my wife," Joab corrected.

Anita watched veins appear on the man's arms as he clenched his fists, preparing to land the first blow.

"It's my fault," Anita interrupted. "I ran into you. Sorry, man."

"The hell you did, Anita," Joab said.

"I did," she insisted, pulling him away and heading to their table.

Both of them sat for a moment and caught their breath, people-watching, until their last drops of warm beer were gone.

"I'm going for another round," Joab shouted.

"I'll come with you," Anita said, rising.

Waiting at the bar, Anita thought she heard someone calling her name. She turned to face a large girl with purple finger waves and a wide, round bottom.

"Hey, Lizzy!" Anita yelled, smiling. "What's happenin', girl?"

Joab placed a second beer in his wife's hand.

"This is my man I told ya 'bout," Anita announced, embracing Joab's upper arm. "Joab, this is Lizzy."

Joab nodded and sipped his beer while the two girls tried to talk over the music which seemed to have gotten louder.

Anita yanked on Joab's sleeve. He leaned over placing his ear close to her lips.

"We're going to the bathroom. See ya at the table."

He nodded again. Joab made his way to the table, sat down and pulled up a second chair with his feet before placing them on it. He watched the people, sipping his beer. Most of the men were wearing jeans that were three sizes too big and those that were on the dance floor hiked them up three or four times a minute as though it were just part of the dance. The folks around the edges of the room were mostly putting the moves on one another and talking trash, hoping to get lucky and get the weekend off to a "good start." A lot of living would take place between now and Monday morning. He thought about his test. Joab would have preferred to have been home studying instead of wasting his time with these people who had nothing better to do with theirs. But he figured Anita needed some R&R with him and he really kind of liked dancing with her when she danced that way. When he looked up, he saw Nita making her way to their table. He watched as some guy grabbed her wrist and turned her around on the dance floor. Anita seemed to recognize him. Joab could tell, from his gestures, that he was asking her to dance. She hesitated and then let her body move with the music for a few bars. The guy placed his hands on her hips. She laughed and removed them but kept on dancing. In a moment he placed his hands on her hips and then slid them back over the swell of her bottom. Joab removed his feet from the chair and rose. But he stood still for a moment, curious to see how his wife would handle herself. For a second or two she seemed not to mind, then she arched her back from her dance partner, laughing as she pulled away and walked back toward the table. The man pursued her. But she kept on walking with quick, decisive strides. Joab went to meet her. She stopped just short of running into him before she saw him.

"Oh, Joab," she broke into a wide, white grin. "Dance with me, Baby." She took his arm and turned around, right into the chest of her previous partner.

"Oop. This is Larry," Anita said, intending to pass him. "He's a friend of . . . "

" . . . Tiesha's," Joab finished the sentence for her.

"C'mon, Nita," he said, ignoring Joab. "Let's finish our dance."

"Larry," Anita giggled, rolling her eyes at him. "This is my husband."

"Oh. Sorry, man. I didn't know you was married." Larry receded into whatever dark corner he'd come from.

Anita was already taking a ride on the music, only this time, her movements were sharp and electric, as though someone had turned her dial up to high. Joab never considered himself a particularly bad dancer, but tonight he could barely keep up with his wife who seemed bound to punctuate each beat of the music with a physical motion. After three songs, Joab decided it was time for another beer. But Anita just laughed, shook her head, and kept right on dancing. Finally, after two more songs, Joab took her hand and headed for the bar. Her chest rose and fell as she worked to catch her breath.

"Baby, you all right?" he asked.

"Fine," she answered, "You're just not used to seeing me have a good time." She didn't know what made her say such a harsh thing, especially when she *was* having a good time.

Joab checked his watch. Quarter of twelve.

"Joab, can't you relax for a little while?" Anita asked.

Back at the table Anita was animated and talkative. This was a bit of a frustration for Joab who might have picked a slightly quieter environment for a conversation. Anita would point to a person and say something. Joab would miss half of it and say, "What?" to which his wife would smile, shrug her shoulders and shout, "Never mind." After the third "never mind," Joab took hold of Anita's hand and pulled her over to sit on his lap. She slipped her arm around his neck and gave his mouth a penetrating kiss.

This is a much more interesting conversation, anyway, he thought. It would have been fine with Joab if everyone else at Don's simply disappeared from the face of the earth.

"I think it's time to go home," he announced between kisses.

"Is that a threat or a promise?" she asked, lips on his ear.

"Later, man," Elvin G. said as they passed. Joab didn't answer.

The cool air was refreshing on Joab's face and he did not mind having the blaring beat fading behind him.

"Come 'ere," Anita said leaning against the side of their car. "I've got an idea."

Joab obeyed. Nita swung her arms around his neck and gave him another long kiss.

"Go home for a little while before we pick the baby up?" Joab guessed.

"How did you know?" Nita asked, genuinely surprised. They stood necking in the parking lot for a few minutes before Joab became aware of several guys walking up behind him. Adrenalin washed through him as he resolved to get Anita in the car quickly, if he was lucky enough to have these guys pass by. They did. Anita seemed oblivious.

They were both half naked by the time Joab got his key to turn in the front door. Joab dropped his coat and his pants and picked up his wife to set her down on the kitchen counter.

Her shirt was already lying on the living room floor.

"Joab!" she shouted, giggling wildly.

"Now, Nita, you just let me help you out a little here," he coaxed and reached his arms around her back to undo her bra.

"No!" she shouted, enjoying the freedom to fill the whole house with her voice. She pushed his arms away.

"Now, Baby, don't you trust me?" he asked with thick sincerity. "I won't tickle you. I promise. You just sit there nice and still."

Anita placed her hands in her lap and tried to obey but as Joab's hands got to the clasp behind her, his lips found the side of her neck.

Anita tensed and let out a high pitched giggle. But she didn't move her hands from her lap.

"I won't tickle you," he whispered as the back of the bra snapped open. Then he took a deep breath and planted a loud, wet smuggie at the base of her neck.

"Joab!" she squealed, finding the place on his rib cage that usually dropped him.

"All right, all right," he said when he'd caught his breath and was able to stand up straight.

"You forget, Joab, I found your tickle spot when we was in the sixth grade."

"I'll be good," he said, raising his hands in surrender.

"I know you will," she said, sliding down off the counter.

Forty five minutes later, Joab woke as Anita slid out of his arms.

"You stay in bed," he offered. "I'll go get her."

"I'm already up," Anita pointed out.

He dozed again until he heard the sound of the front door closing. He rose to brush his teeth and then decided it might be a good idea to drink a cold glass of water. Once in the kitchen, he rediscovered Nita's jeans. He smiled, remembering them sliding off of his wife's hips. When he picked them up, something fell out, hitting the floor with a metallic ping. He retrieved the object and looked at it. It was little more than a short metal straw with a wide rubber band wrapped around one end and a tiny nest of steel wool at the other.

"A crack pipe?" he asked himself in disbelief. They had not been uncommon in Nita's old high school. But Joab had been an athlete, and Nita had always appeared to hold drugs in the same contempt as he had.

He picked up the remaining clothes and dropped them on the floor in the bedroom wondering what he was going to say to his wife. The night was chilly. He got back into bed, still holding the miniature pipe when the front door squeaked open. He heard Anita move down the hall and into Cinda's room. A few moments later she was back in their bedroom.

"I enjoyed our date," she said, heading for the bathroom.

"So did I," he said. It was the truth. "How's the baby girl?"

"Wore out."

Joab waited while Anita brushed her teeth.

"Anita," he said when she was finished. "What was a stem doing in your jeans pocket?"

"A what?"

"A stem, a crack pipe!" he was almost crying.

"Oh, Lizzy asked me to hold it for her. She still lives with her mom."

"C'mon, Anita, you can do better than that. What the hell do you take me for?"

"All right," Anita said, standing in the bathroom door. "I borrowed it from Liz because I thought you might enjoy a little buzz to relax from your school work."

"Enjoy a little buzz? Anita, this is *drugs*. Our daughter is asleep in the next room. We have a life, and you're screwing around with crack? Where is your brain?! We've both seen what this does to people. Remember Sonya Brunson? She'd have cut off both her feet if she thought she could trade them in for her next rock and then bleed to death while she smoked it. In six months, she turned into a lying, stealing hag."

"Sonya Brunson was an idiot. Joab, you know, you think you know what you're talking about, but you're just full of shit because you really have to work at it to get a habit. I've done it three or four times. It's no big deal. Just a little boost when you go out."

"Three or four times!!! Anita, what the hell is going on!? No big deal! No big deal? Well if it's no big deal, then you can stop right now. Promise me, Anita, that you're never gonna touch that shit again."

"Okay, I promise."

"And you're not allowed to go out with Tiesha anymore."

"Fine. And you don't go out with Sammy or his skinny bitch anymore."

Joab's eyes opened wide as he digested what she'd just said, "Sammy and I aren't doing drugs." He finally stammered.

"Fine, but if I give up my friends, you give up yours."

"You know what, Anita, I don't even want to be near you." Joab pulled the comforter and a pillow off the bed and settled in on the sofa.

At 6:00 Cinda, in her footie pajamas, joined him.

Chapter 8

Things remained pretty chilly around the Johnson household for the greater part of the next month. Neither Joab nor Anita spent any social time with their respective friends for the first week. Both resented the other more with each passing day. But by the following Tuesday, Joab needed someone to talk to or burst. In the past, he would have picked up the phone and sought his mother's guidance. Once or twice he had been inspired to pour out a letter into her Email. Joab valued Ruth's opinion and she seemed always to give him a perspective not visible with his own blind spots. Also, she never tried to dictate, but simply offered what she could and graciously accepted whatever course of action he chose. It was easy to return for advice. But he was still very much ashamed of the welfare surrender. He also knew that Ruth would probably never afford any respect to Cinda's mother if she discovered Nita'd been dabbling in crack cocaine. In the long run, he knew he would have to hold his tongue rather than put Anita's and Ruth's relationship under the crushing burden of the truth. He ran into Lesa between classes.

"Sammy and I missed you at *The Pig's Foot* last week," she said.

Joab had given Sammy the short version of what had happened during class. He hoped Sammy had had the sense not to tell Lesa. Poor Sammy. Lesa would neither accept him nor reject him. She may as well just go on and add his balls to the collection of other little trinkets she wore on her charm bracelet.

"Trouble in Paradise?" Lesa asked with her normal, straight-on, bluntness. Joab couldn't tell if she knew or not.

Joab resisted the temptation to spill his churning guts on the first sympathetic shoulders to come along, lovely as her's were, and obeyed the inner warning system which gave him a clear signal to represent his marriage as a united front. He shrugged his shoulders.

"I just had a great idea," Lesa said with one of her rare smiles. "Why don't we both skip our next class so you can give me that bike ride?"

Joab almost instantly rejected such a spontaneous and irresponsible suggestion, but before he could get his mouth to say, no, his mind got a thought caught in it: *Anita had always known his schedule better than he did. She would watch the clock especially closely on Tuesdays and Thursdays. The only time that was really his, was the time he was in class.* He reached into his jeans pocket and came up with the little key ring which he dangled in front of Lesa's sparkling eyes.

Moments later, Joab and Lesa were blasting past the campus entrance and headed for open country. Joab had pretty much explored every inch of paved road that was within forty minutes of Duke as he would often go for a little "pressure trip" on those days when he had a free period between classes and could not bring himself to face the laptop.

It was a beautiful day. One of those when you just have a sense that this is the way God intended the world to stay forever, before that unfortunate fall of man. It was mid-March. Winter had been wet, and for the most part, mild, with only one snowfall - and that one had only been three inches. The leaves along the shoulder rolled over in their wake as Joab and Lesa rode for the joy of riding. Joab had to insist that she wear the helmet. Lesa hadn't liked it, but relented in the end. The air was cool-to-cold making the sun more delicious as it made its presence felt. Joab had chosen one of his favorite country roads. Both thrilled as Joab crested a hill just slightly too fast or leaned into a turn, uniting their bodies with the weight and momentum of the machine. Pastures and barns and dried-out fields of harvested crops fled away to their right and left.

Joab rarely had passengers aboard, and none had ever been female. He was surprised to discover this to be a sensual activity. When Lesa first straddled the bike behind him, he was aware of several inches between them, but now he could feel the helmet pressing against the space between his shoulder blades. Lesa's arms were wrapped snugly around his upper torso. This made him feel strangely exposed as there was little he could do about it without removing his hands from the handle bars. He could feel her small breasts pressed against his back and the heat coming from the inside of her thighs as they embraced the outside of his. He found this a most pleasant sensation and he gave himself permission to drink it in. The ride was innocent enough. He was under no obligation to reveal his thoughts to Lesa . . . or Anita, for that matter.

Hmm, Anita and Lesa must be pretty close to the same height, he conjectured.

Joab loved the vibration and the deep rumbling sound of the power beneath him. It was exhilarating. Even if it was only a tired old bike, it was just what he needed to distract him from the control wars raging within the walls of his singlewide. Eventually, he realized that his passenger had not uttered a word. This was natural. Communication was difficult against the rushing wind. But Lesa was holding him rather tightly. Maybe she was scared.

"You okay?" He shouted over his shoulder.

"Great!" Came the enthusiastic response.

"Am I going too fast?"

"Faster!" She shouted back. "Faster!"

Joab opened the throttle, and Lesa abandoned herself to a joyous laughter which seemed not to want to subside.

"Yaaaaaah!" Joab howled, his blood racing with the bike. He was free, freer than he'd been for a long, long time.

Joab brought the bike to a stop in the dirt parking lot of "BoBobs Quick Stop".

"This is where I usually turn around," Joab told Lesa once he killed the engine. "Seven minutes for a Coke, and we'll be back on campus in time for the next class. Can I get you anything?

"Yeah, I'd like a *Yoo-Hoo*."

"A *Yoo-Hoo*? The chocolate milky stuff?"

"Yeah."

"I never knew anyone who drank that stuff, really."

"Well I drink it, really. I don't like bubbles."

In a minute, Joab emerged from the little store with two drinks. One with bubbles, one with no bubbles. Lesa stood beside the bike. She had taken her helmet off and was shaking out her long, shimmering hair with great flourish.

It was like black satin, Joab thought. He wondered what it might be like to touch it. It was so extremely different in texture from his own head of tight, tiny curls. He had never experienced any other woman besides his own Anita, and she was so much like him, so as to be almost a part of him. Yet, she was so different from him. Not different in the ways a woman is different from a man, though she was that. No. Anita was different in her beliefs, in her motives. If she had been a man, Joab did not think he would have been her friend. *At least, Lesa had a vision for her life,* he thought as she sipped her Yoo-Hoo. *She'll make something of herself. She'll compete in a competitive world and win. You had to respect her for that. Anita will have to be babysat and, if Cinda is to see her Daddy, placated.*

Joab watched as Lesa walked up to him. He thought she was going to ask him if this country shack had a bathroom. She did not. She walked right up to him and kissed him. It was not a friendly type of kiss. It was a deep, passionate kiss and one that held infinite promise. Joab responded in kind. He placed his hand behind her head and felt the silken strands of black between his fingers. His thick arm wrapped around the tiny waist and he was struck by the frailty of a frame that seemed to him might snap were he not to take extreme care. And how difficult that was when her lips were so hungry and her breath so chocolaty.

Joab took a step back. "Now, hold on," he said. "What's going on here?"

"What's going on is I want you. I've wanted you since our first day of class together freshman year."

"Oh, yeah?" he stammered. "What about Sammy?"

"I've never been the least bit interested in Sammy. I mean he's a nice guy and all but - "

"Yeah? . . ." Joab was thoroughly unprepared for the pace at which the afternoon seemed to be progressing. "Well, I'm married," he finally managed to say.

"I know," she said, looking him directly in the eye. "I've met your wife. She seems like a very nice girl. I just want to sleep with you. It's not complicated, really."

"Not complicated?" Joab could not believe what he was hearing. Still, there was something extremely flattering about having Lesa Shemisaki lay it on the table.

"Boy, you don't mince words, do you?"

Lesa just shrugged.

"No, man, I don't cheat on my wife. I think we had better get back to campus."

"Okay."

They mounted the bike. Joab wasn't sure, but he felt like Lesa held him even tighter on the way home. If she could have read his mind she would have seen how thin Joab's resolve really was. Scenarios played on the TV screen of his imagination, flipping channels like a sports fan with a brand new satellite dish. In one moment he was patting himself on the back for having chosen the high moral ground. Click, he saw the two of them comparing class schedules to squeeze out a stolen hour. Click, he was greeting Nita with the sweet, private knowledge of a peculiar martyrdom. Click, he was searching for a room, a bed, a private space, curtains drawn. She was there, silent, with her hair flowing down over her bare shoulders to her thin hips. She was coming to join him under the sheets. It was mid-day, somewhere. Click, she carries the AIDS virus. His bike swerved off onto the shoulder. *She carries the AIDS virus!?! What? Where did that come from? What the hell kind of fantasy was that?* Goosebumps rose on his flesh. Nope, he lived at a point in history when one invisible organism exacted the ultimate price at random. He could not put his family at risk. But he *could* enjoy Lesa blasting through the countryside with him on his bike . . . and the heat of her arms and legs wrapped around him . . . and the pressure of her breasts on his back . . . and the delight of a stolen hour on a perfect, Southern winter's day. He could enjoy it over and over again in his memory. He could dream. And dream he did. Possibilities played out in his mind for weeks to come.

That evening, Anita felt the axis of her world take another tilt, but she could not place the source of its greater imbalance. A plan started taking shape in her mind.

The following week was one that seemed to break the back of the long winter. Days were sunny and mild and a few dogwoods even put out tiny, tentative buds - a silent gamble that Spring was here to stay. Only the spaces within Joab and Anita's mobile home seemed unaffected by hope of an early Spring. Conversation became limited to talk between Cinda and her mother and Cinda and her father, alternately.

Joab generally came home from class, spent an hour at play with his daughter and hit the books. He had taken to eating dinner in his study as well. In some twisted way, he was making Anita pay for all the sexual pleasure he was missing with Lesa. And the home that Anita had longed to keep full-time, began to close in on her.

On campus, Lesa made it clear that her invitation remained open. To Joab's relief, however, she was extremely discreet, seemingly delighting in the stealth of it all. Did she have any idea how sweet her forbidden fruit tasted in his imagination, or how many times a day he went back to the tree of knowledge of good and evil? Once, he could have refused her. But the persistence of an open invitation was more than he could stand. The war was lost well before the surrender, well before the defeated knew he had a need for a swatch of white fabric.

At work, Friday night he decided to check his Email for a letter from his mother. This is what he found:

Joab,

I want you so much that I cannot sleep at night. I want you all day. What a coincidence, my roommate is in class from 8:30 AM until 2:30PM.

Anytime,
Lesa

Joab looked up the number and made the call. He was relieved when Lesa answered.

"Lesa, I got your message. Are you crazy? How could you leave me a message like that!"

"What? Did I misspell something?"

"How did you find out my email address?

"I told Sammy you needed some information from class."

She really is shameless, Joab decided. "What if Anita found it?"

Lesa laughed. "Right. Anita fights you for the laptop. I'll lay odds she doesn't know how to plug it in."

"That's not the point."

"No, that *is* the point. I chose a very safe way to communicate. This should help you trust my judgment. The last thing I would ever want is for Anita to find out. I don't want Anita's rings on my finger, only a few hours with her husband. She'll never even know they're missing."

"Why? Why me?"

"Because you have a great body, a clear enough mind to keep you from getting entangled, and I've never had an African-American before."

"There are other issues."

"Oh?"

Joab stammered and then spit it out. "What about AIDS? What if you have it?"

"What if *you* do?"

"No way," Joab said as a thought crossed his mind: What's Anita been doing while she's been whacked out on crack, those three or four times?

"Have you ever heard of a condom?"

"Oh, yeah," Joab responded before he realized how junior high he sounded.

There was a long silence.

"I can wait," Lesa finally said, "but I won't wait much longer. Bye."

Joab was surprised to hear the recording telling him to hang up and try again if he wished to make a call. He was surprised that Lesa Shemisaki really, *really* wanted him, surprised that he was considering cheating on Anita, surprised at how much he enjoyed considering cheating on Anita and surprised to discover he was *going* to cheat on Anita. Joab was just damned surprised.

✦ ✦ ✦

The rest of the night was pretty much a bust as far as study or sleep was concerned. Joab was more than a bit preoccupied. By 4:30AM he had decided that it might be a good idea to thaw relations with his wife. Nita would have less reason to suspect another woman if they appeared to be getting along better. Joab's computer was all booted up before he realized that he did not have Lesa's email address. The 48 hours of weekend instantly loomed excruciatingly long before him. How could he wait until second period, Monday, to solidify his clandestine meeting with her? Her hair, her hips, her pale skin, her almost-round lips appeared to him a hundred times an hour in a thousand different ways. The sun was rising when the three women of the dayshift punched in.

"See ya Tuesday," the oldest and heaviest of them called after him as he left.

He was back in the door thirty seconds later to retrieve his keys. *Hard to get going without those.* On the way home, he reminded himself to get a grip. After all, he was about to see his wife with adultery on the brain. He needed to cultivate a poker face.

Joab's plan to ease marital relations went well. After sleeping until noon on Saturday, Joab decided to take lunch with his family. He invited Anita along on his outside play time with Cinda. There was almost civil conversation between the parents over dinner, and afterwards, Joab chose one end of the sofa over his garage sale, wingback. This was the week when *The Disney Channel* mercilessly teased the more financially challenged children of the nation by unscrambling their signal for a few blissful days. An outsider, looking in, would have been touched by the scene of little Cinda snuggled between her parents watching Dumbo.

Cinda was asleep before the crows saw an elephant fly. Joab carried her into her room and laid her in the midst of

Winnie-the-Pooh sheets. When he got back to the living room, Nita had switched to MTV and was holding out a beer.

"Tiesha?" Joab asked, accepting it and taking his place at the end of the sofa.

Nita nodded. "Joab," Nita started as they both stared at Madonna, in black leather, rolling around on a floor. "You know me. I ain't into drugs. I just got a little bored and lonely. I promise ya. I won't ever touch 'em again."

Joab was surprised to find she was crying.

"It's just that I miss home and my friends. You have friends here, from school. I don't have no friends. Most of the time I ain't even got you."

Joab never could stand it when she cried. "I don't spend time away from you because I want to," he heard himself say, "I'm working hard to try and build a future for us." He went to the bathroom and came back with a roll of toilet paper for her. Tissues were a luxury item. He sat down beside her and handed it over. Anita gave her nose a long, wet blow. Joab put his arms around her, and she cried like a lost child for the better part of twenty minutes.

"I know you're working for Cinda and me," she wept. "But some days the longer I'm stuck in this house, the more my mind plays tricks on me and pretty soon I'm thinking crazy. I just miss ya, Joab."

"I miss you, too, Babe," he maintained in a gentle voice. She took his hand and led him to the bedroom.

Cinda shuffled in at 5:30AM to find her parents blissfully intertwined. Somewhere within her toddler's heart, she carried a stress sensor, (standard issue in all children). Like a radiation detector in a nuclear power plant, this sensor measures tension between parents and trips alarms when levels become high, and the child's universe is in imminent danger of meltdown. As Cinda heaved her baby on the bed, then climbed up the night table, her stress sensor fell suddenly silent. All three rested in a peace which vanished, for Joab, the second he opened his eyes. For him a delicious torment was just beginning.

He had only meant to thaw relations, not bring them to a boil. How could he hurt Anita? She was so vulnerable, like a child. She was struggling to trust him. How could he betray that trust? Like a *Weight Watcher* in a *Baskin Robbins*, the flavor had already been chosen. Though it had yet to be licked and savored, indeed paid for, the sweet, cool cream was his. In his heart, he had already tasted and the taste made him hunger all the more. Even Anita's sincere repentance could not rebuild Joab's crumbled resolve. *Besides, technically, we're officially separated and that wasn't my idea,* he rationalized. *There it is! As close to a perfect defense as one gets in this life. It was settled then.*

Chapter 9

Monday morning, Joab stopped into Revco to buy condoms. He decided not to wear his helmet the rest of the way to campus. Parking his bike in an obscure parking lot, he tried to make his running into Lesa appear coincidental. She was walking down the hall with three friends.

"Hey, Joab," she called as they passed.

"Uh, Lesa, I've found those notes you wanted."

"Oh?" She said, as she stopped and turned around.

"But I'd like to go over them with you. They're a little confusing."

"When?" She asked.

"Now," he said, wondering if anyone had picked up on the fact that his mouth was bone dry and his heart was about ready to explode in his chest.

"Catch ya later," she said, dismissing her friends casually.

"Where's the bike?" Lesa inquired, falling into step.

"Behind Bryan," he answered, almost running.

"Slow down!" she said, trying to keep up.

"No," he said, laughing.

It was only a short trip to her apartment which was large and obviously high rent. She had her own spacious room, tastefully furnished in blond pine. Joab noticed only the bed—queen size and unmade. He could smell her on its cream-colored sheets. There was one unexpected, awkward moment when both stood in the stark reality of premeditated adultery. Joab walked up to Lesa and kissed her, pulling her body up against his own. Then she dropped to her knees before him and unbuckled his pants.

Joab was not quite sure of condom protocol, but managed to interrupt himself long enough to take care of that business.

Their sex was wild and passionate and left both of them well-satisfied and feeling as if they'd swum a channel. As Joab laid back on a strange bed and felt the exotic sensation of Lesa's satiny hair all over his chest, he compared. Anita knew his body better, but Lesa, with her deceivingly delicate frame, possessed a powerful energy and more than a dash of creativity, he suspected. As Joab's breath came back to him, he slowly ran his long, thick fingers down the length of Lesa's hair. Joab knew the satisfaction would be short lived. He also knew this would be no one-shot deal. He hoped Lesa felt the same. However, there was the problem of cutting class. He couldn't keep doing that. They'd just have to work out a better arrangement.

Less than seventy-five minutes after they left campus, Joab and Lesa were back in their respective classes, though their minds would remain in Lesa's bedroom for the rest of the day.

By Tuesday morning, Joab was convinced that Anita didn't have a clue. This in itself was an astounding thing, as Joab had often suspected that Anita could read his mind. In fact, the bridge reconstruction of Saturday night appeared to be holding up rather well.

Perhaps, Joab reasoned perversely, *a little fling will actually be healthy for my marriage.*

As it turned out, Lesa had felt the same regarding a second rendezvous . . . and a third . . . and a fourth . . . Dates were generally made via email and it wasn't long before Joab had sleuthed out several campus phone jacks through which he could check for messages. He considered Lesa's gift for erotic correspondence a bonus treat.

Soon it was agreed that they simply would not skip any more classes. A forty-five minute lunch break was barely enough time, though it had to suffice on several occasions. Since Lesa's apartment was out of the question after 3:00, they twice tried a cheap hotel following on the heels of their last classes. Lesa picked up the tab. This was the 90s after all.

Anita simply assumed that Joab had been back at *The Pig's Foot* with Sammy and an old, cool wind began to blow through their trailer again. Joab decided he'd just have to work something else out. Besides, he couldn't afford a hotel habit, and it didn't set right for Lesa to have to pay.

Joab did come to dread his Comparative Government and Politics class with Sammy. For the first few weeks, Sammy cornered him to lament the illusive Lesa who had removed him from her social calendar like so much masculine debris. It was little comfort to poor Sammy to discover that Joab had been, too. Joab really did hate brushing Sammy off, especially when he had been such a faithful shoulder in Joab's time of crisis. But Sammy's lovesick churning sharpened the edges of Joab's already pointed guilt. It was much too uncomfortable.

"I told ya she was trouble," was the only comment Joab could offer on the subject. That and, "Sorry, man. Gotta run."

Before long, it was May again and the approach of finals brought with it the perfect excuse to *spend more time at school.* Joab really needed some serious time at the library. He was most convincing.

At home, Anita sensed his stress and assumed it was just his normal reaction to approaching finals. She was mistaken. It was Joab's normal reaction to the thought of losing the regularity of his extramarital squeeze. After all, summer break meant *summer break.*

"You say she misses her mother," Lesa offered from a horizontal position one afternoon during a particularly strenuous study session at *the library.* "Why don't you just send her home? My roommate goes back to Texas right after her last final on Thursday and we'll have the whole place to ourselves until I fly back to Hawaii in a couple of weeks."

"What a great idea!" Joab said sarcastically. "Except that I can't afford to eat and keep the lights turned on, let alone send Cinda and Anita on vacation."

"I can," Lesa answered. "What's it gonna cost for a week? A grand?"

"Lesa!?" Joab couldn't believe what he was hearing.

"More than a thousand?"

"Lesa. I'm not gonna let you pay for a trip for my wife and kid!"

"Well, then, we'll call it a loan. You can pay me back," Lesa lifted her head from his stomach where it had been resting.

"Besides, it wouldn't be like I wasn't buying something for myself, too." She looked Joab directly in the eye. "Don't you think we could have some fun if we could spend, say, forty-eight hours alone, no roommates, no classes?"

"You know, your Daddy must have spoiled you rotten," he said, marveling at her creative deceitfulness.

"He still does," Lesa offered honestly. "Mom, too. You wouldn't believe how I get treated when I go home. Man, it's gonna be a great summer . . . I just wish you could come with me." she added quickly.

Joab wasn't so sure, "Three-fifty ought to do it . . . if the car doesn't break down."

"Is that all? For a whole week?" Lesa was surprised.

Joab narrowly missed Alyson, Lesa's roommate, and decided he may as well get some studying in before going home. When he walked in his front door at 8:00, Nita had supper waiting. She accepted her husband's kiss with her cheek. Cinda had supper ready, too.

"Dada! Dada! I make you food," she announced, leading him over to her kitchen. She was dressed in her Princess Jasmine nightgown. In her pot were muddy green clumps of play dough. She thrust a tiny plastic plate into Joab's right hand and an equally tiny fork into his left. Joab pulled up a chair from the dinette.

"Eat," Cinda commanded, picking up little clumps of play dough and depositing them, one at a time, on the plate.

"Yum!" Joab exclaimed with much conviction, pretending to eat. Nita was not so amused.

Look at him with that child, Anita silently brooded, pulling butter out of the fridge and pushing the door closed just a little too hard. *He might have been able to spend some time with her if he'd come home two hours ago like he said he would.* "Time to eat," she announced.

"Yum, your supper was good but it's time to eat Mama's supper," he told Cinda as he lifted her up into her high chair. Then he filled a real plate and set it down on her tray.

"No!" The child squealed on the verge of a tantrum. "Yuck! I hate cawwots. I hate wice. I hate dat," she said, pointing to some white meat which she could not yet identify. "I no eat Mama food. I eat Cinda food."

Joab hated carrots, too. He tried to keep a straight face.

"Cinda," he said.

She responded to her name by sticking up her chin and pushing out her lower lip.

"Cinda, those are very ugly words. You need to tell Mama you're sorry."

"No!" She said.

"Your Mama's been working very hard to make this meal. You need to eat it."

Cinda was neither impressed nor moved to gratitude. She pushed her plate decisively onto the floor where it shattered, scattering the rejected meal in all directions.

Joab knew something had to be done. He hated the thought of spanking his daughter when he hadn't seen her all day.

"Damn it to hell, Joab! I deal with her all day long! *Do* something with her!"

"Lucinda Ruth Johnson!" He started, his voice sounding strangely like his mother's. "That was an ugly thing to do! You should be ashamed of yourself."

Cinda only raised her chin a little higher and stared down her nose at him. She was adorable in her defiance. He stifled a laugh as he confronted a will that could fly in the face of odds so clearly stacked against it.

"Child, I'm gonna beat your butt! You've been aksin' for it all day," Anita threatened.

Joab lifted his daughter out of her high chair and placed her on the floor in front of her mother. "Cinda, tell your Mama you're sorry," he commanded.

"No," she said.

"Go sit in the naughty spot," he told her.

"No," she answered.

"Now, Cinda, I'll give you one more chance to tell Mama you're sorry." In his tone, Cinda clearly heard her Daddy's plea not to make him spank her. She had come this far. She just had to find his limit.

"No," she repeated.

"That's it!" Anita said, jumping up and starting for the child.

"No. I'll handle it," Joab said, rising and heading for the utensil drawer where a flat wooden spoon was the deterrent of choice. Joab found it, picked up his daughter and started for her bedroom. All the way down the hall, Cinda begged for a pardon. Joab knew Anita was not likely to grant *him* one if he didn't follow through. Cinda's fate was sealed. She bought the ticket. She'd take the ride.

After extracting Cinda's debt to society, Joab returned to the kitchen, warning her not to get off her bed. He held the dust pan for his wife and then the two of them dined to the sound of loud and elaborate sobbing from their two-year-old.

"Man, I just hate having to come home and do that after not seeing her all day," Joab admitted.

"Well, if you'd get home a little earlier, she might not be so cranky. You know she's a brat by the end of the day. Shit, Joab, the last two weeks of school, we may as well not even be here for all the time we get out of you."

Here it comes, Joab thought. "Well, guess what?" He said lightly, hoping to cut this lecture short. "How would you like to go home the week after finals?"

Anita's face lit up. "Really?" She asked.

Joab nodded, smiling.

"Oh, Joab, it's gonna be so good for us to get away. It's been too long. Wait till I tell Mama. And you ain't seen your Mama since when? Two summers ago?"

"Oh, no, Nita. I can't come this time."

Anita's face darkened again.

"I already asked Mr. Davenport for the time off, and he won't give it."

"Why? He knows you work hard all year. He's got to know you need a little time off with your family sometime."

For a moment, Joab thought Anita might cry. She rose quietly and began clearing the table.

Joab hated making Mr. Davenport the bad guy. The fact was that his boss was soft as a teddy bear when it came to his own family. He had a good deal of respect for Joab and would have been more than pleased to give him a break with his wife and child. Joab knew it.

"I'd better not push him," Joab continued. "There's a million college students who would jump at a job that doesn't interfere with classes."

Joab realized that his daughter had quieted. "I'm gonna check on the baby," he said.

✦ ✦ ✦

Anita's sullenness and Joab's absence continued through finals week. Ruth called to find out, firsthand, why Joab would not be visiting home with his family.

"Now, Son, it's just not healthy for a family not to vacation together. It's just not right," she told him in one of her rare, unsolicited lectures. He remained as stubborn in his resolve as his daughter had been in hers. His plan was coming together and he had barely been able to concentrate on finals for the anticipation of a reckless adulterous marathon.

The following Monday he gave Anita, Lesa's three hundred and fifty dollars in traveler's checks, loaded his girls sorrowfully into the little Ford, and kissed them good-bye.

"I'll miss you, Joab," Anita said mournfully. "Let's never do this again. Thank you for working so hard so we could go. I love you, Babe."

"I love you, too. Drive carefully," he said after one final kiss. "Dubby, Cinda."

He waved as the car drove Anita's face out of sight. Then, he jumped the steps to his front door and ran to awaken his laptop. It lay sleeping on his desk, still plugged in. He lifted the screen, an anxious index finger found the power switch and the faint wr-r-r-r of life reached his ears. The blank screen glowed. Then it started searching itself for viral threats to its health.

"C'mon, c'mon, c'mon." Joab urged. But the lengthy process took the usual twenty-two seconds. Joab cursed his beloved machine for being outdated and slow. Within five commands, clicked decisively on the keyboard, Joab found his e-letter.

"PREPARE TO GRATIFY YOUR FLESH," it said.

Joab put the computer back to sleep and picked up the phone. He dialed the phone company.

"Yes," he said to a woman in customer service, "I understand it's possible to have my calls forwarded to another location . . ."

♦ ♦ ♦

Joab shaved a full five minutes off the usual time it took him to get to Lesa's apartment from his trailer. He parked his bike around back and found the door unlocked. The sound of soft music came to him in the foyer. His nose registered the smell of burning candles.

He pushed open the bedroom door. Lesa was waiting for him. Obviously, she was quite prepared to gratify his flesh. It appeared she had been frequenting some well-stocked lingerie stores. Joab had never imagined such stirring combinations of satin and lace, both to the eye and to the touch. And for the rest of his life, this mental photo of Lesa would remain, for better or worse, the one that surfaced most often.

Anita called, right on time, to let him know that he could stop worrying. They were safely at Miss Lucy's. She gave him a brief description of the trip and how Cinda handled it and the look on her mama's face when they got to her door. Lesa did her best to quietly distract Joab from the conversation. She did a mighty good job, too.

"Joab, you all right?" Anita finally asked.

"Just tired, Babe," he responded while making a stern face at Lesa.

Lesa stifled a giggle. Her body was well-satisfied and her soul was well-pleased at the knowledge that she possessed something valued by another. Lesa loved competition. She loved winning and she didn't mind cheating to get her way. She actually considered deception a stimulating enhancement to sex. She rested her head in the crook of Joab's arm and took a deep breath of him while waiting for his conversation to finish up.

"Well, we're all going over to your Mama's for dinner. I miss you. I guess I'll call you in the morning. I love you."

Joab could only grunt.

"Night." She hung up.

"Le-e-e-sa!" Joab reprimanded.

"Let's go out to dinner," she said, leaping from the bed in a dark starburst of hair. "I'm starved!"

To say that Joab was impressed by Lesa's choice of dining establishments would have been an understatement of grand proportions. It was full service French. On his way to the table, Joab discovered he was clearly underdressed and tried not to appear uncomfortable. He had never been anywhere where they didn't offer a clue as to cost.

Joab and Lesa enjoyed a four course meal, complete with two bottles of wine (Lesa's selection), and dessert *with espresso* (Joab's first). Lesa was ever gracious in pointing out which was the appropriate fork.

Somewhere between the rack of lamb and the flan, Joab was overcome by a feeling of unreality. Never in his life had his appetites been so thoroughly indulged. And here he was, eating snails and sitting across from the most gorgeous woman he had ever seen—and brilliant, too! Joab relished watching Lesa's almost-round lips move as she gave an insightful political analysis of the current Senate run-offs taking place in Hawaii.

"Where did you get such an interest in politics?" He asked.

"My father's a fairly successful businessman in Honolulu."

"*Fairly* successful?" Joab questioned.

"Okay, very successful," Lesa admitted. "But his real passion is politics. He's been a pillar of the Democratic structure for decades."

"Tell me about him?"

"Well, his family emigrated from Japan to California just before the First World War. When they got out of the American concentration camps after the Second World War, they moved to Hawaii where there was a growing community of Japanese Americans. It was there that my father and mother met and married. She's pretty close to a true native Hawaiian. We think there might be a couple of generations of French missionaries mixed in there somewhere, but that would have been a few generations back.

Ha! Joab mused, inwardly, *She's Japanese-Hawaiian. Sammy thinks he knows so much!*

"My mother's family owned a farm on Oahu, which my father sold for a long strip of beachfront in the 40s," Lesa continued. "My grandmother disowned him. Everyone thought he was crazy. But ours was one of the first high-rise hotels on Diamond Head. Anyway, that's how Dad got started.

"Hm, sounds a lot like Hilton Head. I wish my Mama had bought some beachfront there. Thirty years ago you couldn't give it away."

"I've been to Hilton Head!" Lesa said, brightly, "I think Dad bought Mom a condo there a couple of years back. It must be pretty close to Savannah."

"Forty-five minutes."

Joab and Lesa talked through a third bottle of wine and the departure of most of the clientele. By the time Lesa signed for the bill, Joab was completely enthralled with her background and lifestyle. She'd done so much, seen so much and knew so much about so many things. He couldn't believe his luck at having won, for a moment, her favor.

Though the following days were physically strenuous, Joab was not displeased to discover that his hunch about Lesa was correct: she possessed more than a little creativity.

Anita's powder blue Ford rolled to a stop amidst the driving rain and rumbling thunder of a severe summer storm. Although Joab knew they were due any moment, little was audible over the sound of the downpour on the thin metal roof, and he was startled out of his thoughts when his wife and daughter were suddenly in the room.

"Anita!" he said in surprise, telling his face to smile.

"Hey, Joab!" She responded, "Oh, it's good to be home!"

Cinda had squirmed out of her mother's arms and ran to embrace her father's leg, "Dada! Dada!" She exclaimed.

Joab squatted down to greet her. Then he stood with the child still clinging to his neck. "Daddy missed you so much!" He said embracing her dripping, little body. "Daddy dubby you!"

"Hey, give Mommy a turn," Nita said, joining her family in a group hug.

"I'm so relieved you're home safely," Joab said after giving his wife a long kiss. I hated the thought of your driving in this mess.

"Everything after South Carolina was tough driving. Man, I still feel like I'm moving!"

"Well, sit down and have a beer. I've almost got supper ready. You need anything out of the car?"

"Nah, nothing that can't wait until it stops raining." Nita took a seat at the kitchen table but set her frothy refreshment aside before taking a sip. Cinda ran down the hall to check and make sure all her babies were still there.

"M-m-m-m, something smells good," Anita commented.

"It's just one of those frozen lasagnas and some garlic bread. I'll have the salad ready in a minute."

"I better call Mama and tell her we're home safe." Anita rose and reached for the phone on the wall.

Joab's mind drifted as his wife spoke and his hands sliced tomatoes. Lesa's plane was due to take off in fifteen minutes. He wondered if it was raining at the airport. He wondered how safe it was to take off under these conditions and if they would delay her flight until the rain let up. He wished he could have been there to see her off, but he couldn't be in two places at once. And besides, they couldn't risk being seen together. The lovers had made their good-byes last night and again this morning and would be held together, through the remaining summer, by the thin line of a modem. Joab would not hear her voice until the first day of class. They had agreed. He missed her touch, her smell, already. Joab sliced the side of his index finger when Anita kissed the base of his neck.

Apparently, she had finished her conversation with Miss Lucy and had walked up behind him.

"OO-oo-oo Joab!" she teased, examining the minor damage done to his finger, "you've been alone too long."

Dinner was relaxed and animated. Cinda babbled about her grannies and her babies and rushed dinner so she could be free to piddle about in her kitchen. This left Anita a moment to relate, in superb detail, all the news from north Georgia. Joab found himself enjoying her company as he hadn't for months. Every now and then she would get to a part of her story where Joab's absence had been greatly felt; "Oh, Joab," she would say, "your mama made such a nice supper for us! We missed you so much." or "I ran into some of your friends from St. Paul's. I wish you could have been there." or "We did this or that but it was no fun without you."

Joab got the distinct impression that he had been missed.

He hadn't realized it, but he had missed his girls, too. He had missed the relentless activities of his Cinda and the quiet knowledge of her secure slumber under his roof at night. He had missed her hugs and her smiles and the droning of her high, shallow voice. And he had missed Anita, too. But not the Anita who had driven away, one week ago. He missed the one who had driven home, and he had been missing her for a long time.

Joab thoroughly enjoyed her lengthy account of her visit. He was reminded of his old best friend. He couldn't put his finger on it, but the trip home had been good for Anita somehow, like a visit to the place of their joyous beginnings had restored a measure of her joy. He wished, now, that he *had* gone, too. This did not mean that he regretted one erotic moment with Lesa, but in a purely masculine mental maneuver, merely lamented his inability to divide himself between two places simultaneously.

Joab and Anita talked, just talked, until 11:00 p.m. Joab fabricated a story of all the job hunting he'd been doing in his wife's absence.

"I'm still waiting to hear from two of them," Joab added, convincingly.

At some point, Cinda had laid several of her dolls out on the sofa, snuggled down in the midst of them, and fallen asleep. Finally, Anita suggested Joab put the baby in her bed while she straightened up the kitchen and they would meet in their bed.

Between the sheets, Anita let Joab know exactly how much she had missed him. Catching his breath, there in the darkness, Anita's head on his arm, Joab tried to recall the last time his wife had been so desperate and passionate.

"Joab," his name broke the silence, "I didn't tell you all the news. There was one other thing . . . you're going to be a daddy again."

Joab was glad she had told him in the dark. His first response was, *shit!* and although he did not say it out loud, he was glad that she did not have the opportunity to read it on his face.

"Joab?"

There was misgiving in her voice. Joab had to say something positive and make it sound sincere.

"Joab? What are you thinking? I didn't know how to tell you." She was crying.

"I'm thinking . . . this is such a surprise."

"Is it okay?"

"Okay? Sure it's okay. It's better than okay. It's just,—just, gonna change things a little bit. But we'll be okay. We'll handle it." He was sure Anita had heard the false note in his optimism.

"Oh, Joab, " she wept, "I wanted to tell you on the phone about a million times this week. But I made myself wait."

"When did you know?"

"I took one of those tests two days after I got home. I told Mama, but I figured you'd want to tell Ruth yourself."

More like you didn't want to face her alone. Joab thought inwardly. "Well, what happened?"

"I thought I was keeping up with my pills. I don't know what happened," Anita lied. In truth, she had been trying to get pregnant for three months.

"Oh, Babe, I'm sorry. But I was hoping all the way home that this could be a new beginning for us. I just wanted you to be happy," Nita continued.

"I *am* happy," Joab said, thinking of Lesa and longing for the freedom from responsibility she represented. She would never be stupid enough to let this happen—twice! "I just need a little time to let it settle in, that's all. 'Course I want another baby, I was just hoping I would be out of school next time."

"I'm sorry," Anita cried, "I'm sorry."

"Don't be sorry." Joab soothed, giving her shoulder a squeeze, "We just got our plans moved up again, is all. Don't ever be sorry over the coming of a baby. Two kids can't be much more trouble than one," Joab said, but he had his doubts . . . "When? Do you know when you're due?"

"Some time 'round mid-December, near as I can guess. I'll have to go and get a doctor to tell me for sure . . . Oh, Joab, I hope it's a boy this time."

"I don't care what it is," Joab continued to lie. "Just as long as it's healthy." In his heart he wanted a son. Joab *wanted* a **son.**

✦ ✦ ✦

The following week, Joab did manage to land a full-time, summer job. He was hired by a building supply company to fill in wherever they needed him. Some days he made deliveries to building sites, some days he performed physical labor, re-organizing and restocking the warehouse, and some days he worked the register. Every day his employer got his money's worth, and Joab went home tired. He also worked the four usual nights for Home Guard.

Once she was sure her husband had digested the news of a second child, Anita set about her domestic duties with renewed delight. All of the restlessness of the preceding year seemed to have melted away. Then, too, she possessed a greater peace knowing that she was not competing with Joab's classmates for his time. Often her voice filled the trailer as she sang while she worked. Through the extraordinary weariness of the first trimester, Anita made it a point to take extra moments with Cinda, knowing time would be less available once the new baby came.

There was a measure of embarrassment in Joab's decision not to email Lisa about the *big news*. How does one break the news of his wife's pregnancy to his lover? Would it change anything? Should it change anything? After pondering these questions, Joab decided he may as well not tell Lesa at all. She, in fact, had been the one who had taught him how to draw a neat line between herself and his family. In any case, the pregnancy really didn't affect Lesa anyway.

Far off in Hawaii, Lesa had made a similar decision.

An only child and the pride of her parents, Lesa received a celebrity's welcome when she stepped off the plane. Two days later, the Shemisaki's hosted a black-tie event for all the establishment cream of island society. Lesa's mother told her it was to welcome her home. Lesa sensed it was to show her off.

The evening of the party, hair piled in shimmering cords on top of her head, Lesa shone like a jewel. Dressed in a strapless, golden gown with a slit in front of one leg, she moved from circle to circle with grace and ease. When she moved with slow, precise steps, a man might be able to catch a glimpse of the long length of her right leg, sumptuously shaped by the height of a five-inch heel. There were few husbands in the room whose eyes hadn't strayed to take in the visual treat. All the while, their wives schemed for ways to introduce their sons.

But who had caught *Lesa's* eye? Aware of the success of her hours of primping, Lesa played social occasions as Joab had played basketball, only better. Had there been an event to measure such skill, Lesa would have been an Olympiad. In her heart she knew she would marry into even greater wealth and power than that in which she had been raised. She would marry into them or create them herself. Perhaps both. And why not? At 20, she was fluent in six languages and had traveled around the world more times than she could recall. She could converse, with some measure of insight on everything from pineapple prices to politics and did so, this evening, with great charm.

As she accepted a wine glass from a waiter, Lesa became aware of someone staring at her without pretense. Ah, it was only William Ianako. His father raised macadamia nuts on his sizable plantation on the Big Island. William's family, however, had been raised mostly on Oahu where he had attended Kamehameha Academy, the finest prep school in the Pacific, with his sisters and Lesa. Lesa couldn't stand his sisters.

"Dirt farmers and Republicans, every last one of them," Lesa thought. Still, William had been a brief object of infatuation in junior high. After a covert inspection, Lesa compared with amusement the pimply wimp of a pre-adolescent he had been, with the smooth-skinned, muscular young man he had grown into.

Who would have thought? Lesa asked herself. *He must be pumping iron.*

Then something tweaked her gut as she remembered he had dumped her for Mary Ellen Gilbreth in the seventh grade. *Hmm.* She stared back.

By 10:00, Lesa had decided there was nothing more interesting at the party than William. There were a few hopeful sons-of-parents-friends on summer break, but they looked boring. By 11:30, Lesa whispered a good-bye to her parents, changed into dance club attire, and slipped out the back door with William. The party had mostly wound down by then and the resort nightlife of Honolulu was just winding up.

As the first light of dawn was considering day, Lesa removed her heels and tip-toed up the stairs to her bedroom. She could squeeze in a few hours of sleep before her promised meeting with William on the beach. Downstairs, her parent's pair of Filipino housemaids (sisters hired fourteen years earlier) had risen from their quarters to finish clean-up from the preceding night. By the time Lesa rose (early afternoon) the grand house had been restored to pre-party immaculateness.

Dressed in a small yellow bikini and a gauzy cotton shirt, Lesa entered the kitchen seeking pineapple juice and a bagel.

"Mom, remember my bagels?" She asked one of the maids in their native language.

"Sure. Sure," came the response in English, "And Missy (pronounced me-see), Missy Shemisaki wants you to be home for dinner (dee-na) and remind you to go shopping tomorrow."

"Okay," Lesa said, pouring the yellow juice over ice. "I'll have my bagel on the lanai."

"Sure. Sure."

Lesa closed the glass door behind her and sat down on a white rattan chair, placing her feet on the top of the railing in front of her. A gentle trade wind danced with wisps of hair as she drew a deep breath of balmy air. *Mmmm, it was good to be home.*

Lesa's parents had built their home on a three acre lot on the slope of a mountain. The side of the house that faced the bay was almost entirely glass. Rightfully so. The view of the resort and business district below was spectacular. Lesa loved it. Today the sun was hot, the clouds were puffy, the water was aqua in the shallows and sapphire in the depths, the island was a lush green where it was green and white hotels stood like geometric sand castles along the shore. *I'd love for Joab to see my island.* Lesa thought, as her bagel arrived.

That was the last thought of him she would have that day. She thought of him briefly that night while admonishing William to use a condom. As long as she did not return to Duke with a venereal disease, Joab would never need to know of her summer activities. Besides, what kind of a fool would accept the burden of faithfulness from a married man? Lesa was sure she was nobody's fool.

Chapter 10

Joab worked hard over the summer. But, Joab liked hard work. His most challenging job, however, proved to be assembling a swing set. Apparently, the buyer for Joab's building supply store had ordered a couple dozen deluxe swing sets, complete with teeter-totter, double bench swing, *and* slide. They usually moved well in the spring when parents were eager to get kids out of the house after the cold months. Joab could see himself pushing Cinda on her very own backyard swing, his child laughing at the thrill. But even when the last few went on sale at the end of June, $114.95 was more than he could spare. Then luck smiled on him. A customer returned one insisting that the box contained an insufficient number of nuts and bolts.

"Hey, Joab," his boss called at the end of the day. "You've got a kid, right?"

"Yeah," Joab answered, not knowing where this was leading.

"I'll let you have that returned swing set, out in the back, if you get it out of the warehouse by Friday."

"Ha!" Joab could hardly believe his good fortune.

The following day, Joab drove the Ford to work and drove home with a great, flat box hanging out of the trunk.

"Dada's got a surprise for his baby girl," he said, wrestling the box in the house. "Your own playground!"

Cinda stared at the box in bewilderment. It didn't look like a playground.

The box read, "some assembly required." Joab couldn't wait for his day off.

It took ten and a half hours, three trips to the hardware store, two bags of cement, and forty-five minutes of shamelessly begging Bubba for help, to perform the required assembly. One hour into the ordeal, Cinda had given up hope and gone inside to play. But just before dusk, just as it began to drizzle, Joab pushed his daughter on her very own swing set. She laughed at the thrill.

For the following weeks, Joab and Anita often spent the end of their long summer days, sitting on plastic chairs behind the trailer, watching Cinda perform astounding feats on her swing set. The first few days, they often held their breaths and rushed to catch the child from an imminent fall. But they eventually came to realize that their daughter had an extraordinary sense of balance and self-preservation. If a foot slipped, a hand was always hanging on.

"She's an athlete, like me," Joab told Anita more than once.

Joab found the time spent with his family relaxing and satisfying, and by the end of break, he had even stashed enough money to pay Lesa back for Anita's trip. Though their email letters had dwindled in the final weeks, Lesa and Joab were both looking forward to fall semester. Anita, alone, dreaded the advent of another endless school year.

Two weeks after their junior year began, Sammy Yu watched Joab and Lesa ride off campus together on his Yamaha. A suspicion was spawned in his sharp little mind and he figured he'd be more observant in the future.

The Tuesday and Thursday schedule was working out wonderfully. Alyson had classes from 10:00 to 4:00, and so she stayed neatly out of the way. Curiously, there seemed to be little about the summer break for either Lesa or Joab to talk about. Anyway, they rarely had time for idle chit-chat.

In the following months, Joab grew secretly smug about the finesse with which he handled all the pieces of his life. His grades remained steady and high, he continued to be the singular source of sexual pleasure for the most desirable woman on campus *and* Mr. Davenport had given him a small raise for no particular reason that Joab could think of.

"It's not much, Joab," his boss had told him, handing him the paycheck, "but you've been here over two years now, and I just wanted you to know I appreciate your good work." Then he added, "you know, Donna and I got married right out of high school, too."

He made room each day for *quality time* with Cinda, whose grasp of life on planet earth was astonishing, considering she'd only been part of it two and a half years. Anita, too, seemed happier and more well-adjusted than she had been since they moved up here. After her initial impulse to indulge frequently in the joy of cautionless love making, Anita's condition soon caught up with her and she came to value the quiet pleasure of sleep over the strenuous pursuit of orgasm. Joab's diminished appetite was generously attributed to his selfless sensitivity to the new baby and Anita's gestative state. As the days grew shorter, the weather grew cooler, Anita's tummy grew rounder and Joab's self-satisfaction grew deeper.

"Not bad for a Georgia boy," he often mused.

All too soon, however, Lesa began to grow restless. Often, Joab's email correspondence contained a definite whininess which, loosely translated, meant: Two times a week is *not* enough.

One afternoon, Joab decided to call Anita and tell her he needed to stay at the library to study for a big test. She told him she and Cinda would miss him, but she understood. Then he waited until he figured Lesa had gotten home and punched in her number. Alyson answered.

"Hey, Alyson?" he asked, "is Lesa in?"

"Who's calling, please?"

"Joab Johnson."

"Sure, one minute."

Joab heard Lesa tell Alyson she'd take it in her room.

"You can hang up, now," Lesa told her roommate. Joab heard a click. "Joab! Why are you calling here?"

"Ah, the hell with it!" Joab said. "She's gonna find out sooner or later. I told Anita I have to study. I want to see you—now."

Fifteen minutes later, Joab was at the front door. Alyson let him in.

"You go on and watch TV," Lesa told her roommate, "we can study in my bedroom."

"Fine," Alyson said without comment, pouring herself a Diet Coke. She was settled in on the sofa in front of *Oprah* when the door closed behind Joab and Lesa.

In a moment, Joab's wedding ring fell to the floor inside his jeans pocket.

"I never realized how loudly your bed squeaks before," Joab whispered.

Lesa giggled and both bodies slid to the carpet on the floor.

Joab was home by eight.

The next morning, Lesa informed Alyson that Joab had been separated from his wife for months. If Alyson had any opinions, she kept them to herself.

Alyson was by no means a prude. She had her own wild streak to blaze and her own itches to scratch. She liked Lesa well enough and considered her an above-average running mate. But what she liked most about Lesa was her apartment. Alyson well understood that the only reason she was tolerated (at less than one-third of the rent) was because Lesa's Mommy and Daddy didn't think it safe for a young woman to live alone. Alyson could keep her mouth shut. Who was she to judge?

In mid-September, Lesa received an early birthday card from her parents. It contained a thousand-dollar check. After a flowery poem about daughters and blessings, the hand-written inscription at the bottom read:

> Your mother and I are sorry we will not be with you for number 21. We hope you'll take this money and throw yourself a little party. If you'd rather take some friends out, be sure to hire a driver.
>
> Happy Birthday! All Our Love,
> Mom & Dad

Lesa chose the party. She set it for the last Friday in September, the twenty-eighth, which just happened to be her birthday. It would be an open bar with a hired bartender and enough food to help people absorb a little alcohol without getting sick. She only wished that Joab could be there. He insisted he could not.

◆ ◆ ◆

Some days later, Anita's pen ran out in the middle of a grocery list. When she opened the kitchen drawer, all she found were two pointless pencils. Obviously Cinda's work. Her daughter had, of late, developed a fascination with writing instruments and no paper, no books, no walls were safe. Pencils lost their points and pens became extinct. Anita's search brought her to Joab's study. She pulled out every desk drawer. No pens. She went through his backpack. No pens. She flipped open the carrying case to his laptop and unzipped a pocket. No pens—condoms. *Condoms*? What would he be doing with rubbers? They had no need of condoms now that she was pregnant. Besides, Joab knew she had been on the pill since Cinda's birth. The implication hit her like Tyson hit Givens.

Anita ran to the living room and looked out the back window. There in the fading light of the day sat Joab, playing with Cinda in the sandbox. Anita wanted to run out there and pull her fingernails across his face. She wanted to punch him in the stomach and bite his ears off. Instead, she ran to the bathroom and threw up.

As her stomach settled, her mind began to work again. She had to find out who he was using them on. She had to *know*. She told herself to get a grip. If she was ever going to find out the truth, she was going to have to act as if nothing had happened. Anita brushed her teeth, washed her face, and set her will. She went to the study, put back all the condoms, except one, and zipped up Joab's computer case. Then she went to the kitchen to start supper.

"Something wrong, Babe?" Joab asked later, between mouthfuls.

Anita realized she'd been staring at him, her mind swirling. "Um, no, the baby's just kicking, is all."

That night, Anita lay beside her husband, staring at the ceiling in the dark. *Maybe he wasn't fooling around with anyone in particular. Maybe he just picked them up to have in case temptation got the best of him. Oh, bullshit! That just doesn't make sense. I'm just making excuses when I should be looking for . . . for . . . who?* Anita realized that she had been kept isolated from Joab's life on campus. She really didn't know who his friends were. The only woman she had met, really, was that Chinese woman with the hair. *What was her name?* For some reason Anita remembered her words exactly: *"Anita, you wouldn't mind if I talked your husband into a little ride one day." What was her name?!* Anita spent most of the rest of the night trying to remember what that woman's name was.

The next morning, while Joab was shaving, Anita closed the lid on the toilet, sat down and tried to casually ask, "Hey, Joab, why don't we stop by *The Pig's Foot* again, one of these days?"

"Sure, we can go if you want. I just didn't think you'd be interested in something like that, since you don't drink while you're pregnant."

"Yeah, but it might be nice to get out of the house sometime and visit with your friends."

"Okay," Joab answered. He was about finished shaving. Anita knew she could not let the subject drop. It would be much more suspicious to bring it up a second time.

"How is your friend, Sammy? Is he still seeing that Chinese girl— Um?"

"She's Japanese," Joab stated immediately, not really knowing why. Then he added, "Yeah, I think they're still seeing each other. I'm not really sure. We don't have any of the same classes this semester and I hardly ever see them."

"Oh," Anita said and decided to finish it. "What was her name? She seemed like such a sweet girl."

Joab felt his pulse pick up. He didn't like this. He reached past his wife and turned the shower on. He tried to think. "Um, I don't remember."

Shazam! Anita knew. In all her life, she had never known Joab to forget a name, not even funny foreign ones.

"She only came to *The Pig's Foot* with us a couple of times," Joab continued, not knowing the game was over. He stepped into a cold shower, not willing to wait for the water to heat up.

"Uh, Shemisaki," came Joab's voice from the other side of the shower curtain, "Lesa Shemisaki." But it was too late. He continued, "I think Sammy was talking about a ring last time I saw him. Lesa Shemisaki-Yu, now there's a name."

Anita didn't laugh. Her eyes narrowed. In a way she *could* read Joab's mind and it had just told her everything. The child wiggled in her womb.

I hope it's a girl, Anita thought venomously. *I'd hate for him to raise up another lying, cheating, son-of-a-bitching dog of a man like his own self. Mama was right. All men are liars and cheats and if I ever get my hands on that skinny, long-haired bitch I'm gonna kill her!*

"Mama, caw-caw miwk." Cinda stood in the bathroom doorway, extending an empty bottle to her mother.

"Good mornin'! How's Mama's girl this mornin'?" Anita asked, scooping her daughter up and setting her in what was left of her lap. "You got any sugar for Mama?" Cinda gave her mama a great big hug.

A few minutes after Joab left for school, Anita looked up Shemisaki in the phone book. As one might expect, there was only one. Then, still in slippers and jams, she ran out to the car and dug up an old map of Durham. Clover Street, it sounded so wholesome and innocuous. Anita could just imagine what was going on on Clover Street. Later that morning, Anita strapped Cinda in her safety seat and they took a nice little drive.

Anita parked across from number 413, a charming, two-story duplex and just watched the front door until Cinda got restless. There was zero activity.

Fine, she thought, *I'll catch them one of these days.* Then she wondered if she was getting paranoid and if her hormones had made up the whole scenario. She took the lone condom out of her purse and stared at it for a long time. "Maximum pleasure" were the words on the little wrapper. Finally Cinda—bored and miserable—began to scream.

Anita drove to Tiesha's for a second opinion.

There were few things Tiesha enjoyed more than throwing gasoline on a fire, especially one which might consume Joab.

"Yo' Mama was right, girl," she told Anita, "men are all liars and cheats. Ain't one good one in the lot of 'em. I know what I'm talking 'bout."

The following Tuesday night, Joab got a call at work at 1:00 a.m. It was Lesa and she was crying.

"Joab?"

"Lesa, what's wrong?"

"Oh, Joab, I just got off the phone with my parents . . . (she took a breath) . . . my mother's got cancer. . . . (Joab waited for her to collect herself and continue) . . . They're going to operate next week and Mom and Dad won't let me come home. I need you, Joab."

"I need you, Joab," was a profound admission coming from his independent lover. His heart went out to her. "You know how to get here?"

"I think so."

Joab gave her directions and waited for her headlights below in the parking lot.

There was an old, plaid couch in the switchboard room of Home Guard. Joab sat Lesa down on the couch and listened to her fears and misgivings, holding her while she cried. Then he laid her back and made soft, sweet love to her. It was close to 4:00 a.m. when she finally fell asleep in his arms.

Joab's eyes shot open when he heard a car roll to a stop in the parking lot.

"Oh, shit!" he said, "Lesa, wake up! Quick! Put on your clothes!" He ran around the room picking up articles of clothing and throwing them at her. Joab's heart sank as he heard Mr. Davenport's foot fall on the steps. He heard his boss try the doorknob.

"Just a minute. I'll be right there," Joab called. He heard the jingle of keys and then the knob turned. Joab had his jeans zipped and his sweater on. He hoped it wasn't on backwards. From the corner of his eye he could see that Lesa had her khakis up and was buttoning her blouse. He spotted her shoes and socks on the floor in front of the door. He took a step towards them just as Mr. Davenport entered.

"Mornin', Joab. Quiet night?" his eye caught Lesa's motion as she pulled her hair out from inside her shirt.

"Good morning," she said, looking him straight in the eye.

"Ah, Joab," Mr. Davenport said in a way which made Joab want to crawl under a rock.

"Uh, Mr. Davenport, this is Lesa—"

"I don't want to know who she is. Just get her out of here before the ladies get in and you embarrass yourself."

Lesa picked up her shoes and left. Both men stood in silence as her engine turned over and drove beyond hearing. The next time Joab looked at his boss, his face was scarlet.

"I won't have any employee of mine shacking up on my time."

Joab gathered his things.

"Your wife is a lovely little lady," he said before Joab could make it out the door. "She's a good mother, too. I don't know who your little side dish is, but only garbage women sleep with married men. I'll mail you your last paycheck."

Joab thought of several arguments for Mr. Davenport. He thought of telling him that he had been separated from Anita for over a year. He thought of telling him that Lesa's mother had been diagnosed with cancer. But the words seemed hollow and he just wanted never to have to face this man again.

Sammy Yu watched Lesa run across campus. She was waiting for Joab, breathless, when he came out the door of his second period class.

"Hey!" she said.

"Hey."

"I'm sorry about your boss," she continued when she was sure no one could hear them. "But this cloud just might have a silver lining."

"I don't want to talk about it," Joab said.

"Good idea. Don't talk about it. You haven't told Anita, have you?"

"No."

"Good. So you can spend the next two nights with me *and* come to my birthday party."

Three free nights sounded pretty good to Joab.

"We'll see," he said.

9:00PM found Joab standing outside of Lesa's apartment door.

✦ ✦ ✦

Friday night Anita could not sleep. In fact, she had not slept well since discovering Joab's stash of birth control devices on Tuesday. After Joab left for work, she put Cinda to bed and plunked her fecund form in front of the TV. Forty-five minutes later, she was still clicking aimlessly through the channels. Her thoughts rolled around and around. She longed to call her mother. Pride had kept her from making the call for a year. Today her anger made her pride seem incidental. She picked up the phone. Then she did a strange thing. She decided to call Home Guard, just to hear the son-of-a-bitch's voice.

"Good evening, Home Guard main switchboard. How may I direct your call?" It was a woman's voice.

"Hey, this is Anita Johnson. Can you put Joab on?"

"Hey, Anita, this is Lois." There was a long silence. "I—I don't know what happened," Lois stammered, "but it looks like Joab got taken off the schedule this week."

"Oh," Anita answered.

"Um, how are you feeling these days? It won't be long now."

"Three more months." Anita managed. "Bye."

Anita went to her bathroom and checked her make-up. Then she laced up her sneakers. Three minutes later, she was knocking on Tiesha's front door with the sleeping Cinda bundled in her arms. She heard the chain lock slide off.

"Anita! Girl, what are you doing?" Tiesha asked.

"Can you take Cinda? I need to take a drive."

"Now?"

"Yep."

"Okay, I guess."

✦ ✦ ✦

It took Anita three trips around the block before she found a parking space. She discovered Joab's bike parked around back and became more angry the second and third time she passed it. Music could be heard coming from 413 and cars lined both sides of the street for two blocks. Nita finally decided to double park beside Joab's bike.

"Fuck 'im," she said as she pulled in.

Lesa's house was crawling with people. No one took any notice as one more body walked in. The bottom floor was a kind of giant rec room from what she could tell. There was a pool table and a keg of beer at the other end. She surveyed the faces. Mostly white. That made things easier. No Joab.

At seven months pregnant, Anita's condition was hard to miss and the staircase was narrow. Several people parted as she ascended to the second floor. One of them was Sammy Yu. A wicked little smile crossed his face as he turned to follow Joab's wife.

The second floor consisted of a living room, a formal dining room and the kitchen. The bedrooms were off to the side. Anita was not prepared to try those doors yet. A woman on a mission, Anita made her way through the crowded rooms. The dining room table was full of food and the kitchen was loaded with liquor. Anita's ears registered *Hootie and the Blowfish* on the stereo. Then she spotted him.

Joab was standing at the far end of the living room. He was leaning with his back against the wall behind him. The bitch stood leaning with her back against Joab, clearly a posture indicating familiarity. They were both talking to an acquaintance who stood in front of them. He must have been saying something amusing because Joab and Lesa laughed as they listened.

Anita felt the blood rush to her face as she strode over to where they were. Lesa's sliver eyes grew almost as round as her lips when she recognized Anita's face. Joab grew almost white. He stood suddenly straight, forcing Lesa's weight onto her own feet.

"Who the hell do you think you are with my husband?" Anita asked at a volume that turned heads.

Joab simply stopped breathing.

"Who the hell do you think *you* are at *my* party?" Lesa asked in a perfectly controlled tone.

"I think I'm somebody who's gonna kick your skinny ass all over this room."

"Look, Darling," Lesa condescended as Hootie sang the last notes of the last cut on his last album, "I'm sorry you can't seem to live with your own decisions, but everyone on campus knows that you and Joab have been separated for months."

The room was stone quiet now. All conversation had ended except this one and the folks down stairs would have regretted what they were missing.

"Oh yeah? Do I look separated to you?" Anita asked, an obvious reference to her obvious pregnancy.

"I don't know," Lesa answered without the least hesitation. "Whose is it?"

With that, Anita drew back and smacked Lesa across the face with such force as to draw blood from somewhere on Lesa's almost-round lips. The crack of flesh resounded across an otherwise silent room.

Joab, finally moved to action, grabbed his wife's wrists before she could inflict any more damage.

"Let go! Let me go, Joab!" Anita screamed, squirming, "I'm gonna kill her, and then I'm gonna kill you!"

"You listen to me," Lesa said in a manner that commanded obedience, "If you don't leave my house right now, I'll press charges, and you'll deliver your kid in a jail cell. Now, get out."

"C'mon, Anita," Joab said, quietly. "Let's go."

"You gonna let that woman threaten me?" Anita asked her husband.

Sammy watched with sweet satisfaction as Joab led his hysterical wife, by the wrist, down the stairs.

Several female acquaintances rushed forward to fuss over Lesa's busted lip and collectively bristle over Anita's nerve.

Ayah, Sammy reflected. *Joab was right. That woman is trouble with a capital 'T.' Better his balls than mine. I'll have to remember to thank him sometime.*

Sammy was among the last to leave. He had thoroughly enjoyed Lesa's 21st birthday celebration.

Chapter 11

By the time they reached the car, Anita had run, temporarily, out of words.

"Give me the keys," Joab told his wife, "you're too upset to drive. You might hurt yourself"

"As if you give a damn!"

"I do give a damn, but let's just get in the car."

"What? Afraid you won't get no respect now that everyone knows what a lyin', cheatin' son-of-a-bitch you are? You don't deserve no respect."

"Anita, just get in the car." His voice was low and flat.

"Joab Johnson is a lyin', cheatin', son-of-a-bitch!" she shouted at the top of her voice. A few people, smoking a joint around the side of Lesa's house, turned to look. A light went on across the street.

"Are you embarrassed, Joab? You embarrassed in front of your rich, college slut and her friends?" Anita asked over the roof of the car.

"Yeah," Joab said in the heat of anger and humiliation, "I'm embarrassed that I have a wife who will come into a party and make a scene like a typical welfare broodmare from the slums of Savannah. You make this nice neighborhood sound like a tenement. Now, get in the damn car."

Anita had been hit. She stood mute as verbal shrapnel tore into her soul. There were no words. Her husband was ashamed of her. That's why he didn't include her in his social life. He was ashamed. She opened the car door and sat staring at the windshield.

"I wanna go home," she said, "I want my Mama."

Joab drove at exactly the speed limit all the way to their home. After he cut the engine, he sat still and silent as his wife wept. She wept with utter abandon and with great heaving sobs. Her eyes streamed and her nose ran. Her swollen belly convulsed with each breath. Joab could only reflect on the fact that he felt nothing - no compassion, no animosity, no remorse, only a distant sense of responsibility for this woman. After a half hour, as there was no end in sight, Joab announced that he was going to get Cinda.

Joab did not respond to Tiesha's attitude, but simply pushed past her to gather up his daughter.

Wrapped in her Winnie-the-Pooh blanket, half-asleep in her father's arms, Cinda's internal alarms began to sound. Something was wrong. Something was wrong in the dark, in the night. She didn't know what it was. She only knew that it was.

When Joab entered the trailer, Anita was on the phone with her mother. Anita was trying to make her voice sound normal though her sinuses were full of fluid. Nita fooled her mother about as much as she fooled her daughter.

"I can't explain now, Mama . . . No, I didn't lose the baby. I'll be home sometime tomorrow afternoon. Bye."

"Mama cry?" Cinda asked, in a thin voice, from beneath the blanket.

"Mama no cry," Joab soothed as he lay the child in her bed. "Go to sleep now. Sh-sh-sh." He knelt beside her bed, stroking her hair, until he was sure she was sound asleep. When he went to his room, Anita was packing.

"Anita, please don't leave until you've gotten some sleep," he asked.

"I'm leaving now," she answered.

"Now, Anita, you'll have Cinda and the new baby in the car with you. You need to get some rest. I'll sleep on the sofa tonight. In the morning, I'll go to the bank, first thing, and get enough money for you to get home safely. Okay?"

Anita nodded.

Joab closed the door quietly behind him. He fell asleep to the sound of opening and closing dresser drawers.

He woke to the sound of the first bird at dawn. He opened his bedroom door and peeked in. Anita was lying across the bed between two suitcases, still dressed from the night before.

Joab went to the kitchen and prepared a warm bottle of chocolate milk. Then he took it to Cinda's room and laid it in the crook of her arm. She would find it when she stirred. Joab stared at her for a moment. He loved to watch her sleep. Her little lips almost looked like they were smiling. Her skin was so perfect and smooth. She had kicked all her covers off, and her chubby, miniature feet lay bare beneath the hem of her favorite Princess Jasmine nightgown. He wondered when Anita would bring her back. He wondered *if* Anita would bring her back. The seriousness of his situation hit him and a lump formed in his throat. If he had his bike, he would have gone for a ride. He went for a walk instead.

A little over an hour later, when he walked into the trailer, he could smell coffee and hear the sounds of Anita packing Cinda's clothes. He poked his head in his daughter's room and told Anita he was going to the bank.

"Go," she said.

"Go wiff you, Dada?" Cinda asked, still half-asleep under the covers.

"No, Dada will be right back." Joab warmed a second bottle of chocolate milk, and presented it to his daughter, before he left.

"I checked the tire pressure, the oil and the radiator, and filled the tank," he told Anita later, as she made some instant oatmeal for Cinda. At some point, the size of her front had made it necessary to rock her weight back onto her heels. She had the characteristic waddle as she moved around her kitchen. Cinda sat unusually still as she waited in her high chair for breakfast.

"It's going through oil fast," Joab continued. "Be sure to check it every time you fill up. You've got three new quarts in the trunk, along with a rag. Okay?"

"Sure. The stuff by the door needs to go in the car." There was no emotion in her voice.

Joab packed the car and double-checked to make sure Cinda's safety seat was securely fastened. Then he prepared five bottles of chocolate milk and put them, and a baggie of seedless grapes, in a small cooler with ice. Finally, he set the cooler on the front passenger floor, strapped Cinda into her seat, set her two favorite babies beside her, and gave her a kiss.

"Dada's gonna miss his baby girl," he said, not expecting the rush of tears. "But you have a good time on your vacation. Give your grannies great big hugs for me."

Joab rolled down her window (still without A/C after more than a year), pressed down the lock and swung her door closed.

"Dubby you," he said.

"Dubby, Dada," she responded.

Soon, Anita and Joab were standing beside the car.

"Oh, here's the money I took out. Two hundred and twenty was all that was in there."

Anita shoved it into her maternity dress pocket. "You got your map? You know where you're going?"

"We made this trip twice without you," Anita reminded. "Call my Mama and let her know what time we left.

"Right."

"Call me when you get there." Joab took a step towards his wife. He intended to kiss her. She backed away from him and opened the car door.

"I'll miss you," he said.

Anita just started the car and was gone.

Joab thought about trying to get Bubba to give him a lift to his bike. He thought about picking up a paper to look for a job. Mostly, he spent the day thinking about how badly he had screwed things up.

Real good, Georgia boy, he told himself, *now wha' cha gonna do?*

The more Joab thought about it, the more afraid he became that he was in love with Lesa. He hadn't meant to fall in love, but he might have. In any case, he was sure Lesa, at least, had stuck to the original plan. He wished he could conjure up some emotion for Anita. He could not. Two things he was sure of, though, he loved his little Cinda and the child Anita now carried was just as much his. This led to the big question: Did he have a responsibility to his children to live with a woman he might no longer love?

Joab was attempting to absorb some of Dubois' *Black Reconstruction in America*, when Ruth appeared at her son's front door the following afternoon. Once inside, she fixed a big pot of coffee and, as the day grew old, Ruth got confirmation of the troubles she had long suspected.

By the next morning, Joab had made the decision to do the right thing. His mother dropped him off to pick up his bike on her way out back to Savannah.

Armed with a firm resolve, Joab decided not to put off the call. He detected soft weeping when he told Lesa he would not be seeing her anymore. This surprised him a bit, as he knew the call could not have been unexpected. Then all that was left to do was to phone Anita, swear that his affair with Lesa was over, and ask her to come home. Miss Lucy answered. Her greeting was predictably icy. However, Joab was not prepared for his wife's flat refusal to return.

"No. I'm staying here with Mama until my baby comes," she announced. She could not be persuaded otherwise. Joab noted Anita's indication that "our baby" had suddenly become "my baby." He was beginning to get a handle on just how complicated human relationships could become. He was discovering how swift and easy it is to destroy trust and how long and arduous it is to build. Obviously, his wife was not willing to let him off the hook with a simple slap of hand.

Another stand-off. Joab ended up doing the only things he could see to do; he got a job, worked hard, studied hard, kept his mind off of Lesa (some days were tougher than others) and waited for his wife to relent. He missed Cinda terribly. Days turned into weeks, weeks turned into months. Without Anita's signature, the welfare checks were no good to Joab. He mailed them promptly down to Anita who had little inclination to mail any portion of them back.

"She'll need to buy some things for Cinda and the baby," he reasoned.

Joab fell a month behind on the rent but managed to scrape together enough to keep the lights and phone turned on. There was little left over for food. No matter, Joab didn't have much of an appetite these days.

Ruth, meanwhile, was doing all *she* could see to do; she counseled Joab long distance, did her best to keep communications open with Anita, enjoyed as many hours with Cinda as work would allow, and she prayed. Then she enlisted some of her closest friends from church to pray with her.

Finally, when Ruth could stand it no longer, she took action. It was 6:00AM when Joab answered the phone.

"Do you know what today is?" Ruth asked, by-passing the convention of a, hello.

"December 8th, I think." His mind wasn't quite awake." Joab, this is Anita's due date," Ruth stated, incredulously. "This thing has gone on long enough! You need to get down here, now. It's only by the grace of God that this baby hasn't been born already. Now, I've got a ticket waiting for you at the American Airlines counter. I've booked you on flight 1312 departing at 6:23 this evening and arriving in Savannah at 8:37 after one stop. I'll be there to pick you up."

"Mom, Anita told me she doesn't really want me there and I've got a new job and final exams starting next week!"

"To hell with exams!" Ruth almost shouted. Joab could only remember hearing her curse once before, and that was when the football coach had thought he'd broken his leg again. "Shit" his mother had said, and then covered her mouth as though she were as shocked as the rest of them. Somehow Joab did not think she was covering her mouth now.

"What do I tell my professors?" he stammered.

"Tell them your wife is having a baby! Joab, you *must* be at the birth. This is your child, too. If you aren't there, you'll never be able to make it up to Anita or the baby. Your professors will understand."

Joab wasn't so sure. The only acceptable excuse for a missed final at Duke was death—and it had better be your own.

After his first two classes, Joab spent the block of time, which used to be reserved for Lesa, camped outside of Dr.

Morse's office. His secretary said he was in a class and then he was booked for an appointment, but Joab was welcome to wait.

An hour and fifteen minutes later, the secretary told Joab he could go in.

"Hey, Doc," Joab said, entering, "I didn't mean to cut into your lunch, but I need to talk to you."

"Quite all right." The older man motioned for the younger to have a seat on the other side of the desk. "Before we get started, is this gonna take long? I can get the courier to deliver lunch."

"No, sir, I don't think it should take long. I just need to be excused from some of my finals."

"Which ones?"

"I don't know yet."

Dr. Morse held up a finger and pressed the intercom button with another. "Hey, Sally, could you have a couple of chicken salad sandwiches, two bags of chips, and two Cokes sent up from the cafeteria? Thanks."

"All right," he said, clasping his hands behind his head and leaning back in his leather chair. "Spill it."

Joab looked at the floor and shook his head. "Ah, Doc, my wife left me a few weeks ago, and she's due to deliver our baby today. She won't come home, and I just gotta be there for the birth. . . You know how these things go. She could have it tonight or two weeks from now. She's down in Savannah and if I wait until she goes into labor I'll probably get there too late. It was pretty fast last time."

"I see." There was a long silence while Dr. Morse nodded and appeared to be thinking. "Tell me, Joab," he finally continued, "are you in love with Lesa Shemisaki? She is a beautiful woman, and very bright."

Did Joab detect a note of envy? He could not have known that his mentor had seduced Lesa the second semester of her freshman year and had, in fact, made love to her on the very desk that stood between them now.

Dr. Morse had taken more than a professional interest in several female students over the course of his twenty-three years in advanced education: four to be exact; and if asked, he would have defended four as a number indicative of great restraint. After all, he was still a man and his attraction to this or that young woman was as natural as theirs to him. What was four compared to annual waves of impressionable young girls, fresh from the shelter of Daddy's protective wing, hungry for new thoughts and new experiences? Four was nothing when considering the hundreds of sweet young things who had swept through his classroom doors and swooned to his progressive philosophies, so liberated from the black and white confines of the Bible-belt mentality. Ah, yes, a backwards and irrelevant faith yet beat in the heart of Dixie. But the heartbeat grew more faint with each freshman class and would, Morse was convinced, flat line one of these years, finally freeing the Southern mainstream to flow into the twenty-first century.

Four. Only four. But each of them had been exceptional beauties, screened for emotional maturity and a sense that they were well beyond the first blush of virginity and had come to accept sex as the purely physical act that all intellectually honest adults knew it to be.

Upon reflection, Dr. Morse could never quite decide whether he or Lesa had done the seducing. But he *was* certain who had done the walking. After only a very few, all too brief encounters, which Morse remembered well and often, Lesa had simply stopped keeping her appointments with him. *He* had always done the walking before, letting his student-lovers down easily, of course, taking care to ensure that he would be remembered as a positive growth experience. It still made him uncomfortable, though, to think that he might be slipping a bit at forty-four.

Anyway, Morse considered himself a moral man. His snubbing by a nineteen-year-old, still smarting, had been set aside when it came time to give out grades. The "A's" he had given Lesa were "A's" she had earned—in his honest and objective opinion. After all, he was a professional.

In his soul, Morse craved a description of all the intimate details of Joab's affair with Lesa. He did envy Joab. He knew he had to be careful.

"You know about me and Lesa?" Joab asked, surprised.

Morse nodded, smiling. "You weren't exactly discrete," he said. Joab took a deep breath and shook his head again. "I know. So, can you fix it so I can take my exams when I get back?"

"I think I'll be able to work it out."

"Oh, man, thanks."

"When are you leaving?"

"Tonight."

Morse's secretary knocked on the door and entered with lunch. She handed a white paper bag to Joab and one to her boss. She closed the door on her way out. Morse unwrapped half of his sandwich and took a bite. Joab did likewise.

"So, what are you going to do? I mean after the baby comes?" the older man asked.

"This will be my second kid. I guess I'm going to try and put my marriage back together, for the children."

"Good, good." Morse said, chewing. He swallowed, "Divorce is a tough thing."

Joab listened closely. He had a deep respect for Dr. Morse and was glad to get some advice from another man.

"Of course, there comes a time when a bad marriage is harder on kids than just getting out. I had no kids from my first wife, but I've got two boys by my second wife. 'Course, I don't see them much anymore. Their mother got a job in Miami a couple of years ago. I just have them for a few weeks in the summer and a few days over Christmas break. They're in highschool now. Ah, they went through the normal adolescent problems, but they seem to be doing fine now. It was the best thing . . . Do you still love her?"

"Who?"

"Your wife."

"I don't know."

"Oh. How about Lesa?"

"I don't know. I sure hope not."

✦ ✦ ✦

Joab saw his mother's face before he was out of the flight ramp. His eyes searched for a glimpse of Cinda but could not find her. That was strange, Ruth had said she would bring the child, and Joab had thought of nothing but her lovely little face, and a great bear hug, during the flight. His heart began to race.

"Welcome home, son. Thank the Lord you're in safely," Ruth said, reaching up around Joab's neck. "Lord, but you look like one of those poor refugees from Somalia. Didn't I teach you how to cook?"

"I'm fine, Mama. Where's Cinda? You said you'd bring her."

"She's with her Aunt Annie at my house. Do you have any other bags?"

"Nope. This is it," he said, referring to a small canvas suitcase, filled to the seams.

"Good. Let's get going. Miss Lucy called to tell me that Anita's water broke at around two. We're going straight to the hospital." Ruth set a brisk pace.

This was Joab's first visit to the new airport. He could not help but be impressed by the contrast between this vast, modern terminal and the simple, cinder block structure that had served Savannah adequately for so long. He had been gone less than three years, yet the changes in his home city had been hard to keep up with. No one had told him when the old terminal had become obsolete. It felt vaguely like he had landed in the wrong place.

"I didn't tell Miss Lucy you were coming," Ruth continued. "I wasn't sure she'd call me if she knew."

"Miss Lucy still upset with me?"

"Wouldn't you be if it was your Cinda?"

Anita was in the middle of a moderate contraction when Joab walked in the door.

"Wha-choo doin' here?" Anita asked through gritted teeth. A nurse who had looked up to see the father quickly lowered her eyes again and busied about her work. Miss Lucy shot Ruth a deadly look that Ruth decided not to catch.

"Miss Lucy!", she said. "You look all wrung out. You must be starving! When was the last time you ate something?"

"Well, I never did get lunch," the other grandma admitted, "but I don't think I should leave Anita right now."

"Oh, you still have a little time. I'd be surprised if the baby gets here much before the next hour, at least," the nurse offered.

Sweet girl. Ruth thought.

Miss Lucy looked to Anita who, between contractions, nodded grudgingly. Ruth whisked the other grandma out the door.

"So. How ya doing?" Joab started, awkwardly.

Anita rolled her eyes.

"Annie has Cinda. I guess you already know that."

"Yeah."

"How far along are you?"

"Six centimeters about a half hour ago."

Joab could hear the fetal heart monitor pick up speed. He looked to the graph paper and saw the jagged line begin to rise. Anita bit her lower lip and let out a squeak. His heart filled with compassion. He took his wife's hand. Incredibly, some Lamaze came back to him.

"C'mon, now, Neet, breathe."

"Don't touch me," she said through a constricted throat, but she held tight to his hand.

"C'mon, Nita, hoo-hoo-hoo, hee-hee-hee."

"Hoo-hoo-hoo," Nita responded. Unable to afford the luxury of real pain relief, she knew managed breathing would help.

"When do they move you to the operating room?" Joab asked after the contraction.

"This is a birthing room. The doctor will come and deliver the baby here when it's time. I only go to the operating room if there's trouble."

After several more contractions, Anita informed the nurse that she might need to check her dilation again.

"Oh, my goodness!" the woman exclaimed, "that was quick. I'll call Dr. Freemont right now. Hang on, Honey. Don't push yet."

In the next few moments the room was a flurry of activity. Three more nurses appeared. One pushed a cart with a clear, plastic box on top for the baby. Another removed the bottom third of the table and flipped up stirrups for Nita's feet. Joab went to the top of the table to coach his wife and stay out of the way. Dr. Freemont materialized, rolled his little stool between Nita's legs, and prepared to guide and catch the baby. Joab couldn't see much blood from where he stood. He liked it that way.

"Wait! I can't push until Mama gets back!" Anita exclaimed.

"Well, she better come back soon," one of the nurses commented.

The next few contractions were difficult but productive. Then the baby seemed to get stuck.

"I can't do it, Joab. I can't do it," Anita cried.

"You can do it, Baby. Just push one more time," he encouraged, close to her ear.

"No, it hurts. It hurts. Oh, no, here it comes again. Oh, it's gonna hurt." There was panic and raw fear in her voice.

"You can do it, now. C'mon, Anita, you're doing great," Joab told her.

"Okay, bear down, hard," the doctor commanded.

"Please, Dear God—" Joab heard himself beg before he could stop himself.

"Okay, one more time. Push as hard as you can, now. It's almost here." Dr. Freemont instructed.

"I love you," Anita whispered to her husband. Then she drew breath and held it as she pushed until her whole body trembled. She squeezed Joab's fingers. He was wondering if she really had the strength to break them when the strained cry of a baby filled the room.

"It's a girl!" the doctor and the nurse announced at the same time.

Joab chastised himself for his disappointment.

"I know you wanted a son," Anita whispered.

"We can try again," he answered, knowing it was pointless to argue. She knew him too well. Both doubted if there would ever be another child between them.

"Would the father like to cut the cord?" The doctor asked.

✦ ✦ ✦

Anita looked to her husband. Joab accepted the stainless scissors and performed the task.

"Welcome to the family, little one," he said, smiling softly at the writhing little body. There was a sadness in his heart as he remembered the purity of the joy he had experienced in the first moments of Cinda's life.

Then the grandmothers were in the room.

✦ ✦ ✦

Joab went home to fetch Cinda.

"Daddy! Daddy!" She hollered as she heard his voice greet Aunt Annie at the front door. She ran into his arms.

"Daddy missed his baby girl!" He said, honestly as his big arms wrapped around her small frame. He pulled back and looked into her clear, dark eyes. "You have a baby sister!" He said, "She wants to meet you!"

"My Mama! My new baby sister!" Cinda exclaimed as she entered the hospital room. Both grandmothers snapped pictures furiously as the sisters met for the first time. Cinda was completely captivated by the baby. It was only under protest that she let Grandma Lucy take the wonderful bundle from her lap. Watching his daughters, Joab knew he had no choice but to do whatever it took to put his family back together again. He resolved to jump through any and all hoops Anita required.

"Are you sure you don't want me to stay?" Miss Lucy asked her daughter when it was time to leave.

"I'll be okay with Joab," Anita answered. After the grannies took Cinda home, the nurses came to wheel the new baby down to the nursery.

In a few minutes, Anita was alone with her husband for the first time in over two months.

"You did a fine job," Joab told her. "She's beautiful. What did you decide to call her?"

"Amanda, just 'cause I like it, and 'Nicole' for my brother."

"Amanda Nicole, that's real pretty."

"Mandy's cute for a little girl, too."
"Yeah, real cute."

Savannah Memorial released Anita and the baby the next morning. They went home to Miss Lucy's house. This was particularly difficult for Joab as his mother-in-law had been known to carry a grudge for decades against anyone who had done one of her children wrong. As far as Miss Lucy was concerned, Joab's penance was just beginning. He could well imagine the advice she had given his wife concerning pay-back for infidelity. Even so, Joab was relieved to have his new daughter here safely, and his family reunited—geographically anyway.

The following evening he stepped off a plane in Raleigh/Durham having missed only one day of finals and having extracted a solemn promise that his wife would come home once she felt well enough to travel. He had even managed to hang on to his new job.

Back within the walls of his mobile home, Joab was keenly aware of Cinda's absence and the hollow silence grew louder with each moment. He longed to hold his new baby and share snuggle time with Anita as she nursed at all hours of the night. In his loneliness, he yearned for Lesa, too, just a few moments with her—one kiss, one touch. He dared not. He would not even let himself check his email. He could not afford to compromise his Cinda *or* his Mandy, again. It was difficult to concentrate on finals. He was sure he had done more poorly than ever before and found it hard to give a damn. He made up the one he had missed and they were over, at last.

After work one day, Joab decided to assemble the crib for the baby. Next, he pulled out the Christmas decorations to do up the house in grand fashion. Until this year, the chore had always fallen on Anita who seemed to enjoy that kind of thing. Joab had always been too busy. This year, he wanted Cinda's homecoming to leave an impression she would not soon forget. Also, he wanted to send the message to Anita that he would be thankful to have his family home for the holidays.

Joab went to K-mart and returned with an additional twenty dollars worth of colored lights. By the time he was finished, they zig-zagged up and down the side of the trailer, across the top, down the back, squiggled all over Anita's neglected little shrubs, and encircled the living room window. Then he started on the tree. Joab had no idea how time-consuming it was to decorate a Christmas tree, but he enjoyed the diversion and the speculation on how his surprise would be received by his girls.

That night on the phone, he shared his secret with Anita.

"I can't wait for you and Cinda to see it!" He told her excitedly.

"Well, Joab," she said, "I'm still real sore where the baby came out and I don't think I'll be able to take that long drive before Christmas... Joab? You still there?"

He knew that his voice would crack if he spoke.

"Joab?"

He swallowed, "Yeah."

"I mean, I'll talk to the doctor, but I don't think he'll let me."

He had a feeling she was stalling, a feeling payback had begun, and a sense that he must not give away the extent of damage.

"Fine," he said, "you just take your time." Then he added, "I'll try and keep busy. . . I'll call you tomorrow."

"Bye."

"Bye."

Joab hung up the phone, slumped down in a chair and wept.

The next time the phone rang, it was Ruth.

"She can't do that, Mama, can she?" He asked after explaining his most recent conversation with his wife. "She can't keep them away from me at Christmas, can she? You think she's really that sore?"

Ruth heard the anguish in her son's voice. "You can always come home," she offered.

"Mama, I just barely managed to hold on to my job last time. And I need the money or I won't make rent and there won't be any home to come back to."

"Well, I can always lend you a little money, son."

"I know, Mama, but I already owe you a fortune and I just want my family back home," Ruth heard his soft weeping. She hadn't known him to cry since he was a little boy.

"Ah, Mom, what have I done?" He asked.

"Joab, you're not still seeing that woman, are you?"

"No, Mama, I swear."

"All right, I'll see what I can do."

Chapter 12

Ruth prevailed. On the evening of the 24th, she arrived at Shady Oaks with Anita, and Baby Mandy packed in her car. Miss Lucy and Cinda were right behind in the exhausted, blue Escort. Joab had his lights blinking festively and he felt as though he was waiting for St. Nick himself as he stared through the window, anticipating the first embrace of his little Cinda. When he saw the headlights come to a stop outside the trailer, Joab made a mental note to kiss Anita first.

"Welcome home, Neet," he said, helping her out of the car. "How do you feel?"

"Fine," she answered, accepting a dry kiss. She bent over, back into the car, and unstrapped the baby carrier.

"How'd she do with the trip?"

"Not too bad."

"Well, you and the baby get on to the house. I'll bring your things."

By that time, the rest of the passengers had emerged. Cinda ran around both cars and clung to her daddy's thigh.

"Hey, baby girl!" He said, "How do you like all your Christmas lights?"

Cinda's eyes sparkled in the near dark. "Pretty!" She said.

Joab held his daughter in one arm as he gave hugs to the grandmothers and invited them out of the cold.

Joab had the table set. The smell of baking turkey and the velvety voice of Nat King Cole greeted the travelers as they passed through the door. Cinda did not miss the colorfully wrapped boxes beneath the tree.

Anita was touched. Even Miss Lucy thawed a few degrees. The ladies busied about the final meal preparations as Joab emptied the car.

Over dinner, all the adults took care to keep the conversation light and non confrontational. Ruth was a little concerned about the other grandparent, but even Miss Lucy managed to find a soft tip to her sharp tongue.

After dinner, Anita zipped Cinda into her teddy bear sleeping bag and snuggled her down on the floor of her room. Grandma Lucy would take Cinda's bed and Ruth would sleep on the sofa. Joab set up the bassinet beside the master bed while the older women straightened the kitchen.

Finally, everyone was settled and Joab and Anita closed the door to their room. Joab peeked in on the baby. She slept soundly in her frilly basket. Walking up behind his wife, Joab put his arms around her waist, and kissed her neck.

"I'm so glad you're home," he whispered.

She removed his arms and turned to face him. "Look, Joab," she said, "Supper was very nice, and all, but just 'cause your mother talked me into coming home for Christmas doesn't mean that you get to fuck me like everything is all fixed up. Understand?"

Joab cringed at her choice of words. He found the "F" word particularly crass and degrading. Enslaved to instinct, *dogs fucked.* People *chose* their lovers.

"Yeah. I understand," he said.

✦ ✦ ✦

The excitement of Christmas morning rendered Cinda oblivious to the tense undercurrents swirling around her mother and father. Ruth and Miss Lucy sensed, immediately, that things could not have gone well last night. Even little Mandy seemed unable to find peace. She remained fussy and irritable through most of the gift giving.

Anita had decided not to buy a gift for her husband this year. "I figured a baby was enough," she announced.

Joab exchanged looks with his mother, took a breath, and made himself shake it off.

"And it's the most wonderful gift you've given me since Cinda. Thank you, Anita." He said with sincerity. "*Your* present is in the hall closet. Go on and get it. Go on."

Anita handed him the baby who instantly began to cry. She rose, walked down the hall, and slid the folding doors open. Drawing breath, she put her hand to her mouth.

"It's a washer and dryer," she told the mothers when she returned. "Thank you, Joab," she said, not looking him in the eye. "That was very nice of you."

"They're used, but Bubba said they're good for a few thousand more loads. I thought it might make things a little easier for you with another baby and all."

"Thank you." Anita repeated. Joab couldn't tell for sure but it looked, for a moment, like Anita might cry. She did not.

As soon as the grandmothers returned from Christmas church services with their beloved Cinda, they had a simple lunch of leftover turkey sandwiches, and Ruth started packing the car.

"Are you sure you can't stay for just one more day?" Anita was almost whining.

Miss Lucy gave Ruth a pleading look.

"I'm sorry, Anita, but the court system barely slows down for the holidays. Charlie needs me to finish typing a brief by tomorrow morning." Ruth offered apologetically.

Grandma Lucy felt like she was losing her daughter, all over again, and that was painful enough, but the thought of leaving her grandbabies behind was almost more than she could bear. It had been a pure joy to be able to dote on Anita and Cinda. Once the baby came, she had been only too pleased to let Nita rest while she bathed and rocked the darling Mandy. Fact was, Lucy's house seemed very empty once Nicholas had finally moved to Atlanta. Oh, Lucy Twedell was relieved not to have to worry over him anymore, but she had always found it easy to get along with her daughter and God hadn't created two more perfect children than hers.

Ruth Johnson's heart swelled with similar emotions, but she knew Anita's place was with her husband, and she would not permit herself to shed even one tear in selfishness.

"Give me your keys, and I'll load that stuff in the trunk," Joab offered.

Ruth produced the keys and followed her son out to the car.

"Thanks for getting my family home, Mama," Joab said, opening the trunk.

Ruth gave him a tight hug, her left cheek pressed against his hard chest.

"There's going to be some rough waters ahead," she warned, stepping back to look him in the eye, "but you bought the ticket and Anita has good reason to be angry with you. Every time she lashes out, commit to love her through it, rise above it, and go on. Love is not a thing you catch, Joab, like some kind of virus. Love is a choice you make. Otherwise, how could Jesus command us to do it? Persevere. Overcome Anita's insecurities, and the two of you will be stronger for it. In His own time, God will rain down blessings on your marriage again. Only be patient."

Joab wondered how his mother presumed to be such an expert, having never been married herself. *Mama's never been on the receiving end of Anita's temper*, Joab thought, and he suspected she could tote a grudge longer than Miss Lucy. Anyway, he was deeply grateful to Ruth and he was in no position to argue. He just kicked a pebble around with the side of his Reeboks.

"Yes, Mama," he said.

❖ ❖ ❖

The screen door hissed behind his mother-in-law. Joab slammed the trunk and helped her load a cooler on the floor behind the front seat. Ruth returned to the trailer for her purse and her farewells.

Ruth could not abide long good-byes. Anita's mother had already kissed Cinda and Mandy three times each, had soaked a hankie clear through, and was going in for round four. Ruth started the car. In moments, the two grandmothers were on their way and Joab was left to stand at the helm of his household, once more.

His mother had been right in her prediction of rough waters. There was a powerful tempest in his mobile home—her name was Anita.

Soon second semester classes started. Rumor had it that Lesa was dating some Blue Devil basketball star. Joab wondered if he was white or black. He chewed on that thought for about two hours before he decided that he didn't want to know, and forced his mind to spit Lesa out.

After two weeks, Anita finally relented on the sex. However, nuptial rights remained severely restricted and the relationship strained. Joab's 21st birthday passed without observance save a call from his mother. In spite of her husband's humble repentance, Anita proved unable to let go of her bitterness. Joab had given her permission to make him eat crow and it looked like she intended to dish it out until the caldron was empty. In her mind, her unfaithful husband deserved every rebuff and every snide remark. He had been her best friend since childhood. Anyone who would do their best friend that way deserved to be treated like a dog, but at the core was a far more crucial issue. It had been the reason she had run to the one person who loved her unconditionally and the reason she had been afraid to return to Durham and it was this: Joab knew her better than anyone alive, better than she knew herself. If he rejected her, after knowing her so completely, there would be no safe place for her to hide, no corner of her being protected from his judgment. Truly everything, for Anita, was at stake and she was unsure she could withstand the assault of absolute rejection. *Does he still love me?* Repeated in her conscious thoughts almost by the minute. Each time he willingly suffered before the slings and arrows of her outrage, something within her cried out, *See!! See? He must love me. He has to love me, because no man would put up with this for anything less.*

✦ ✦ ✦

One day, Lesa caught up with Joab in the Student Union quadrangle.

"Joab, I need to talk to you," she said, trying to keep up with his brisk pace.

"Lesa, I don't want to be late for my next class," he said.

"Please, Joab, I won't keep you long." She was as close to begging as he'd ever heard her. He turned and faced her beside the trunk of a great sycamore. Tiny buds were barely visible upon the tangle of naked branches. A gust of wind caught Lesa's hair and she drew her thin shoulders up around her neck. Joab yearned to put his arm around them.

"I love you, Joab," she said. "These have been the longest four months of my life."

"Tell it to your basketball star."

"There'd be no basketball star if you'd come back. I didn't mean to love you."

"Yeah and I've got two little girls to raise."

"What about you, Joab? Do you really love Anita?"

"Look, Lesa, this is difficult enough. You go have fun with your basketball player. I'm gonna try and put my family back together and we'll just pretend like none of this ever happened. Okay? I'm late for class now." Joab turned to go.

"Joab, kids or no kids, you're too young to waste your life on a bad marriage. You deserve better."

"How's your mother doing?" Joab asked. It had been on his mind.

"They think they got to it before it spread. Mom's doing well. Thank you for asking."

"I really have to go," he said.

✦ ✦ ✦

Joab spent the rest of the day trying not to think of Lesa. He tried not to think of her silken hair, her narrow hips, her delicate hands, her almost-round lips, her long, smooth legs. He tried not to think of her mischievous smile, the smell of her sheets, the bite of her humor, the keenness of her mind, the ingenuity of her play, the texture of her lace, the passion of her—nope! He was trying not to think about that.

As Joab turned the corner into Shady Oak Trailer Park, he could almost see the cloud that hung over his house. He could hear the combative tones of rap music before he opened the door. The baby was crying.

"I'm on the phone with Mama, Joab," Anita hollered from the kitchen. "Go get the baby."

Cinda turned away from the bare-chested, angry-sounding man pointing his finger at her from inside the box in the living room. Her face instantly brightened.

"Daddy's home! Daddy's home!" She announced to no one in particular, leaping up and rushing at him.

"How's my baby girl?" Joab asked, throwing her up until her head just grazed the low ceiling.

"I'm not a baby girl," she said firmly, "Mandy is the baby."

"Oh, that's right." Joab said, slapping his forehead. "You're the *big girl.* Mandy's the *baby* girl. Let's go see if we can cheer the baby up."

Anita watched with a small but expanding contempt as her husband carried his adoring daughter into her room. Only a few years earlier, Anita would have thought it impossible for parents to be jealous for the affections of their children. Naturally, she had assumed that a wife's joy multiplies as the bonds of love strengthen the whole of her family. But that was before Joab's treachery had loosed the demon of disunity in her household. The uncertainty of Joab's affection drove Anita to a new possessiveness of the love of her daughters who, by right, she believed belonged to her, first.

Right ear against the phone, Anita's left ear heard the baby quiet.

"Look, Mom, Joab's home and I gotta go," she said, "I love you, too . . . I will. Bye."

Anita stood in the doorway of her bedroom and watched her family. Little Mandy lay on her back in the middle of her parent's bed. Cinda sat hovering over her, bowing every now and then, to kiss the round, little face. Joab changed the diaper with an expert hand. Well into her third month, the baby delighted in eye contact and struggled to find sound in her mouth, intrinsically longing for the connection of conversation even without the understanding of a single word.

"Ah, Cinda loves little Mandy," Joab crooned as Cinda succumbed again to the urge to kiss the cherished face.

"Daddy's gonna fix his baby right up," Joab continued in a voice that seemed to please. "Nobody likes a stinky diaper. We'll just get rid of that old thing." Joab knew his words were silly and he also knew it didn't matter a wink to Mandy. What she loved was the sound of his voice. She beamed and kicked at the bliss of being personally addressed.

"Gu-u-u," she said, locking onto her father's eyes.

Joab had almost forgotten how much he loved three-month-old babies. It was a pure kind of satisfaction to watch them emerge from the isolation of the womb and discover human affinity. First the parent's voice, then the eyes, then the hands learned to obey the yearning to reach out and touch. She could already roll over. Soon she would be sitting up. Then she would be crawling, then walking, then running—words! Somewhere along the way she would say her first word. Joab wondered what it would be. Through words he could know what she thinks about, what's important to her, who she is. And it occurred to him that a child is like a gift with brand new surprises morning by morning because they grow and they learn and they change every day. Little wonder Anita had been miserable spending so much time away from her Cinda when she had to work. Joab bent over and kissed his daughter's tiny chest.

"Mandy's laughing, Daddy!" Cinda said, joyously stating the obvious. Indeed she was.

Joab set the little bottom on a clean diaper and commenced sprinkling powder.

"Look at you getting powder all over the bed," Anita scolded, "You're as bad as Cinda! Couldn't you think to put a towel or something down first?" Anita crossed over to her husband and snatched the powder out of his hand.

"Cinda, could you please throw this diaper away in the diaper pail for Daddy?" Joab asked. "You're such a big help to

Mommy and me," he added as she left the room. Then Joab turned his attention to his wife.

"Look, Anita, I screwed up bad. I know it, and I'm sorry. I'm sorry!" Joab checked the decibel level that had crept up, "Okay? But don't you ever talk to me like that in front of our daughter again. You will not teach my daughters to disrespect me in my own home."

"Oh, yeah? And what have you done to deserve our respect, huh? Were you respecting me when you were screwin' that skinny bitch while I was blowing up like a fat sow with your baby? Huh? Your home! This ain't *your home*. A man *pays* for his home. You don't pay nothing and your Mama's still picking up the bill for your school books. Your precious daughters eat from food stamps. Hell, you're so smart you can't even find a part-time job!"

"You told me you needed help with the baby."

"Well, maybe I don't. Maybe I don't need your help with nothing!"

Anita paused to breathe. Her last words hung in the air. She could feel the tension in her jaw and the acid in her stomach. She knew she had said too much and had better shut up before it was too late—if it wasn't already.

Unable to hold her tongue, she took a different tack, instead. "You don't change to get a baby. I'm the one who has to watch myself get all stretched out and ugly."

"Well, you wouldn't if you weren't too stupid to remember to take a simple pill once a day. Whose fault is that? Mine? Or maybe it wasn't accidental."

"What are you saying, Joab? That I tricked you? Is that what you're saying? Go on and say it. It's what your mother's thought from the start and she's mad at me cause your daddy wouldn't marry her."

Joab couldn't believe the kind of twisted logic he was hearing coming out of his wife's mouth.

Anita continued, "And I didn't have to use no tricks, you was always gonna marry me, anyway . . . weren't you?"

Joab knew the truth and he remembered it well; no, she had not gotten pregnant on purpose, and yes, he would have married her anyway. But she had been so malicious toward him that he could not resist a clean jab when she exposed her vulnerability. Joab withheld the answer. His silence was thick in the room.

"Weren't you?" Anita repeated. Joab noted, with a cruel pleasure the anxiety in her voice. After weeks of sucking it up, the scent of vengeance smelled sweet.

Anita reacted with instant nausea. Her head felt light and a sweet saliva rushed into her mouth. The baby began to cry and she saw a stony-faced Cinda out of the corner of her eye. Joab's answer was clear; he had married her for the baby. Anita willed herself not to vomit. She would not give Joab that satisfaction.

Anita sat down on the edge of the bed. Mechanically, she unfastened her bra, gathered up the baby, and held her to the breast. Mandy quieted.

Anita's mind swirled. She had to know if Joab would fight to keep her. She knew she loved him with all her being. She also knew the doubt of his love would eat away at her until there was nothing left. She had to know if he loved her. Anita formed her words with a false confidence.

"You know, Joab, I can get along just fine without you. I want a divorce."

There was a long pause and Anita almost breathed a sigh of relief. Then he asked, "Would you keep the girls in Durham until I graduate?"

The girls!! All this time he's only put up with me for Cinda— and now Mandy. Anita turned her head away so he could not see her face.

Like hell I will, she thought. "Sure," she said.

"Okay, Nita. If that's what you want."

"Just like that? You'll divorce me just like that?"

"You're divorcing me, and what the hell choice did I have when *you* wanted a separation?"

◆ ◆ ◆

For the following two days, few words passed between Joab and Anita. Cinda was unusually subdued. On the third day, Joab came home from school to discover that Anita had packed up most of the household and was gone.

She must have rented a U-Haul and hired some help, Joab decided. Except for the furniture that came with the trailer, 'most everything was gone. She left a dish, a glass, one place setting of flatware and a Duke coffee mug for him in the kitchen. She hadn't touched anything in his study. In his bedroom, she had taken his dresser and left his clothes in a pile on the floor.

Thankfully, she hadn't touched the six-pack in the fridge. Joab grabbed it and went out the back door. He sat down on one of two plastic chairs and popped the top on the first Bud.

He figured she couldn't have finished much before he got home. That would put her in at Miss Lucy's around 10:00 or 11:00PM. He knew he'd better call his mother but decided to put it off until morning. He'd also need to call Mr. Keylar to ask about visitation rights. He knew enough about the law to know he *had* visitation rights . . .

At dusk, Tiesha appeared.

"Missing something?" She asked sarcastically.

"Go... Now." Joab demanded flatley. She did.

Joab began figuring. He figured he'd messed things up pretty badly and Anita just couldn't get past being mad at him. He guessed Lesa wouldn't mind. He figured he may as well go on and get a job and see if he could find an empty dorm room. What he hadn't figured on was missing his little girls so much.

The sun was setting fast. Joab popped the top on his last beer. He noticed Cinda's toys scattered 'round her sandbox. A gust of wind pulled at her swing as though a ghost child had given it a sudden push.

Joab Johnson hung his head and cried.

Part Two

A Son is Born

Chapter 13

She stood alone in the girl's lavatory, in the only stall with a dependable lock. Each of the close walls was covered with declarations of love, scratched or scribbled in haste. There were hearts around initials paired by a plus sign. There were statements of possession:

Zonnie is Tonya's man!!!!!

And others of enduring commitment:

Jamie belongs to Sharrie 4 Ever !!!!!!!!

There were lots of exclamation points as though the more there were, the truer the love. On another day, Ruth might have looked for a space to add one more heart. Not today. The metal wall was cool on her shoulder as she leaned against it. The first steamy tear made its way over the high, smooth swell of her cheekbone and down to the corner of her wide mouth. Her delicate frame, hunched and shaking, could not contain the cloudburst. It came. She tried to weep softly. No one must know. Thankfully, third period found no other teenage girl in this bathroom. Everyone was in class. It was time for Ruth to get back, too. Any longer and she'd be in trouble. She ran a finger under each eye, blew her nose, and washed her hands, more out of habit than need, but the cold water felt good. She drew in a deep breath before pushing open the door and heading down the empty hall to face the end of Social Studies.

The yellow bus labored down the windy country road at its max speed of forty miles per hour. It was almost time for summer break. If you weren't used to the heat of the

Lowcountry, the humidity would have been oppressive. But these children were used to it. Had there been a Yankee around to make the observation, he would have been impressed by the activity on the bus. Teasing and giggling could have been heard floating on the wind blowing through the open windows. Once, a ball of paper, having missed its innocent target, carried with the children's voices over the edge of a metal sill and became lost among other pieces of trash on the side of the road. But there was no such Yankee there today. Not even one car to get stuck behind the old bus and peek out around every curve, eager to pass.

The old bus turned right down a dirt road. A cloud of dust rose up behind it to meet the canopy of tree limbs. Silvery clumps of Spanish moss hung from their branches and remained motionless in the thick air. The bus drove past an inlet where a view of the marsh could be seen with its tufts of straight, green reeds and shimmering, flat water glistening under the brilliant sun. A shrimp boat sat on the horizon like a winged water bug. Not one child even took notice. This was their native land and its familiarity had rendered them blind to its extraordinary beauty.

Ruth's house was the first stop on Gibbit Road (named for her mother's half brother). The hinges of the school bus door shrieked as they were forced, ungreased, to swing open one more time. Jethro, fourteen, John, ten, Lyndon, nine, and Abe, six, all hopped lightly down the deep steps to freedom. Ruth, fifteen, and the oldest now that Annie had moved out on her own, followed without enthusiasm. Most two-dozen chickens of various ages fled across the dirt yard to hide under the house at the sound of the bus. The twins, Sarah and Maybell, (four) played barefooted on the sagging porch. They were aggravating each other, as usual - each pinching the other's forearm, each squealing and neither willing to let go first. John and Lyndon grabbed one each and threw them over a shoulder, leaving the rusty screen door to slam as they disappeared into the shack, then, to slam again after Jethro and Abe.

Ruth had never really considered her home. It was a typical dwelling for the folks she knew, most of whom were kin to her in one way or another. It was built on family land; built without floor plans or blueprints by her mother's first husband, the father she shared with Annie. Mama had a few pictures of him and her uncles hammering together boards of wood and laying bricks for the chimney. There was even one with Annie, as a toddler, sitting on their father's wide shoulders in front of the brand new house. The walls had yet to lean and the whitewash was fresh and crisp as a cotton shirt, bleached and starched. Ruth always got a stab of jealousy whenever she was drawn to look again at the old photo. Annie had experienced the security of an embrace within those strong arms and had sat astride the muscular young shoulders of a father who had vanished by the time Ruth was born. *Was it her arrival that drove him away?* Whenever Ruth put the question to her mother, she was scolded for foolishness and then Mama would laugh and say, "Mans jus' need to go they own way, sometime."

The house had been built under the great, sprawling limbs of an ancient Live Oak, a tire swing hanging from one of them. A Plymouth station wagon, a decade beyond new, was parked under another. Even in the picture of Annie and Daddy, the oak was just the same. So many years had passed, that the fifteen which had grown Ruth into young womanhood, had barely left any impression on the old tree at all. On early summer days, the bright sun would shine past good-natured clouds and make lacy patterns through the twisting limbs and dark, shiny leaves of the oak. But in late summer, 'round about dusk, the same billowing clouds would join together in a sinister alliance. In moments, they would turn from white, to gray, to a washed-out violet blue. The electricity of a southern summer storm was terrifying. Under darkened skies, the gracious old tree looked entirely different. The limbs reached out in silent agony with a multitude of swollen, arthritic joints.

One October night, Ruth made up a story about the tree. Not to be outdone by Annie in scaring "the babies" out of sleep for a week, she explained how the haints turned little children into old people overnight and when they got so old they shriveled up to die, the ghosts would gather up their gray hair and beards and decorate the trees.

"Folks call it Spanish Moss," Ruth crooned to six pairs of wide eyes, "but look yonder at that tree. That gray stuff is the hair of children, who died of old age one Halloween night."

Truth was, Ruth half believed her own story, and was never again of much comfort to those babies whenever the wind set the silvery clumps to swaying and thunder shook the house.

Ruth never considered her house at all, until third grade. That was the year busing became mandatory in Georgia. At first Ruth didn't know what to think of it, "integration," a big word her Mama defined as, "mixin' folks all up." Some big men in Washington thought it needed a push, so they decided to push it on the kids. Suddenly, half her schoolmates were being driven forty-five minutes across the city, and white kids she didn't even know were taking their places. She missed her best friend, Shaval, lost to busing. No one liked it, kids least of all, but big men in Washington had made up their minds that it was for America's own good. Ruth wondered how their own kids liked it. It never crossed her mind that maybe the childen of "The Big Men in Washington" didn't go to public schools.

Before busing, Ruth didn't think of herself as poor or oppressed. Poor folks didn't have any food to eat. Poor folks didn't have anyone to take care of them. But for Ruth and her family, there were always fresh eggs for breakfast, a chicken for Sunday supper, vegetables from Mama's garden 'most year round, and watermelons when days got long and hot. Every now and then, an uncle would drop by with a half of a swamp hog he'd shot. There were plenty of crabs, fish, and shrimp in the creeks, and all the oysters you could gather from their slick, mud beds in the winter. Best of all, there was plenty of family everywhere.

After busing, though, Ruth wasn't the only one to notice that some of the white folks had shiny, new cars and fancy clothes. They talked differently, too. Ruth liked their stuff well enough, but she didn't want to *be* like them. She wanted to be with her own people. She wanted to be with Shaval. She wanted to go back to the way it was before she was poor. 'Course there were some poor white folks, too. They were the ones who resented busing the most. No. Ruth liked it the old way. She decided "Big Men in Washington" were changing things too much too fast. Now here she was, a sophomore in high school and half the kids were still getting bused across the city and all of them still hated it. Ruth's thoughts drifted to Shaval. Ruth had long since lost track of her. It's hard for an eight-year-old to stay in touch. She wondered what Shaval was doing now.

Ruth was still thinking about her old best friend when the screen door slammed behind her. Inside, Mama was hollering over the steady drone of the TV and the wailing of the twins, about bad children who pinch each other and should be trying to get along. Ruth knew what would happen next, the same thing that Mama used to do when she and Annie got to beatin'-up on each other. Mama would punish the twins by making them kiss each other. First they would refuse. Mama would threaten no TV for a week. Then they would pout. Mama would threaten a whippin'. Then they would look at each other considering the unthinkable. In a moment one would point to the other and beg to kiss a pig instead. The other would plead to press lips to a dead fish, then a toad, dirty feet, or a big, slimy worm. Inevitably, a funny bone would be hit. The girls would be stricken with the giggles and deliver the token kiss.

Ruth closed the door to the room she shared with her little sisters, thankful they were elsewhere for the moment. She started to change out of her school clothes. Slowly, she began to unbutton her white blouse. Her breasts were so sore. She popped the snap of her good jeans. There was an impression of the seam in the flesh around her waist. She paused to look at her upper body in the mirror over the dresser. Her breasts had not finished growing. The newness and wonder of them had not yet worn off. And now something else was happening to them. The tightly stretched stomach of a gawky adolescent had been replaced by a definite convexness, which was undeniable. Something had taken her body away from her. Something was growing inside.

But I'm not done growing yet! she thought almost out loud.

Panic and fear gripped the pit of her stomach again. She resented this thing. She had prayed through several nights that God would make it go away. In desperation, she paid a visit to Dr. Buzzard, the local Voodoo man, in hopes that he might cast a spell sparing her this terrible tribulation. He told her ten dollars would probably not buy strong enough magic. She told him it was all she had. He took her money anyway. No luck. Finally, she made a thousand promises to Jesus. One day, she felt the dull ache in her abdomen and ran to the bathroom, begging for blood and finding none. Now she knew this cup would not pass.

There was something in there. It never asked. It just came and took what it needed from her body. She hated it. She hated it for making her tell her mother. She hated it for what the relatives would say to her mother. She hated it for coming from her first attempt at sex and for embarrassing her in front of her friends. She hated it because she had tried to act older and had told her boyfriend that she was "on the pill," and he would know that she had lied. Most of all, she hated it for growing into her body before she had had the chance to. Sarah and Maybell burst into the room, out of breath and giggling.

"Don't y'all ever knock?" Ruth spat, as she searched for something comfortable to wear.

In the end, Ruth decided never to tell the father. He was the cousin of her friend, Channel. He had come down for a visit over Easter break. His name was Ben. He was from New York and he was 17. Channel said he was on the football team in his school. Ruth remembered being impressed even before she met him. When she did meet him, he looked so large and grown-up, like a man. When she looked at him, her face flushed warm and she wondered what it must be like to be held in a man's arms. That was all she had really wanted, to be wrapped in those arms, but by the time she was she became aware that something else was expected of her.

He's 17. He comes from Brooklyn, New York. I bet all the girls up there do it and he'll think I'm an ignorant, farm Negro if I don't, she thought.

"Yes," she lied when he asked if she was on the pill.

"Yes," she answered when he pressed.

If her virginity surprised him, he gave no indication. When he was done, his arms slipped away from her, and she would never feel them around her again. Next time he saw her, he seemed not to remember her name. Then, he went home to New York. Embarrassed, Ruth never even told his cousin, Channel, about the encounter. Three months pregnant and even more embarrassed, Ruth decided Ben would never be told either. It was her lie, her gamble, and her own horrible mistake.

Mama was another story. How to tell Mama?

She didn't have to. Mama knew.

Less than a week later, Mama had a talk with her second-born. Supper was just finishing up, and it was Ruth's turn to dry the dishes. Mama turned the job over to Jethro, who had done it the night before. She offered no explanation..

"Ruth, I'll see you on the porch," she said.

Sarah and Maybell were sure Ruth was in for the belt. Their older brothers weren't so sure, but they were relieved, and almost smug, that it was Ruth and not one of them this time. The silence was broken by the slam of the screen door behind Ruth and Mama. The idea of eavesdropping flashed across the minds of Jethro, John, Lyndon, and Abe in the same instant and was simultaneously rejected an instant later. The only thing worse than a call to the porch was being caught spying on a call to the porch. In this crowded dwelling, the code of privacy in discipline was strictly enforced.

"Sit down, Chil'," 'Mama commanded. She stood in front of the flowered armchair so Ruth chose one end of the old Naugahyde sofa under the window. These two pieces had become outdoor furniture when Mama bought a new living room set from the fire sale at Farmers Furniture, just before Abe was born.

That would make the new furniture six years old already, thought Ruth as she sat.

Mama walked over and sat down beside her daughter. She leaned over to look Ruth in the eyes. Mama's skin was smooth and warm looking. It was the color and texture of milk chocolate, not the bitter, dark kind, but more golden in the slanting sun, more like the color of unrefined sugar. Her eyes were dark and kind and knowing. Ruth's own could not meet them.

"Somethin's botherin' ya, baby," she observed quietly, "I have a good idea what it is, but I think it's time you be tellin' me yo'sef."

Ruth could feel tears swell. Silence.

"When was the last time you had yo' flow?"

Ruth began to rock, very slightly, but no words would come.

"Does the boy know?"

Ruth shook her head, no.

"Don't you think he ought to?"

"No." Ruth leveled her eyes at Mama. "No," she repeated.

Ruth's resolve was clear. Mama had seen that look in cornered animals when they turned to fight. There would be another time to bring up the issue.

"All right. All right." Mama took her child into her arms and held her while she cried. All the fear melted away, drop by drop, until there was nothing left of it but a salty wet spot on the shoulder of Mama's house dress.

"Where is Mama's treasure?" She asked after a while. It was a family question. Mama had never played "hide-and-seek" with her children. The Johnson kids played "treasure hunt" because they were Mama's treasure.

"Right here," came the response Ruth had learned almost before she could talk.

"Where?" Mama asked again, gently teasing.

"Here, Mama, I'm right here," Ruth answered through heaves of breath.

Then came Ruth's tears of relief as she realized she was not alone anymore. Mama would not let anything hurt her. Mama would take care of her, and Mama loved her in spite of what she'd done.

"You just go on and cry, Chil'," Mama crooned as she rocked, "Mama'll take care of her baby. Why, Mama wasn't much older than you when she started getting big with Annie. Nah, not much older at all."

Inside, Ruth's brothers were disappointed in the realization there would be no beating. Nope, if there were no hollering and shouting by now, there wouldn't be any. Probably just a girl kind of talk like Annie and Mama had a lot before Annie moved out. Nope, Ruth was a good girl. Ruth got good grades in school. Ruth never cut class. Ruth never sassed Mama. Ruth never stole nothin'. They'd heard it a million times from teachers and aunts and cousins. Ruth is a good girl. They should have known better than to think she'd get in trouble.

Later, after all the children were asleep, it was Mama's turn to cry. She cried because she knew every stone and pit in the road her daughter would travel. She cried for the men she had loved but could never make stay - sexy and lying and appealing in their lies - and her wanting to believe their words when she was far too old to be fooled again. She cried for the loss of her little girl and the loss of the little girl she had been. And just before dawn, she cried for her first grandchild.

One day turned into the next. Soon school was out for the summer. Ruth was relieved. None of her friends had seemed to notice the changes in her body. This was both surprising and not at all surprising. Half the time she, herself, felt as though there couldn't possibly be another person within her. Sometimes she felt as though her body would realize its mistake, and she would wake to find her flow had finally appeared. Still, there was this indomitable fatigue. It was a strange and powerful kind of tired. Sleep did not surface from her mind or eyes as it always had, but it called to her from every muscle. If she pushed them too hard, her calves would retaliate with a tight, painful cramp.

This must be what it's like to be old. Ruth decided.

After sixty-three total months of gestation, Ruth's mama was a walking treasury of homespun remedies and old wives' tales.

"Eat mo' bananas, Chil'," she would say when Ruth cried out in pain. "Yo' body's aksin' ya fo' bananas."

By midsummer, Ruth's tummy left no doubt as to the truth of her condition. Her brothers long since sensed a clear and well-defined change in Ruth's relationship with Mama. Ever since that talk on the porch, Mama had started treating her like a grown-up while babying her at the same time. It was puzzling to them. By mid-summer, however, Abe was the only one of them who had not connected the changes in Mama with Ruth's tummy. Jethro, John, and Lyndon whispered between themselves but remained mum. While not grasping the full social implications, they were able to discern an opportunity for some powerfully stinging teasing. They longed to let it fly. How many times had they each endured comparisons to "Saint Ruth"? Ah, this was a rare and sweet opportunity indeed. But there would be Mama to contend with. For John and Lyndon, the tug of self-preservation proved too powerful for the lure of turn-about.

Jethro, almost one year younger than Ruth to the day, was a different story. His initial response of "serves her right" quickly gave way to something else. No, it didn't serve her right. She just made a mistake and got caught. Ruth was still a good girl, and he knew that he would just have to punch the lights out on anyone who said otherwise.

Finally, one evening at supper, the silence was broken. John and Lyndon sat on either side of Abe. Each of the older boys whispered things into the six-year-old's ears. Mama eyed them suspiciously as giggles bubbled up past the resolve of tight lips.

"She did not!" Abe burst out.

"She sure did," responded Lyndon.

Abe looked up at John who raised his eyebrows and nodded solemnly. In an instant, the giggles were gone. Horror flashed on Abe's face as he looked to Mama.

"Lyndon says that Ruthie swallowed a watermelon seed and there's a watermelon growin' in her and that I did, too, and there will be one growin' in me!" He held his little stomach as tears of fear welled up in his eyes.

John and Lyndon stared at their laps and bit their lips. Jethro took a long look at his lap, too. Sarah and Maybell stared wide-eyed at Mama.

Ruth wasn't paying attention. *There it was again.* It was like butterfly kisses from the inside, a kind of fluttering. All at once, the baby was real. It was there, growing and moving and completely other, inside of her. It slept on its own schedule and wiggled when it felt like it. For the first time, her mind's eye could see a baby. A face was born in her imagination with smooth, soft skin, a tiny, flat nose and a frilly white bonnet.

Oh, God, make it a girl, Ruth prayed silently.

Ruth could see her infant daughter all dressed up for church services with tiny, white shoes with silky bows on them and a lacy, pink dress. Mama was holding her and everyone was standing around making a fuss over the new baby and braggin' on how pretty she was.

"That's enough." Mama's voice was low and threatening. Instinctively, Ruth looked up. Mama pushed back her chair and opened her soft arms to Abe who rushed into them.

"How'd you let John and Lyndon get away with tellin' ya somethin' so silly? You know they're nothin' but a couple of liars tellin' tales. You 'member 'bout when Sarah and Maybell got here. You 'member what happened to yo ol' Mama's big tummy, don't ya? I didn't give birth to no ol' watermelon, did I?"

Abe shook his head and smiled as the pieces came together in his mind.

"When they were big and strong enough to do without me, I pushed them out into the air and y'all got to meet yo' pretty little sisters. Not just one, but two presents sent down from heaven from the Lawd."

"And Aunt Josephine helped. And we got to stay at her house with our cousins," added Abe brightly.

"That's right," said Mama. Sarah and Maybell smiled proudly from their chairs.

"Well, the Lawd's growin' us another present inside of Ruthie. He's gonna give us another little brother or sister in our family."

The twins clapped and cheered at the prospect of a live baby doll. Ruth looked for a reaction from Jethro who just kept his head bowed. John and Lyndon served themselves up another helping of grits 'n brown gravy.

Soon after, Mama decided Ruth was "showing" enough to take her down to the welfare office. The appropriate papers were filled out, and because Ruth was still Mama's dependent, the increase in government support was simply included in Mama's check.

Ruth made only one prenatal visit to an obstetrician. He listened to Ruth's heart, let her listen to the baby's heart, drew some blood for testing, and offered some advice to give to the hospital at which the baby was to be born. Mama just nodded. She had gotten the information she had come for. Mama had heard the doctor say "normal" about the pregnancy and "healthy" about Ruth. There was no reason why Ruth's baby could not be delivered by a midwife at home. Miss Pritchard had delivered all of Mama's young'uns and she could birth Mama's first grand young'un, too.

As the end of summer break approached, Ruth became more and more depressed. She knew that everyone at school had already found out about her condition. She could imagine the rumors as to who the father was. She dreaded facing them, but Mama would not hear of Ruth missing a year.

"Big or not, you're the smartest chil' on my side of the family! You gonna need book learnin' if you got a baby to bring up. You wanna wind up po' like me?" Mama would holler whenever the subject came up.

"I'm not gonna quit school forever, Mama," Ruth would plead, "I'll just stay out one year, just one. I'll go right back, Mama, I swear."

"You be goin' back *this* year, and I'll hear no mo' 'bout it!" Mama would walk off mumbling about fighting every last school board member if they tried to keep her Ruthie out.

Ruth's heart sank at the thought of a school board battle. How could she bear the attention?

A week before the first day of school, Ruth could not eat and she could not sleep. In the end, fearing for the health of the baby, Mama reluctantly gave in. Not, however, before she'd extracted a solemn promise, on the Bible, that Ruth start her junior year the following August. Ruth was delighted to agree. Mama took the opportunity to cut another deal. If Ruth could manage to graduate top in her class, Mama promised to raise the baby as one of her own. Mama figured that if Ruth graduated top in her class, she was sure to be offered a scholarship and Mama'd wind up raising the baby anyway. Ruth's appetite rebounded almost immediately.

Ruth had always been a shy child. With the onset of adolescence, her insecurities had grown until she was positively invisible. If the truth had been known, Ruth did not miss the social pressures of school in the least. She did, however, miss the education. Although she enjoyed the luxury of so much of Mama's time and she was happy enough to lighten her mother's burden by doing chores and caring for the twins, her mind soon became desperate for stimulation. It wasn't long before Ruth took it upon herself to help her little brothers with their homework. Once, when Jethro came home with his first 100 on a term paper, Mama had to caution Ruth that *helping* with homework didn't mean *doing* the homework. After that, Ruth became quite a good teacher and by the end of the year, Jethro, John, Lyndon, and even little Abe had all raised their grades by at least one letter. Even so, after chores it was not unusual for Ruth to finish off a novel a day.

Although Mama counted reading as a pure labor and waste of time, she knew she must not quench Ruth's fire for books. On Wednesdays, Mama soon found herself making the trip to the public library in downtown Savannah. Ruth considered this an awesome blessing and was always sure to help Sarah and Maybell select several treasured bedtime stories of their own. Mama considered the weekly trip her duty to Ruth and a good excuse to visit Annie who, lacking a car, could rarely get home.

It was a curiosity to Mama where Ruth came by her love of learning, and it was also Mama's greatest source of pride. But in her heart, she often wondered why the good Lord had decided to give all the smarts to a girl when it was the boys who would need to support a family one day.

Everyone enjoyed the trip to town. Having been one of the first planned cities in the country, Savannah maintained a contrived grandeur that had been a part of her character since conception. Coming in on Abercorn Street, one would encounter one square per block. This made the driving slow and monotonous, but the twins loved to see the fountains or monuments at the center of each well-manicured, little lawn. Huge antebellum mansions were neatly arranged around each square. By the early seventies, most of them had received desperately needed restoration. For structures that were still waiting, their tiny cracks and peeling paint were generally obscured by the grand stature of oaks lining Savannah's streets and the maturity of the gardens gracing her parks and courtyards. The Historic District could take your breath away in early April when the blossoming of thousands of azalea bushes lavished long banks of pink, white, and lavender, or bright patches of fuchsia around every corner.

Raised the royal daughter of King Cotton, the city was graced by the Savannah River which gave her beauty and wealth as an international seaport.

Still, her armies were defeated and on December 21, 1864, Major-Gen. William T. Sherman presented the city as a Christmas gift to President Abraham Lincoln. Although Sherman proved more gracious to Savannah than he had been to Atlanta, her fall from grace was swift and brutal. The city was treated as a conquered province and federal troops, many of whom were Negroes, were kept in occupation. Bitter resentment surged silently through the hearts of ex-Confederate whites forced to submit to the authority of a uniform worn by a former slave.

The war that had freed Ruth's ancestors had also left behind devastating poverty. Vast slums spread from beneath Savannah's tattered silken skirts. Hungry, the city offered herself to any who could pay. By the late 1960's, she had attracted shipping companies. Huge metal cranes suddenly spring up over expansive dusty yards stacked with cargo containers to be disbursed by noisy semi-trucks. A large paper company set up camp at Savannah's doorstep, replacing her sweet saline fragrance with a foul-smelling mist and buying as much Georgia land as worn-out farmers would sell. But though it took advantage of the fallen city, like Sherman, it did not rape her and took care to replenish the pine forests that produced its product. The paper mill also offered honest work to many of her people. A sugar cane plant came, and Dixie Crystals hit the market.

Ruth's kin became sharecroppers, eventually saving enough money to buy some cheap, undesirable land on Savannah's barrier islands. They purchased it for what now would be considered a pittance of back taxes. It was this land, subdivided through ensuing generations, upon which sat Mama's shack. It was this land, and the life in its surrounding waters, which had sustained Ruth's grandparents and great grandparents.

Savannah's real chance for restoration, indeed the restoration of the entire South, came with the discovery of Freon as a cooling agent. Suddenly the thick, wet heat of the Lowcountry could be managed. Soon Yankees, on their way to Florida beaches, viewed the beauty of the Southern coast from the comfort of air-conditioned automobiles. Some crazy young entrepreneur by the name of Charles Fraser had even purchased a nearby island and was turning its swamps into golf courses in hopes of marketing it as a resort destination. Imagine!

Slowly Savannah rose to her feet. It had taken the better part of a century. Running parallel to the river, Bay Street's majestic government, bank, and hotel buildings were restored while modern ones joined them. A couple of blocks inland, businesses on Broughton Street thrived. Lined with exclusive women's clothing stores and fine men's tailors, it was Savannah's version of Main Street. They were also accompanied by shoe stores, where one pair of footwear would have cost Mama a month's worth of provision for the whole family. The Johnsons never ventured into any of these shops. It made Mama visibly nervous just to walk by them, and her nervousness was like a thick fog over the children.

Unbeknownst to Ruth and her sisters, there was already a new dragon on the old city's horizon. Her river made her as accessible to illegal drugs as she had been to other commerce. Urban housing projects were rapidly becoming local distribution centers, escalating the crime rates for blocks. The viability of these small businesses in historic downtown already threatened as illegal commerce began beating back the legal.

Mama always walked in silence from the parking lot, down Broughton, and into Woolworth's Department Store, where the fog lifted. Mama would purchase a dime's worth of treasure for each of the twins and maybe buy herself a Sunday lipstick. Then she would treat everyone to a cafeteria lunch with Annie. The twins always occupied the hallowed seats on either side of their biggest sister. It was the most special day of the week. The fact wasn't wasted on Ruth that it was an outing she'd have missed if she had been in school with her brothers.

Enjoyable as Wednesdays were, though, it saddened Ruth that she never really got to talk to Annie about the baby. Although they shared the same parents, she and Annie could not have been more different. Their faces looked similar enough with high, well-defined cheekbones and strong, square jaw lines. But Ruth was smaller and leaner and almost appeared frail next to Annie whose frame was that of an athlete. Socially, Annie was as gregarious as her sister was shy. Ruth longed to get Annie's opinion about names and such, but the twins would never let her get close enough and anyway, no one would bring the subject up outside the house.

Ruth lately felt a strange loneliness when she thought about Annie. They had never really been close, but Ruth had never really missed the closeness, until now.

The little flutterings turned into soft internal jabs and kicks by Halloween, and by Christmas, even the grand dimensions of Ruth's abdomen were becoming too confining for the "little one."

Ruth felt very left out of the Christmas of '73. At sixteen, there were a multitude of things she was hoping to see on Christmas morning. Instead, what she discovered beneath the tree were all gifts for the baby. From her mother, the family cradle with a fresh coat of white paint and new, hand-sewn linens. From Annie, a miniature, cotton nightie with a drawstring at the bottom. From the boys, infant size blankets and tiny, fuzzy socks. And to add insult, all the gifts were in white or pale green or yellow. Nothing was in pink, although Ruth was certain that it would be a girl. By the time she had opened her present from Sarah and Maybell - a rattle - it was hard to disguise her resentment.

This baby had invaded the secret places inside of her, sapped much of her energy, stretched her thin body beyond recognition, filled her breasts to aching, made her feet and her hands swell, and woke her nightly with internal blows of such force that she wondered if the intention was malicious. It was now taking up so much of the room in Ruth's body that it was difficult for her to eat, sleep, breathe, digest food, or even just sit in one place very long. It had interrupted her life, her education, her growth, and now it was outgrowing its dependence on her body and would soon seek an escape at an expense of tremendous pain - hers! (She'd been doing a little reading up on childbirth.)

As if all this weren't enough, it had now succeeded in stealing Ruth's Christmas, too! Ruth was not very good at holding back her tears lately and ran from the room, crying. She would have thrown herself across the bed but this was impossible on her stomach and if she laid flat on her back, the baby put such pressure on her lungs that it was difficult to breathe.

She sat leaning against the headboard, picking at a thread on the bedspread and weeping. When she saw Mama at the door, she held her breath to stifle the sobs, the corners of her mouth turning down, trembling with the effort. Mama sat down on the bed and put her arms around her daughter.

"Oh, Mama," Ruth wept, "I hate this baby! I do. I can't help it. She's come along and taken everything from me, and now she's taken Christmas, too!"

"Now, Chil', I don't ever want to hear you use that word again," Mama gently scolded, "You do not *hate* your baby. You will love your baby just the same way I love you and your brothers and sisters. God gives it to women to love our babies and you will love yours."

"I don't see how, Mama. I wish He had never given me this one."

"You know what the Bible says about babies?" Mama asked, "It says that they're a reward. You must have done something mighty good to have God to give ya one."

"No, I did something bad. He's punishing me," Ruth wept.

"What a thing to say on Christmas! Christmas is all about a baby. You know Jesus' mother couldn't have been much older than you when God started our Savior to grow inside her - His greatest gift. Every woman who carries a baby carries a little Christmas inside of her. Shoo, chill', I'll bet even Mary was a little afraid of giving birth."

"Oh, Mama, it's gonna hurt. I know it's gonna hurt."

"Yes, Ruth, it's gonna hurt. But no woman ever remembers the pain, really. And your body is young and strong. It will heal before you know it."

Mama held Ruth for a long time. Then she pulled a little wrapped box from her pocket and put it under Ruth's nose.

"Not all the gifts were for the baby," she said.

Ruth unwrapped it quickly and drew breath when she opened the box. There inside was one of Mama's two gold rings. One was a plain wedding band from Jethro's father. She never took that one off. The other was a small, dark, oval sapphire with two round diamonds on either side. She only wore this one on Sundays or at weddings, and this was the one that sparkled from the box Ruth held. Ruth's eyes filled with tears all over again.

"It was a gift from your father to me on my 19th birthday. I'd always figured to give it to you on graduation day. But maybe you should have it for giving me my first grandbaby.

Ruth slipped it on the ring finger of her right hand. It fit perfectly. She felt suddenly beautiful, forgetting for a moment the enormity of her belly. She moved her hand to catch the light, sending out blue sparks.

"Annie's not gonna like it," she said, "Annie always said you'd give it to her."

"Well, *I* never said that. Annie's lost anything good I ever give her. I know you'll take care of it. . . Now, help me get the twins ready for church. Can't even make it on time for

Christmas services... Time to get ready for church!" Mama hollered as she hurried down the hall.

Ruth took a moment to admire her ring. The baby rolled. Ruth shifted her gaze to her belly. Under an old, thin, maternity nightie of Mama's, Ruth was astonished to see a bulge visibly shift from the right side to the left side. Then a little elbow, fist, or foot pushed against the tightly stretched flesh of her tummy. She pressed at it with her index finger. It withdrew. Ruth giggled in spite of herself. She wondered how much longer it could possibly remain inside and how much more her abdomen could possibly stretch. Then she hurried to get herself and the twins ready for Christmas services.

Two weeks later, on January 8th, 1974, Ruth's baby was born.

Chapter 14

Ruth had woken in the dark, early hours of a chilly morning with the sensation that she had wet the bed. She checked the sheets and found some dark stains. She could almost hear her own heart beat by the time she made it down the short hall to Mama's room.

"Mama, something's happening!" Ruth whispered from beside Mama's old bed.

"What's happenin', Chil'?" Mama asked in a soft voice. Ruth explained about the sheets.

"Well, you just run on to the bathroom. Then c'mon back and lay down with me for a while. We'll just see if this baby's ready to meet the rest of the family yet."

By the time Ruth returned from the bathroom, Mama had found a fresh nightie for her and had covered the left side of the bed with towels. Ruth put her head on Mama's shoulder and snuggled close to her. She couldn't remember the last time she had snuggled with her mother in this big, soft bed, but it felt safe and warm, there in the dark.

Mama's voice came soft and steady, "Now, Ruth, pay attention to your belly and tell me if you're feelin' anything different."

The two women lay in silence for several minutes. Ruth stared at the moving shadows of the moon through the moss on the oak outside. She remembered the little girl who used to run to Mama's room on the heels of a bad dream. No matter which men had come and stayed and ultimately gone from Mama's room, it had always remained Mama's bed. It was the bed upon which Ruth had been conceived and delivered, and it was as timeless in this family as the old tree outside. Through the years, Mama had always made sure no child was turned away from its safe haven when the midnight monsters of the young subconscious came a-callin'. Ruth had all but forgotten the rich security it offered. But that thought suddenly vanished with the realization that she was having a contraction. Ruth wondered how fear could have crossed beyond the threshold of Mama's room.

"I think it's time to call Miss Pritchard," she said through a tight throat, her mouth instantly dry.

"Not just yet, Chil'," Mama laughed softly. "I think we might have a little time left. Let's see how long it is before your next cramp."

Ruth rolled over into Mama. Her head on the older woman's chest rose and fell with each breath. They waited in the darkness.

By the time the sun came up, Ruth's contractions were seventeen minutes apart and intensifying. The other children were sent to school with overnight bags and instructions to go straight to Aunt Jo's house until Mama came for them.

By 8:30, Aunt Jo arrived with old Miss Pritchard. She gave Ruth three hugs and several encouraging words before departing with the twins.

Ruth found her examination by Miss Pritchard to be humiliating and keenly embarrassing. By the time Annie arrived just before noon, Ruth was rapidly approaching transition and the easy part was over. She would not hear of having her baby anywhere but on Mama's bed. From the porch, Annie could hear her sister's cries. When she entered Mama's room, Ruth had just finished a severe contraction. Mama was sitting beside the bed reading from the Bible. Ruth's face was all beaded up with sweat, but it brightened when Annie entered.

"How'd ja get off work?" Ruth asked.

"I'm sick. Can't ya tell?" Annie answered. "Stomach bug."

"I'm the one with the stomach bug," Ruth responded, attempting to smile.

Miss Pritchard, after having set up her birthing things to her liking, plugged in her portable, black and white TV and commenced to watching General Hospital. Annie grabbed a chair from the dinner table and took her place on the other side of her sister. She could tell that Ruth was pleased to have her come. Annie knew that nothing could have kept her from being with her little sister today. This was the glue that kept family together through a succession of men. This was where the bond of blood and of kin was forged. And the women of this household had carried its meaning way deeper down in their souls than its men had.

Annie's gaze shifted to her sister's right hand as it clutched the sheet. Unaffected by the girl it adorned, the sapphire ring remained cool and beautiful, flashing blue when the light hit it. Annie was still feeling a sharp sting from Mama's giving it to Ruth.

I'm the oldest, she thought. *That ring is mine. Any woman can have a baby.*

Ruth struggled to breathe through her contraction.

"Whatcha gonna name it?" Annie asked.

"Shaval," came the answer through gritted teeth.

"Keep breathing, Chil'," Mama prompted, "and try not to push yet. Not just yet."

"Shaval, that's real pretty," Annie commented trying to take her sister's mind off of her pain. "What if it's a boy?"

"It ain't gonna be no boy," Ruth answered with narrow eyes.

At exactly 2:47 p.m., Ruth pushed her son out into the light of day.

Miss Pritchard's stern, no-nonsense face broke into a tender smile.

"Ah, Chil', ya done yo' se'f proud. He's a fine-lookin' boy! And listen to those lungs! No doubt he's strong as a bull."

Ruth leaned up on one elbow to view her son, grateful that the pushing was over. Except for stature, he did not in the least resemble the baby of her daydreams. This baby was purple and bloody and kind of slimy looking. The thing hanging off his belly button was disgusting. His face looked right-angry and he screamed with a strength that was astonishing for his size.

A boy! Thought Ruth. *What can you do with a boy? You can't even dress them up in pretty clothes. . . Well, at least it's over.*

His pinched little face floated away on Mama's soothing voice.

"Now, Darlin' one more push." It was Miss Pritchard, "We're almost done."

Almost?! Ruth bristled inwardly. *How could she mean, almost?*

Finally, it *was* all over. Ruth rolled gingerly over to one side while Mama and Miss Pritchard tidied up the bed cloths. Annie held her nephew who weighed in at 7 lbs 11 oz. He had dried off completely and settled down somewhat. His mouth had found his fist, and he was sucking furiously on his knuckles. Through her disappointment, and in spite of the fact that his head was a little coned from the force of delivery, Ruth could not help but notice that he had an appealing face.

"I'll need a name for the birth certificate," announced Miss Pritchard.

"Well, Ruthie?" inquired Mama placing the infant beside her.

"Oh, I don't know. How about Godzilla? It sure felt like I gave birth to a monster." Ruth touched the soft skin of his cheek. He turned his head to the touch with his mouth open.

"He's ready for some supper," Mama observed.

"Can't we send Annie to the store for some formula, Mama?" Ruth asked, knowing the answer.

"Shoo, Chil', do you think some smart man in a laboratory could come up with better food for yo' baby than the Good Lawd Hisse'f? And it's a free gift to both of you."

With that, Mama gathered up the infant and laid him across Ruth's chest. For her part, Ruth was too tired to argue and since all modesty had departed at seven centimeters, Ruth prepared herself for the inevitable first feeding. Mama showed her how to get started and how to break the suction without irritating her nipples. Ruth's son was a naturally hearty eater.

Ruth cradled her baby to her breast, leaned back against the pillows, and closed her eyes. The sensation was not at all unpleasant.

"How about naming him after his father?" Suggested Annie.

Ruth forced her eyelids up long enough to shoot Annie full of daggers.

"The Good Book's full of fine names fo' boys," Mama quickly interjected.

"What were you reading before, Mama?" Ruth's tongue was thick and she could not get her eyes to open again.

"Let's see," Mama opened her tired, old Bible and began reading where she had left off.

"The second book of Samuel, Chapter 10, verse 9:

Now when Joab saw that the battle was set against him in front and in the rear, he selected from all the choice men of Israel, and arrayed them against the Arameans. But the remainder of the people he placed in the hand of Abishai his brother, and he arrayed them against the sons of Ammon.
And he said, "If the Arameans are too strong for me . . .

Mama's voice faded from Ruth's consciousness. She fought back the invading sleep. *I must settle this matter*, she determined. *Then I'll be done. Then I can sleep.*

... Be strong, and let us show ourselves courageous for the sake of our people and for the cities of our God; and may the Lord do what is good in His sight."'

"Who said that?" Asked Ruth.

"Said what?" Asked Annie.

"Be strong and courageous for our people."

"That was Joab." Mama answered. "He was King David's right-hand man for a long time. He was a mighty general over the King's armies."

"Well, did they win?" Ruth enquired weakly.

"Sure enough. They won this battle and 'most every one after."

"Fine." With a long "o" and a short "a" the name had an appealing, open sound. "The baby's name will be Joab," Ruth announced. "Joab Samuel Johnson. Please tell Miss Pritchard."

Mama smiled, gathering up her grandson and placing him in the white cradle beside her old bed. Annie motioned that she would stay. Before Mama could close the door behind her, both Ruth and tiny Joab had fallen heavily into a deep, peaceful sleep.

Annie sat beside her sister watching her. All the tension and pain of the previous twelve hours had vanished from Ruth's beautiful face. Not the smallest hint of a wrinkle could be found in her forehead or at the corners of her eyes. The peace and innocence of childhood had returned to Ruth, but only in slumber. Annie felt a knot swell in her throat. It had been hard to watch her little sister in such agony. Annie now understood, in part, what every person who loves learns: that even the most willing heart cannot bear the suffering of another. Annie, too, was relieved to have the great ordeal over.

Joab pulled his legs up under him, his bottom forming a raised lump under the fuzzy, white blanket. Annie's heart filled with pride in her family and respect for her little sister. Ruth's hand lay across her chest. Annie took one last, long look at Mama's sapphire ring. Then she released any covetousness she had ever had for it.

If that ring is for having a baby, then Ruthie earned it and deserves at least ten or twenty more, she thought.

✦ ✦ ✦

At four months, two tiny, white teeth pushed up, front and center, through the tender flesh of Joab's lower jaw. By five months, Ruth had him completely weaned and transferred to formula.

"Teeth are God's way of saying he's ready for solid food." she told Mama, knowing the older woman wouldn't argue with God's maternal plan.

From the day that Joab was forced to give up his last demand on Ruth's body, he was also forced to give up his demand on her time. If he became restless in the middle of the night, Ruth let him cry knowing that Mama's feet would not be long before hitting the floor. Ruth would simply roll over and enjoy the luxury of a full night's sleep. As the milk in her breasts diminished and her body resumed the shape of a woman not far beyond adolescence, so too, diminished her sensitivity to his nocturnal cries until they could no longer even wake her.

It was difficult for Mama to watch Ruth become more and more detached from her son. Time and again she would make herself hesitate that extra moment, hoping that Ruth would see about his fussing, but it didn't take long to realize that Ruth could not be bluffed into raising a son she did not want. Ruth knew full-well that no child's needs would go unmet, no boo-boo unkissed or tear unhugged, so long as Mama drew breath. The self-absorption of youth blinded her to the weariness in Mama's eye and the slowness of her step. Anyway, Mama's heart was especially tender to her grandson. It would recognize no thinning of blood between her first and second generations.

Ruth's gettin' excited about school again, Mama imagined, *I suppose she's got a right to what's left of her childhood.*

There was one time, when Joab was seven months old, when Ruth did feel a tugging at her heart on his account. The twins were just getting over chicken pox. Little scabs had formed over the itchy blisters on their faces and arms and the fevers of the past week were already forgotten. Mama had just left for the grocery store when Joab's temperature started to rise. Ruth administered one half dropper of Tempera, filled a bottle with apple juice, settled herself with the baby in the rocking chair, and waited on the temperature to break. By the time Mama's car rolled to a stop under the old oak, Joab had been screaming for an hour and fifteen minutes. The thermometer was reading 103.5 and Ruth was beside herself. She was greatly relieved to hear Mama's footfalls on the porch and the slam of the screen door. Mama quickly set the grocery bags on the table and gathered up her grandson. Her voice crooned deep, sweet assurance and in under a minute, miraculously, the child quieted.

"Carry in the rest of the groceries, Ruthie." Mama ordered.

Ruth had been dismissed. What was that prick in her heart? Jealousy? Possessiveness? Ruth knew the transition had been made. Joab now observed no difference between Ruth's arms and the arms of her siblings, each pair doting and adoring, but none as comforting as Mama's. Rejection stung. It was one thing for Ruth to move on with *her* life and quite another for her son to move on with *his*. Hadn't she sacrificed a whole year on his account? Where was the gratitude due her?

Fine, she thought, spitefully, *if being valedictorian is my official ticket to freedom from you, then I'll buy one. I don't need you either.*

Ruth set her mind on the coming school year. Her own class would go on to their senior year without her. She wondered how Jethro's class would treat her. She expected they would not accept her. No matter, Ruth had no regrets about dropping out for a year. Besides, she knew she could always count on Jethro.

In her big sister's mind, she couldn't see how her little brother's schoolmates could be so tough to rise above. From what Jethro had told her, a white girl by the name of Samantha Freeman would be her only real academic competition. Ruth knew Samantha. Her daddy was a dentist who had apparently endeavored to raise a daughter with a superiority complex. *Good going, Dr. Freeman.* Silently, Ruth loathed Samantha. No one would ever have guessed what a giant competitive spirit resided in little Ruth. Not even Jethro would have guessed how much "Saint Ruth" enjoyed plotting her victory over Miss Samantha Freeman and the class of '76.

Academically, Ruth's junior year did turn out to be a success. With only a little extra effort, she was able to pull one or two points ahead of Freeman in every subject except art and gym. Natural talent went a long way in both, and application of study time and logic simply could not impact the B+ that felt like a brick wall to Ruth. Still, she did manage to hang on to her lead.

Socially, the year was hurtful and bitter. In the first few months, Ruth was met by all but one of her classmates with face-to-face silence and behind-the-back whispers. By Christmas break, the girls had polarized into two groups: those who were contemptuously judgmental of her child's illegitimacy and those who silently respected the courage with which Ruth handled pregnancy and motherhood. The latter, however, were too cowardly to lend support when the former struck out at Ruth like social copperheads.

The boys treated her differently, too. Aware of her year on them as well as her academic prowess, few addressed her directly. The bold ones would make lewd remarks under their breath as she hurried by them in the halls.

Ruth was more alienated than ever before. She thanked God daily for Jethro who was her closest friend, sharing in her social exile. More than once, he'd been sent home for fighting. He never said why, and Mama and Ruth never pressed. If he missed his friends, he made sure it didn't show. Ruth reciprocated in the only way she could. She helped Jethro with his schoolwork. By May, he had developed a real pride in his grades and an amazing enjoyment of math. He had become as disciplined in his studies as he was in athletics, which both he and Ruth enjoyed; Ruth from the stands.

By summer break, Joab was sixteen and a half months old. He called Ruth "Mama," although the name lacked substance. For it was Ruth's mother Joab ran to when he wanted to show-out that he could "wun fass," or jump up with both feet off the floor, or (almost) do a somersault.

"Look me, Big Mama," he would say, grasping a pinkie and tugging his grandmother away from her endless chores. "Watch I do!" Then he would perform yet another astounding feat of toddlerhood. Big Mama was always a gracious audience.

"Ain't you somethin'!" She would exclaim with a twinkle in her eye. Then she would shuffle back to her work, mumbling things about how smart and strong Joab was. "You be careful, now, Joab," she'd warn over her shoulder while washing dishes, folding laundry, or sweeping floors.

Except for an occasional changed diaper, during which, to Ruth's considerable consternation, the boy would unfailingly reach down and feel his male parts, Ruth had had little to do with her son's development. She vaguely recalled that his first word had been "chicken" pronounced "sicken." She knew there had been a playpen in the kitchen but she could not have told you when he first learned to climb out of it and when, exactly, Mama decided it was useless and gave it to her cousin in the next town. Nor could she have told you when his infatuation with basketballs, baseballs, and footballs had started. She was not aware that he had a powerful temper and an iron will and liked to move furniture just because he could. She hardly suspected that all the information collected as he reached out to touch and taste and discover was filed in an exceptionally bright new mind. But Mama did. And in so many ways, she fondly considered him reminiscent of her own second born. Ruth did know, as did the rest of the family, that Joab had a quick smile, a charming disposition, a handsome cherub's face and an unstoppable enthusiasm for exploring his world and mastering physical skills. He was the unchallenged darling of his household and the apple of his grandmother's eye. Even Sarah and Maybell adored him to the point that Mama's lavished attention was not a source of jealousy to the usurped-babies of the family.

✦ ✦ ✦

By Halloween, the following year, Mama had little doubt Ruth would meet the terms of their agreement. Mama faced Ruth's impending emancipation from her son with mixed emotions and often questioned the wisdom of that agreement. On occasion of sleeplessness, the very thought of her own part in Ruth's abdication was a torment.

"Lord, I just gotta leave it in your lovin' hands," she would ultimately whisper in the dark. Only then could she find rest.

It was also around mid-term of their senior year that Jethro and Janice got together. She was a pretty girl who had enjoyed almost instant popularity when she had transferred in from Atlanta for her sophomore year. Jethro had been infatuated with her from the moment he had laid eyes on her. Many were the occasions when he had spoken longingly of her to Ruth. Neither of them thought she would ever give Jethro a second look. But then the star quarterback tore up the ligaments in his left ankle, and Jethro was the natural choice to replace him. Suddenly, Janice took notice of Jethro and she wasn't the only one, though he was completely oblivious to the flirtations of any other female. From the first kiss, Jethro was completely smitten. In class or on the football field, his mind would float away on the slightest reminder of her. They had planned meeting points in the halls between classes and were always together in fifth period study hall on Tuesdays and Thursdays. In the evenings, they would tie up the phone lines in two households, speaking in hushed tones and devising ways to squeeze a few extra moments out of the following day.

Although she kept it to herself, Mama was not unaware of the changes in Jethro. Her first son was growing up. She was charmed by the sweetness and abandon of his naiveté. Time had yet to teach him that love was, to the heart, like a double-edged sword and pain pierced as deeply as pleasure. It was a lesson Mama hoped Jethro would never have to learn, all the while knowing that both must come if one dared love at all.

John, Lyndon, and Abe were aware of the changes, too. More than one dinner was interrupted by spontaneous wrestling matches brought on by the name, Janice. Jethro, now 6'3" and the idol of his little brothers, would jump up in mock outrage to silence their tauntings. Abe was generally the last one left standing. Through the snaggle-toothed smile of a mouth still trying to close the gaps left by the loss of baby teeth, Abe teased from behind the living room chair, "Jethro lo-oves Janice. Jethro lo-oves Janice. Poor, poor Janice!"

Then he'd spin in a hail of breathless, you-can't-get-me giggles and be gone out the front door, leaping off the porch and scattering the chickens. Jethro routinely returned, ten minutes later, the skinny eight-year-old locked in a fetal position within his arms.

"Who is Janice?" Jethro demanded.

"A goddess," Abe would reply through a restricted throat.

"What else?" Jethro would ask with a squeeze.

"The prettiest girl on the face of the earth," Abe would shout. Upon which Jethro would set him gently on his feet.

Once in a while, when Abe was feeling particularly indestructible, he'd circle casually to the far side of the table and add, "Sure makes ya wonder what she's doing with a goon like you."

The chase would resume.

All of this Joab would observe from his high chair, equipped with a sure-enough child-proof seat belt. When things seemed to him to be getting out of hand, he'd tuck his chin and demand, "You no hurt my Abe," in his deepest baby voice.

Touched by the fortitude of the littlest male, Jethro would obediently break off the chase and resume his place at the table.

"I no hurt your Abe," Jethro would assure the small protector. "Only pretend."

"It's okay, Joab. I'm tough. I can handle him," Abe would offer puffing up his narrow, ribby chest.

Ruth could not help but be happy that her beloved brother had found something wonderful in Janice. Yet, her happiness for him could not fill the void created by his girlfriend. It had seemed to happen so abruptly. One moment she had been more of an illusion of Jethro's imagination, and the next, she had become real. Although Jethro was aware of the impact of his neglect upon Ruth, he lacked the Herculean strength-of-will to divert, even one moment, from his sweetheart. Sometimes, he would try to include Ruth on their dates. Ruth mostly refused. But one Friday evening, she decided to accompany the happy couple to a victory party after a big game. It was a B.Y.O.B. affair. After draining his savings, Jethro made sure he had enough "B" for his girls. Neither really liked the taste of the stuff so even two women were still a pretty cheap date.

The party was a casual gathering and consisted of a wide circle of cars around a bonfire in a fallow field. The location was considered ideal because it was accessible only by a 1.5 mile dirt road or a tractor. With any luck, the kids figured, they could consume their alcoholic beverages undiscovered by law enforcement officials for another two or three victory celebrations. Then, of course, a new field would be scouted out. And next year, when the farmer came to prepare his soil, he'd discover a charred spot in the middle of his field, scattered beer cans, and his own inadvertent hospitality.

A black LTD had become the unofficial winner of the stereo competition. All four of its doors were swung wide as though the volume of the music had just blown them open. Some of the kids were dancing beside it. Ruth felt awkward but she instinctively moved to the music as though she were oblivious to her solitude. Jethro and Janice were among the dancing couples. To any observer, they were a striking pair. They matched like bookends. Both bodies tall, on the lean side, and extremely well-formed. Both shared medium dark brown skin which was rarely ever plagued by even the tiniest blemish. Each of their attractive faces had a pair of beautiful, wide, full lips which often came together. Each, a pair of misty, dark eyes which could see no other. Looking at them, Ruth's loneliness increased by contrast.

"Ja like a beer?" came a question from beside her. It was Jimmy Simmons, one of Jethro's teammates, and he had a silver can extended to her. This would be her second beer. She had never been able to endure more than one before.

Oh, why the hell not? thought Ruth. "Thanks," she said, popping the top and taking a sip. She hoped Jimmy hadn't seen her grimace. She didn't mind the first flavor of beer but it sure left a bitter taste in your mouth after the rest went down your throat.

"You're Jethro's sister, aren't you?" Jimmy asked.

"Yep," came Ruth's shy response.

"He sure can play ball."

"Yep"

"I'm Jimmy Simmons. I'm on the team."

"I know. Tight end." Ruth offered softly.

"Wow. You speak football!"

"I know the positions if that's what you mean."

"The positions, huh?" Ruth sensed something dirty in his last remark but failed to understand his implication.

"Hey, my brother just bought a car. He let me borrow it. Wanna see?" Jimmy, picked up the rest of the six packs, took her by the elbow and was guiding her toward an ancient, full-size, Chevrolet coup on the outer circle of the field. He unlocked the door and offered Ruth a seat in the front. Then he slid in beside her. Ruth became instantly uneasy but hoped it didn't show. She had always thought Jimmy was cute.

"Man, wait 'till you hear this sound system. My brother put in six new speakers. I helped him. Let's see," Jimmy rummaged through a cardboard box filled with cassettes, "You like <u>Earth, Wind and Fire</u>?"

Jimmy didn't wait for her response but fast-forwarded until he found the beginning of, "That's the Way of the World" and turned the volume up to the point that further conversation would be impossible. Ruth did like <u>Earth, Wind and Fire</u>, and the song Jimmy had chosen was one of her favorites. She leaned her head back and let her ears drink in the easy rhythm of the music and its advice: stay young at heart. Ruth realized she was relaxed. Her head was swimming slightly as she recognized the symptom of a second beer. It felt good. At the end of the song, Jimmy turned the volume down.

"So, were you at the game?" he asked.

"You mean tonight?"

"No, last week."

Ruth took a gulp of her beer while digesting his sarcasm.

"Yeah, I mean, I was at the game. The Tigers are a tough team."

"They sure the hell are," he agreed heartily. "They beat us the last four years straight. Not this year, though. Nope, this year we creamed 'em. 'Ja see me make that tackle on Forty-one in the last quarter?"

"I don't think so," Ruth offered honestly. She usually only watched Jethro.

"Forty-one, he's big and he's fast but not enough to get by me, this time."

For the next few moments, Ruth just listened and nodded in the dark, wondering what to say that Jimmy hadn't already said. Then she felt his arm slip around her shoulder.

"Come'ere," he said, pulling her to him. Suddenly his tongue was in her mouth. Ruth was instantly anxious. Her mind and her body sent out conflicting signals. One less beer and she would have been more responsive to her mind.

Okay, three more kisses and I'm out of here, she decided.

They were long kisses.

"Well, Jethro's probably looking for me," she said, sliding across the seat and placing her hand on the latch.

"I doubt it. Him and Janice are probably off doing the same thing we're doing." Jimmy's lips were on hers again. It was like he had two pairs of hands. One pair was rubbing the top of her thigh and the other pair was up her shirt. Ruth marked the depth and rate of his breaths. She remembered the price of her last indiscretion. A panic seized her which could not be masked.

"Stop." It was her own voice loud and firm. He obeyed.

"What?" He asked as though he honestly didn't know.

"No. No. This is just not—not—"Ruth stammered. Jimmy did not throw her a line. "It's too fast."

"Fast?" He said. "It might seem that way to you, but I've been watchin' you all year. I just didn't think you was ready before."

Ruth was instantly touched.

"All year?" She repeated.

"Yeah, man, why not? You're good-lookin' and smart. Everybody knows you're the smartest girl in the whole damn school."

He was kissing her again. After a moment, she pulled back.

"We need to stop now," Ruth stammered breathlessly.

"Why? We ain't doing nuttin'."

"Because I ain't gonna have no more babies!" Ruth blurted it out. It was the truth.

"You know I kinda respect what you've been through, man, with a baby and all. But you don't have to worry about that with me. I wouldn't let anything happen to you." He was fumbling for something in his wallet. "You can't get pregnant with one of these."

Ruth was not prepared for this response.

"Hey, it ain't like you're a virgin no more."

His last comment stung. But at least he had said it to her face.

"C'mon, baby, I've been wantin' you for so long."

He could not have said anything more appealing to Ruth. Could it be that someone had really been wanting her this whole lonely year? Suddenly the possibility flashed in her mind, she could be half of a couple, too. Perhaps she and Jimmy could be like Jethro and Janice and she would have someone of her own. They could go to parties together and she could pull for him at football games and they could talk on the phone.

Oh, why not? Ruth rationalized. *May as well just enjoy the reputation I already have.* Without the disarming effects of alcohol, this argument would never have reached conscious thought.

"You sure we're safe?" she asked.

"Trust me, baby. I'll take care of you," Jimmy assured.

Jimmy and Ruth saw each other several times over the next three weeks. But the relationship never got the chance to blossom before Jimmy lost interest and turned his attention to a curvy, brainless freshman.

That's fine with me, Ruth told herself. *I'll have a brand new start in college next year and Jimmy will be stuck here flipping burgers in Hardees. And after I graduate, I'm never coming back.*

Inwardly, Ruth felt betrayal from the soles of her feet to the crown of her head. Outwardly, there was no sign of the slightest pang. Besides, there were several other young men who were suddenly anxious for her company. As long as they brought along a condom, her answer was always, yes.

Had Jethro been less distracted with Janice, he would have suspected something was wrong. But the guys on his team took care to guard their tongues rather than risk a fight. There were no changes in Ruth's grades, and Mama was pleased to see her daughter stepping out a little.

Graduation was only one month away, and Ruth was top in her class by a clean four points, when she missed a period.

Oh, God, no, Ruth thought as she checked the calendar again. A week had come and gone since her period was due. *I've been careful. I've been so careful.* She declared inwardly as that old, trapped feeling gripped her again.

When she was ten days late, she put in a call to Annie.

"Hi, Annie. It's me, Ruth . . . I'm fine. How are you? Good. Listen, if I got Mama to drop me off, could I spend the weekend at your place? . . . No reason. I just miss you, that's all. Well, you don't have to work all night, too. Do ya? . . . No, nothing's wrong. Just leave the key under the mat and I'll have Mama or Jethro drop me off some time after school."

Mama thought it was a great idea for her two oldest to spend some time together. After all, Ruth would be setting off for college in the fall. She had been offered several full scholarships and would likely be far from home for the next few years - maybe forever. Mama was delighted to drop Ruth at Annie's apartment.

Annie knew something was wrong, but Ruth could not bring herself to say the words until Sunday evening, just before Mama was due to pick her up.

"I'm pregnant," Ruth said from across the small, kitchen table in Annie's tiny, hot apartment.

"Oh, not again," was Annie's immediate response. "How?"
Ruth shrugged.

"I mean, girl, don't you know nothin' 'bout birth control? It's not like it was when Mama was comin' up. How could you be so smart and so stupid at the same time?"

"I don't know," Ruth started to cry. "I thought I *was* being smart. I never did it without a rubber! I swear."

"All right, all right. Just settle down. We need to think."

"What am I gonna do? What'll I tell Mama? I'll just have to tell her I'm in college and go as far away as I can. That's what I'll do. I'll just go away and have it. Maybe someone will adopt it and I can go back to college somehow. Oh, Annie, I don't see how I can keep my scholarships!"

"No, wait, I've got an idea." There was a long pause before Annie continued. "You can have an abortion. You know they're legal now."

"You mean kill the baby?" Ruth asked, horrified, trying to grasp her sister's meaning.

"I mean stop the pregnancy. A clinic just opened. A friend of mine had one. She was back to work in two days. No one even knew. You're eighteen now, Ruth. Mama wouldn't ever have to know.

"No. I can't. It's not right." Ruth said, more to herself. She was thinking of Joab's smile, of the first time she felt him move within her.

Both girls jumped at a knock at the door.

"It's Mama. I'm going to the bathroom. I'll be out in a second."

Ruth ran from the room wiping her eyes. From the bathroom, she could hear Annie greet Mama and invite her to stay for coffee. Ruth gathered herself together, then went out to hug her mother.

Ruth knew she'd have the abortion before she would even admit it to herself. The solution was just too easy to reject. There was little that Ruth would not have done just to keep from disappointing Mama again. Still, she needed time to rationalize. Over the course of the following week, Ruth's sharp mind put itself to the task of justifying the elective termination of the person who was due to draw his or her first breath in approximately seven and a half more months (give or take). Her intellect twisted and turned and spun in a million directions, chasing down the fleeting rabbits of logic that would permit her to live with the decision she had already made. But like a fleet-footed rabbit, the logic always darted this way and that and ultimately vanished down a dark hole in her brain before she could really lay hold of it.

The decision was made all the more difficult because the collective wisdom of the feminist movement had not yet been crystallized into sound bites. The ability to see her fetus as part of some nameless, faceless mass of unwanted humanity was a crutch not yet made available. Ruth could only think of the life she carried in personal terms. Then, too, Joab's birth had made it quite impossible to imagine a formless blob of protoplasm. Even this early on, Ruth knew that the life she carried was human. Hadn't Mama taught her that *all* people of all colors, shapes, and sizes were made in the image of God? How precious was this baby, really?

In the end, Ruth abdicated her responsibility for the decision.

The government of the United States has made abortion legal. Surely, if abortion were murder, our government would not permit it. Therefore, it cannot be wrong to have one, she reasoned dispassionately.

The secret call was made to Annie who agreed to front Ruth the money and make the appointment. The clinic would be unable to take Ruth on a weekend before Saturday, June 13th. Graduation would be six days later. Ruth was relieved to think it would all be over by then.

"Y'all have a good time together," Mama told her two daughters at Annie's apartment on the evening of the 12th. "Annie, you help Ruthie pick out something real pretty for her graduation speech. Don't you worry about the price tag neither, Ruthie. It's not every day a mama gets to see her daughter graduate *first in the class*." Mama paused as she gave her girls hugs and kisses. "You know it warms my heart to see y'all two spending some time together."

With that she was gone down the three flights of stairs to the old station wagon, double-parked, below.

Next morning, Big Mama stood at her dining room table, folding the next basket of endless laundry, as her second grandchild was being killed. Other than that, the day passed as one of no particular consequence.

The sisters had taken a city bus to the small clinic on the edge of town. The inside looked like a regular doctor's office and it had the smell of a hospital, but there was little conversation for the dozen or so mostly white girls who awaited their abortions. Ruth's eyes swept the waiting room. Thankfully, there was no one here she knew. Ruth took a clipboard from the nurse-looking woman behind the counter. She must have anticipated Ruth's question.

"The information is just for our doctor. It will be completely confidential," the woman assured in a smooth, hushed tone.

All the same, Ruth recorded a false last name and address at the top of her medical background questionnaire. She calculated the days since her last period as best she could remember, and filled in the space. When she had filled in all the other spaces, she returned it to the woman behind the counter who asked if she had a way to get home and someone to accompany her. Ruth indicated her sister.

"Let's see," the woman said, looking at the chart. "First trimester... that will be $265.00. We accept Visa, American Express or cash but we do not take personal checks."

Ruth took Annie's money from her pocket and placed it on the counter. She watched as the lady counted it out. Then she was given one five milligram Valium to help her relax and was told to take a seat. There was no point in trying to read any of the magazines. Ruth knew she would not be able to concentrate. Annie was no reader anyway and Ruth knew her sister felt awkward because there was nothing more to say about the baby and nothing else to talk about. The decision had been made. Finally, Annie took Ruth's hand and held it tight until the nurse came for her. She couldn't tell if Annie was praying or not.

Ruth was escorted to a small room with a padded, paper covered table equipped with stirrups. The room also contained a small counter with a sink, a free-standing, adjustable lamp, and a swivel stool. The nurse gave her a cotton hospital robe and told her to put it on. She directed her to lay down on the table and told her that she would be back with the doctor in a little while.

Ruth was puzzled as to whether the opening for the robe should be in the back or in the front. She decided on the back because she would not have to worry about its falling open during, what the nurse referred to as "the procedure."

It seemed like an eternity before the doctor appeared. While Ruth waited, her mind spun with dizzying acceleration over all the rationalizations of the previous week. She had almost overwhelming misgivings. More than once she considered flight. Only the thought of telling Mama kept her on the table. It was a fragile resolve.

Ruth was startled when she heard the metallic turn of the doorknob. Surprisingly, the doctor was a woman. She was of medium height with a fresh scrubbed appearance and a professional manner. Her dark wavy hair was pulled back into a low ponytail and fastened with a wide, frilly, red clip. In

Ruth's eyes, she was an angel of mercy. Here was a deliverer who could fix her mistake, spare her from telling Mama, and enable her to get to college. No more thinking. She was almost home free.

"Good afternoon. I'm Dr. Cork," she announced, "Nurse Richards will assist me with your procedure (Richards nodded and smiled compassionately). You are (she consulted her chart) Ruth Gilbert."

Ruth nodded.

"Before we get started, Ruth, do you have any medical conditions that you may not have included on your questionnaire and that you think I should be aware of?"

Ruth shook her head, no.

"Fine. Then let's get on with the procedure, shall we? Saturdays are always so busy. I'll be lucky to get out of here by seven tonight." She sat down on her stool at the foot of the table. "Please place your feet in the stirrups, bring your bottom all the way down to the edge of the table, and let your knees relax and fall open."

The paper crinkled as Ruth complied self-consciously. Dr. Cork adjusted the lamp.

"You may feel some discomfort, but it will be over quickly."

"You're welcome to squeeze my hand," offered Nurse Richards, taking hers.

Ruth closed her eyes as she felt cold metal slide up inside. Oddly, she remembered a baby chick Mama had let her hatch and raise when she was a young child. Ruth had stolen the egg from a plump, red hen. The old bird squawked and pecked at Ruth's intruding hand.

"I'll take good care of it," Ruth promised as the pale, brown prize slipped out from under the warmth of its mother's body. She had taken good care of it, too. She made a little nest for it from an old flannel shirt and placed it in a box on the top of her dresser. Then, she set the egg in the nest and placed a lamp over the box, faithfully turning it every so many hours. Ruth remembered running in the house every day after school to check on her egg. One afternoon she heard a tiny peep-peep before she reached it. Her chick had hatched! Ruth had taken great pleasure in caring for her fragile, fuzzy baby. When it was a few weeks old, she took it outside in the yard. She had just finished pushing Lyndon on the tire swing and was crossing the yard to gather up her chick when a shadow fell over it, and in an instant, it was gone in a flurry of brown hawk feathers.

Mama'd come running when she heard Ruth's screams, but there was nothing to be done and Ruth, trembling at the thought of a sharp beak tearing her soft chick apart, would not be comforted. The horror cut as a fresh wound. The little girl still grieved.

Ruth made herself open her eyes. The ceiling was a series of white panels. It sounded like someone switched on a vacuum cleaner. Ruth squeezed the hand, and held her breath as a sharp pain pierced her womb. Then, in an instant, it was over. All over.

"You will experience mild cramping and some bleeding for a couple of days. We recommend Tylenol for the pain. And be sure to drink plenty of fluids," explained the nurse as she led Ruth to a recovery room of sorts. The room contained about a dozen small beds of which more than half were occupied. Ruth lay down on the one she was directed to. She quickly curled around her cramps in the fetal position.

"We would like you to stay for at least forty minutes, then you are free to leave. But you are welcome to take as much time as you need. There is a dressing room in the corner when you are ready to go. I'll be back in a moment with your clothes."

"Thank you." Ruth said, closing her eyes. Instantly, she saw Joab's face. Her eyes sprang back open. Lying on her left side, she could see three other girls. One black and two white. The blonde sat, chewing gum and filing her nails. The fat brunette was reading an issue of <u>Cosmo</u>, and the other black girl just lay on her back staring up at the ceiling. Ruth closed her eyes again. This time her relentless mind conjured up an image of Joab on Mama's lap, in the big rocking chair. Ruth began to weep with relief which soon turned into sorrow. Somehow she had to cry. There was no one else to do it. Mama's second grandchild had been lost to her today, and no one knew to grieve. Only she and Annie, and she would never mourn in front of Annie. Yet, even as the tears made their way down her face, she had no regret. The sun would rise, brand new, tomorrow and add the first layer of distance to the events of this day. And in the fall, she would be away from this place. She would be starting college and working towards a bright new future.

Annie settled her sister in her own bed and set a cold RC on the night table. She switched the standing fan to high and turned it on Ruth, cursing the place for its lack of an A/C. Then she went out shopping for Ruth's graduation dress.

Chapter 15

Monday morning, Ruth forced herself to get up and help Mama get her little brothers and sisters off to school. It was always a challenge catching the bus on time and Mama had long since come to depend on Ruth's as her second pair of hands.

Ruth had exempted all her exams and enjoyed the privilege of a week off before the graduation ceremony on Friday afternoon. She had hoped to use the time to work on her valedictorian speech. After the screen door slammed behind Sarah, Ruth set Joab in his high chair and popped the seal on a jar of Gerber rice cereal with bananas. Mama turned from the breakfast dishes to examine her second-born.

"You feelin' alright, Chil'? You look a little weak."

"I just got the flow, Mama," Ruth answered.

"Well, why don't you just go back to bed for a while. I'll finish feeding little Joab here. You sure Annie didn't keep you out too late last weekend?" Mama smiled.

When Ruth hadn't risen by noon, Mama came into her room to check on her, Joab on her hip. With the temperature in the mid-90s, and every window in the house open, Ruthie was wrapped in a blanket and shivering.

Looks like you're coming down with something, Chil'," Mama said, putting a palm to Ruth's forehead. It was well above normal. Mama had a hand like a thermometer. About 101 she guessed.

"I'll get the aspirin," she said on her way out of the room.

At 3:13 p.m. the yellow bus swung open its doors for the Johnson kids.

"Ruthie's not feeling too good. I want y'all to keep quiet and let her get some rest. Ya hear?" Mama cautioned each child entering the house.

At 4:30, Mama entered Ruth's room with a cold RC. Her daughter was sound asleep. Mama placed a hand on her forehead. Ruth was pushing 104°. She stood, watching her daughter sleep for four or five minutes before deciding to wake her up.

"Ruthie, I want you to drink this RC." No response. Louder, "Ruth, Chil', I think you should try and drink somethin'."

No response. Mama rolled back the cover. She fought panic when she saw the pooled blood soaking through the sheets.

"Jethro!" She hollered. "Jethro!" The boy entered, sensing an emergency.

"Call 911. Something's bad wrong with your sister. And, for God's sake, boy, give them good directions. Make sure they don't get los'!"

Ruth opened her eyes ten hours later in a room at Savannah Memorial Hospital. Mama was standing over her bed before Ruth could register her surroundings.

"Oh, thank God. Thank you, Sweet Jesus. Thank you, Jesus. Thank you, Jesus. Thank you, Jesus," she repeated until Ruth interrupted her.

"Mama, what happened? Am I in a hospital?"

"Ah, Chil', you had me so scared. Thank God. Baby, . . . they had to operate. You've had an operation. But you're gonna be just fine, just fine."

"An operation?" Ruth closed her eyes and tried to listen to her body. There was a powerful ache in her abdomen. There were tubes releasing a steady flow of oxygen into her nose. There was an IV in her right forearm.

"What? Why?" She asked.

"There was a problem with your female parts. They couldn't fix 'em."

Ruth remembered *the procedure*.

"I just had some heavy cramping is all," she lied.

"No, Chil', that's not all. They said that you'd had an abortion. The Doctor said they put a hole in your womb and you had a bad infection. You lost a lot of blood. You almost lost your life."

At that moment, Ruth wished she had.

"Lawd, Chil', you had me scared. Why didn't you tell me? You could have told me."

"No I couldn't, Mama, not after Joab," Ruth said, turning her face away.

"Everyone makes mistakes."

"Twice?"

"Ruthie, most folks don't learn but by mistakes. The smart ones make lots and lots of 'em . . . But you made someone else pay fo' yours. Someone who never wished you no harm. And they paid a dear price... God can always fill one mo' plate at our table."

Ruth wondered if she would ever be able to look her mother in the eye again.

"Do ya hate me, Mama?" She asked through the blur of tears.

"Hate you? Ah, Chil', where's Mama's treasure?"

Ruth's throat tightened at the question.

"Where?" Mama persisted, tenderly.

"Right here, Mama, I'm right here," Ruth finally responded, "and I'm so sorry."

✦ ✦ ✦

Graduation day dawned bright and clear with a cool breeze promising some unseasonal relief from the thick heat. It was 5:30 AM when Mama's feet hit the worn spot beside her bed. There was much to be done.

Mama made the decision to go on with the graduation party. There was little enough in her life to celebrate. Today, two of her children would graduate from highschool, both bound for college. Jethro would be attending Clemson University on a football scholarship. And Ruth would be accepting a full academic scholarship to Furman. In four years, God willin', they would be the first college graduates in the family that anyone could remember.

It will be good to get Ruthie's mind off her troubles, Mama reasoned.

Truth was, Mama had endured more than one pointed remark from family during Ruth's pregnancy, and it wouldn't hurt her kin any to have to look her in the face and offer the appropriate accolades under more positive circumstances. This was one day Mama would simply not be cheated out of.

Her heart was light as she busied herself around the kitchen, making final preparations for the feast to follow the graduation ceremony. Mama's rich, deep, voice seemed to carry her from task to task.

"Amazing grace, how sweet the sound . . ." she emptied a five pound bag of sugar into a giant, borrowed urn. "that saved a wretch like me. . ." She chose one of a dozen jars and pitchers that had been brewing through the night and poured the black-brown tea into the urn. "Hmm Hmm-hm Hmm-hm lost . . ." she opened the fridge to check the Jell-O fruit salad. It had congealed nicely. "But, now, I'm found . . ." she turned up the heat under the pot of vegetable oil and began preparing her own special, secret coating for the last several batches of fried chicken to the remaining bars of her song.

Jethro had been ringing necks for a week and everyone else had plucked feathers until their pluckers were sore. It was a shame to serve chicken cold, but there would be no time to cook for so many people. Aunts, Uncles and cousins, most of 'em would be in her yard by mid-afternoon. She figured about sixty-five, not counting little ones. Most every woman would be bringing an offering of signature cakes or casseroles, and it was safe to say that no tummy would go unfilled. Some of the men would brown bag whisky, and more likely than not, a collection would be taken for a cold keg of beer. The celebrating was likely to dance on past the wee hours.

Amid beds of sleeping sisters, Ruth stared at the ceiling, absently listening to the rise and fall of Mama's voice and going over her valedictorian speech in her mind. She was not pleased with it. She longed to say something of substance, to communicate to her class the enduring lessons which had cost her so dearly. And she longed to be understood. Yet, how could they understand? The issues they were dealing with seemed so distant from her own experience of the past two years. In the end, there was not enough trust for Ruth to span the canyon between herself and her peers. It was hard enough simply to stand before them and speak, at all.

Ruth chose safe ground, composing a speech designed to deliver what she thought her classmates wanted to hear. It was seasoned liberally with references to black pride, white tolerance and racial harmony. In it, Ruth quoted no less than three lyrics by black vocalists currently topping the charts. Each time Ruth went over her speech, it sounded more trite and superficial than the last. She was on her fifth silent rehearsal when Mama appeared in the door frame.

"How ya feeling today, Chil'?" Mama whispered.

"I'm fine, Mama." Ruth's statement was close to the truth. At 18, her body was extremely resilient. Her recovery from the surgery had been swift and dramatic. Ruth had decided that Tylenol and grit would be enough to get her through her speech. She wanted her mind to be clear. Afterwards, she would let herself return to the prescription pain relief and relax into comfortable movement. She just had to remember not to pick up anything heavy.

"Well, your big day is here," Mama beamed.

Ruth managed a smile.

"I'm so proud of you and Jethro I could just burst wide open. Stop fretting about that speech. You're gonna do jus' fine. Now, come and help me in the kitchen." Mama raised her voice a little, "Sarah. Maybell. Mama's gonna be needing yo' help, too."

The little sisters stirred sleepily at their names. Then Mama was off down the hall to enlist some muscle from the boys.

Soon the house was a hive of activity. Each body was sent to work and Mama had no lack of jobs.

"Jethro, I'll need you to find a table and set up the big radio on the porch," she ordered, "Mind you be careful. John and Lyndon, come with me and I'll show you where you can set up the three folding tables cousin Eliza give us."

Suddenly, there was a loud clatter from the kitchen. Joab clung precariously to the almost-top-shelf of the pantry closet.

Below him was a sea of brightly colored breakfast cereal circles.

"I get it myself, Big Mama." Joab offered, smiling proudly from his shelf.

"Sweet Jesus in heaven!" Mama exclaimed hurrying to catch the toddler before he lost his grip, "Thank God he didn't want fried chicken. Abe, will you help Joab, here, with his breakfast and, clean up this mess for me? I'm counting on you to keep him out of trouble so the res' of us can finish gettin' ready for this party."

Abe hung his head. "Oh, Mama, how come I always gotta watch 'im?" He asked.

"Because you got more patience than all the other children put together and he loves to play with you mos'."

Abe rolled his eyes and accepted his nephew from his mother. Then he placed him gently into the high chair.

"Sarah! Maybell!" Mama hollered. "Wipe off the tables and put on these tablecloths. Be sure to put somethin' on 'em so the wind don't carry 'em away. Ruth, you feel up to cleanin' the bathroom?"

Abe got the broom.

By 9:30, Mama had sent each child to get dressed.

As soon as the bathroom was fit for company, Ruth was charged with dressing her son. Mama had bought him a navy blue suit complete with a vest and tie. It looked like it might belong to a Bay Street lawyer except for its size and the clip on the red paisley bow tie.

"A red bow tie! Don't you look sharp!" Ruth swooned over her little man. "Go show Big Mama how handsome you are."

With that, Joab tucked his chin and marched out of Ruth's bedroom door.

"I got bow tie. I handsome, Big Mama," Ruth could hear his little-boy's voice down the hall. She smiled as she listened to Big Mama stroking the youngest male ego in the house, though maybe not the smallest.

A few minutes later, Ruth and Jethro appeared in Mama's doorway for inspection. They were both in their caps and gowns. The girls in her class had chosen white and the boys, navy blue. Pulling on her gloves, Mama's eyes glistened when she saw them.

"I'm very proud of you, Ruthie," Mama said, putting her hands on the girl's shoulders and looking straight into her eyes. "I'm proud of who you are. And you, Jethro, there just ain't much boy left in you." She stepped back to take him in from head to foot. "You're a fine young man, a *fine* young man." Flustered at her own unexpected wash of emotion, Mama shooed her near-graduates out the door and turned to search her top drawer for her fancy handkerchief.

"Y'all go keep an eye on Joab before he finds trouble. I think he's in with the boys."

John, Lyndon and Abe were tearing their room apart looking for one of Lyndon's twice-handed-down dress shoes. Jethro decided he'd better engage in the search before Mama was ready to load up the car.

Joab wasn't in with the boys. When Ruth found him, he was hanging through the middle of the tire swing, dangling from the old oak. Miraculously, the brightly covered tables had not attracted his attention and he had chosen swinging over table jumping this morning. As Ruth watched from the parlor window, Joab spun himself in circles. She laughed when he tried to walk and staggered like a drunk. His shirttails were already untucked and his suit had collected a good bit of dust. He started at the suspended tire, arms raised over his head, and dove, running with all his strength until his feet left the ground. He swung. There was nothing tentative about Joab. Everything he did, he did with absolute commitment, abandon, and joy.

A lump formed in Ruth's throat as she watched her son. He would be the only one. The solid ground of shared familial experience would never fully be his. Ruth knew how to walk away from outsiders, but she could never turn from family. Who would teach Joab how to love a peer when you didn't like him and how to keep on loving him until he became likable again? He would never know the abiding friendship of an Annie or the strong, quiet support of a Jethro or the pride and protectiveness of big brotherhood. He would be alone in a generation of strangers. And she had made it so.

"You better run and get 'im before he ruins that new suit or upsets the tables," Mama suggested. She was peeking out the window behind Ruth.

"Oh, Mama," Ruth burst. "He'll always be playing all by himself."

"Oh, nonsense. He's got plenty of kin to play with after school."

"Mama, you know what I mean. He's an only child. My only child, and the only one I'll ever have. I don't blame God for punishing me for what I done. But Joab's getting punished, too."

"God's not punishing you, chil'. He might be letting you live with your choices. He might be trying to teach you somethin'. But Jesus came to forgive and restore. He ain't punishin' you."

"I've been thinking, Mama," Ruth paused. "You know our agreement about Joab?"

Mama nodded and said a silent prayer.

"Well, I decided *I* want to raise him. I want him to be mine. I mean, if you don't mind. Can I have him back, Mama?"

"I won't hold you to our agreement so long as you still make the valedictorian speech."

Suddenly, there was a disturbance among the chickens. Mama and Ruth looked out the window to see Joab standing in a circle of poultry. Two pullets fled in a flurry of flapping and squalling as the toddler took aim and a yellow stream found, precisely, the head of his next target.

"He's pissin' on the chickens!" Ruth squeaked in disbelief.

"Good shot, too!" Mama observed with a resonant burst of laughter, "I'll go save them chickens. You go and freshen your face."

Ruth watched Mama try to approach the boy with a straight face and muster some kind of sincerity while scolding the evils of chicken pissin'. She watched the older woman wiping off the dimpled hands and tucking in the child-sized man-shirt. It was Ruth's turn to pray.

"Oh, Lord," she started, "I'm so sorry for what I did to that other baby you tried to give me. But, I promise, Jesus, if you'll forgive me, I'll do right by Joab. You'll see. If you'll just help me, I'll do my best to raise him up in a way that'll make you proud."

✦ ✦ ✦

A raised platform had been erected down one end of the football field for the graduation ceremony. There were 347 students participating in Wade-Hampton High School commencement exercises. Ruth sat beneath a square white cap lost in the midst of approximately 180 identical ones to the right side of the platform. Jethro was under one of the navy caps on the left side.

Ruth's heart raced as the principal's voice droned on in the high sun. She sat up straight and peeked out over the rows ahead of her to the sea of parents beyond. Relatives and loved ones spilled out of the rows of folding chairs into the bleachers. Even then, some were standing. Ruth wondered how many of them were her people. Half-sized, white papers fluttered back and forth as the women fanned themselves with their programs. Ruth spotted Mama in her brand new, dark pink dress and matching hat.

". . . our valedictorian, graduating with a 4.1 cumulative grade point average for the 1975-76 school year, and a 3.98 cumulative average over her four year high school career, Miss Ruth Chantell Johnson."

Ruth stood. Instantly, her mouth went dry. She would not have had enough spit to lick a stamp. Everyone clapped as she made her way to the podium, front and center. She stepped up on a wooden milk carton which had been preset for her. Still, Mr. Ford, the principal, lowered the angle of the microphone before taking his seat. She set her papers down before her.

"Fellow students," her voice thundered over the P.A. system. Ruth must have jumped because there was a low rumble of laughter in the audience. She began again, this time leaving a little distance between her lips and the microphone.

"Fellow students, Principal Ford, honored faculty, parents and loved ones, I am both humbled and honored to stand before you today and to have the privilege of speaking on behalf of my class, the Wade-Hampton High class of 1976."

"At tender ages, my classmates and I were witness to the turbulence of our era. Could it really have been over a decade since an assassin's bullet took the life of John F. Kennedy? We were less than a decade old when Martin Luther King, Jr. and Robert F. Kennedy were cut down. Since then, many of our brightest young men have been lost in the Vietnam War. But has our hope died with them? Were mere bullets able to stop their work, extinguish their vision? Clearly the answer is, 'no.'

"Now, in 1976, the fruits of their labor are just becoming ripe. Our young men have long been home from Vietnam and those graduating today need not fear the draft. The dream that Martin Luther King, Jr. had is fast becoming a reality. I, as a black American, can look with optimism to a culture struggling to embrace the principles of the Equal Rights Movement of the 60s. The gaps in education and income between black America and white America are closing. My prayer is that they disappear completely in my lifetime. As an American woman, in four years I can anticipate entering the workforce in a marketplace which welcomes us into an ever-broadening range of professions. Equal pay for equal work is clearly becoming the rule rather than the exception."

Ruth scanned the remainder of her speech. She scanned her audience. Programs rhythmically fanning. Faces clearly bored. Ruth honored an impulse.

"John, could you bring Joab up here?" She asked.

People looked up as their ears registered silence while John made his way to the platform carrying little Joab. Ruth pulled an empty chair over beside the podium. John set the boy down on it.

"This is my son, Joab," Ruth heard her own voice announce.

Joab commenced swinging his legs over the edge of the metal seat.

"Most of you already know that I took time off between my sophomore and junior years. I wanted to show y'all why I am glad I got the grades I did. Because good grades got me into a good college and graduating from a good college will give me a chance at a good career. And that'll give me a chance to take good care of my son. And for that I thank God . . . So, I guess, I really just wanted to thank my teachers and especially my Mama for challenging me to be the best I can be. And also my brother, Jethro, for being the best big brother a sister ever had. Thank you."

Ruth stepped down off of the milk carton and extended an index finger to Joab who grabbed it and jumped down off his chair. On their way back to her seat, Ruth thought of ten other things she might have said in her speech. But by the time she sat down and helped Joab onto her lap, her tongue quit sticking to the roof of her mouth, and she was quite pleased with her speech.

All Big Mama's work and preparation paid off in a fine party. After stomachs had been satisfied, Abe cleared a spot on one of the tables and stood Joab on it.

"Hey, Joab," he asked the smaller boy, pointing to a woman, "Who's 'at?"

" 'at's Aunt Jo."

" 'at's right!" Abe announced, like a man at the carnival, "And who's 'at?"

" 'at's Mr. George from up the skreet."

Soon all the guests gathered round to ask the toddler if he could identify them. Abe puffed his skinny chest out bigger and bigger with each correct answer.

"I taught 'im, myse'f,' Abe admitted proudly after the child had rattled off more than a dozen names, some from folks he'd only seen once.

Big Mama winked at Ruth, "Ain't no wonder the boy's as smart as his Mama," she said. Ruth was as amazed as the rest of the folks. But the thought pleased her.

As Big Mama had predicted, the graduation party rocked on long after the little ones fell into limp heaps of exhaustion. No one had a better time than Big Mama, herself. Only the few remaining chickens seemed unmoved by the celebratory spirit of the moment.

Chapter 16

Several days later, Ruth sat beside her mother on a dark green, leather sofa in the waiting room of the law offices of Dunn, Smoot and Reeves. Mama had decided on funeral attire. Her brightly colored, Sunday prints had been pushed aside as too gay for this appointment. She even wore her black hat with the wide band of netting around the brim and her black cotton gloves. These accessories were generally reserved for only the most solemn of funerals. While Ruth had not reached an age that required hats, she was admonished to wear her black gloves.

Both women sat on the edge of the antique sofa, backs straight, hands folded in their laps. Neither was willing to lean on the ancient furniture or risk fingerprints on the rich patina of the freshly waxed coffee table - even through gloves.

After a gracious greeting by a tall, well groomed receptionist, followed by an invitation to "Sit and make yourselves comfortable," the woman went about her business behind her high, bank teller's desk. She answered the phone in hushed tones and either asked the caller to "leave a message" or "please hold." Once, she put someone "right through." Twice she greeted businessmen in navy, pinstriped suits with red ties and invited them to have a seat, assuring them that Mr. So and So would be with them in a moment. Both men, in turn, sat down. Both men, in turn, swung his leather briefcase on his knees, released both spring-loaded locks simultaneously, retrieved a small stack of paper stapled together in the upper left corner, locked his case, swung it down beside his chair, and began reading the papers in earnest. Neither gentleman got to read his papers for more than seven or eight minutes before the receptionist invited him down a hallway to the left rear of her desk. She seemed, to Ruth, not unlike Carol Marrol on <u>Let's Make a Deal</u>, but with a little more class and a lot less glitz.

All of this, Ruth observed with keen interest. Ruth liked this place. She liked the library feel of it. She liked the formality of it. She liked the way people spoke to each other here. The environment, though intimidating, seemed the antithesis of her own. And in so being, it appealed to her.

After twenty minutes, Mama decided to risk messing up the magazines. Disappointed in not finding <u>People</u>, she chose a current edition of <u>Architectural Digest</u> and began looking at pictures. Ruth was absorbed in the details of the waiting room. Under the coffee table was an ornate carpet with rich, dark colors and an exotic pattern. On the other side of it were arranged a matching pair of chairs upholstered in a floral tapestry that didn't exactly match the fancy carpet, but looked like they belonged with it. Beyond them was a bit of an open area and beyond it, against the wall, stood a long, thin, table adorned at the center with a great Chinese vase. The brightly colored vase was filled to extravagance with a fresh arrangement. Ruth could just catch the scent of gardenia from where she sat. The walls of the entire room were paneled about a third of the way up with dark wood that was rubbed and varnished until waves of grain glowed in the soft light. The rest of the walls were covered in creamy, textured wallpaper. Ruth turned around to view the pictures over the sofa. They were Audubon bird prints in gold frames. Now she was really impressed.

"Mama," Ruth whispered, breaking the long silence, "Look! These are pictures of Carolina Parakeets!"

"Very nice," Mama whispered, barely turning around to see the image of the bygone birds which had captured Ruth's imagination since she was five and an Uncle swore he had seen some in a nearby cypress swamp. In the seventh grade, Ruth had done her science research paper on them.

Like the buffalo of the great plains, Carolina Parakeets were once countless, filling the skies of the southeastern United States in swiftly shifting, living clouds. Ruth still kept a small flock in her imagination. They were similar to the popular "lovebird," only this kind had been more streamline and measured almost a foot long. Their curved beaks were pale yellow. The front of their faces were a bright orange which faded into a yellow hood. The rest of their bodies were lime or emerald green with some blue and yellow in the wings. They must have been beautiful to see.

It wasn't their striking appearance that had smitten Ruth, though; it was the jester spirit of the parrot she loved. They had been very social, screeching and chattering in ceaseless banter with one another. They often roosted in groups, hanging by their beaks inside the hollow of trees while they slept. Ruth figured this was probably the only way they could make themselves quit fussing and fooling long enough to get some rest.

From time to time, Ruth had tried to envision what the character of the southern forests might have been like while hosting such gregarious personalities. In Ruth's imagination, they still flourished, hanging upside down from branches by one foot while using the other like a hand to eat, cracking open hard seeds and prickly pods with those curious beaks of theirs. Ruth remembered reading that each bird had a preference for one foot over the other which made them right-handed or left-handed, like people. She respected the species, too, because the females had not accepted the faded plumage of their sex, but flaunted bold, clownish colors just like the males. Having lingered at the cockatoo exhibit at the zoo during a class trip, Ruth concluded there is something in the psyche of parrots which turns everything they touch into toys and everything they do into play.

There was one thing they took seriously, though, and that was death. In the mid 1800s, the bright green and yellow feathers of the Carolina Parakeet became a fashion rage in the great cities of the Northeast and even Europe. Farmers already despised the little creatures who had, by this time, developed a taste for cultivated food, descending like locusts on orchards and fields and tearing a harvest apart to devour the seeds within. While Ruth could certainly sympathize with poor farmers laboring to scratch out an existence, she wished there could have been another way.

Soon, orchards and fields became bait for a more lucrative cash crop, as hunters opened fire. In a short while, as though in mourning, the surviving birds would pass a second time over the fields of their fallen companions. Rifles would be reloaded and waiting. And so, whole flocks, one morning thick as a thundercloud, would be destroyed by evening. True, some hunters caught the birds alive to sell as pets. But they did not breed well in captivity and scientists would discover, too late, that the only native North American parrot needed large numbers to maintain their species. Ruth missed them, though she had never really known them.

"Mr. Keylar will see you now." The receptionist's smooth voice woke Ruth from her daydreams. Mama placed her magazine neatly on the coffee table and both women rose.

"I'm sorry you had to wait so long," she apologized as she led them to Mr. Keylar's office. But Mama didn't mind. In truth, she never trusted the ability of any professional who didn't make her wait.

"Must not be very good at what he does," she reasoned, "if he ain't busy." If Mama entered a doctor's office that wasn't packed, she left and never returned.

Mr. Charles R. Keylar, Esquire, shook hands with Mama and Ruth over a massive, leather-topped desk, and motioned them to take a seat on the other side.

Mr. Keylar wore the uniform of his profession. He was not very tall and neither too thin nor too thick. He looked to be in his late-twenties and had prominently displayed on his enormous desk a framed picture of a pretty young woman with a head full of long, blond curls. Ruth checked his left hand for the ring. He had wavy, brown hair that was on the verge of being too long, under which were eyebrows that were on the verge of being too thick. His lips were thin, but gave expression to a deep, resonant, speaking voice; an invaluable asset to a trial lawyer of such unimpressive stature. Charlie Keylar was, in fact, the most junior associate of the firm, having passed the bar only months ago.

"Okay, I'll tell you what I remember from our phone conversation, then you can fill in the blanks from there."

Ruth watched his eyes as he spoke. They were golden brown, and warm. He had a direct, but gentle manner. Ruth trusted him. He consulted a lined, yellow tablet for notes.

"Let's see . . . On the morning of Saturday, June 12th of this year, you entered the Savannah Woman's Clinic on North Abercorn and received an abortion. You were discharged the same day and went home. The following Monday evening you were admitted to Savannah Memorial Hospital where you underwent an emergency partial hysterectomy due to complications from the abortion procedure. You are now permanently infertile at eighteen years of age."

When Charlie Keylar looked up from his notes he found his client sullen-faced with downcast eyes.

"I'm sorry," he said with genuine conviction. He and the pretty little blonde had been trying to conceive for well over two years. He believed a woman had a right to do as she pleased with her own body, but maintained a shelf in his heart for the childless. "If we're ever gonna hold the abortionist accountable, you're gonna have to give me the details."

Ruth nodded.

"Do you remember the name of the doctor who gave you the abortion?"

"Dr. Cork. She was a lady doctor," Ruth answered, not looking up.

"Do you recall the names of any of the other people at the clinic?"

"The nurse's name was Richards. She was a lady, too."

"Did they tell you about any risks?"

Ruth shook her head, no.

"Did they have you sign anything?"

Ruth nodded, yes.

"Do you remember anything about the paper you signed?"

"No, sir."

"You didn't happen to keep a copy, did you?"

"No, sir. I wouldn't have kept a copy, anyhow. I didn't want anyone to find out. I just didn't want any more babies."

"Any MORE babies? Do you have children?"

"Yes, sir, I have a son, Joab."

Charlie Keylar put down the pen he'd been taking notes with and fell back against his chair, dwarfed behind his giant desk.

"How old were you when you gave birth to Joab?" he asked.

"Sixteen."

"Okay," he took a deep breath, leaned forward, and began taking notes again. "Who was the surgeon who performed your hysterectomy?"

"Dr. Lamb." Mama offered.

"Did he offer any opinion as to why the surgery was necessary?"

"Yes, sir," Mama continued, "He said it was on account of the infection in her womb from a cut she got from the abortion. And she'd lost a lot o' blood."

"Good. Well, that's enough information to get me started," he said, rising. "I'll have to get some files from the hospital and the clinic, and I'll be in touch in a few weeks. I must tell you that I can only accept contingency work with the approval of the senior partners of the firm. They decide which cases to take on."

He shook hands with Mama.

"I'm awfully sorry for what happened to you, Miss Johnson," he said, taking her hand. "I'll do the best I can for you."

Ruth nodded.

✦ ✦ ✦

Two weeks later, Ruth and Mama sat across the large desk from Charlie Keylar again.

"I have to tell you that the senior partners will not permit me to accept your case," he said. Mama felt like she'd been punched in the stomach.

"I asked you to come in because I wanted to give you an explanation . . . Abortions have just been legalized. Regulations haven't been hammered out yet. That means it's basically a brand new area of the law. The right to privacy, however, is a well-established concept in association with health care.

Doctors hate being made to hand over their files to lawyers. We did receive your files from the hospital but the clinic insists that they have no records of any Ruth C. Johnson and is threatening a counter suit if we press. Between depositions and expert witnesses, the overhead in a case like yours can run into the tens of thousands and the senior partners just feel that the existence of one illegitimate child will ultimately make a jury less sympathetic to your plight. I'm truly sorry. It's out of my hands."

"You mean," Mama interrupted, "that your bosses don't think folks will give a damn if one poor black girl can't have no mo' babies."

"Like I said—"

Mama stood. "Thank you for your time, Mr. Keylar. Tell your bosses that we'll find ourselves some *real* lawyers."

Ruth followed her mother, sheepishly, down the hall.

"I left my gloves," she announced when they reached the elevator. Then she raced back to Mr. Keylar's office.

"It's not your fault, Mr. Keylar. I didn't give the clinic my real name," Ruth confessed.

"I know," he answered, coming all the way around the desk to shake her hand. "I wish I could help."

"It's okay," Ruth said. She picked up her gloves and left.

Mama walked down Bull Street toward the parked car with fast, angry steps, speaking more to herself than to Ruth.

"Don't you worry, Ruthie, we'll find ourselves some *good* lawyers. We'll make that woman pay for what she done to you."

"No, Mama, the fault is mine and I just want to move on now," Ruth said, "I don't want any court fight. I'm taking Joab and I'm going to college and I'm going to make a life for us."

And she did.

Part Three

Manhood

Chapter 17

True to form, when Anita ran, she ran home. Miss Lucy stone-walled Joab's attempts to communicate with his wife by phone and simply stated, "She's not here," before abruptly hanging up on him. Ruth, however, would not be so easily put off, appearing often outside Mrs. Twedell's door until there was nothing to do but call the police or let the woman in. Anita finally relented, allowing her mother-in-law Friday overnights and most of Saturday with the grands. Early Saturday mornings, Ruth usually put in a call to Joab and let him speak to Cinda who considered this a rare and grown-up treat, indeed.

After a phone consultation with Charlie Keylar, it was decided that the divorce proceedings would be greatly simplified if kept in state. Charlie drew up preliminary papers and advised Joab to plan on coming home for the summer, during which time, he felt sure, he could set the final hearing. Joab was anxious for the day when enforceable visitation rights would be afforded him. His heart cried out for his Cinda and he often wondered what stepping stones toward toddlerhood he had forever missed in Mandy's life. Resentment puffed itself up like yeast in dough each time his plea for communication was rejected by the Twedell women.

"But they're my daughters, too!" he screamed into the phone one day.

"Maybe," came Miss Lucy's smug response, over Cinda's voice in the background, "but they're not here."—Click.

Joab slammed the receiver down and put his fist through the thin trailer wall. Charlie Keylar insisted he had little recourse until details of the divorce were final.

Predictably, Anita was less than cooperative with Joab's attorney. It took four tries before divorce papers could be properly served. Charlie absorbed the expense of the process server without mentioning it to Joab or Ruth.

Twice before finals, Ruth flew Joab home to steal a Saturday with his girls. They were joyous hours as Joab soaked in the sweet company of his eldest and delighted in the care of his youngest. Anita was spitting mad both times. However, there was little she could do after the fact, but fuss. Cinda wept for a week for her Daddy after each visit.

"Your Daddy doesn't want to live with us anymore," Anita told the child, "but don't worry. Mommy will never leave you. Mommy loves you."

✦ ✦ ✦

Back in Durham, Joab settled up with Bubba (who had turned out to be quite a true friend in spite of the rosy color of his neck) and found himself a small, but whole room in the co-ed dorm. It wasn't difficult, late in the year, when many of the non-freshmen had made the jump to apartments. Lesa was the first to visit him. It was a steamy, tempestuous reunion in spite of the dimensions of a single bed in a closet-size room. Overnight, Blue Devil basketball became history for Lesa. She, like Ruth, had never really possessed the soul of a true fan anyway.

Dr. Morse pulled some strings, and the school hired Joab to work, part time, in the library. On Saturdays he gave campus tours to prospective freshmen and their parents. Because of the comparative luxury of Lesa's apartment, Joab wound up spending little time in his dorm room. Often, Lesa would urge Joab to simply let go of it and move in with her, officially. He would have, too, if he had had the means to pay the rent. But something about moving under a roof that was so completely *hers* was vaguely unsettling. He accepted a key to Lesa's place but continued to maintain his dorm room, as a kind of escape hatch, should things turn nasty.

For the first time in his college education, Joab almost enjoyed finals. It approached pleasure to study with someone for whom education was embraced, not merely tolerated. Lesa and Joab sometimes found themselves launched into lengthy discussions of political theory which lasted late into the night. One day it would be the rise of Stalin. Two hours later, Alexander the Great or Richard Nixon. The next day it would be Fidel Castro or the path to lasting peace between Israel and her neighbors. Both shared a passion for politics and both had to take care lest they spent all their study time in discussion which, while immensely entertaining, would not improve their grades. Then too, during particularly strenuous cramming sessions, break time often included brief, wild sex, followed by a fifteen to twenty minute nap. Next, Lesa ran a fresh pot of coffee and back to the books.

Lesa was looking forward to the frivolity of her last summer break before the responsibilities of post-graduate life set in. She knew Joab had to return to Georgia and she knew why. She also knew there was a slim chance that Anita might win him back. Great was her lament that Joab could not accompany her home to her beautiful island. Inwardly, she didn't mind the thought of his absence nearly so much. It was only eight weeks, after all.

Mr. Shemisaki sent Lesa airline tickets for the Sunday following finals week. With no space for luggage on his bike, Joab had mailed a box of clothes home a few days earlier. Saturday night they went out for an early dinner, showed up at a graduation party, and closed a club where they danced until 3:30 in the morning. Sunday was spent in bed until it was time to get Lesa to the airport around 4:00. Joab carried her luggage to the desk and checked her in. He gave her a long kiss at the gate and watched her 737 become airborne. Then he drove her white Beemer into the garage at her apartment and hid the key. Alyson had already graduated and was responsible for dropping off her house key to a neighbor who would keep an eye on things and water the plants over the summer. Alyson's departure was set for Monday afternoon.

At 5:35 Monday morning, just before dawn, Joab's bike roared out of Lesa's garage and he was South-bound. It was a hot day and a glorious trip, though for an older man it might have been a bit grueling. Mile after mile, Joab anticipated, with great excitement, his homecoming. Oh, he was looking forward to seeing his mother, of course, but his heart raced as he imagined Cinda's face when she first laid eyes on her Daddy. As thousands of broken, yellow lines sped by, Joab tried to anticipate all the changes which little Amanda might have grown through since he last saw her. The date had been set for weeks. Anita had promised to let Ruth pick the girls up at noon and spend the night. That meant they would be there when their father arrived. Joab's bike whined steadily at seventy miles per hour. He had to keep reminding himself not to push the old thing much harder than that.

At last his bike hit the old dirt road, dust rising up behind him. He passed the little inlet where he could see, for a second, beyond the marsh to the ocean. The sun glittered on the water and Joab saw, for the first time, the magnificent beauty of the Savannah delta. Patches of sun filtered down through tree limbs as a sudden gust of warm wind set Spanish moss in motion. There was Big Mama's great, ancient oak and his old tire swing. He'd have to be sure to give Cinda a few pushes before the sun went down. Ol' Boog was lying, flat out in the shade of the sprawling tree. He pulled himself stiffly to his feet and barked twice at the strange motorcycle. When Joab glanced at the front of Big Mama's house, her form appeared on the porch, but only in his memory. A keen longing for the cherished woman mingled with his longing for his daughters.

"I wish you could have met my girls," he whispered under his helmet.

And then his own Mama's double-wide appeared. The grass had been freshly mowed and hedges looked as neat as ever. He wondered who she was paying to keep the yard these days. Up at Shady Oaks, the grass would have grown right over the trailer if Anita hadn't borrowed the mower from Bubba once in a while. And look at that, Mama had bought herself a carport. It was really just an aluminum roof on legs, but it was white to match the house and the posts were embellished with wrought iron frills. Under it, Mama had had a slab of concrete poured. A good job, too. It gave the house an appearance of permanency.

Joab's lower cheeks were still vibrating when he took the porch steps three at a time. Ruth was at the door. Joab put his arm around her waist and lifted her off the ground in an exuberant greeting.

"Where are my girls?" he asked as he set her down.

"Anita wouldn't let them come," Ruth answered as though it pained her to speak the words.

"To hell with that!" Joab said. "Go get your car keys and we'll go and get 'em."

"We can't."

"Why not?"

"Because I don't know where they are."

"Aren't they at Miss Lucy's?"

Ruth shook her head.

"Maybe she just took them out for the afternoon or something," Joab speculated hopefully.

"No. Lucy let me in to see. Anita's gone and she's taken the playpen, the high chair—everything. Miss Lucy's as put out about it as you are. It seems they couldn't agree on who was to raise the kids and Anita decided it was time to be on her own again."

"Well, where'd she go?"

"You think they'd tell me?"

Joab put his hands to his head and rubbed his temples. It was all he could do to keep expletives from filling his mother's living room. He clenched his fists which craved one clean shot at a wall.

"I'm sorry, son," Ruth offered. "Come, sit down a while, and let your bones relax."

Joab took a deep breath and obeyed.

"I guess the next question is; where's Nicholas?" he said, leaning back in the sofa. "Is he still in Atlanta?"

"Last I heard; but who knows?"

To Joab's surprise, Ruth served him a beer—in a frosted mug, no less.

"What's this?" he asked.

"You're 21. You ought to be able to handle a beer by now. This is still your house, son. You're welcome to live in it."

"Thanks, Mama." Joab was touched by such an observance of his coming of age. It might be his house, but it was still under his mother's roof. "What do the ladies of the church have to say about all this?" Joab teased.

"Oh, some of them have been known to back-slide a little during the week, and I reckon there are things that just aren't much their business."

"You sure you don't keep a few cold ones around for your own self?"

Ruth turned away and smiled like a schoolgirl. "Now, you go on," she said.

It was good to have the tension dissipate a bit.

✦ ✦ ✦

Joab stayed with his mother for a week, during which time he met with Charlie Keylar.

"I sure am sorry about all this, Joab," he said.

"Me too," Joab answered. "So what now?"

Charlie leaned back in his leather chair and almost disappeared behind his expansive, old desk. "Well, assuming she fails to appear before the judge on June 19th, he'll probably just issue a standard divorce settlement."

"What about visitation rights?" Joab asked, hopefully.

"I'm sure they'll be reasonable, but it'll be awful hard to make her comply until she reappears. Let's hope she *does* turn up in Atlanta, at least that's *in state*. I've put in a few calls to some folks I know there, but they can't find any Nicholas Twedell or Anita Johnson listed."

"Isn't there some judge who can make Mrs. Twedell tell us where she is?"

"Not if she says she doesn't know."

"Well, I'm sure she's still getting her welfare checks. Can't you trace her through those?"

"Not legally. The government is pretty strict about things like that unless, of course, it serves their own purposes."

Charlie became heartsick when he saw the despair on the younger man's face. He hated domestic law. He had always avoided it. He wished that he had avoided it now. He just didn't have the stomach for it. It got too dirty, too painful, too real. He couldn't imagine life without Susan and the kids, though the kids were almost grown now. If his wife ever turned on him that would simply be the end of Charles Keylar. She would know exactly where to place the blade in order to pierce his heart. And though he had never been unfaithful, he well understood the weakness of men and the availability of women in a culture which seemed to have come to exist within a great moral void. Often, on business trips, he had taken his meals in his room and literally bolted his door against it.

Charlie had taken Joab's case as a favor to Ruth and because he knew the boy had no one else to turn to. But he decided, then and there, that this would be his last divorce case ever. He had lent Joab his Lincoln to take Nita to the junior prom, had danced at their wedding, and had given gifts when their children were born, for God's sake. It was just too hard.

"You can hire a private investigator, but they can run up a bill in no time. And I mean more than pocket change," he said honestly. "C'mon, Joab let me take you to lunch."

With no father to talk to and very little good news from his attorney, Charlie hoped he could at least offer some comfort. It would not have been the first time the older man had offered the boy a wing to run under. In a very real way, Charlie had seen Joab grow up. Several times he had advised his mother on the psychological phases of male adolescence (such as he could remember) or on a particular aspect of child-rearing. With three children of his own who enjoyed the benefits of a stable two-parent family as well as the luxury of a stay-at-home mom, Charlie still considered the raising of healthy, responsible citizens to be the greatest challenge of his life. He had no small respect for the job that Ruth had done. In Charlie Keylar's estimation, Joab had clearly screwed things up. But he was still a bright young man and a fine one, too. Charlie had every confidence that Joab would land on his feet and that, when he did, he would be much wiser.

"Thanks very much, Mr. Keylar, but I think I just better go home."

Charlie stood to reach across the desk and shake Joab's hand, "Why don't you call me Charlie?" he asked.

Joab broke out in a wide grin and shook his head. "Oh, I don't know if I can." he said.

"Well, try. This kind of formality is for children, not for friends.

Joab kissed his mother on the way out. Before going home, he decided to stop by his mother-in-law's to beg.

She would not invite him in, so he stood on the front stoop and pleaded, "Please, Mrs. Twedell, I just want to see my kids."

"You should have thought of that before," she said. *Before you slept with that other woman,* was implied.

"My God! Don't you Twedell women have any room for forgiveness? What the hell do you want me to do?"

Joab thought he detected a slight softening. "Look, Joab, she made me swear I won't tell. I just can't. You know how she is."

"They're my kids, too, damn it!" He shouted, breaking a promise to himself.

Miss Lucy's face turned to stone again. "I think you'd better leave 'fore I call the po-leeze."

Joab spent the afternoon sitting in the home of his childhood. Ultimately, he concluded that he couldn't stay without his girls. He just wanted to be away from here. The plan was to go back to Durham and try to make a little money before senior year cranked up. Just before his mother got home, Joab finished giving Lesa an update by phone. She had insisted he go ahead and use the apartment for the summer. Ruth was greatly disappointed at the news of his departure, but she understood.

Although Joab would never know it, that day, Ruth instituted a weekly day of prayer and fasting. Each week, from sunset Tuesday evening to sunset Wednesday, Ruth would abstain from all food and drink, save water, and rise early to intercede on behalf of her son's marriage and his children.

Once on his bike, Joab decided to head west on I-16.

He didn't really know what he was going to do once he got to Atlanta. But if Nicholas was still there, he couldn't think where else Anita might have run. When he got within the city limits, he pulled his bike into a convenience store with a phone booth outside. As Charlie had indicated, there was no listing for a "Nicholas" or "N. Twedell." He looked for Anita's name and was not surprised to find it absent. There were two "A. Johnsons." He ripped out the page deciding it wouldn't hurt to try later. Then he looked up "Minks."

Joab had remembered, on a particularly boring stretch of I-16, that it was Jojo Minks who had talked Nicholas into the move to Atlanta. Joab recalled with disdain, Nicholas bragging on how Jojo was gonna get him this "excellent" job as a bouncer at some big club and how Nicholas was gonna find him a rich girlfriend—Nope, no "J" or "Jojo" or "Joseph Minks." *Scummy drug addicts like Jojo never get legitimate enough to have a phone listing*, Joab thought. *They mostly prefer to sleep uninterrupted during the hours of sunlight, only emerging at night to scavenge for their next 24 hours worth of subsistence.*

Finally, Joab found a Motel-6 and decided to pull in to wait for nightfall. He spent part of the hundred his mother had slipped him for a ground floor room. He put a towel down on the floor and walked his bike right in. Based on his experience in Savannah, Joab knew how quickly big things can disappear in a city, and how incapable the authorities can be at finding them. And some parts of Atlanta had a far rougher reputation than little, old Savannah. Being so far from his destination, Joab was taking no chances with his transportation. If anyone noticed, they didn't care enough to report him to the desk.

Next, Joab left a message on Ruth's answering machine as to his whereabouts, hung the *do-not-disturb* sign on his doorknob and crossed the street to a Huddle House where he enjoyed a giant, greasy lunch and a milkshake. When he returned to his room he tried the two "A. Johnsons" to no avail. At last, he settled in for a long nap before his search continued nocturnally.

The clock read 9:42 when Joab awoke. He brushed his teeth, washed his face and went to the front desk for some directions to the "Hotlanta" nightlife.

"Out for some adventure, tonight, huh?" The guy at the desk asked. He was an average looking white male with about ten years on Joab. "Atlanta's got all the fun and all the trouble one man can stand in one night, but you better have some cash; the cover charges can be pretty steep these days." he continued. He reached over to a tourist brochure rack and pulled one with a map. "I remember when you could have a hell of a time in this town for thirty bucks. Damn business conventions drove the price of a drink out of sight."

Joab didn't care much to commiserate; he just wanted to find a bouncer. But he did appreciate the fact that this guy knew most every watering hole in the city. Joab studied the map and took notes for twenty minutes.

"You know any places where the brothers hang?" Joab asked when the guy's knowledge seemed to be exhausted.

"No, man, I used to go to one when I was in high school, but that was when I was immortal. I got a wife now and a kid on the way. She don't let me tempt fate much anymore."

"I know what you're sayin', man." Joab empathized. The man noticed the ring on Joab's left hand for the first time.

"Where ya from?" he asked.

"Durham, North Carolina."

The guy gave Joab a sly smile. "Well, drink one for me and have yourself a real good time. Check out's not till eleven."

Joab's first three or four stops were at huge dance clubs. The vast majority of clientele were white, but the places were not altogether without African-American representation. The guy hadn't been kidding about the cover charges. The first couple of times, Joab just waited in line until he was close enough to get a look at the men keeping the door. Joab was shocked to find that lines had formed halfway around the block. They moved very slowly, and the people waiting seemed to accept this as part of the experience. Apparently, the hot clubs all had long lines and who wanted to go to one which had fallen out of favor? Sober and alone, Joab had a hard time getting caught up in the social aspects of the line. At one place he watched as a white limousine pulled up and a party of six emerged (one being a very striking black girl) and walked casually to the front of the line where, without explanation, they cut in front of the next party and were allowed right in. Joab could still be surprised at what money could buy. Apparently, he was the only one pissed-off about it.

Finally at the door and unwilling to meet the price of a peek inside, Joab asked if anyone knew a brother by the name of Nicholas who was supposed to work here.

The response was always "no" followed by an impatient "are you coming in or not?"

When the cover got under ten bucks, Joab decided to go in. He paid the bouncer, flashed his driver's license with a cool confidence, and proceeded down into the expansive basement of a seven story office building. The sound system, which had been causing rhythmic quakes under the sidewalk outside, now sent its steady beat pounding in his chest like some unifying pulse from an entity greater than the individual heart. The interior was large, sparse, and futuristic. Joab found the lighting of interest; it was excessively dim and patchy except over the dance floor where a series of theatrical fixtures, programmed to shift and flash to the music, hung from a grid. Animated by the single mind of a computer, the synchronized robotics of the fixtures were a show in themselves. Joab parted with four dollars for a beer and found a seat at the bar.

Suddenly a woman appeared before him. She had thin red lips, bobbed black hair, a short, black dress, black strappy shoes with chunky heels, and thick, black eyeliner. All contrasted with pale white skin that nearly glowed in the dark. In spite of her creature-of-the-night fashion statement, and a medium sized, indistinguishable tattoo on her left shoulder, she was not unattractive.

"Dance with me," she said.

Joab gulped half of his four-dollar beer, in fear that, once abandoned, he would never find it again, and followed her to the dance floor where they waded into the low mist of dry ice. She turned out to have a fairly erotic style which Joab found pleasant enough.

"Come back to our table," she said when the DJ mixed in a fifth song.

Joab followed.

"I'm here with some friends but they must be dancing," she shouted as she slid into a dark booth surrounding an aluminum covered table. "What's your name?"

"Joab."

"Oh," she said, though she wasn't sure she heard it right. It sounded like Joe or Bob or something. She nodded, staring at the dancers for a while.

"You from Atlanta?"

"No. Savannah."

"Oh. I always go to St. Patrick's Day on River Street."

"Yeah?"

"Yeah."

"It's a great party . . . . on River Street."

"Gets bigger every year." True enough, but Joab had grown bored with the peculiar Irish festivities by his second year of high school.

"'Ja like a bump?"

Joab wondered, for a second, if she was propositioning him. "'xcuse me?"

She put a finger to her nose, closing off one nostril. Then she lifted a fist to the other and did a quick intake of air.

"Bullet," she said, reaching under the table to place a small vial with a rounded plastic cap in the palm of his hand.

"Uh, thanks, but I'm really looking for somebody." Disappointment made itself obvious on her face. He found her hand and replaced the vial. She sniffled.

"Oh."

"My brother." Joab's omission of the 'in-law' part made his statement a Clinton truth at best. But it was still the truth—mostly.

"Oh." She brightened to find he wasn't waiting on a woman. "Was he supposed to meet you here?"

"No," he shouted close to her ear, "I couldn't reach him to tell him I was coming. He's supposed to work in one of these clubs. His name is Nicholas. Nicholas Twedell."

"Nicholas Twedell?" She repeated.

"Yeah. Kind of a big guy—big."

"Nope. I don't know any big Nicholases."

Joab looked at his watch. It was pushing 1:00 already. He thought about Cinda. Part of him was close to despair. *I'll never find that big son of a bitch in this damned town! And what if I did? What's he gonna do? Give me a high five and drop me off at Anita's for a nice scrambled eggs and grits? What am I doing here?* He thought.

During his years at St. Paul's, Joab had been to Atlanta twice for Conference Basketball Championships. He found most folks from Atlanta had an attitude about their city. He considered it greatly inflated for a town that couldn't even handle its traffic. He looked at... at... ???

"What's your name?"

"Mary." A thin smile and more nodding.

I could probably bed this willing waif and at least salvage the trip as something more than a total waste of time, he thought, though he half suspected she'd need to be back in her coffin well before the sun came up. He wondered if he still had those two condoms out in the bags of his bike. He wondered if, outside, he still *had* his bike.

"I gotta go," he said.

"Are you sure?" she asked with a coy tilt of her head and an attempt at pouty lips.

Now, Joab was fairly certain that he could bed her, although, he conjectured, like a long basketball shot, you never really knew until you were through the hoop.

"Yeah," he repeated. "I gotta go."

Joab decided he didn't have enough time for any more lines or ladies or enough money for any more beers. After that, he went straight to the door to ask about his brother-in-law. Towards the end of his list, he made some inquiries and worked his way down to a couple of dives. No Nicholas. No leads. No luck.

The sun was rising as he walked his bike into his motel room. He slept until around 10:30, brushed his teeth, washed his face, (to hell with the shower until he got back), turned in his key card, and headed northeast on I-85. It was a long, rigorous drive, especially after so little sleep. Round about Charlotte, when he hit the two lane part of the trip, Joab became thankful that Atlanta hadn't afforded him more than one beer. It was approaching dusk, and he was exhausted when his key turned in Lesa's lock. Without her in it, Lesa's bed had never felt better.

Joab looked up an old employer and was hired, on the spot for $9.50 an hour doing construction. He enjoyed the work. Failing to possess that exceptional spark which would have enabled him to play college ball, Joab missed the physical discipline and challenge of sports. Working outside with his hands and the strength of his young back enabled him to sweat out some of his rage at Anita so he could sleep.

Most of the men on his work crew were decent enough sorts who didn't mind hard work so long as it earned them enough money to support an official or common-law woman, a couple of kids or a fast car, a weekend pot habit, and an endless river of Budweiser. Summer by summer, they'd seen college boys come, and they'd seen 'em go. After graduation, not one of them ever came back. This bred a grain of resentment that grew with the passing of years. It could be held in check, however, if a kid took the job seriously and could be trusted not to make the rest of them look bad by screwing something up. Joab was just such a kid. He soon proved himself as a quick study and a hard worker. This made everybody's job easier and afforded Joab great blocks of time without supervision or interruption. He was refreshed for the long hours his body carried the load, freeing his mind to take a vacation – when it wasn't seething over Anita. So the summer passed.

Before long, Joab was greeting Lesa at the airport and they were immersed in the intellectual calisthenics of their senior year. Lesa had convinced Joab not to keep a dorm room, but only upon his insistence that he pay Alyson's portion of the rent. The school rehired him to work in the library, part time. Thus terms were set and met and life for the couple looked like it might fall into a pleasurable routine.

Chapter 18

Just after classes had resumed for Joab and Lesa's senior year, Mr. Shemisaki flew into Charlotte for a business meeting. When his dealings were concluded, he chartered a small plane and flew to Durham for dinner with his daughter. Both she and Joab met him at the airport.

"Am I supposed to bow or something?" Joab whispered, in a panic, as they walked toward the diminutive, black-haired man.

Lesa laughed. "I think a hand-shake will do," she whispered back.

While Lesa had made her parents aware of her cohabitation, she had not mentioned Joab's ethnic heritage. Joab was much darker than Mr. Shemisaki had expected and, in truth, Mr. Shemisaki was much shorter than Joab had expected (standing barely as tall as his daughter). It was obvious where Lesa had gotten her thin frame. A well-concealed shock of apprehension went through the older man's body as he pictured African genes mixing into his grandchildren.

Now, Jules, he reprimanded himself silently, *there was a time when Japanese genes weren't considered much more desirable.*

Having succeeded in wrapping her father around her finger by the age of three, his thoughts were almost audible to Lesa. She knew he would soon come around to his normal response of *whatever makes her happy.*

Invisible to the outsider's eye, Joab was oblivious to all of these goings on and just assumed that Mr. Shemisaki had been told of his color long ago. Lesa had briefed Joab, however, not to mention his marriage or his children to her father. That information was on a need-to-know basis and her father really *didn't* need to know.

As one might expect, Lesa chose one of the three finest restaurants in the Raleigh/Durham area. The atmosphere was formal yet intimate. After ordering, Jules Shemisaki started his cordial interrogation. He broke the ice with a brief summary of his wife's health and a few moments of note-worthy information on friends and family followed by an apology for indulging in conversation which left Joab rather out of the loop.

"And what do you call your hometown, Joab?" He asked, though he clearly remembered it as being Savannah. Jules smiled and nodded congenially through Joab's responses, adding his own comments from time to time, and asking ever more personal questions until striking upon ones which elicited more passionate responses. Then he would casually dine, eyes sparkling through thin slits and ears listening intently to each word.

In his nervousness, Joab had to guard himself against babbling. Lesa, well aware of her father's tactics, was pleased to discover that Joab rarely needed bailing out. Still, she listened vigilantly, counting the refills in his wine glass. Using sign language, Lesa cut him off at three glasses, which, in spite of her best efforts, did not escape her father's notice.

By the time Joab stood to help Lesa with her chair, (a gesture counter to her feminist leanings but which scored big with her dad) Jules felt like he had a pretty good handle on what made the boy tick.

Obviously disadvantaged by upper class standards, Joab's mother deserves credit for making private schools a priority. Not much social polish, but he has basic manners and an appealing graciousness in his adherence to Southeastern conventions of respect, most notably the use of, "ma'am" and "sir"... and treating women like ladies.

This, too, he counted to Ruth's credit.

...The boy's not afraid to look another man in the eye and seems to carry only a small chip on his shoulder for his race. Though tall, he neither apologizes for his size nor uses it to intimidate, but will likely carry himself with the posture

developed as a high school athlete, until old age rounds his shoulders... Doubtless, his straight teeth are a direct gift of fate, Juels mused, remembering how costly Lesa's flawless bite had been. His eyes became crescents when they shifted toward her. *Worth every penny, too.*

... Clearly, the young man's passion and his college education are parallel rails of the same track; political science and history, in that order. This explains Lesa's attraction to him. He chuckled inwardly as he remembered his only child setting her course for politics when barely an adolescent. *Her combination of intellect, savvy, and beauty will open many doors of power,* he conjectured with pride. *And if she ever finds one locked, I'll make sure I know where to find the keys. Whatever makes her happy.*

On the way to Lesa's car, Joab was relieved when Mr. Shemisaki inquired as to hotels.

"But, Dad, there's still a double bed in Alyson's old room. You're *not* going to stay in a hotel." She protested. Joab bumped her with his elbow. Lesa ignored him and continued. "If we're lucky, Joab, I'll be able to talk Dad into omelets in the morning. My father makes the best omelets on the face of the earth."

Omelets! Joab didn't want omelets with this man! And certainly not after just having slept with his precious daughter – without benefit of marriage – under the roof he was (mostly) paying for.

"Maybe your father needs some rest after his long trip. He might not want to be disturbed early in the morning." Joab suggested hopefully.

"You don't know Daddy," Lesa jumped in, "He'll be up at 5:30, drinking a cup of decaf and pacing the floor until the paper comes."

"Okay, Lesa," her father relented, "I'll stay at the apartment. But let's stop at a grocery store on the way home. I'll need the proper ingredients if I'm to retain my reputation for omelets."

Once in bed, Joab was a bit surprised to find Lesa in an exceptionally amorous mood.

"Stop that!" He whispered, "Your father is in the next room!"

"So? Joab, he knows we do it."

"Well, you know how this bed squeaks. He doesn't have to know we *are* doing it."

"Joab! You're being ridiculous."

"Fine. Then I'm ridiculous. But I'm not going to stick it to his daughter while he's under the same roof."

At this point, Lesa rolled over, sulking, and went to sleep. Joab knew she would be grouchy most of the next day. If so, that would just have to be the price he paid.

Joab lay awake staring at the ceiling and wondering if his percentage of the rent was enough to cover the square footage of Lesa's bedroom.

Down the hall in the other bedroom, Mr. Shemisaki checked in with Mrs. Shemisaki, clicked off the light and lay staring at the ceiling in the dark. .

Maybe I can pull some strings and bring the boy along, he conjectured, his mind spinning. *Black politicians are at no disadvantage these days. Our party will nominate an African-American for president in the foreseeable future. If Clinton can pull off a second term, I'll be the only insider against the nomination of the endlessly boring Al Gore. I'll place my bets on Amos Webster...*

Mr. Shemisaki owned the dominant newspaper in the Hawaiian Islands and he well understood its influence. He had, in fact, seen Governor Webster rising, four years earlier, and had made it a point to become a close, personal friend.

... If Lesa were ever to marry Joab and still expect a career in politics, she would be well served to know what kind of instincts the boy has for the acquisition of power, he speculated. *An inter-racial marriage, during the first African-American presidency, could prove quite advantageous. And a similar genetic mix produced Tiger Woods, after all.*

Mr. Shemisaki drifted off to dreams of gifted grandsons playing golf. By the time the newspaper arrived on Lesa's doorstep, Jules had formulated a plan.

✦ ✦ ✦

A few days after his departure, Joab and Lesa got a call from a school secretary. One of the tenured professors in the Poly-Sci department wanted to see them, together. Both Joab and Lesa had taken classes under Glenda Blackwell. She was known on campus and off as a militant feminist and she had earned her reputation. Lesa thought she was brilliant and was awed by the woman's ability to take charge and be heard. What Lesa didn't understand, and what Joab couldn't articulate, was that all the men in her path deferred to her authority out of a single motivation—fear. Her every gesture sent out one message: Cross me and find out what it's like to defend a sexual harassment lawsuit. Guilty or innocent, few professors could remain employed with such institution-damaging litigation pending. Blackwell knew it, and Blackwell used it. Not many of her male co-workers weren't visibly nervous in her presence.

"Have a seat," she commanded when the students entered her office. They obeyed.

"I guess you're wondering why you're here."

Lesa and Joab exchanged eye contact and nodded.

"Well, it's quite simple, really; a friend of mine is running for a hotly contested state senate seat. She's running against a Republican who is clearly beatable, but she has asked me if I knew any students who might benefit from volunteering a few hours a week for her campaign. This is a fine opportunity to see how political theory plays out in the real world *and* it would be an invaluable experience. Of course, the two of you came to mind right away. However, I do understand how limited your time is, so I got permission from the Dean to let me treat the job like a practicum and offer you two credits each, should you decide to take it."

Lesa looked at Joab and beamed. Joab was a little more reserved. He could hear his mother's voice, "Anything that seems to be too good to be true, is."

"What exactly would be involved in this job?" Joab inquired.

Ms. Blackwell was mildly exasperated at the question. She had declared this a sweet plumb of an opportunity and that should have been enough.

"You can expect to hand out candidate information and issues flyers, man phone banks, post signs, set-up for public forums, etc. Also, you will be permitted to listen in on strategy sessions. I have asked that you get as much exposure to the process as possible. But I will need you to make your decision now." Blackwell continued. "We're already a week into the semester and if I'm going to offer this opportunity to anyone else, I need to get going."

The fact was, this opportunity would not be offered to anyone else. It had been tailored specifically for Lesa and Joab. Though the dean had not said it in so many words, Ms. Blackwell was no newcomer to the world of politics or higher education. You didn't need a doctorate in social engineering to see that someone wanted a political Head Start Program for his or her child. Joab's background suggested that his parents wouldn't have enough pull to get a parking ticket fixed. The Shemisaki's, however, were obviously a different story.

"There won't be a conflict with our other classes?" Joab asked.

"Of course not," Ms. Blackwell responded. "Most of the time required will be late afternoon or evening."

Joab got a knot in his stomach as he realized that a choice had to be made between *this opportunity* and his job. He had managed to save up a few months' rent over the summer.

"Great! We'd love to do it." Lesa announced.

"Good. It's settled then. I think you'll find the experience enlightening and fun. It's very exciting, actually, in an understated kind of way."

Ms. Blackwell scribbled a name and phone number on a piece of paper and handed it to Lesa as if Joab were invisible. Her name is Liz Straddlethorp. She'll be expecting a call tonight so you can get started."

Lesa rose and shook her hand enthusiastically. "Thank you very much, Ms. Blackwell," she said.

Instinctively avoiding physical contact, Joab just nodded in agreement and mumbled his own thank you, as he reached for the doorknob.

"Wow. What an opportunity!" Lesa enthused as they stepped out of the air conditioned building into the balmy air of the late summer afternoon. "I've never worked on a campaign before. 'Course Daddy and I have always stayed up together to watch election results come in."

"Really!? I remember going to the polls to vote with my mom when I was a kid, but I don't think she cared much about who won or who lost."

"Hmm, I'm surprised to hear she voted at all. I'd have thought hers was the generation that understood religion and politics don't mix. The damn Christian extremists have made it so tough to get anything good accomplished anymore. How somebody can profess feeding the poor out of one side of their mouth, and advocate the cutting of social programs out of the other side of their mouth, is hypocrisy beyond my comprehension! I guess that's our challenge! This is going to be great fun."

Joab had never heard Lesa come so close to cursing his mother before. He actually didn't know which party Ruth Johnson belonged to, but he thought it unfair for Lesa to assume that she voted Republican just because she was a Christian. And he knew the woman too well to think the word hypocrite could apply to her character. He made a mental note to discuss these things with his mother the next time they were face to face.

Lesa didn't know where she had lost Joab. "Don't you think this is going to be fun?"

"Oh, yeah. Yeah, I'm looking forward to it," he said.

And it did turn out to be fun, although it was a lot of work. Along with their regular course load, Joab and Lesa spent four or five evenings a week setting up for and/or attending meetings, posting signs all over town, calling lists upon lists of people to elicit support, and performing every form of "gofer-type" responsibility, including preparing and serving coffee.

Joab did regret the necessity of giving up his job. Life with Lesa included frequent restaurant dining and the consumption of above-average wine. While the meals were a great pleasure, Joab could never get quite comfortable with his inability to pick up even one check. As the months passed, Joab had the growing feeling that he was being kept, and one thin rent check was not much of a barricade against such an impression.

On the campaign trail, it wasn't long before State Senate candidate Straddlethorp sniffed out Joab's extraordinary gift for correctly remembering names and faces and determined to keep him close at hand in social situations. Lesa's cordial smile and gracious manner were exploited at the information table where she handed out buttons, bumper stickers, and flyers and took in campaign donations. A portion of the checks carried the signatures of men who considered a brief conversation with the charming young woman well worth the price of a modest contribution.

Before long, Joab and Lesa had Liz' issue positions and speech memorized better than Liz herself. But Liz, with almost vaudevillian flair, knew how to work a crowd.

"And folks," she would say, "let's be honest. There are plenty of places in our budget where we can cut wasteful spending, but NOT AT THE EXPENSE OF OUR POOREST CITIZENS (pause for audience response). THAT'S where I draw the line, and THAT'S where most good Americans draw the line, too. (Pause for applause). And you know I'll work hard to bring industry into our district, to promote our economic growth and cultivate well-paying jobs, but NOT AT THE EXPENSE OF OUR ENVIRONMENT AND THE HEALTH OF OUR CHILDREN! (pause for applause, shift to soft sensitive tone) Because that's why we're really here tonight, isn't it? For our children? To protect their future. That's why *I'm* here. Because I want their future to be bright with hope and promise. (Building to forceful conviction) But I'll tell you right now; this is NOT the time to abandon public education. We have invested too many hard-earned tax dollars in our educational system and there's a lot about it that works and works well. (stone silence) Of course, our educational successes don't get much press these days. Now, I'm not denying that we've got problems—and BIG problems, but unlike my opponent, I say, FIX WHAT'S BROKEN AND HANG ON TO THE REST!! I'M NOT GONNA FALL VICTIM TO A RIGHT WING EXTREMIST PLOY TO GET ME TO PAY FOR THEIR KIDS TO GO TO CHRISTIAN SCHOOLS! (pause for applause) Did anybody ever hear of the separation of church and state? Hello? (pause for applause) And I'll tell you something else . . .

✦ ✦ ✦

(The and-I'll-tell-you-something-else part is where Joab found himself continually squirming.) *Somewhere, his Cinda walked the earth because Anita had chosen life, and the earth was a better place for it. Big Mama had stood firmly against abortion. Then, too, Joab still blamed abortion for the life-long absence of brothers or sisters. You've just got to take the good with the bad,* Joab ultimately concluded. *Neither party gets it all right. And the Democratic Party happens to be the party of reproductive rights, plain and simple.*

✦ ✦ ✦

. . . I've got a daughter in junior high, and God forbid she should get pregnant; I want to make sure she's got options. NO RELIGIOUS EXTREMIST IS GOING TO TELL ME OR MY DAUGHTER WHAT TO DO WITH OUR OWN BODIES! (pause for wild applause) It's a fact that most Americans believe that this is a decision between a woman, her doctor, her God AND NOBODY ELSE. (pause for very wild applause) And what's the first thing the Republicans did when they took the House and the Senate? PUSH FOR A BAN ON PARTIAL BIRTH ABORTION AND FORCE SOME WOMEN TO DELIVER UNDER LIFE-THREATENING CIRCUMSTANCES! (at this point, some booing generally occurred) and, folks, this is only the first step. You know they won't be happy until they've pushed choice back into the back alley. My job, as your senator, will be to protect your rights and honor the will of my constituents and THAT'S JUST WHAT I'LL DO! YOU HAVE MY WORD! (pause for more wild applause) So, I hope you'll vote for me, Liz Straddlethorp, in November. Thank you very much.

◆ ◆ ◆

What Joab and Lesa considered the coolest thing about the whole deal, though, were strategy planning sessions. Before the college students were admitted to attend, Liz, herself, had given them a strict confidentiality briefing. It had been short and to the point, "Everything mentioned in these meetings is to be considered secret and is not to be discussed with anyone outside of you. Leaks will not be tolerated. Clear?"

Joab and Lesa had nodded like small children being cautioned by a stern mother. Strategy planning sessions were held once a week, generally in the home of a well-to-do core supporter whose grand house impressed the shoes off Joab, but which Lesa took for granted. They were always attended by about a dozen committed and connected Democrats from the community. Occasionally, they got input from a player from state headquarters, and several times from the DNC. The core people were considered power citizens who had their fingers on the pulse of various levels of local society. Most of them belonged to one of the more liberal-leaning churches. To everyone's considerable frustration, Catholic and evangelical churches had seemed to close ranks in recent election cycles and had proven almost impenetrable since.

Another cause for nervousness was the small but steady trickle of traditionally liberal blacks and Hispanics joining the Republican Party. One or two were even running for office! Wider polling statistics indicated the same trend all across Dixie and was generally attributed to the thin but tightening Bible belt. So far, social pressure had kept the numbers in check. Titles like "Uncle Tom" and "Judas" were resurrected to label such traitors. Ironically and inexplicably, many such traitors and their families often sat stiff-backed in the pews while preachers who had baptized them railed against them from pulpits.

On the choice-vs-life front, the gruesome details of the procedure known as Partial Birth Abortion had many formerly pro-choice voters suddenly leaning toward life. Promotion of the fear of the total repeal of *Roe v Wade*, while largely unfounded, was considered the way to go by most political handlers.

Everyone was responsible for clipping out any newspaper articles mentioning Liz or relating to her issues. Strengths and weaknesses were discussed, though it was a well-known fact that the chain which owned *The Atlanta Chronicle* was, in fact, owned by a multi-billionaire whose socialistic views were advanced between each line. Almost all conservative spin was reserved for a small corner of the opinion editorial page. Even letters to the editor were "modified due to the confines of space," and few pro-conservative views ever got printed before first getting their teeth pulled, a fact generally unknown to the public. Still, a peanut had to be thrown to the elephants from time to time, and in politics, nothing could be assumed.

Around dining room tables designed for large dinner parties, Straddlethorp's advisors cautioned: "Try not to alienate business too much, but be sure to maintain environmental concerns as a Democratic issue," Liz's campaign manager cautioned at the last meeting.

Another advisor jumped in, "Stay pro-gun control but avoid the issue if at all possible. You know how rednecks love their shotguns. If it's unavoidable, use the death of little Jimmy Swanson as the basis for your position—."

"A picture of you at the funeral is due to run in the paper tomorrow," the press person inserted.

"-- South Carolina's crime numbers, since they passed that concealed weapon legislation, are hard to argue with. So DO NOT be sucked into a battle on statistics. This issue is only winnable if framed in terms of personal human cost."

"You're doing great on balancing taxes with public security issues," another encouraged.

None of this was wasted on Joab or Lesa. It was very heady to know things before they happened and to manipulate how they happened. It was like a great gambling game in which both sides were permitted (even expected!) to hedge as much as possible.

Lesa, in particular, found the experience exciting almost to the point of eroticism. Climax came on November third. Joab and Lesa had been drafted to take a poll managing course and had spent all of Election Day at their precinct poll. Once the precious voting boxes were on their way to county headquarters, the couple went home, indulged in a quicky, showered and headed for Liz's house to watch the results come in with "the core".

Liz, single mother of one, had made her small fortune in real estate and owned a lovely home in the most elite section of Durham. There was an open bar and a pervasive attitude that all had been done and there was nothing left but to enjoy their box seats and watch the race. Liz had two TVs stacked in a large family room so as to view national and local results at the same time. Ms. Straddlethorp's closest allies sat on her sofa sipping twenty-year-old scotches and very dry martinis. The men loosened their ties and unbuttoned their collar while the women kicked off their shoes. Sinking ever deeper in the cushions they discussed opinions on national races, sharing Straddlethorp campaign reminiscences and inside jokes, and hoping to pop the cork on champagne. Whenever Liz's district was mentioned, or the phone rang, a cry of "Sh-sh-sh!!!" hissed through the room until, in silence, all ears strained for the latest information.

By 11:00 p.m., it was clear that this was going to be a close race and a long night. About half the people and most of the press cleared out. Liz finally sat down, kicked off her heels and put her feet up on her coffee table as her 14-year-old daughter snuck a third round of beers from the bar for herself and her best friend who was waiting, up in her room. By quarter after one, eighty-five percent of the precinct ballots had been counted, and Straddlethorp was declared the winner. A cheer went up in the Straddlethorp family room, backs were patted, and the corks were popped at last. It was an exhilarating moment.

As Joab and Lesa departed, Liz shook their hands at the front door and reiterated what a fine job they had done. She would be sending along an in-depth evaluation to her friend Ms. Blackwell, within the week, and it would be a bright one.

"Oh, we enjoyed it, and we learned *so* much. Thank you for making the opportunity available to us!" Lesa said with a warm smile.

"And Mr. Johnson," Liz said, turning to him, "how in the hell do you remember all those names!?"

Joab shrugged his shoulders, embarrassed.

"Well, be sure to keep them all filed for the next six years, and I'll be looking you up."

"Congratulations again, Ms. Straddlethorp, and thank you," he said.

"Thank you both."

That night, Lesa's tendencies towards politics escalated into addiction. She babbled excitedly all the way home as Joab just smiled and nodded with charmed amusement. On the way up the stairs from the garage, clothes started peeling. Joab carried his laughing lover up the last two steps and threw her, giggling, on the sofa where they fooled around playfully for the better part of an hour. When she was still spouting political hoopla at 4:30 a.m., Joab knew what he had to do. He picked up the lean length of her naked body and carried her into the bedroom where, after about fifteen minutes, Lesa finally relaxed into slumber. Joab's last impression of Election Day, just as the sun was lightening another morning, was a sudden realization that tomorrow—today was Wednesday - class in 3 short hours.

About the time Joab closed his eyes, down in Savannah, Ruth pressed the headlight button of her new Buick LaSabre, backed out from under her carport, and began making her way to I-16.

"Praise you, Jesus," she spoke out loud as lavender-pink clouds rippled across a paling sky and reflected on strands of tidal water twisting through the golden marsh. A Great Blue Heron, aptly named, lifted gracefully on wide wings that pushed the earth away in natural slow-motion.

"Glory!" she uttered under her breath, ever astonished at the endless artistry conceived in the inexhaustible imagination of Jesus, Creator God. A few moments after her tires rolled onto the smooth pavement of the Interstate, Ruth began praying in a language she did not understand, but was sure could move mountains. She considered this day to be the result of many such hours of prayer. For it to be successful, a whole lot more prayer would be necessary.

By midday, her heart was sinking as she made her way down the narrow, pitted streets of an old and neglected section of Atlanta, searching for an address, and hoping she was lost. A group of boys in oversized clothes, topped by matching purple bandannas worn tied over their closely-shaven heads, watched her shiny, golden car pass by with undisguised greed and resentment. She was glad for the car phone, the automatic locks, the tint on the windows that hid the fear on her face, and the latest automotive security system. There it was number 2773. Ruth found a space across the street, parallel parked, and pressed the security button on her keychain, noting with satisfaction the soft hiccup which indicated that the doors were locked and the alarm engaged. The boys began migrating in her direction as she knocked on the door.

Ruth heard a succession of sliding deadbolts and then Anita was standing in the doorway. "Hey, Mom," Anita said awkwardly, not knowing what else to call her. Ruth gave the younger woman a warm embrace and kissed her on the cheek.

"You look fine, Anita," she said.

At the sound of Ruth's voice a cry rang out, "Grandmama's here! Grandmama's here!" Anita stepped back as Cinda ran at her grandmother. Ruth scooped up the child and gave her a long, delicious hug.

"Where's your baby sister?" Ruth asked, at last putting Cinda down.

"C'mon in," Anita invited. Ruth was pleasantly surprised to discover that the inside of the house was in much better repair than the outside. The place was clean, well-kept and equipped with a state-of-the-art entertainment system. Mandy was walking around the edges of a playpen in the center of the living room. Anita smiled as Ruth lifted the youngest grandchild to fuss over her.

"Great day! Look how big she's gotten!" Ruth said.

"One year next month. Can you believe it?"

"It doesn't seem possible."

"Sit down, Mom. Can I get you a cup of tea?"

"In a minute. I've got a few things in the car for the children."

"Oh. Put Mandy back in the playpen, and I'll help you in with it."

The boys, now standing around at the other end of the block, stared as the two women crossed the street. Anita stared back.

"Is this a safe neighborhood?" Ruth asked, popping the trunk from her keychain.

"They won't mess with you," Anita assured. "They don't want to face Nicholas. Ooo, you got a new car! It's beautiful."

"Thank you," Ruth answered, handing Anita a bag full of gift boxes and slamming the trunk. "The best part of the car is the keychain." Anita liked the leather seats and the new car smell.

Once in the house, Cinda jumped up and down with excitement until Ruth handed her a box. She made short work of the paper and swooned over her latest adopted daughter. Three more little packages, all brightly wrapped, contained two changes of clothing and more plastic baby bottles. Ruth held little Amanda Nicole and helped her open her gift: a farm animal book that made farm animal sounds. Mandy liked the wrapping paper best. Next, Ruth pulled a foil-wrapped offering from her bag of goodies.

"Oh, Anita, I almost forgot. I made you a little pound cake."

Anita smiled warmly at her mother-in-law. She hadn't known what to expect of this visit. She had spent the last two days dreading it as her mind replayed her own harsh words and her often irrational behavior of the past year. But what Ruth seemed to have chosen to remember was simply that her daughter-in-law loved Big Mama's sour cream pound cake. Accepting it, Anita headed for the kitchen.

"I'll put on the water for tea," she called back over her shoulder.

When she returned to the living room, she found a box sitting on her chair.

"Oh, Mom, what did you do?" She asked, placing the box on her lap and sliding a finger under the paper. In a moment, she lifted a lovely, red dress from the box. She stood and held it to her body. It had been a long, long time since anyone had bought her an impractical gift and much longer since she had been able to afford a new dress.

"Oh, it's so pretty!" she almost squealed.

"Well, go try it on, child," Ruth insisted.

The dress was stunning on Anita. It was made of a finely woven wool fabric that had weight and movement but was not coarse. It was fully lined and had padded shoulders, a slightly scooped neck and was tailored to the waist and flared to the ankle. It gave Anita's long frame a classic beauty. In the living room, Anita spun once, and Ruth handed her a matching red hat with a wide black band and a wide black belt. Now Anita *did* squeal.

"All you have to do is pick up a pair of black heels and you should be set for the holiday season," Ruth suggested, well-pleased with her surprises.

"Oh, Mom . . .," Anita started not really knowing what to say. She bent over and gave her a hug.

The teapot began to whistle, and by the time Anita had changed back into her sweater and jeans, Ruth had two cups of tea fixed and two slices of pound cake all set on the kitchen table. Mandy sat in her high chair, carefully picking up the cake crumbs set before her while the two women talked. Cinda declined the snack, wanting to get acquainted with her new baby instead. Subject matter was kept simple and superficial and neither woman dared mention the name, Joab.

When Ruth inquired as to Nickolas, Anita said he had been good to take them in. She said he seemed to have a good job, though she was vague about the details. He did fairly well putting up with kids, but had a girlfriend and spent most nights over at her house. Ruth sensed tension between the women but did not press.

"How many bedrooms does this house have?" Ruth asked.

"Only two," Anita responded, "but the guest room has enough space for each of us to have our own bed and I really sleep better with the girls in the same room at night. After living in Shady Oaks, I guess I'm not used to city sounds. Besides, with bars on the windows, I worry about getting the girls out in case of a fire."

Ruth never could fault Nita on her maternal instincts.

More than once, Anita mentioned looking for a job and getting a place of her own, but Ruth wouldn't count on it until Mandy was in school full time.

Anita also asked for Ruth's opinion on placing Cinda in some kind of part-time K-4 program next year. Ruth thought it would be a fine idea *if* a good program could be found in a safe place.

Later in the afternoon, Ruth spent some time playing on the floor with Cinda and helping care for all her children. She marveled at Mandy's ability to pull herself up on the edge of the coffee table and walk, on straight, plump legs around it.

"She'll be taking her first steps any day," Ruth proclaimed while Anita agreed.

'Long about 4:30, Ruth decided it was time to go.

"We'll walk you out to your car," Anita insisted after Ruth had gathered up her coat and purse.

Nita scooped up Mandy. Cinda crossed the street holding her Grandmama Ruth's index finger. After administering jovial hugs and kisses to the children, Ruth faced her daughter-in-law on the sidewalk.

"Thanks again for my beautiful dress," Anita said.

"You make it beautiful," Ruth answered.

"Thank you for coming."

"It has been a great blessing to be here. Thank you for letting me come." Anita detected no bitterness in Ruth's voice.

There was a wide silence. Mandy pulled at her mother's nose.

"Can I come for a Christmas visit?" Ruth asked, her voice cracking on the last syllable and her eyes suddenly glistening.

"Sure. Of course, Mama will probably be coming up here this year. I'll call you, okay?" All at once Anita saw the depth of this woman's loss and her heart melted. Still, one issue had to be put on the table, "But Joab had better not find out." It was a clear threat.

"You have my word," Ruth responded.

Anita knew Ruth's word didn't bend, and it never broke. "I'll call you next week and we'll pick out a day."

Cinda began skipping down the block.

"Cinda, you c'mon back here," her mother called. Ruth pulled open the car door.

"Uh, I almost forgot," Anita shifted the baby as she pulled at a finger. "Here. I think it's time you have this back," she said, holding out Big Mama's sapphire ring.

Ruth looked down at the ring and shook her head. Her voice dropped almost to a whisper, "That ring became yours the day Lucinda Ruth was born. Nothing can change that. . . . Cinda!" she called, raising her voice, "You skip on over here and give Grandma Ruth one last hug."

Ruth squatted down as the child ran into her arms. In a moment she watched the three crossing the street to their house in her rear view mirror.

"Thank you, Jesus," she said, "thank you, Jesus."

Lesa's parents decided to go on a cruise for the holidays. Joab knew, though it had not been spoken, that his mother would never honor Lesa with a visit. Lesa was well aware of the snubbing and regarded Ruth with a keen resentment. Who was this woman, born to the benevolence of the state, and bearer of a bastard herself, to judge Lesa Shemisaki for the provincial sin of adultery in a society whose mantra had become, tolerance? Lesa credited it to the woman's fundamentalist Christian ethic and never missed an opportunity to poke fun at the obvious simplicity of a mind feeble enough to be taken in by such antiquated superstition.

"Observe tradition. Go on and buy a heavenly fire insurance policy if you must, but a boat filled with creatures in pairs? Really! The earth created in six days? Any thinking person could easily distinguish between probable fact and obvious myth. And what kind of a small mind did it take to believe that *your* way was the *only* way to God?" Lesa often argued.   Ruth's faith became Lesa's only point of entry for a wedge between her lover and his mother.

Had Ruth known, she would have been neither surprised nor perturbed. But night by night, on her knees, Ruth beseeched the God of her mother to resurrect her son's marriage.

As Christmas approached, a heaviness fell upon Joab that neither he nor Lesa had known. In an effort to throw it off, Lesa had gone out and bought a giant blue spruce which filled the house with the crisp scent of pine. Then she picked out silver and white ornaments, covered the tree with tiny white lights, and created a magnificent work of Yuletide art. And though Joab appreciated it in his head, his heart longed for the gaudy warmth of colored lights, tasteless and twinkling in his daughter's delighted eyes. He longed for the Rudolph and Frosty wrapping paper and the Santa Claus secrets. Finally, he talked Lesa into accompanying him on "the pilgrimage."

In awe, Lesa braved parental masses driven like crazed lemmings to toy outlets to leap over the edge of credit limits. The first thing she picked out for Cinda was a beautiful, porcelain doll in traditional African clothing. Joab smiled graciously and placed it back on the shelf. Then he went and found a soft and cuddly baby with her own diapers and bottle and three changes of clothing. He bought a miniature changing table and a child size baby carrier so Cinda could carry her Christmas doll all through the holidays and still enjoy free hands for play.

"These are all so. . . so domestic," Lesa protested, "Maybe she'd like an electric train set or something."

Joab smiled, "She's a very conscientious mother and she's got more children than the old woman who lived in a shoe."

Lesa had to strain her memory to make sense out of Joab's last statement.

"Well, at least throw this in."

Joab accepted into the cart an electronic alphabet game. He knew it would be beyond Cinda yet, but she'd grow into it.

Mandy was next. Joab tried to recall the specifics of Cinda at fourteen months, only to discover what a miserable recording device the human memory can be. How could the details have faded so quickly? He did not *know* his second child, and so he picked out a few things guided only by the age level suggestion printed on the package.

Joab and Lesa wrapped the children's gifts the next day, packed them in a large box, and mailed it down to Miss Lucy with a letter imploring her to deliver it. Lesa's name, of course, was omitted.

Christmas Eve afternoon, when Lesa went to the store for some last-minute provisions, Joab rolled the dial on the stereo until he found something familiar. Joab was aware of his own quirk, but he could not abide contemporary rock during the holidays. There was something far too disingenuous about his militantly rebellious generation scraping the dregs of their feelings to embrace family traditions for one month—or worse, just going on railing against them as usual.

Ah, there it was, the soothing, fatherly notes of a man whose voice kept wrapping its rich warmth around Christmas after Christmas, like an exquisite, golden ribbon from an endless spool. . . . *"Jack Frost nipping at your nose. Tiny tots with their eyes all aglow will find it hard to sleep tonight . . .,"* The voice, like a spirit hand, found the play button of Joab's memory and the ghosts of Christmas Past were released with torturous clarity.

When Lesa returned, she found a note which explained that Joab was out finishing up a little shopping of his own and would not be gone long. At 1:30 a.m. she was still waiting. Finally, lying on the sofa before the soft, white glow of the giant blue spruce, Lesa heard a sound at the front door.

"Joab," she said, rising up on an elbow, "I was beginning to get worried. Where have you been?"

"Just shoppin'." He crossed the room and sat down beside her. "Hey, Lees, how about we have Christmas now?!" he said with the first spark of real enthusiasm she'd seen in days. Lesa's compassion was about spent on this lost-kids thing. *Get over it,* she thought with no small margin of jealousy for the little females who had made her holiday season less than jolly. Had her ear picked up a slight slur on her name?

"Have you been drinking?" she asked.

"A little. What do you say?"

"C'mon, Joab. I say we go to bed and open our presents in the morning when you've sobered up a little."

"I'm sober now," he insisted in a way that clearly indicated he was not. "Ple-e-e-ease?" he begged in a child-like way which she had not seen before. She didn't like it. In fact, she didn't like dealing with drunken men at all. Especially without the benefit of alcohol herself. They were too easy to manipulate, too willing and sloppy in their affection, like a puppy. Lesa reached down inside of herself for some tolerance. After all, this was the first time she'd seen him really drunk.

"Okay," she said, deciding to play, "But only one gift, and I get to give you yours first."

Joab waited while she climbed to the top of her closet for a beautifully wrapped, large, flat box. What he unwrapped was a brand new, state of the art, IBM laptop computer with every conceivable bell and whistle.

"Oh, wow. Lesa, wow. I don't know what to say. It's too much. I mean, do you know what these things cost? Of course you know. You just bought one," he babbled to himself. "Oh, wow. Thank you." He gave her a kiss. Then he pulled a small square box from his pocket. It was covered with plain red paper with a silver bow. Joab beamed and bit his lip while he held it out to her.

Uh-oh, Lesa thought, accepting the gift with hidden reservation. *Yep, there it was.*

"Oh, Joab, it's lovely," she said, viewing the plain little diamond ring winking at her from within the black box.

"Marry me, Lesa?" Joab asked with the puppy dog eyes. "I know it's small," he said, gazing at the quarter karat, "and you deserve a great, big rock on your beautiful hand, but I'll get you one someday, I promise."

"Ah, Joab," Lesa started, "You know how I feel about marriage. I told you from the beginning I wasn't looking for a ring."

"I know. But that seems like so long ago, now . . . Just think about it—and wear the ring while you are. It's my Christmas gift."

Lesa had already made up her mind, but she slipped the ring on anyway.

On the 26th, Joab went back to the jewelry store and had Lesa's little stone set in a pendant to be worn on a chain around her neck. In his sock drawer in Lesa's room, Joab kept the empty ring tucked in its box for the day when Lesa changed her mind.

The following week, UPS returned Cinda and Mandy's Christmas box, unopened.

Chapter 19

About the second week of his second semester, it occurred to Joab that his endless college career was, in fact, coming to an end. There was something surreal about the thought. Months earlier, he and Lesa had discussed going to law school together. Something in Joab's soul recoiled at the idea of three years in Hawaii. Every time he looked at a globe, the islands seemed so small and alone as though the earth itself had pulled away and abandoned a forgotten speck of itself in an inconceivably vast expanse of water. Joab was surprised at the strength of his desire to return to Georgia. Months earlier he had applied to Emory University Law School, his first choice, but Lesa, wishing to waste no time in making the local connections so crucial to a successful political career, would consider no alternative for herself. Finally, he applied to school in Hawaii as well. Still, there was a new tentativeness to Joab and Lesa's relationship, and the larger graduation appeared on the horizon, the less Lesa would be drawn into a conversation about their future.

One morning, Joab awoke to the sound of Lesa vomiting in the bathroom. He knew immediately what was the cause.

"Hey, Lees," he said after she had brushed her teeth and had come back to bed, "can I get you anything?"

"I don't think I'll be able to make it to class today," was her only answer.

All that day, Joab racked his brain to recall the last time Lesa had had her period. He couldn't recall with certainty, but he had a sense that it had been longer than usual. Well, if she *was* pregnant, there was only one thing to do.

"I must have had some kind of flu or something," Lesa said that evening over a dinner she barely touched.

Three days later, she came down with the same flu.

"Maybe, you should take one of those tests," Joab suggested.

"Look, Joab," she answered with a sharp edge, "it's just some kind of a bug, alright?"

That evening in bed, Joab carefully broached the subject again. He snuggled close to Lesa and put his lips close to her ear.

"You know, Lesa, if you are pregnant, it would be just fine with me," he whispered. "You know I want to marry you, and we would make a beautiful baby."

"Oh great words coming from a man! It's not *your* body," Lesa said with a piercing resentment he did not understand. With Anita, this statement would not have found voice as he and his wife had exchanged their bodies as gifts, one to the other, on their wedding day. This made his adultery, in fact, a very literal theft. The depth of his treason seared him afresh, in this most unexpected moment. His mind fumbled in the dark for the right words to help his lover grasp this alien concept.

"I love you, Lesa," failed miserably to communicate the message, but were all the words he could find. He knew Lesa would view a baby as a very real threat to her life's aspirations. Joab tried a different tactic.

"We could still finish law school. People have done it before. A baby would make things a little tougher, but if anyone could handle it, we could, and I know—"

"*We* could? As though *you* would be any help. Great job you're doing with the first two!"

Her sarcasm sliced through the darkness like a razor.

"Thank you very much," she continued, "But I'm NOT pregnant!"

"Then why not take the test?" Joab pressed, though her tone had clearly indicated consequences for pursuit. Still, he knew much was at stake, "Suppose you are?"

"No," came the defiant response. Lesa rose with the comforter wrapped around her long body and left the room.

"Where are you going?" Joab asked.

"I'm sleeping in Alyson's room."

That was Thursday night. Friday morning, the door to Alyson's room was still closed. Joab dared not open it. After class, Lesa stayed gone until 11:30 Friday night. Joab was waiting up in front of the TV when her key turned in the lock.

"Lesa," he said as she entered the living room, "I've been so worried. Are you all right?"

"Just great," she said, not slowing down on her path to her bedroom, "I'm very tired. I'm going to bed."

Well, at least she was going to the right room, Joab thought. He decided to keep the TV on until she got settled in, then he would slip in beside her and just hold her. Perhaps she would find that more comforting than words. In a moment, Joab heard a floorboard squeak behind the sofa. He turned in time to see Lesa's form, illuminated only by the blue/green light of the TV screen, pass like a lovely phantom into Alyson's room. The door closed silently behind her.

The door was still closed when Joab arose the following morning. It was still closed at 10:00 when Joab decided this had gone on long enough and knocked. No answer. Joab's heart skipped twice as he turned the knob, half expecting it to be locked. Alyson's bed was unmade but Lesa was not in it.

Late afternoon, Lesa appeared holding a bag from the drugstore. Joab rose from his books to greet her. He had been reading for two hours and could not have told her the first thing about the subject of his study.

"Hey," he said.

"Hey." Lesa looked white and frail.

"Where ya been?"

"I finally decided to go to the doctor. He said I have a severe virus that's been going around and I just need to stay in bed."

"Oh, Lesa, I'm sorry. Would you do me a favor?"

Lesa nodded once.

"Sleep in your own room? You'll feel better and so will I. I won't bother you. I'll sleep in Alyson's room until you forgive me or until I turn thirty-one, whichever comes first."

Lesa cracked the first smile Joab had seen for days.

"Okay," she said.

"Can I get you anything?"

"Sure. How about some pineapple juice on ice?"

When Joab got to her bedroom, she was in the bathroom. He set the juice on the night table as Lesa emerged in one of his favorite flannel shirts. This was her preferred winter sleeping attire, (in summer, she preferred nothing) and it might prove to be the first signal that she could be considering a truce. Joab watched as she slipped between the sheets.

"Want me to close the blinds?" He asked.

She nodded with her eyes closed.

He lowered the shade and noticed that she had left the light on in the bathroom. There was a pink box sitting beside the sink. It was a product foreign to Lesa's house, but he was sure he'd seen it before. As his finger flicked the light switch, he remembered. This was a product that only appeared directly after the birth of a baby. His mouth went dry and a rush of goosebumps rose up on his flesh. He picked up the box.

"You don't use these," he said, walking over to the bed.

"What?" Lesa asked, opening her eyes and trying to focus on the pink box. "I do, too."

"No you don't."

"Yeah? Well, I told you I wasn't pregnant."

"Only you were!"

"Oh, don't be stupid—"

"Stupid? What kind of an idiot do I look like? I can't tell when you've had an abortion? Why? Why did you do this? Why, when I would have married you?"

"Because I don't want to be married." She stated this slowly, as though she were trying to convey a difficult concept to a four-year-old. "I don't know how many times I've told you that."

Joab stared at the floor. It was true. She had told him this their first day together, out on that glorious bike ride. It was he who had changed his mind.

"But it was a baby, our baby," he pleaded, close to tears.

"Oh, bullshit," she spat, having had enough of defense, "Look, Joab, I'm gonna be a senator or a governor or an ambassador someday. I've got no room for mistakes. I have to do everything right. I can't afford any skeletons in my closet.

"Unless they're the tiny, little legal kind!"

"Look, Joab, I'm not gonna saddle myself with a mulatto bastard because you've got some romantic delusions of fatherhood."

The words sounded more harsh than she had intended, but Lesa felt weak and at a disadvantage.

"It wouldn't be a bastard if you would let me marry you!"

"Oh, right!" Lesa took a breath and continued in sharp condescension, "Joab, I had to teach you which damn fork to pick up, for Christ's sake; you'd be some whiz at international protocol."

Joab threw the sanitary napkins on the bed and left the room.

Lesa screamed after him, "I've got a right to my dream!"

Once on his bike in the chilly air, Joab began to think clearly again. His checking account had been holding at twenty-three bucks for over a month now. He'd have to see what was available on campus and call his mother for deposits and the like. Not an appealing thought at this point in his life. The only thought more distasteful was one of returning to Lesa. He decided he had to scrounge up a job ASAP and promised himself never to be without one again. At least he could be back in his home state, Joab thought, relieved in the knowledge that Emory would be happy to have him and had recommended him for a full academic scholarship.

Using his mother's credit card number, Joab checked himself into a cheap hotel. The next morning he found another dorm room. It was a suite full of freshmen, one of whom had a small pick-up truck and was promptly recruited to help him get his stuff out of Lesa's. When he was sure she was in class, Joab let himself into her apartment, and he and his new buddy were out of there in an hour. He left her key and the empty engagement ring in the mailbox in an envelope which read simply, "Miss Shemisaki." Joab did have one indecisive moment as he considered leaving the dandy little computer Lesa had given him for Christmas. Before long, he decided he'd better not let emotion get the best of prudence. He'd need the thing in law school, sure enough.

Duke personnel found an opening for him in the bookstore.

So passed the final days of Joab Johnson's undergraduate career. It had been a long four years, and Joab had finished under even more humble circumstances than he had begun. But through it all, his grades had remained generally high and he hoped to enter law school under somewhat more optimistic circumstances.

For graduation, Ruth had managed to persuade Annie and Maybell to take the road trip with her. Joab was both touched and embarrassed to have the three ladies fussing around him like a swarm of happy bees. As divine providence might have it, Ruth's Buick and Lesa's BMW were only two spaces apart in the parking lot. Just after commencement, as his two aunts paused to recount, for the third time, that Joab had graduated "cum laude," he looked up to discover that Lesa and her parents stood close by. Lesa must have seen him first. She delivered to him a direct look which communicated confidant defiance and gave no hint of regret. Her black hair shimmered against her white graduation gown as it fell over one shoulder. Her lovely face almost shone in the sun. A sudden shadow fell over Joab as he considered the cool heart which warmed only for itself. Mr. Shemisaki followed Lesa's gaze to Joab and to her surprise, walked over to his circle of women.

"Congratulations, Joab," he said with the remainder of an accent no amount of American culture would neutralize.

"Thank you," Joab responded, shaking his hand. "Uh, Ladies, this is Mr. Shemisaki. He is the father of a friend of mine. Mr. Shemisaki, this is my Aunt Annie, my Aunt Maybell and my mother, Ruth Johnson."

"Ah, this is your mother," he said, turning to Ruth and bowing ever so slightly, "I have wanted to meet you. You have raised a fine young man, Mrs. Johnson."

"Thank you," she said as Lesa's car pulled up beside them with the top down and her mother chattering in the passenger seat, "And you, a charming beauty."

"Well, it looks like my ride's here."

Ruth turned to see the infamous Lesa for the first time. For all of her resolve, Lesa could not, in the end, stand up under the scrutiny, but stared straight ahead rather than look Ruth Johnson in the eye.

"Well, good luck to you, Joab. Perhaps we will see you in the House or the Senate someday," he said.

Joab smiled broadly and kicked a pebble with the side of his black, dress shoe, "Now, I don't know about that, Sir," he said.

Mr. Shemisaki slid into the back seat of the chic, luxury import he had bought for his daughter. They rolled forward in the line of cars waiting to exit.

A moment later, Joab, Ruth, Aunt Annie, and Aunt Maybell all watched as Lesa pulled out onto the road, hair streaming in the wind.

Lord God, bless that young woman, Ruth prayed in silent compliance with the Biblical admonition to pray for your enemies.

Aunt Annie and Aunt Maybell raised their eyebrows and exchanged glances which said, "*So that's the hoochie mama who broke up Joab's marriage.*"

Joab realized that this was likely the last time he would ever lay eyes on the beautiful Lesa and decided that this was fine with him.

Joab took a job with his Uncle Jethro, doing construction in Charleston for the summer. Jethro's wife, Bea, had offered him the guest room and, in the interest of saving money, he took it. He was treated like the oldest of Jethro's three sons and a daughter. His nephews, the oldest of whom was now a sophomore in high school, worshiped him; and his niece just giggled whenever he was in the same room. Joab found he enjoyed being part of what felt like a big family. Whenever his uncle gave him two days off in a row, he traveled down the coast to Savannah to spend a little time with his mother. Out of pure gratitude, Joab accepted one of her many invitations to Sunday church.

To his amazement, it became quite clear that one of the church elders had more than a ministerial interest in his mother. He was a large, quiet man, a widower in his early fifties. He was greeting the church members as they entered. His face broke into a warm, wide smile when he turned to discover Ruth and Joab.

"Ah, this must be your Joab," he said.

"Joab, I'd like you to meet Deacon Jefferson Christopher Pinckney," Ruth said.

"Please, please, call me JC," the Deacon insisted. "It's good to finally meet you. Sister Ruth speaks of you often... in the best way." He sat on the other side of her during the service.

"You know, Mom," Joab said, on their way home, "I think Mr. Pinckney likes you."

"Oh, now Joab," she said, with a giggle reminiscent of his niece.

Once or twice, over the course of the summer, the subject of Anita and the children came up. Joab asked his mother if she had succeeded in getting any information out of Miss Lucy as to the whereabouts of his ex-wife and their children. Ruth said the woman had given her a general update every now and then but was careful to omit any reference to location. These were extremely difficult conversations for Ruth, as she generally visited Anita and the girls about once a month now, and was in the habit of slipping hundred dollar bills to her ex-daughter-in-law whenever she sensed the need. Still, she had given her word, and the only information she was released to offer was that the girls were alive and well. Ruth's hands were tied. She continued the Wednesday fast and found peace only by commending the situation into her God's powerful and loving hands.

The past year and a half demonstrated two things to Joab. First, a welfare check had enabled his family to get by with him, and they were still getting by without him. The hole in his life, left by Cinda, remained empty. His mind often wondered about little Mandy, but the sun continued to rise day-by-day, the moon grew round, waned to nothing, and grew round once more. Joab came to accept the fact that Anita would not be found as long as she did not want to be. Second, women were a whole lot more trouble than he was equipped to handle. He made a vow to keep his dealings with the weaker sex light, simple, and as infrequent as possible—at least until he was out of school. For the most part, it was a vow he kept.

Chapter 20

One afternoon, in September of his second year at Emory, as Joab sat in his Constitutional Law class, a secretary came for him.

Once outside of the classroom, the woman anticipated his question and spoke as they walked at a brisk pace, "A Ruth Johnson is waiting in my office. She said there is some kind of emergency, and she needed to see you now."

Ruth rose from a lobby bench when Joab entered the administration building.

"Hey, Mama," he said, offering a kiss on the cheek. "What's going on?"

"Cinda is in the hospital. Anita called this morning."

"Where?"

"Here in Atlanta."

"I knew she was here!"

"My car's right outside."

In moments, Ruth's Buick was speeding into the city.

"She's not dying or anything?"

"No. They put her in ICU for a little while after surgery last night, but they say she's doing well this morning."

"Surgery! What happened? Was there a car accident? What?" Joab asked.

"I don't have all the details, but apparently she got beat up pretty badly."

"Beat up? At school?"

"Anita has been cleaning houses to make some extra money. Sometimes she runs a little late and Cinda knows to let herself in the house and lock the door. Anita said she's never been more than twenty minutes late."

"What the hell does she think, leaving a little girl home alone!? What the hell kind of a mother leaves—"

"Now, Joab, you stop right there," Ruth broke in. "Anita's always been a good mother and she's doing all she knows how to get by, and her car just broke down is all. Anyway, a man knocked on the door. Cinda recognized him as one of Nicholas' friends, so she let him in."

"Oh, God." Joab felt all the blood drain from his head. He was suddenly nauseous. "Oh, God. He didn't . . . didn't . . . "

"There is evidence of rape."

"Oh, God, she's only a baby."

"Six."

Joab wanted to cry. Tears welled up in his eyes with a rage greater than grief. "He's a dead man. I just hope Nicholas hasn't gotten to him first."

"Nicholas is gone. He pulled out in the middle of the night, over a month ago. Anita said she figured he'd been dealing drugs and came up short one too many times. No one knows where he went."

"Did she tell his name?"

"Anita thinks it was Jojo Minks."

Joab stared out the window for a long time. "Does Nita know I'm coming?"

"No. Miss Lucy, God bless her, tripped and broke her ankle two days ago and couldn't come. At least you won't have to deal with both of them."

"Thank God for small favors." Joab said sarcastically.

Ruth made no comment.

A nurse directed them to a waiting room on the fourth floor. Anita stood staring out a window. She must have detected movement reflected in the pane. She turned when they entered the room. Joab saw visible relief wash across her face.

Joab hadn't known what to expect. It had been over two and a half years since Anita had left him. Most of that time he had spent hating her for taking his children away. During that time, thoughts of her generally lead to fantasies of circumstances under which he might achieve revenge. Often he indulged in thoughts of personally suing her for custody, once he passed the bar. Today she proved his case. He would delight in demonstrating her an unfit mother and see how *she* liked being locked out of her own family… All at once, what his heart recognized as he entered the room, was not his adversary, not the mother of his children, not even the naive and passionate lover of his boyhood. What his heart recognized, in the lean figure of his ex-wife, was his oldest, best friend and he was astonished in the realization that he had missed her very much.

From the expression on her face, he felt sure she must have missed him, too. But her face, almost as familiar as his own, had aged. The smooth arcs of her cheeks had melted away into planes. Her jaw line was more pronounced and there were dark circles under her eyes. A great and terrible pain was visible to his knowing eye, and an inexplicable desire to hold her and protect her from any more, gripped him.

She extended her hands as she walked toward him.

"Oh, Mom, thank God you're here." Anita said, as though Ruth had entered alone. She took her ex-mother-in-law's hands and began to cry.

Mom? Joab thought, as he stood there. *She's not Anita's mother anymore. She's my mother.*

Ruth led Anita to a row of chairs, and the two women sat down. Ruth held Anita's hands in her lap while the younger woman wept.

"Oh, Mom, it's my entire fault. It's my fault."

"Don't say such things. It couldn't possibly be your fault."

"You don't know," Anita sobbed, "you don't know some of the things I've done."

"I know you're a fine mother. You always have been. Terrible things just happen in a fallen world. It's no one's fault."

"I'm going to see my daughter," he interrupted.

"It's bad, Joab," Nita warned. "Don't you upset her."

Nothing could have prepared Joab for what he saw when he pushed open the door. The eye closest to him was black/purple and completely swollen shut. Cinda had to turn her face full toward him in order to see who had made the door squeak. She had a crescent of stitches under the left eye and more across the inside of her lower lip. There was a cast on her right arm. Tubing blew oxygen up her nostrils, and an IV dripped clear fluid into a vein just above the left wrist. Even so, Joab knew that the greatest damage was that which could not be seen.

It struck Joab as a gracious long way from the top of her head to the tip of the toes under the sheets.

"Daddy?" she said. It was a question, as though she was not quite sure.

"Hey, Baby Girl," he managed.

A sudden smile pulled at the corners of her mouth, revealing emptiness where front teeth had once been. Joab vowed again to kill the man who had done this. The smile disappeared in a wince of pain. Joab considered the possibility that Cinda's two front teeth had been pushed out by adult ones, needing room. He vaguely recalled six as the age when things like this began happening. *Which was it? Had they fallen out naturally or had they been punched out by Minks?* Joab didn't know—had no way of knowing. A molten hatred for Anita erupted anew like an undersea volcano.

Joab pulled up a chair and took his daughter's left hand, reminding himself of the old Little League trick that regular breathing was the best way to avoid crying. Somewhere under the swelling and the stitches and the passage of unknown seasons was the face of his Cinda. Joab searched for it.

"Does it hurt much, baby?" he managed to ask.

"Not too much," she said through dry, thick lips. "I don't mind 'cause it made you come. I knew it would make my Daddy come."

Joab stuffed an impulse to flight. Cinda's eyes, one sparkling from between swollen lids, held none of the emotions that warred within her father. There was no judgment, no resentment, no anger, only the abiding trust that had always been there.

"Where's Daddy's treasure?" The old question came softly as he leaned close and looked into those precious eyes. Cinda did not answer but continued gazing up at him. *Could it be that she had forgotten the answer? Right here in this bed. That was the answer. His mama had always known the right answer when Big Mama had asked her. He had always known when his mama had asked him. How could it be that the chain was broken? How could she not know that his treasure was right here in this bed? ANITA! That's why she did not know. Anita, damn her!*

Joab sat leaning over the bed for what seemed like a long time.

"Don't leave, Daddy," Cinda begged.

Joab reassured her that he would not. Then she was asleep.

When her breathing was deep and even, Joab uncurled the thin fingers and set them on the bed. He took one look back before closing the door quietly and striding down the hall to the waiting room. Ruth sat praying in the same seat in which he had left her. If Joab could have heard her silent words he would have heard this: *Lord, your ways are not our ways. This was meant for evil but You can use it for good.*

Anita stood staring out the window.

"What the hell kind of a mother leaves a six-year-old alone in a house?" Joab was suddenly in Anita's face. "Have you seen her?! Have you seen what that son-of-a-bitch did to her face? I hope you took a good look 'cause *you* did this to her. You're damn right it's your fault!" Joab had never wanted to hit a woman so badly in his life. He longed to unload two years worth of rage and outrage upon this woman. He longed to hit somebody—something. But he made himself hold his fists at his sides, knowing that, if he lost control for a second, there was a good chance he might kill her.

Ruth quickly ran to stand between them.

"Shut up, Joab," she commanded. "You just hold your tongue."

"She knows it, Mama. She knows I never would have let this happen to Cinda."

"Go ahead. Hit me, Joab," Anita screamed with desperate remorse. "Hit me! I deserve it! Go on!"

Ruth put her arms around her ex-daughter-in-law and urged her to calm down. "Joab, get out of here," she ordered.

"Go take a walk or go down to the cafeteria or something. Just go away for a while."

When Joab returned to Cinda's room an hour and fifteen minutes later, both women were sitting silently on either side of the bed. Cinda was still sleeping. Joab scavenged a third chair from an empty room and joined the vigil.

"What kind of surgery did she have?" he finally whispered.

"She had a concussion. They set the bone in her arm, stitched her face and went up inside of her to repair some damage. The doctors think she will be able to have children someday."

"If she can ever let a man touch her."

"When can she leave?"

"Tomorrow evening or the following morning."

"Who's got Mandy?"

"My neighbor, Loretta, but I think Mom is planning on picking her up and keeping her at the house."

"Can I go with her for a little while? I'd like to see Mandy."

"Sure."

Around four, a nurse came in and took Cinda's blood pressure and pulse and examined her eyes.

"I think it's time to get rid of that old IV," she announced happily. "What do you think?"

"Fine with me," Cinda said.

"But you'll have to take your pain medication by mouth. Think you can do it?"

"Sure!"

Once the tubes were gone, Cinda brightened somewhat. By and by, Joab made a trip to the gift shop and returned with a pink teddy bear and a silly children's book called, *What Do You Do With a Kangaroo?* It had many animal characters. Joab created funny voices for them all and it was tough to figure who enjoyed it more, the reader or the listener. Anita had forgotten how much Joab loved to tell the bedtime story.

Just after six, Cinda's first solid meal arrived and by 6:30 Ruth told Joab that it was time to pick up Mandy.

"Stay, Daddy," Cinda implored.

"I'm just gonna have a short visit with your baby sister. I'll be right back. I promise."

Reluctantly, Cinda accepted a kiss good-bye.

"Anita, can I talk to you for a moment?" Joab asked on his way out. Anita followed him out to the hallway.

"Are you sure it was Minks?"

Anita nodded.

"I want to know where he lives."

"Nicholas used to pay me to pick up stuff from his house. He lives up in Buckhead, 187 Ulmer Street. It's a rundown, white house with dark green shutters and an overgrown yard. He lives alone unless he's shacking up with someone, but he never takes them to his house. If he goes out, he won't be back until after three . . . Get him, Joab."

On the way to Anita's house, Ruth warned her son not to yield to any more such outbreaks as she heard this afternoon.

"This is difficult enough without laying blame on anyone. It's time to show some self-control and do what's best for Cinda. She doesn't need you attacking each other. She's seen enough violence."

"Yes, Mama," he said. He knew she was right. He resolved to be careful in front of the children.

Joab eyed the street apprehensively as his mother looked for a parking space. "Rough neighborhood," he observed.

"Yes, it is."

Ruth let him into Anita's before going next door to gather up Mandy. Joab was overcome with a nervous excitement as he anticipated seeing his youngest daughter. She had possessed the generic face of an infant, the last time he had seen her. *Now she is over two. Was she talking? What did she like to play, to eat? Will she look like Anita or me or neither of us?*

He heard the front door close behind his mother. Ruth placed the toddler on her feet and Joab squatted down to appear less threatening and to meet her eyes.

"Hey, Mandy," Ruth crooned, "I have someone special for you to meet. This is grandma's little boy. This is your daddy."

Joab smiled broadly and extended an open hand to the child—*my face. Amanda Nicole has my face. She doesn't smile easily. She doesn't trust me; doesn't know me. How could it be that someone so like me could be growing up so apart from me?* Mandy took one look at the stranger in her living room and backed away until she backed into Ruth. She wrapped her arms around Ruth's thigh and buried her face. No amount of coaxing could get her to turn around and look at the man again. Ruth finally unwrapped the child's arms and lifted her up, where she rewrapped them around Ruth's neck and clung as though life depended on it. All this time she uttered not a sound.

"I guess she's not used to strangers in the house," Ruth offered.

"Well, she goes to you easily enough," Joab said before he realized how childish it sounded.

"Well, she knows me," Ruth answered before she thought to stop herself.

"She *knows* you?"

Mandy's Grandmama drew a deep breath and sat down with the child.

"I've been here to visit several times. Anita made it clear that my visitation rights would end the day you found out where she lives. I gave my word."

"You gave your word and sided against me when she was right here in Atlanta the whole time!?"

"It's been a long day, son." Ruth cautioned, "Watch your tone in front of the child. Cinda and Mandy had lost their father. They never knew a grandfather. Anita offered me the opportunity to make sure they didn't lose one of their grandmothers, too. I didn't side against you. I just sided *with* the children."

Joab shook his head. "You're something, Ruth Johnson," he said, "I don't know whether I'm supposed to curse you or kiss you. . . . But I have a feeling Big Mama would have done the same."

"Why don't you see what you can find for supper and I'll hold the baby awhile.

Mandy watched cautiously as Joab cut up little pieces of food and placed them on the tray table of her high chair. She stared at him with furrowed eyebrows for a full ten minutes before she put anything in her mouth.

"Does she talk?" Joab asked.

"Like a chatterbox when she knows you," Ruth answered, honestly.

"She doesn't seem to warm up to people right away, does she?"

"Some things can't be rushed, son," Ruth smiled, "she'll come 'round – in time."

With Ruth's words came the awareness that his children were back in his life for good. The events of the day had been horrible and irreversible, but there was this at least: Joab's children were back in his life.

After dinner, Joab put in a brief call to Anita while Ruth put the baby to bed. Cinda had requested a second cup of Jell-O and was sleeping soundly. The swelling in her eye had gone down considerably.

"I think I'm gonna take your car and go back to the hospital," Joab said. "I'll call you in the morning or if there's any change."

"That will be fine," Ruth answered.

"I hate to leave you in this neighborhood all alone."

"Oh, don't worry about me," Ruth said, fishing in her purse for what Joab assumed must be the keys, "There are bars on the windows and good locks on the doors and I never go on a long car trip without this." Ruth held up a Glock semi-automatic pistol, chambered a round with an expert hand, and placed it on a high shelf of the TV cabinet.

Joab's eyes grew round. "When did you get that thing?"

"'Long about the time you were eight or nine."

"How come you never told me?"

"Loaded guns and curious boys are a dangerous combination."

"You know how to use it?"

"I take a brush up course every couple of years or so."

"I don't mind telling you, Mama. You've surprised the hell out of me today."

"Women will do that from time to time. Now remember what I told you about Anita. Mind your tongue."

"Okay."

Joab listened as his mother slid the dead bolts into place once he was on the other side of the door. It was full dark now. He began to appreciate the security system on his mother's car. There was a real value in the ability to get in and lock up without fumbling for keys. Joab pictured the pistol up on the cabinet shelf in Anita's living room and wondered, briefly, if there was any way to sneak it out. He couldn't come up with a feasible enough lie. Bullets were too quick anyway. Joab was actually looking forward to a violent release. Still, he would need a weapon—a baseball bat or something.

From inside the house, Ruth watched her son change direction and head to the shed behind the house. It contained little more than a few rusty tools and some piles of junk. Not even worth locking up. A few moments later she watched her son cross the street to her car. When he passed under the streetlamp, she could make out a length of heavy pipe. Ruth knew where Joab was going and she knew that he had to go. She checked on the baby and settled herself on the sofa to do some serious intercession.

"Sweet Jesus," she started, "Don't let him kill that man. . . And if he does, don't let him get caught."

Joab made one stop at a Wal-Mart for a pair of gloves. He found a map of Atlanta in the glove-box and looked up Ulmer Street. The house was unusually run down for the neighborhood. There was no need for bars on the windows in Buckhead. Joab parked his mother's car around the corner of the next street and walked once by the house. There was a light on beside the front door and no lights within. There was no garage and no car in the driveway. Joab slipped around back and tried to peek in the window – darkness. The overgrown weeds and shrubs gave him good cover and there were several mature trees in the front yard. He tapped on a back window with the pipe until it broke, reached a gloved hand inside, unlocked it, and climbed in. Once inside, he identified the light connected to the switch just inside the door, and removed the bulb. He checked to make sure all the blinds were down and rotated for maximum privacy. Then he sat on the floor to wait. The only light was a soft glow that filtered in through the living room window from beside the front door. The hours passed. Joab stretched his legs every now and again.

All at once, the glare of headlights swept across the living room mini-blinds. When a car engine cut off beside the house, Joab discovered his own heartbeat was audible in the near dark. He split the blinds to peek out. He had to be sure it was Minks and that Minks was alone. A light went on as the driver's door swung open. Joab's pulse picked up when he saw the face and fought the image of this scummy bastard upon his little girl.

Minks had aged predictably rough. He was average height but appeared smaller due to fifteen years of substituting alcohol, nicotine, and cocaine for food. His large hands bore witness to a frame which, if given the least consideration, would have well carried another thirty pounds. His dirty blond hair was thinning and four to six months late for cutting. Joab did not need to see those shallow, pale green eyes.

Next instant, the light was consumed by the sound of the door slamming. Carefully, Joab picked up the pipe and positioned himself behind the door—*the jingle of keys.* He raised the pipe and checked his baseball grip—*the thunk of a deadbolt hitting home.* He held his breath—*the door swung open.* A triangle of light split the floor against Minks' shadow. The click of the switch seemed loud.

"Fuck," Minks commented when no light happened. He took a step towards the kitchen and heard the door slam behind him. His eyes registered a burst of red and yellow as a thick metal pipe shattered his right kneecap. The joint bent backwards for the first time in his life. The wordless sound of his voice filled the room. He had fallen back against the closed door when a second impact forced his left knee backwards. He fell to the floor.

Jojo Minks remembered words. "Oh, my God. Oh, my God." He was crying.

Joab could make out his form. He was sprawled with his upper body rolled halfway up to hold his right knee, but afraid to move either of them.

"What do you want, man?" There was terror in his voice. Joab could feel him straining to adjust his eyes to the dark. "I got money—cash! I hide it in the freezer in a fish stick box. I swear, man. Go get it. Anything you want."

"I didn't come for money," Joab answered.

"You one of Keefe's guys? 'Cause if you are, you got the wrong guy, man. I'm all paid up. I swear I'm paid up. Call 'im, man."

Joab went to the kitchen and turned the light on. Backlit, Jojo Minks saw his silhouette.

"You don't remember me, do you?"

Minks shook his head furiously.

"I'm Joab Johnson. My daughter is lying in a bed in Atlanta Memorial."

Jojo placed his palms on the floor behind him and began pulling himself backwards.

"What I really want to do," Joab continued, "is to cut off your balls, then do the world a favor and bash your brains out all over this room."

"Look, man, Nicholas owed me big. Anita, too. Did you know Anita's a crack whore? She is. She needs it, man. She told me when the kid would be there, man. And what to say to get her to open the door. She traded me for a fix. I swear."

"You're lying," Joab whispered. "Shut up."

"Oh, yeah?" Minks questioned, all the tension disappearing from his voice. "You've been gone a long time. How do you know?"

For one split second, Joab was strangely aware of his ankles. It was the same awareness he had had once as a child; barefooted, near the marsh, looking down to see a cottonmouth ready to strike. *Could Anita do such a thing?* The thought was so thoroughly repulsive that he knew Anita's mind could not have conceived it. Yet, he had no doubt Minks would slit his mother's throat to save his own skin. *Had this been the voice Eve had known in the garden? Void of conscience, cool, more relaxed in a lie than in the truth.*

"Because I know Anita," Joab answered flatly.

Minks started screaming.

Joab's gloved hand caught him in the jaw. Then he squatted down to communicate his message. He formed the words slowly and evenly. "If you ever come near my wife or my daughters again, or if I ever hear of you laying a hand on any other man's kid, I'll track you down, put a bullet between your eyes, and laugh all the way to prison. Is that clear?"

"Yeah, man. I swear."

Joab swung the pipe one last time. This time the blow landed squarely and forcefully between Minks' crippled legs. Jojo Minks passed out.

Calmly, Joab switched off the outside light, locked the front door, yanked the phone cord out of the wall, shut the kitchen light, and slipped out the back door.

Joab felt exhilarated in the cool night air. He had to force himself to walk slowly to the car. Some distance away, a dog barked. Otherwise, the houses were dark and the neighborhood undisturbed. Crickets chirped and the car hiccupped once as the security system disarmed and the locks popped up. Once in the car, Joab spread out the map and wrapped the pipe in it.

Joab drove around the hospital until he found a dumpster. He threw in the pipe, still in the map, and the pair of gloves.

It was pushing 4:00AM when Joab entered the hospital. The lobby was locked and he had to enter through the emergency room. An anxious woman with a screaming baby paced the floor. Another woman looked up from behind the desk and inquired, "Can I help you?"

She was a woman of color. She looked tough. Joab hoped she'd cut him some slack. He gave her a wide smile. "Evenin'. Uh, I know you have visiting hours and all, but my daughter's up on the fourth floor, and I promised my wife that I'd be here as soon as I got off work."

The woman leaned back in her chair and crossed her arms. "Yeah? What do you do?"

"I'm a student at Emory, but I work at a convenience store at night."

"Yeah? What are you taking?"

"I'm a graduate student. Law."

"Good for you. What's your daughter's name?" The nurse leaned forward and placed her fingertips on a computer keyboard in front of her.

"Cinda. She's probably listed as Lucinda Ruth Johnson, age six. . . room 415."

The woman looked at the screen. "You got any ID that tells me who you are?"

Joab pulled his student ID from his wallet and handed it to the woman. "How do you pronounce your first name?"

"Long 'o', short 'a', Jo-ab."

"Umm." The woman nodded and handed him back the plastic card. "Go through those double doors and head straight down until you come to a pair of elevators on your right. Go to the fourth floor and follow the signs. I'll call the nurse's station and let 'em know you're on the way. They get a little nervous when strange men walk in after 4:00, know what I mean?"

"Thanks."

On his way, he passed by a men's room and decided to go in. On his way out, he paused to wash his hands and throw some cool water on his face. The adrenaline high was letting down and exhaustion was settling into his muscles. A distant headache gathered like storm clouds on the horizon. Joab rubbed his forehead and wondered where he could find a couple of aspirin.

"You're in a hospital, stupid," he told himself, out loud. He knew his mind must be getting desperate for sleep. He tried to prepare himself to face Anita. How he hated her. He remembered with satisfaction, Minks passing out. *I fixed him, I'll fix her, too, one of these days,* he thought, *but I'll use a law book on her.* Still, his mother was right. He'd need to bite his tongue for the time being. He had to do whatever it took to make Cinda better.

"You'll make nice to the ignorant bitch," he told himself in the mirror. The water felt good on his face. He stared at his reflection. Rendered defenseless by fatigue, a horrible truth rose unstoppably, like a bubble of breath from the darkest abyss of his consciousness: *Look at your household. One daughter lies raped and beaten in a hospital bed down the hall. One daughter doesn't even know who you are, and a third child*

was disposed of as medical waste. You don't even know if it was a boy or a girl... It was your hand that opened the door to the destruction of your children, your adultery, your failure to make Anita understand about the separation.
The enemy of your household is you.

Cinda's room was dark. Anita had two of the chairs pushed together and was sleeping uncomfortably under an inadequate hospital blanket. Joab was amazed to realize the pit in his stomach was gone. He looked upon his ex-wife with a tender compassion he would have thought impossible only moments earlier. Cinda seemed to be sleeping soundly. Joab left the door cracked so he could make out the features of her face in the dim light. The swelling continued to abate. Joab drank in the wonder of looking upon his daughter again. As he stood beside her bed, the events of life-since-Cinda began to play out in his memory. He saw himself holding her in blue, paper scrubs only moments after her birth. He had almost squeezed the blood out of Anita's fingers. He remembered the ear infections and the chicken pox and the night they drove to the emergency room in the rain with the roof of the old Le Baron slit. He remembered Anita's anguish as she faced the necessity of day care. He remembered Lesa, all in satin and lace, on her bed. He remembered, with heaviness, little Mandy's birth and the suspicion in her eyes this afternoon. He saw Cinda's terrible struggle with Minks and the broken self-condemnation in the dullness of his own Anita's eyes. . .

Joab knew what he had known the day he signed the separation papers that would start the flow of someone else's money to his own household: his family did not belong to the government. They belonged to him. They were his responsibility, his and Nita's. They were his treasure. The world beyond the borders of his roof was a dangerous place. Without him, his girls had no protector, no champion. No social program or bureaucrat knew his children or loved them. The government was an indifferent provider at best, and a poor one at that. A pride swelled in Joab which he had not felt in a long, long time. "They need me," he whispered. The realization formed words. "They need me."

"Joab?" Anita's soft whisper startled him out of his thoughts.

"Anita, I need to talk to you," he said.

"Is she okay?"

"Yeah. She's sleeping fine."

Anita sat up and tried to roll a crick out of her neck. "What time is it?"

"Pushing 5:00 I think."

"Now?"

"Before she wakes up. I want to be here when she opens her eyes."

"Okay." There was a flat resolve in the word. "I doubt there's anyone in the waiting room at this hour."

When they reached it, she turned and gave him a look which meant, "Okay, I'm listening."

"Anita, I want to put our marriage back together."

Anita looked at the floor and shook her head.

"We owe it to the children to at least give it a try."

"Joab, it's been a hard twenty-four hours. You're talking off the top of your head. Go get some sleep."

"I'm serious, Nita."

"Yeah? And just what am I supposed to do? Give up my kids to the big man and live in a house with nothing for me? No! I won't do it. I won't do it."

"It's not just the girls. I want you back, Nita. I love you."

"Ha. Yeah, right."

"I do, Nita, I never stopped loving you, I swear it."

"Yeah? Well, what if *I* don't love *you*?"

"I'll make you love me. I'll make you fall in love with me all over again. I'll never cheat on you as long as I live. I swear."

Anita just stared at the floor shaking her head.

Joab wanted this like nothing he'd ever wanted in his life. He had to make her see, to believe in him again, to try.

"Please, Anita," he pleaded. He fell to his knees before her, put his arms around her waist, and wept. He had no pride before her, no face worth saving if it would cost him this chance. She stared, dry-eyed, out the window. The sky began to pale. Her hands held the back of his head as tears soaked through her clothes.

Chapter 21

The following Friday, Joab got the night off from work and his second courtship of Anita commenced. He appeared at the front door of her house bearing gifts for all his girls. For Anita, a single red rose. For Cinda and Mandy, a bag each of Gummy Worms, a rare and highly favored childhood delicacy at the convenience store.

"Hey, Joab," Anita said, answering the door. "I can't believe that damn bike is still running."

"It's just standing there craving asphalt," he teased. "I can't believe that damn Ford is still alive."

"It's just standing there craving a mechanic with a Jack Kevorkian touch."

Joab smiled. He was cautiously encouraged by the casual summer dress and the meticulous application of make-up. Both good signs.

"Cinda! Mandy! Your father's here," she announced.

"Daddy!" Cinda exclaimed emerging from a bedroom and running to wrap her arms around him like a forty-five pound linebacker. The cast on her right arm did not seem to slow her down much, yet it would be years before terror and an impulse to hide would fail to accompany each knock on the doors of Cinda's life. Mandy watched this enthusiastic greeting with obvious skepticism.

Joab observed as his gifts hit their intended marks. Anita almost caught herself smiling as she set her flower, its stem freshly clipped, in a glass of Sprite, and placed it on the dining room table. Cinda graciously offered to help her little sister open her bag of candy and immediately started trading green worms for red.

"Cinda, count out five pieces each, and give me the rest to put up 'till tomorrow," Anita commanded. "Supper is still a few minutes out, Joab. Why don't you visit with the girls while I finish up?"

Joab squatted down before his youngest. "Hey, Mandy," he said in his warmest voice, extending open hands. The child just furrowed her brows and stared at him with wide, dark eyes. When he leaned forward to pick her up, she leaned away.

"Cinda," he said standing up empty handed, "why don't you show me your babies?"

"C'mon, Mandy," Cinda said, paying no mind to her broken arm, and carrying her sister to a toy chest in the corner. "I don't really play with babies too much no more. Me and Mama gave a bunch of 'em to the poor for Christmas, las' year. I mostly play with Barbies now. Mama didn't useta let me play with none of the little Barbie stuff, though, 'cause Mandy could choke. But she's not doing that much no more."

Joab sat on the floor accepting skinny, little, female dolls, most of them appeared to be of African descent, except for the long, straight, black hair. As his daughter placed them, one by one, in his hands, she told him their names and gave him a brief bio on each.

". . . and this is Shameeka. I got her from my best friend, Shameeka, who lives next door. She give it to me fo' my fif' birffday party. She be a Splash Barbie. . . . and this is Tamera. I got her from my friend, Tamera. I traded two Polly Pocket houses and a white Pizza Party Barbie for her. . . This here's her baby sister, Amanda Nicole. You could call her Mandy. All these ones babysit, sometime, fo' Mandy."

Joab's ear picked up each misuse of language, and he cringed inwardly. *How can her teachers let her fall into such poor verbal habits?* he wondered. *How do they expect our children to compete?* Joab decided a talk with Cinda's teacher would soon be in order. He also figured he could begin to correct his daughter's language once he and Nita were remarried.

Still, Joab was captivated by his daughter, as usual. He marveled at the level of detail created and filed in Cinda's heart for each little doll. The swelling had long disappeared and the bruising was fading rapidly. The doctor had done a fine job with the stitches under her eye and promised the scar would become less noticeable with each year. Joab wondered at the scarring on her soul, though, and he vowed again, as he had done several times a day since her attack, to protect her from any more such ugliness and to provide her with a safe place to grow and thrive. He'd do the same for Mandy, whether she liked it or not. And Anita? She would always be his best friend. Home was no longer a place or a concept. Home was wherever Nita set her foot. Joab didn't know whether she understood, yet. He guessed that he, himself, was only just beginning to. But he would outlast her anger and distrust, and he would never compromise her again. Joab was not fearful of the challenge. She'd come around. He'd make her come around because life without his girls was no longer an option. He also knew the truth—they needed him as much as he wanted them.

Mandy maintained her silence all through dinner. Cinda was more than equal to the task of filling the void. Anita, too, was quiet, observing the interactions of a father in her household with casual indifference. Joab searched her face. She was giving nothing away.

After dinner, Joab offered to do the dishes and easily recruited Cinda to help. Anita went to the bedroom to change Mandy into her night clothes and ready her for a visit next door. After Cinda had cleared the table, she too was dressed in jammies.

"Tell Daddy night-night," Anita told them as she unlocked the side door in the kitchen, Mandy on one hip.

"Night-night," Mandy whispered in obedience.

Cinda's face was sullen. "Are you comin' back?" she asked softly.

"Maybe not tonight, but I'm always coming back. Okay?"

"Okay." The door closed behind her as she followed her mother across the cement walkway between the houses.

In a few moments, Anita reappeared.

"I need to do something," she said, "I'll be out in a minute."

"Take your time," Joab answered with his arms in sudsy dish water to the elbow, "I've got at least another fifteen minutes here."

Anita emerged from the bedroom in a light, sleeveless, summer shirt and a pair of jeans. On her feet she wore a pair of biker-type boots. A single sapphire stud adorned her nose.

"Why'd you change?" Joab asked, surprised.

"Well, if that damned bike won't die, I may as well make my peace with it."

"I won't mind taking the car," Joab offered.

"Trust me," she said, "we have a much better chance of getting where we're going on the bike."

"Them's phat boots!" he commented, on their way out the door.

Once Anita subdued her fear, she managed to enjoy the sensation of the ride much more than she would have imagined. Then, too, it was no small pleasure to have her arms around her ex-husband's waist again, though it would be a while before she'd admit to enjoying either the ride or the embrace.

Joab's plan was to take his wife out for dessert and a drink and catch a movie at 9:00. He decided on a Pub-type restaurant, close to a cinema, where he knew he could find a booth with high seat backs and low lights.

"How about a double-fudge Sundae?" he asked Nita as they were being seated.

"No-o-o," she answered.

"They have a great peanut butter pie."

Anita shook her head.

"I've got an idea. How about a great, big strawberry colada?"

"Nah," Nita said. But it was too late. Joab had seen the way she raised her eyebrows before her refusal.

When the waitress appeared, he ordered one great, big strawberry colada, a piece of pecan pie and a "Pete's Wicked Summer Brew".

"Jo-o-oab," she reprimanded weakly. "They charge $4.25 for one of them fancy frozen drinks!"

"You're worth it," he answered.

Joab and Nita never made it to the cinema. They sat in that same booth for the next five hours, raising only to sneak to the bathroom. By 1:30 a.m., Nita had enjoyed more than four of those fancy drinks and appeared quite a bit more relaxed than she had been when Joab had knocked on her front door. Joab switched to Dr. Pepper after his third Wicked Brew, not wishing to justify Nita's fear just when she was warming up to his wicked bike. Besides, she had two little girls who needed her.

Neither of them spoke much about the past two years. From where they stood, some of the water passing under their bridge smelled pretty foul. Much more comfortable was talk of a past they shared, talk of childhood crushes, football victories and victory parties, the old Le Baron, their first visit to Disney World . . . .

"I can't wait till we take the girls next time," Anita said before she could filter the implication. She hadn't meant to stumble onto the unsure footing of the future. But there she was.

"I can't wait, either," Joab said. "Maybe this summer after school gets out."

Nita didn't answer, but only stirred the pink slush in the bottom of her glass.

"Anita," Joab started, dreading his next words, "You been messing around with crack?"

"No, Joab, that night up in Durham was the last time," she answered. Then she continued, "Nicholas broke off with Loretta just before I got up here. He left her with a bad habit. I watched her kids while she went to a place to get past it. I visited her once while she was in there. It was terrible. We made a pact with each other and we hold each other to it."

"I'm sorry. I just had to know from you."

Anita stared past him and shrugged her shoulders.

The trip home turned out to be an educational experience for Joab. He had never really been out in the truly depressed areas of Atlanta late at night. He was astonished at the activity. All around him was evidence that his restless and angry generation had taken possession of the night. Groups of teens and young adults loitered around street lamps and stoops, talking trash and smoking substances which, if they did not take life outright, surely eroded the quality of it with every breath. Portable music blared defiantly, challenging any who presumed authority to return peace to the hour. Domestic sedans, glistening under street lamps, circled the streets like mechanical sharks, scanning their domain for the scent of blood or the vibrations of fear. Joab knew he was in over his head. Twice, he ran a red light rather than risk the vulnerability of inertia. Thankfully, Nita's street appeared comparatively innocuous. Joab parked his bike and gave Nita a long kiss at her door. He could tell she was nervous.

"You okay?" he asked.

"We shouldn't stay out here too long," she said.

"If nothing else, Nita, you have to let me help you get the girls out of this neighborhood."

"I know."

"Want me to help you carry them back from next door?"

"No. Loretta will call me in the morning, when they wake up."

Anita had already decided Joab would not spend the night. She was sure that once he knew that the girls were gone until morning, he would push for access. Anita had anticipated, with great satisfaction, the necessity to turn him down flat. But Joab gave her no such opportunity.

"Good night, Nita," he said, "I enjoyed this very much. Can we do it again?"

She nodded, "I guess so."

"I'll call you tomorrow. Now, get inside and lock the door."

Anita peeked out the window as his bike pulled away.

The next day, Joab called his ex to set up a second date for the following week. Between classes and studying and hours at Speedy Gas, as well as the demands of the Vice Presidency of the Young Democrats, there was precious little time for dating. Then, too, Joab gave himself one more job to do. He had to find a respectable engagement ring - cheap. Instinctively, Joab entered pawn shops with apprehension. Represented in the abandoned collections of stuff were scores of broken hopes, salvaged for a fraction under the grim circumstances of reality. Joab couldn't help but sense, as he perused the non-essential trinkets of other people's lives, the stories, like the sorrowful lyrics of so many Country and Western ballads, left forever unsung. But he needed a ring, something special this time. And he knew his best chance, given the constraints of his wallet, was within the case of a pawn shop. Systematically, Joab began his search until he found one that had just opened and had made the mistake of becoming more cash-poor than its clientele. There, after much bartering, he picked up an above average, marquis cut diamond in a custom setting. The stone was just under a half carat and he got the ring for the incredible price of $365.00. *What luck!* Joab hadn't spent much less than that on Anita's first engagement ring and its diamond had been a speck by comparison. He wondered, briefly, what poor non-fiancé had had his proposal rejected, or worse, whose marriage had ended in ruin. Perhaps the ring had been stolen and some woman, somewhere, longed for a possession that's true worth could never be covered by an insurance policy. Joab derailed his train of thoughts. This lovely ring, purchased through a measure of his own good fortune, was getting a fresh start today. Henceforth, if Anita could accept his terms, it would be the symbol of something difficult but victorious, something that would outlast even the diamond itself. Joab wanted to use his original wedding band. He wondered if Anita still had hers. Or had it, too, been recycled into someone else's dreams?

On their third date, Joab popped the question - again. He parked his bike along an inlet of Lake Lanier and found a beautiful place to sit and spread out a blanket. He had talked Nita into lunch and a day trip because he had to work at 3:00. He considered the possibility of waiting for an evening date, but he was too excited to delay.

Joab savored Nita's reaction when she opened the box.

"Oh, Joab," she whispered, astonished, "Mom lent you the money, right?"

Joab shook his head.

"You're in hock for the rest of your life."

Joab shook his head. "Don't worry about how I got it. I just lucked into a really good deal."

"That's what Nicholas used to say. Man, it's pretty!"

"You might not want it. We need to get some things straight, first, if we're gonna make it this time."

Anita crossed her legs and turned to sit facing her ex-husband.

"First, you can't give me any more ultimatums," he said. "No more unilateral decisions."

"What does *unilateral* mean?"

"It means that you can't make decisions, on your own, and threaten to leave if I don't accept them. We have to talk things over and reach an agreement. I'll have to bend and you'll have to bend and in those places where we just can't come together . . . you'll have to yield to me. I've got to be able to be the head of our family. You have to let me lead."

There was a long silence as Anita struggled to get her brain around the long term implications of such a concession.

Joab saw her set her jaw and continued, "Anita, I swear, I'll break my back to meet you where you are. I'll do everything I know how to defer to you. But on the big things, I have to be the tie-breaker."

"What else?" she asked, dead sober and looking him square in the eye.

"No more welfare checks."

Anita threw her head back, as thought she'd been cuffed on the chin, and stared up at a cloudless sky.

"Anita," Joab started to try and articulate something which had been, for over three and a half years, mostly just a gripping misgiving, "Lucinda and Amanda are *our* children. They may not have been planned, but they are not mistakes. They are not burdens to be thrown off on the government like some kind load that's too much for us to bear."

"Ah, shit, Joab! Here we go again. I don't understand what your big problem is with this!" Anita cut in, "We've both worked. We might not have made much, but we paid our fair share of tax. 'sides, our people worked as slaves here for two hundred years. What the hell do we owe this damn country, anyway?"

"We don't owe this country, Nita. But we *do* owe our children. It's our responsibility to raise our own kids; our honor, our right. And it's the next guy's responsibility to raise *his own* kids and I'm not going to take from *his* family to raise *my* family. It's wrong and it's the wrong message to send our children!"

"It's just your damn pride again!" Anita spat.

"You're damn right it is! I *am* proud, Anita, and you should be, too! We're both young and strong and smart. Why should we let ourselves be treated like some kind of pathetic, sort of cripples who can't survive without the more *competent* people made to carry us? It's an insult. And it's crumbs, Anita! It's not worth it. We'll get by just fine if we only stay committed and work together."

"Oh, Joab, *it's so hard.*" This was a point of fact and there was resignation in Anita's voice.

"I know. But hard is good. It makes you strong and it satisfies. Besides, we're almost there! I'll be out of law school in a year and a half. Then we can go home to Savannah if you want. Mr. Keylar has offered me an associate's position as soon as I pass the bar."

"Really?" Anita brightened.

Joab nodded.

"Okay, well, what if I have some rules of my own?" Anita challenged.

"All right." Joab crossed his arms and listened.

"I started going to Loretta's church a while back. I like it and I think it's good for the girls. Now, I won't make you to go with us, but I want to keep taking the girls and I don't want you bad-mouthin' it."

"Agreed." Joab said, inwardly relieved that her demand wasn't something more important.

"And you won't ever do me like that—cheatin' again?"

"I promise, Nita. If you take me back, never again."

"Because I'll kill ya next time. You know that."

"I'll load the gun and hand it to ya."

There was a long, long silence. Joab watched points of light glittering on the water. He let Nita take all the time she needed.

"Can I put it on now?" she asked, at last, staring down at the ring.

"I don't know. It's up to you," he answered.

Anita pulled the ring from its slot in the box and slipped it on the fourth finger of her left hand. Then she threw her arms around her ex-husband and nearly knocked him over.

"Hoo-wee! It's the prettiest thing I ever seen in my life!" she squealed. Then she gave him a full-body kiss, the likes of which he hadn't tasted in way too long. "Oh, shit!" she said, suddenly, "How am I gonna tell Mama?"

"That's your problem," he laughed, "I'm staying out of that one."

"Joab, you don't know some of the stuff we said about you."

"Oh, I got a pretty good idea," he told her honestly.

Anita leaned over to whisper in his ear, "Why don't you come by the house after work tonight? I can send the kids back to Loretta's."

Joab laughed and shook his head. He pushed his woman down on the blanket and lay upon her.

"Nope. Not this time," he said. "This time we're gonna do it right. 'Sides, knowing us, you'd probably go to the altar pregnant again. Speaking of altars, how about next weekend? I think we're gonna have to do it fast if we're gonna do it right."

Nita just laughed and wrapped her arms and legs around her oldest, best friend.

Preparations for the wedding, modest as they were, could not be made in less than three weeks. Miss Lucy was, by no means in agreement with the reunion, but held her tongue. Joab decided it wasn't too early to set an appointment with Cinda's teacher. In light of the upheaval of her recent ordeal, her parents agreed not to pull Cinda from her school before the end of the year. This meant that a safer neighborhood within their price and within the same school district would have to be found. Both knew this task would be close to impossible. Joab was counting on luck. Nita took a cue from Ruth and Loretta and started to pray for a miracle.

Joab's first visit to Cinda's school proved as educational as his 2:00AM bike ride in Nita's neighborhood. It was called the Dr. Martin Luther King, Jr., Primary School. Though the facility had only recently been completed, evidence of the habitation of budding vandals had embezzled the freshness due a new building. Miscalculations in growth projections had rendered the facility prematurely obsolete, resulting in the proliferation of "portable classrooms" even before the last brick had been laid. A high, chain link fence crowned in razor wire encircled the campus. Within, metal detectors adorned the main entrance and metal bars remained retracted in the ceiling, waiting to descend, dividing the hallways and classrooms into so many jail cells, in case of a riot.

"Good God," Joab thought as he made his way down the deserted hallway to Cinda's classroom, *"this is only the primary school. What does the high school look like?"*

Cinda's teacher, Ms. Wills, sat behind her desk, filling out some kind of form when Joab entered her room.

"Hello," he said, standing beside her desk, "I'm Joab Johnson. I'm Cinda's father."

"Uh-huh," the woman grunted, unimpressed. She did not look up.

"I believe we have an appointment."

"That's why I ain't home yet. All we got is these little chairs for the kids. You can go on and sit on a desk if you want." She still did not look up.

Well, at least he knew why Cinda's language skills were so poor. Joab remained standing.

Finally, the woman finished her work, leaned back in her chair, crossed her arms, looked at Joab and asked, "What's the problem?"

"The problem is, Ms. Wills, that my daughter barely recognizes the letters of the alphabet. She has no idea what sound is associated with them, and she can't identify a plus or minus sign, for starters."

"A lot of parents who were taught the old phonics system have a hard time understandin' our approach. We use the "whole word" method. Basically, we show the kid how to recognize words by looking at them, not by sounding it out. That's the new way. Anyway, I don't know what your problem is, she's getting good scores."

"She can't read."

"She's not supposed to be able to read. This is only the second quarter of first grade. None of her class reads yet. Some of them won't read until the end of second grade."

"Yeah? And some of them never will."

"Look, Mr. Johnson, I'm sorry for what happened to her and all, but it ain't my fault that your chil' missed a lot of days already. And her self-esteem counseling is taking up even more of her time."

"Self-esteem counseling?"

"We keep a certified child psychologist on staff for victims of violent crimes."

"Well, what if I'd rather have her spend the time in reading class?"

"You wouldn't be able to make that decision. Only the principal can decide that."

"But I'm her *father*."

"Yeah, how come I never met ya 'fo now?"

Joab could not believe the level on which Ms. Wills had just placed this conversation. He took a breath and gathered his thoughts. "Cinda's mother and I are to be remarried next weekend."

"I know. Children talk more than people think they do. And I'm very happy for you and Ms. Johnson. I hope it lasts, this time. But we are qualified teachers here, and our program has the best interest of your daughter in mind."

"And I don't?" Joab checked his outrage. It would be pointless to antagonize this woman.

"I'm sure you do. All parents want to see their kid do good. You just need to bring your expectations in line with reality. At this point, your girl just needs to develop a desire to learn and feel good about hersef." Ms. Wills' tone warmed some as she prepared to dismiss her 4:00 appointment. "Trus' me, Mr. Johnson, I've been at this fo' nine years, now. Yo' kid will read when she's ready."

Joab allowed himself to be dismissed. The meeting had not gone at all as he had expected, but he had learned what he had come to find out. By the time his bike stopped for the first red light, Joab was talking to himself—out loud.

"Bring my expectations in line with reality!?!? I'll tell you what I'll do," he said to the chrome bumper in front of him, "I'll bring reality in line with my expectations or be damned!"

The next day, Joab made an appointment with Charlie Keylar.

✦ ✦ ✦

In the weeks before his re-marriage, Joab seized the opportunity to spend time with his girls. Several nights were passed in front of the TV, snuggling Cinda and Anita, and catching up on the last three years of Disney offerings. Mandy considered herself a close personal friend of all the main characters and jumped up to point at the screen and formally announce the entrance of each. Variations on the names Pocahontas, Quasimodo, Hercules, and Esmeralda were particularly entertaining in toddler-speak. But Joab took great care to reflect his daughter's enthusiasm each time she made a comment, and in so doing, discovered in the cartoon landscapes of such places as the American Frontier, Paris, France, and Ancient Greece, the first places of common ground with his second born.

One evening, after he and Nita had put the children to bed and after they had necked like teenagers on the sofa and fallen asleep there, Joab awoke to a wet spot on his chest. Anita was crying.

"Babe? What's wrong?" he whispered.

"Nothing," came the response.

"Tell me," he said, sitting up and making her sit up as well.

All at once she started pounding his chest with her fists. This behavior confirmed, for the thousand and first time,

Joab's notion that women are indeed strange and unpredictable creations.

"What did I do, now?" he asked while receiving the near-harmless blows without any effort to restrain them.

"You've done it to me again," she wept.

"What?" he asked.

"I've lost myself in you," she said, "I promised I'd never do it again. You better not turn back into a shit. You better never leave me again."

"But *you* left *me*."

"No. You lef' me, first," she said as the pounding subsided, "That's why I couldn't stay."

"I'm so sorry," he said, holding her, "I won't let you down this time."

Appropriately, Joab and Anita's second wedding was held at their family church in Savannah, the same site as was their first. The ceremony was simple and the guests were few. Joab wore the navy, pin-striped suit Ruth had bought him for graduation from Duke. Anita wore a stunning cream-colored formal dress and the little girls were in lavender.

Ruth had driven up a week before the wedding to take Anita and the girls on a shopping trip. The first place they went was Phipps Plaza, a fancy, high-rise shopping mall which Nita had only ever seen through the windows of her old car or a city bus. Though Mandy was clearly a bit young to appreciate the process of clothing selection, Cinda could not remember ever having been so fussed over. She modeled dress after dress, beaming and taking elaborate turns, and by the end of the day, a consumer had been born. The price tag for Anita's purchase was $230.00, but Ruth knew they would never find a more beautiful dress, if they searched the whole city. She insisted. It was the most expensive thing Anita had ever had on her body. Her cheeks burned each time she thought of the expense, and yet the expense made her feel elegant and lovely each time she slipped the dress on. To Ruth, it was a particular joy to watch her ex-daughter-in-law blossom into a bride and to see the spark of hope bring spring to a soul that had resigned itself to an early winter.

Cinda consented to accepting the duties of ring bearer only after being convinced that it was not an office held strictly by boys and that it required the particular talents of a first grader. Mandy was the flower girl. JC accompanied Ruth. Charlie and Susan Keylar came to baptize the union in a second round of tears, and Miss Lucy came by herself. The small group let out of the church to a bright, blustery September morning. The first chill of fall was in the air and Joab watched with amusement as JC took off his jacket and placed it over his mother's narrow shoulders. Joab winked at the most splendid of brides—his. Truly, he had never seen Nita more lovely. Relief and keen anticipation swept over him as he considered, again, that consummation was close at hand. The small company divided up in cars, Cinda and Mandy with the bride and groom in Ruth's Buick, drove to Miss Lucy's where she served the most elaborate champagne brunch ever to grace her table. After much toasting and laughter, JC gave Ruth and the granddaughters a lift to her house where the little girls were to spend the night, and the party broke up. For their wedding gift, Charlie and Susan Keylar provided one night's stay at the Hyatt Regency on River Street. Rarely had a hotel room ever been so thoroughly well-enjoyed.

Check out was at 11:00AM. Ruth had just gotten the girls home from Sunday church when Joab and Anita pulled off the dirt road in front of Big Mama's house. Mandy, in a frilly, floral dress, ran with all her strength and dove through the center of the old tire swing, still dangling from the limb of the ancient oak. Her mother and father stopped to watch before throwing the door open to call to her from the car.

"Mama!" she hollered, running toward them, her face suddenly bright.

After his mother served up a delicious fried chicken lunch (his grandmother's recipe), Joab left Anita to pack things up while he kept an appointment with Mr. Keylar.

◆ ◆ ◆

"Sorry to make you come in on a Sunday afternoon," Joab apologized, shaking hands as Charlie greeted him at the front door.

"No trouble at all. Why don't we go sit down in the small conference room. I've got a pot of coffee brewing."

After mixing in sugar and cream to their liking, both men took a seat at a small, round, mahogany table. Charlie had a fresh, yellow legal pad in front of him and a silver pen.

"I sure am glad to see you and Anita back together again. And your girls are beautiful. I don't think I've ever been to a better wedding."

Joab looked down at his lap and shook his head, half-embarrassed. "Well, we sure appreciated y'all coming. And we darn sure enjoyed your present."

"That one was my idea." Now Joab was full-embarrassed. Charlie Keylar read Joab's thoughts, and the two men shared a laugh.

"So, what's on your mind?" Charlie finally asked. "You still planning on working for me after graduation?"

"Oh, yes, sir. Nita can't wait to get back home. It's not about that."

"Good. Okay?"

"Mr. Keylar, I just gotta get Cinda out of public school. You ought to see the place, razor wire around it, metal detectors. Two kids got shot by another student at the high school down the street last week. It's bad. The children are lucky to survive, never mind learn anything. It's a tough place. And after what she's been through, I don't know if she can handle it. And she's not learning anything. Her teachers spend more time counseling her and filling out forms than they do teaching her what sound goes with "B." I want to put her in a private school with basic reading and math and rules for discipline, like I went to. There are a few good ones in our area."

"I'm sure a lot of those schools have scholarships programs," Charlie suggested hopefully.

"Yeah, and a waiting list a mile long from people who have lived in the neighborhood since the foundations were poured."

"Is there any way Anita could home school?"

"She's scared to death of the thought. But I've been doing some research, and the state of Georgia is openly hostile to home schoolers. Anyway, even with the best curriculum in the world, they'd never approve Nita without a high school diploma. Besides, as long as I'm in school, we need her working."

"Okay. That's not an option. Most folks just move to a better school district."

"I know. We're looking into it. But how about the people who can't move? Our school district in Atlanta gets $5,245.00 per student. Why can't they just give me the money, and let me decide where to educate my own daughter? Hell, I could get her into a good private school for a lot less than that. "

"Oh, Joab, you make it sound so simple. Let me give you a few reasons why. First, the National Educators Association is the most powerful union in the country with a membership somewhere around two and a quarter million, last time I heard. They have a government monopoly on education which gives them decent pay, mind-blowing job security, solid government benefits and comfortable retirement. They're not gonna walk away from all that without a fight. Then, at the federal and local levels billions have been invested in buildings and property. Scrapping all that would be a pretty hard sell to taxpayers. Add to that a majority of kids who come from single-parent households and you've got a huge complacency problem. Otherwise parents wouldn't put up with the psycho-garbage that passes for public education in the first place."

Joab stared at the patina of the wooden table in front of him. His jaw muscles worked as he ground his back molars together, absently.

"You sent your kids to private schools, right?" Joab asked.

"Yeah. About broke me once or twice, too. And that's another thing, white-flight folks who *can* afford a private education for their kids are perfectly happy with things the way they are. And every one of these parents and teachers are hiding behind this notion of the separation of church and state ..."

"I can tell you it's not working. You know me, Mr. Keylar, I'm not real religious, not like my mother, but at least in a Catholic school I know my girls would be given some form of discipline. I mean they'll kick you out if you don't behave. The kids at MLK Primary are just plain out of control. No one can learn in an environment like that. I mean what kid likes to work?"

"Man, Joab, I know you're right but I just don't see how we could take this one on and win. And going against the government? Hell, I'd be better off just to give you the money to put Cinda in school. I mean it's a real David and Goliath scenario."

"Well, I guess if Cinda's trapped, she's just trapped is all," the younger father stated, sadly.

Then Charlie Keylar heard himself utter the phrase which always became a declaration of war within his soul, "Man, I'd really like to help you, but ..."

Charlie-the-idealist and Charlie-the-realist locked in combat.

Chapter 22

By and by, up in Durham, Professor Glenda Blackwell of Duke University met Senator Liz Straddlethorp, in a posh restaurant for a ladies' power lunch. They were like-minded on issues and agendas and each greatly enjoyed the opportunity to relax into candid conversation before a socially kindred sister. Sadly, packed schedules permitted such outings only rarely. There was much ground to be covered. Over an appetizer and the first glasses of white wine, Liz gave the professor an insider's view of the recent skirmishes and victories of North Carolina policy-makers. By the main course and the second glass of wine, both women were relating tales of their latest sexual encounters with stark frankness and not a few chuckles. The third glass of wine led them through a winding trail of mutual acquaintances and shared interests. Eventually, their conversation stumbled upon Lesa Shemisaki and Joab Johnson.

"So, did their love survive graduation?" Liz asked, batting her eyes sarcastically.

"Nah."

"So sad," Liz commented, "Shit. What I wouldn't give for her skinny waist. I'll bet that little bitch can eat anything she wants."

"Don't worry. Forty will happen to her someday, too. And if the calories don't get her, at least we can count on gravity. Last I heard she was in some law school in Hawaii."

"Oh, yeah, she's from Hawaii," Liz remembered while savoring a bite of white chocolate cheesecake.

"And he's at Emory in Atlanta."

"I wonder if he stayed busy in politics?"

"Oh, yeah. He's hooked, VP of their campus chapter of Young Democrats down there."

"Man, that kid's incredible with names! Half the politicians in this country would cut off their right nut if that would help them remember names. Hell, that kid clinched the cocktail party set for me. 'Course, I'd never tell him that."

Now, Liz Straddlethorp got to thinking. She knew that making a personal recommendation was always a tricky business. People are just so damned unpredictable! You never know if someone will make you look great or screw things up and embarrass the hell out of you. On the other hand, a good favor never goes uncompensated and one can't have too many allies. Liz liked to keep things friendly with her Dixieland neighbors and she judged Joab to be a pretty safe bet, as black boys go. The call went out Friday morning.

✦ ✦ ✦

Anita found a cleaning company, run by a friend of a friend, and accepted work as a domestic cleaning woman in a few of the more affluent homes in Buckhead. She chose the job because she liked her boss - a single mom with three kids. During the interview, she promised that if Anita worked efficiently, she would be off in time to pick Cinda up from school. She understood that children caught bugs and needed tonsillectomies, and she would not begrudge sick days so long as Anita never lied to her. She paid a fair wage.

Eventually, Anita was able to ferret out several homes where Mandy would be welcomed. Next she cut a deal with her three-year-old, that she would be able to "go with Mama " so long as she stayed in her old playpen and played with her toys so Mama could work. It was a tough deal for a toddler, but Mandy accepted the discipline after only one brief return to daycare. Though awkward at times, this arrangement turned out to be a double blessing: not only was Anita more relaxed while watching her own daughter, but the savings in child care expenses made a real difference. Joab continued to work three days a week at the Speedy Gas, from 5:00PM to 12 midnight. On his days off, Anita and the girls were already home by the time class let out. Thus, the pieces came together that would enable the Johnson family to get by.

Unfortunately, the housing search was not nearly as successful. Finally, it was abandoned, all together, and the Johnsons stayed put for lack of a viable alternative.

One day, Joab walked in his front door to the sound of the phone ringing. Cinda ran at her father to offer the daily linebacker hug, announcing his arrival as she went.

"Joab? Telephone." Anita called from the kitchen.

Joab kissed his wife and took the receiver. "Hello. This is Joab . . . The governor? Well, yes, sir. I'm Vice President this year . . . Sure, sure. I'd love to . . . okay. Saturday the 16th at 12:00. Oh, yeah, I'm pretty sure I can make it . . . Thank you."

Anita stopped peeling potatoes and turned to face him.

"What was that all about?" she asked.

"It was a guy by the name of Scott Houghton. He's one of Theodore Cummings' aids and he invited me to the Governor's mansion for a hamburger barbecue on the 16th. He said Gov. Cummings is interested in Young Democrats or something."

"You're going to lunch with the Governor?!" Anita asked, astonished.

"I guess so. You're going, too!"

"No! I'm not!"

"Oh yes, you are."

"Joab, what could I possibly think of to say to those people? Did you know that clear ammonia is still the best thing for washing windows?"

"You wouldn't have to say anything at all. Just stand there and look beautiful."

Anita rolled her eyes.

Joab decided not to argue, but went to hunt for Mandy. He made it a point to greet her each time he walked in the door, a ritual he would observe until *she* came to greet *him*. He found her quietly undressing Barbies beside the toy box, an activity which infuriated Cinda who shivered at the sight of naked dolls.

"Daddy missed you today," he said, scooping her up. "Give Daddy a great, big neck hug." Each day the child responded with a more generous measure of enthusiasm. He was coming to know her, and she, him. Her personality was, in many respects, the antithesis of her big sister's. Where Cinda thrived on the social interaction of friends, Mandy was quiet, observant and content with long periods of solitary play. But one was mistaken if he interpreted her quiet self-containment as dullness of mind. Animated spurts of conversation often revealed a crunching of information previously assumed to have gone whizzing over the top of her little head.

Joab had missed her potty training by months. So had Anita, for that matter. One day, just before turning two, Mandy had simply refused to wear another diaper. She had presented a pink pair of Cinda's Cinderella underpants to her mother, accepted assistance in stepping into them and had had remarkably few accidents thereafter. Up until her encounter with Jojo Minks, Cinda had met few strangers. But Mandy's approach to unfamiliar faces had always been one of caution. Joab had a sense that once Mandy accepted you, her heart locked you in for keeps. He hoped it would pop open to him one day soon. He knew it had not taken her nearly this long to warm up to his mother and considered the innate foreignness of his gender to be the cause of her lingering skepticism. Apparently, Nicholas had had little real interaction with the girls, working most of the night and sleeping most of the day, often at a lover's house. Joab found the search for the tiny key to his youngest daughter's heart to be a particularly sweet challenge and looked forward to the day when, in need of comfort, she would seek his arms as easily as her mother's.

Ultimately, Joab decided not to push Anita into going to the governor's cookout. He knew she would come around in time if he was patient and careful in building her confidence. Shiny new cars lined the sidewalk outside the walled grounds of the governor's mansion. Joab drove once around it trying to discover the place of access. Then he drove his decaying Ford around the corner (out of sight) and parked. A security guard at the gate checked his name off a list and directed him to the back of the main house. It was hard not to be intimidated by the grandeur of the estate. Even in mid-fall, an over-seeding of rye kept the grass bright and lush and it was manicured to golf-course perfection.

Joab had worked enough fundraisers with Liz to know what to expect - or so he thought. But instead of a crowd of 200-250, what he found on the back terrace was a small group of no more than forty people. Most of them looked like young professionals, mostly male but some females, in casual attire. There was one family with small children. Joab was one of four of African-American descent and one of them was a waiter. A man in a white chef's uniform tended hot dogs and burgers from the center of three propane grills and sent them over to the buffet table when they were ready to be served. A bartender took orders from behind another well-stocked table.

Joab stood at the edge of the gathering, taking a deep breath and trying not to look nervous. He was relieved to discover that he was dressed properly. His first impulse had been to wear a suit and tie to meet the Governor of Georgia, but he quickly realized that khakis were more appropriate for a cookout, though not as totally informal as jeans. It had taken him over an hour to choose between a sport coat without a tie or a sweater. Finally, the weather made up his mind for him. It was a crisp, sunny day, windy, a bit late in the season for a cookout, actually. It was a day made for a thick cotton sweater, definitely. Anita had ironed a dress shirt for him though she was sure only the rim of the collar would ever be seen.

"You look fine, Joab," she had told him again and again. "I'm sure glad I ain't going."

Joab's dress shoes looked entirely too black next to the beige khakis and sand-colored sweater. His Wal Mart sneakers were now over two years old, and the soles were having a hard time remaining bound to the rest of the shoes. That left only his biking boots, and they had a hole that had progressed through the first layer of leather on the right bottom. He'd just have to make sure he kept his feet flat while sitting down.

Joab had been in the same room with the governor on a couple of other occasions. Both had been large fundraisers held in enormous rooms in which Joab and other YDs had handed out bumper stickers and written out name tags. Both times, Theo Cummings had entered the building through a private entrance behind the table of honor that had been set on a raised platform. He had exited the same way, soon after delivering his speech. Theo Cummings was an attractive, silver-haired man in his mid-sixties. His Southern accent and manner favored "gentleman" over "good-old-boy." He was a gracious man and a widower. His wife of over forty years had died of cancer four years earlier. Rumors of girlfriends abounded, but Theo was discreet. Joab remembered thinking how much smaller he appeared in person than on TV. And now here Joab was, eating a burger right there at a table in *the governor's backyard*. Joab sorely wished for a beer to settle his nerves but decided that, under the circumstances, he'd better not head for the bar first thing, maybe not at all. He was on his way to the buffet table when a thirtyish, yuppie-type walked up to him extending a hand.

"Hi. You must be Joab. Am I pronouncing that right?"

Joab nodded, grasping the hand firmly.

"I'm Scott Houghton."

"Oh, you were the one who called. Pleased to meet you, Mr. Houghton!"

Scott had already taken in everything about Joab from his wedding band to his biker boots.

"Was that your wife who answered the phone?"

"Yes."

"Oh, I meant to invite her, too."

"You did," Joab smiled. "One of our girls woke up with a fever last night. She decided she'd better stay home. She sure did hate to miss this though."

"Oh, I hope it's nothing serious."

"Nah, just a little bug or something."

"How many girls do you have, Mr. Johnson?"

"Anita and I have two."

"I've got three boys."

"I'm hoping to have one of those, myself, someday. If I ever get out of school."

"Ah, one's never enough."

"I don't know about that. My mama only had one, and I've heard her say he was a right, big handful." Both men laughed.

"So, can I get you a beer or something?" Scott offered.

"Uh, just a Coke, I think."

"Fine. Why don't you get yourself something to eat and I'll meet you over at that table," Scott indicated a round table, occupied but for three seats.

"Can I get you something from the buffet?" Joab offered.

"No. I've already eaten. But, thanks."

Joab lingered over the food table until he saw Scott set down his Coke and take a seat.

Mingling comfortably with his guests, Theo Cummings kept a loose eye on the tall, attractive, black boy in his midst. Over his years in politics, Mr. Cummings had had many of these small, informal get-togethers with staff and close supporters. He found they encouraged his people to retract the claws and curb the back-biting, often found in tight circles where much was at stake. The governor was also a keenly intuitive people watcher. He had long since come to appreciate the value of such gatherings in assessing the worthiness of a potential employee or political ally.

Gov. Cummings appraised Joab. *The boy presented well, smiled easily, and could hold his own in a social setting. Just like Liz said.*

By the late 1990s, Democrat incumbents were under mounting pressure to surround themselves with more minority bodies; a practice unnatural to the Governor's personal preferences. This fact, if not well hidden, would mean death in the Democratic Party. With the political tidal surge gathering behind Amos Webster, the handwriting on the wall was hard to miss. Any public official who wasn't scrambling to pick up a few aides of African-American descent was either imprudent or just plain stupid.

I owe Straddlethorp a favor for covering my blindspot, the Governor conceded in his mind.

The United States of America was very close to the election of its first black Presidential candidate, and the Clinton Administration was grappling with a serious miscalculation. While it was indisputable that the media had gone to extraordinary lengths to keep their impeached President from being kicked out of the White House, Hillary and Bill had made a grave error in perceiving media bias as social approval. An honest mistake. After all, hadn't NBC kept the Juanita Broaddrick rape story from breaking until after the senate vote? You just don't get better friends than that. Now, as they prepared Al Gore to grasp the baton, they realized that media loyalty was more indicative of a loathing of conservatism than a love for Clinton. And William Jefferson Clinton had cost them dearly. All major news shows were losing their credibility and their ratings. America was tuning them out or turning to alternative sources.

After seven long years of reaching ever deeper into the reserves of human creativity for damage control angles and image reconstruction, there was an almost tangible letdown after Judge Rehnquist's gavel finally fell silent. Spin fatigue swept through news organizations faster than runny noses through a day care center. Bernie, Katie, Peter, Larry, Dan and even Geraldo were just flat wore-out. Only the feisty James Carvil seemed undaunted at the prospect of keeping those approval polls up and November 2000 was suddenly looking very far off. Media operatives hungered for a new figure to move their progressive agenda forward. Desperately, they scanned the political horizon. Then, there he was: Amos Webster; solid, credible, charming—*monogamous*. Besides, Al Gore just couldn't sell papers and airtime like his charismatic predecessor. He was... well... dull. The best handlers couldn't project him as anything more than a mildly passionate geek. So day after day the hapless vice-president muddled along in bewilderment as the press adopted Amos Webster as the new apple of their camera's eye. In the end, they turned on him as if he were a Republican. Unfounded rumors of his desire to spend more time with his family and his failing health abounded. From the safety of the private sector, Dan Quayle secretly pitied him. The undercurrents of a cultural feeding frenzy were being stirred up. And, although Governor Cummings knew that anything could happen in eighteen months, he'd also been playing this game too long to be caught unprepared.

There was a second reason he had a need for a new staff person; Cummings had felt himself slowing down since his wife's death. He was getting tired. Historically, the challenge of remembering the personal details of all key people had fallen into Helen's domain. They had been a dynamic team, and he missed her terribly. He supposed he should be considering retirement, but he was used to being a celebrity. Without Helen, he needed the buzz of the press, the fuss of the public, and the sport of the race more than ever. If this boy was really as good as Liz had indicated, he just might improve the odds.

Lost in light conversation about kids and jurisprudence, Joab was caught by surprise when the governor was suddenly standing behind him.

"Oh, Theo, this is Joab Johnson from the Emory Law School chapter of Young Democrats," Scott announced, suddenly.

Joab rose hastily, swallowed his mouthful before it was fully chewed, wiped his mouth with a napkin, and extended his hand.

Gov. Cummings pumped Joab's arm and patted his back.

"Good to meet you, Joab," he said, with flawless authenticity. "Sit down. Sit down. Eat."

Joab sat, but turned his chair around to face the governor.

"I always like to keep up with what's going on with our young folks. Our party needs enthusiasm and fresh ideas. Don't be afraid to let Scott, here, know what you think. I'll be sure to ask him about it."

"Yes, sir," Joab said.

Cummings made several friendly comments to others at the table before drifting to the next.

Joab harbored a great respect for Cummings, who was known in Georgia as "the Education Governor." He had a well publicized interest in improving public education, a subject which had become of deep concern to Joab, of late. Joab had read a recent article about him in *The Atlanta Chronicle*. It stated that he had increased the budget for public schools by over seven percent, in his first term, and had upped it another two point five percent in his second. The article, however, praising the abiding commitment of the Governor to this issue, failed to give any solid indications of the improvements resulting from the increased flow of tax money to the schools. Joab assumed that there were improvements and they were, or would soon become, evident.

✦ ✦ ✦

The following morning, Governor Cummings called Scott Houghton in for a little conference.

"So, how'd the boy do?" the governor asked.

"Johnson?"

"The black boy."

"Joab Johnson. He did great. I hate to tell you, but the kid is good. I must have introduced him to 25 people yesterday, and every indication I got was that he not only had total recollection of their names, first and last, but he can retain reams of information on families and wives - all kinds of stuff."

"Is he married?"

"Happily, from the sound of it, with two daughters."

"Two? They must have gotten an early start."

"High school."

"Hmm. How come she didn't come?"

"Sick child."

The governor bobbed his head thoughtfully. "Okay," he said, reaching a decision. "I've got a cocktail party with those execs from Mitsubishi next week. Schedule him to come along. Let's see how he handles those impossible oriental names. Tell him that I expect him to absorb names and personal details and cue me on them discreetly. Jeanna has particulars of time and place. Get her to send a car around for him. Oh, and be sure to indicate appropriate attire. The Japanese are damned sensitive to that kind of thing. Questions or comments?"

Houghton shook his head.

"Good enough. Thanks."

✦ ✦ ✦

That evening, Joab received two surprising phone calls out of what seemed like nowhere.

He had barely concluded his conversation with Scott Houghton, when a call came in from Charlie Keylar.

"Hey, Mr. Keylar. Guess who I just got off the phone with?" he boasted, still astounded. "The governor's office. He invited me to a cocktail party with some guys from Mitsubishi."

"Well, congratulations, Joab. Good for you!"

"Thanks."

"How are Anita and the girls?"

"Great. And Susan?"

"Fine. Fine. The reason I called," Charlie went on, "was concerning what we talked about at our meeting. I'll tell you, Joab, you've really got me bothered. I'd hate to have to send one of my kids to an urban public school, especially after all that Cinda's been through, so I've been looking into it. Do you have a minute?"

"Sure!" Joab grabbed a pen, the message pad, a kitchenette chair, and cleared a spot on the table from the recently concluded dinner. He prepared to take notes.

"See, the problem is that not only do you want the government to let you decide where to spend your child's tax allocation for education, but your particular choice would be a specifically religious school. This is going to have institutions like the American Civil Liberties Union raising all kinds of hell over the so-called separation of church and state. This is really where the battle's going to be won or lost and we have no choice but to take it head on. I've come up with an argument, it's a giant long shot, but there are a few supporting decisions and common sense is heavily weighted on our side. Here goes:"

"I'm listening."

"See, the discipline problem you've witnessed in the classroom is really just a superficial manifestation with a much deeper root. Actually, it's just the outward indication of an inward acceptance of the religion of Secular Humanism. Let me explain. The most basic premise of Secular Humanism is a substitution of faith in man for faith in God. Now, while this seems innocuous to a tolerant society, and I've always considered myself to be a tolerant man, the implications of it spin out in every direction. I'm really only just beginning to scratch the surface."

At this point Joab noticed his daughters, freshly bathed and dressed in pink nighties, staring at him from the kitchen doorway.

"Can you hang on for just a second," he asked Charlie.

"Sure."

"Daddy's got an important phone call from Mr. Keylar," he told his daughters. "You know who Mr. Keylar is?"

At this, Cinda shook her head, "yes," and Mandy shook hers," no."

"He's Granny Ruth's boss," Nita offered, walking up behind them.

"He's the white dude at Mama and Daddy's wedding," Cinda informed her sister proudly.

"Right," Joab agreed. "Well he's got important business with Daddy so Mama will read you the story tonight and tuck you in. I'll be in to give y'all a kiss as soon as I'm off the phone. Okay?"

The girls nodded and disappeared with their mother.

"Okay, I'm back," Joab said, raising the receiver to his ear. "Sorry for the interruption."

"Quite all right. Let's see, where was I?... –Oh, yeah, the implications of this basic premise: faith in man instead of faith in God, are tremendously far-reaching, but the one which you're most concerned with stems from the Humanist assertion that man's highest purpose is to seek personal fulfillment and that the only legitimate rules governing human behavior are dictated by an individual's circumstance. So, traditional standards for behavior are rejected and the lines between right and wrong become blurred. In our public schools, this assertion manifests itself as a severe discipline problem.

"But, with regard to public education, it's more insidious than that. Since all codes of discipline have their foundation in some form of religion, and the Supreme Court has insisted on religious neutrality since the 1960s, no real codes of discipline can legally be implemented. Let's take the Ten Commandments, for example, okay? Most everybody can agree that it's wrong to murder or steal or sleep with your neighbor's wife, but because these rules were codified in religious scripture, they are banned from being posted on public school property. But the reality of it is this: a code of behavior, consistent with Secular Humanism, has been fostered and is obviously flourishing in our public schools today. Ah, I'm getting ahead of myself. Man, this is so big to try and get your arms around! There's so much stuff. I can't believe I've never heard all this before. I mean I can't be the first guy to be digging through this!

"Here's my point, Joab. An extremely strong and shockingly well-documentable case can be made that the Federal Government has, in fact, been using the public education system to indoctrinate our children into a state religion; Secular Humanism. And that, my boy, is a crystal-clear violation of the Establishment Clause of the First Amendment of the United States Constitution."

Joab wondered if he was going to take a breath.

"Listen to this:," Keylar continued, "one of the first public signers of the Humanist Manifesto I of 1933 was an American by the name of John Dewey. He is known today as the Father of Modern Education, and he openly set out to infiltrate public schools with Humanist dogma over sixty years ago. Another example: the Goals 2000: Educate America Act passed by the Clinton Administration back in 1994, effectively compelled states to implement federal dictates on public education by tying compliance to federal funding. In other words, no compliance, no money. This is a blatant violation of Title 20, section 432a, US Code, setting forth federal education law which, believe it or not, specifically forbids the U.S. government, quote, 'to exercise any direction, supervision, or control over curriculum,' unquote. . . as well as a whole host of other educational specifics Uncle Sam's supposed to be keeping his long, sticky fingers out of. And Goals 2000 is replete with Secular Humanistic doctrine.

"Joab," he went on excitedly, "that's just the tip of the iceberg. But the incredible thing is that in several 'conscientious objector' cases, the U.S. Supreme Court has defined 'religion' broadly enough to easily encompass Secular Humanism. Do you know what that means? That means, we have a really credible case."

"Mr. Keylar, you're really fired up about this!" Joab observed when he could get a word in.

"I don't know, Joab. I'm somewhere between pissed-off and fired-up, but I can tell you, I haven't been this excited about a case since... since... well, maybe never. But now let's follow the chain of logic which leads us to our goal. Once we've established that Secular Humanism *is* a religion forced upon the less privileged masses by a government which compels its citizens to make their children attend school or face prosecution, we *must* get the court to accept the fact that a religion-free education is an impossible and unattainable goal, which it is. After that, it's a cakewalk, because the question then becomes whose religion is the child to be raised in - the state's or the parent's? And unless I woke up in a Communist China this morning, which, frankly, I'm beginning to wonder, the answer is clearly, the parent's.

"Hell, in a perfect world, we'd prosecute the largest class action suit known to man and bankrupt this government with damages! They'd deserve it, too, Joab. This country was founded by boatloads of desperate people searching for religious freedom. It's the first thing our Constitution addresses, and the language is *not* ambiguous. This separation of church and state thing was supposed to protect religion from the government and our educational system has used it to usher in the very thing it was designed to prevent! Shit! I'm beginning to sound like one of those damned religious fanatics!" Charlie took a deep breath and reined in his enthusiasm. "Anyway, precedent for a no-strings-attached voucher has been well established by the post-WWII GI Bill. It worked and it worked well. In fact, that's how my daddy got through Notre Dame and, God willing, that's how Cinda and Mandy and maybe a whole bunch of others will get through elementary school."

"So you think we can really win?"

"Well, don't start celebrating yet. Not only are we setting ourselves up against the most powerful government on earth, but also the third most powerful union in that nation. A lot of people have a lot to lose if we win, and I'm not talking about the kids. We could get shot down at any time. If we make it to the U.S. Supreme Court, I can guarantee a long and bloody fight. Courts tend to try to find a way to uphold and legitimize what the government is doing."

"What about money, Mr. Keylar?" Joab asked, afraid to hear the answer.

"Ah, what's money, Joab? If it gets too expensive, I'll just let you work for free the first five or six years."

There was a pause in conversation as Joab wondered whether he should laugh or not.

Charlie's laughter burst out first. "I'm kidding. Joab, lighten up. Look, in these cynical times, it's not often an attorney gets to fight one just because it's right. I think I can finance this one. I might call on you to help with some research, though. It'll actually be a good experience for you. And, hey, if we win, I get a national reputation. If we lose, it's not the end of the world, except that Cinda stays trapped in a bad school. I'll start framing the briefs in my spare time - like I have any - and file the case as soon as I can. Man, it's gonna have to be airtight, though."

"Good luck, Mr. Keylar. But I don't really know how I can thank you or repay you... even if we do win... maybe, especially if we don't win..."

"Strap in, Joab, this might be a wild ride."

"I don't know how to thank you."

"Just start praying for a judge with balls."

Charlie Keylar hung up the phone, rocked back in his executive chair, crossed his feet on the leather top of his massive desk, placed his hands behind his head and stared at the ceiling of his office. He had consulted his partner about this case last night. He had held nothing back but explained, at length, the projected cost of trying such a case in terms of time commitment, emotional energy, and financial resources. Susan never flinched, but feeling the heat from the fire in her husband's belly, told him she was prepared to back him through the ordeal and gladly abide by the consequences. Charlie pondered, again, the unfathomable wealth which was Susan. For him, it was a humbling thing to be the object of the rare and unshakable devotion of such a fine woman.

Had Joab had any prophetic insight into the enormity of the personal cost of his lawsuit, he too, may have had a talk with his partner. But still in his second year of law school, he was blind to most issues not printed between the covers of law books.

"Mr. Keylar thinks he may have found a way to force the government to let us choose where Cinda goes to school," he told Anita in bed that night, when she asked why Charlie had called. "It has something to do with First Amendment rights and proving that the federal government is using public education to impose a state religion and is he evermore fired-up about it!"

"Great. I hate that school. It's a dangerous place," Anita said, snuggling down under his arm and resting her head on his shoulder. Then she was asleep.

Having indulged in, perhaps, one too many Louis L'Amour novels, Charlie Keylar often fancied the parallels between modern attorneys and the hired gunfighters of the Old West. Experience told this hired gun that once the initial shots had been fired, the returning rounds would come in the form of a motion to dismiss the case and/or for summary judgment. He was betting on drawing a judge seasoned enough to know that any decision was sure to be appealed, so he may as well just go on and let both sides prepare for the fight. Charlie knew you had better have all cylinders loaded, with plenty of back-up ammo, when you're calling out the government! Over the next three months, the lights in Charlie's office often stayed on long into the night and an on-line legal research company started billing considerable sums to Charles R. Keylar, Attorney at Law. The longer Charlie pored over his pleadings and briefs, the more he was convinced that the Federal Government had greatly overstepped the boundaries of the Constitution, had become brazen from the lack of public resistance, and was decades overdue for a stiff rebuke by a people yet free.

Finally, when the jurisdiction had been established, when background and supporting facts had been mined and refined into the purest form, when legal theory and precedent came together to point the finger of guilt, and when a compelling prayer for specific relief had been drafted, perfected and redrafted several times over, Charlie decided it was time to file the case.

Joab got the call at work. He answered the phone, "Speedy Gas, downtown."

"Hey, Joab. This is Charlie Keylar."

"Hey, Mr. Keylar."

"I just wanted you to know, I'm filing it tomorrow. I wanted to make sure you're in 'cause once it's filed, we're in 'till it's over. It's time to lock and load or walk, right now."

"File it," Joab said, a bit surprised by Mr. Keylar's peculiar sense of drama.

"Oh, and I thought I might file it under a fictitious name, probably, John Doe in order to protect Cinda from hostility or bias in the classroom and from publicity."

"Great idea, Mr. Keylar!" Joab heartily agreed. He was instantly impressed by his counselor's sensitivity and forethought.

On October 31, 1998, Charles R. Keylar filed <u>Doe v. Pickens Co. School Board</u> in the Federal District Court in Atlanta.

The case was immediately recognized as one worthy of the attention of a U.S. District Court judge. The rotation fell to the honorable Earnest M. Dowling, III. Charlie couldn't believe his luck. Not only was this Federal Judge known to have had an ample supply of testosterone, but he was leaning more to the right with each passing year *and* (unknown to all but his oldest friends) he had a vendetta against The Education Governor. History was that the two men had been classmates in Wake

Forest Law School back in the 50s. Both had come from powerful families endowed with plenty of old money. Though they had been on friendly terms, they had been natural rivals. Moving in the same circles, the beautiful and gracious Helen Calhoun had quite fancied Ernest Dowling before the winsome Theo Cummings had convinced her to become his bride. Forty years later, and still moving in similar circles, neither had abandoned the old rivalry.

As expected, Federal Judge Dowling, III, denied the motion to dismiss and seized control of the case with great interest, requesting that both sides suggest a discovery plan and trial date. Since Charlie had already done the bulk of his homework, it was time to hurry up and wait until the opposing side revealed the position from which its first attack would come. Charlie Keylar could well imagine the danger alerts going out to the legal strategists and big guns of the National Education Association and the American Federation of Teachers. With dues payments from over three million combined members, there was no lack of financial resources for legal talent. Charlie had to consciously guard himself against the invisible, but very real, danger of intimidation. It comes to this, he reminded himself daily while shaving, *the education machine is immense and formidable, but it has betrayed the people it was created to serve. And a free man or woman has a right to decide where to send their child to school.*

Charlie's confidence improved when the Supreme Court refused to hear an appeal against the constitutionality of Wisconsin's voucher. For the Johnsons, it seemed at first, as though little had changed since the lawsuit had been filed. There was a short article that made its way into *The Atlanta Chronicle*, but it was given no prominence. The media didn't seem to take much interest in the matter and the education establishment certainly didn't seem to be creating any publicity about it.

The days flew by in a flurry of activity and deadlines. Anita's exhausted Escort was daily coerced into rolling itself from home to work to MLK Elementary to the grocery store, and back home again. Joab, gloved, hooded, helmeted, and heavily coated, could be seen on his own languishing two-wheels, making the rounds between home, Emory, and the Speedy Gas convenience store.

Once committed and in full view of the home stretch of Joab's education, the Johnsons lowered their heads and plowed through resistance, like a well-matched pair of powerful, young draft horses. No longer fighting the harness and driven by faith in the harvest, they threw the full weight of their strength forward, turning up the dark, fertile soil of their lives.

Christmas brought with it a renewed joy and wholeness which had not been known since Cinda's first. Although Nicholas' absence continued to pain Miss Lucy, all three generations rejoiced in the blessings of a family reunited-- none so much as the children.

Back in school, Joab no longer submitted to the tyranny of the urgent, but made himself maintain the priority of his family above all else. Sweating over stacks of books and mock briefs on the nights that he did not work, Joab would force himself to close the computer and read his children the bedtime story. Then, he would lie down with his wife, permitting himself a few moments of the pleasure and release she offered, bringing to her a tender ending to a grueling day and the knowledge that she was greatly desired. Once the stress had been purged from her muscles and her breathing had become slow and even, Joab would gently unwrap her arms from about him and return his attention to his studies. And the price for all of this? - the exchange of As for Bs. It was a high price for Joab to accept at first but he reminded himself that Mr. Keylar already had a job waiting for him and his real goals were to reconcile his family and, then, to pass the bar.

Often, while studying, Joab would stop to enjoy the peace of his household. Often it felt as though his family's dwelling was the eye of the tempest which raged all around it in the lawless violence of his neighborhood. A new awareness of the value and fragility of the lives of his wife and daughters, birthed in Joab a desire to pray that he had not known. It was a desire he denied.

The governor's office called on him with increasing frequency until, by the end of the school year, conflicts with Joab's job made a conference with Scott Houghton imperative, though unwelcome.

"What's the problem?" the governor asked impatiently when Scott made an impromptu visit on a busy day.

"It's Johnson, Sir." came the answer.

"What's wrong with Joab? He's not sick is he? I'm going to need him at his best for the Chamber of Commerce gala this week," Cummings grumbled.

"No, sir, he's not sick. It's his job. Our meetings are, apparently, impacting his work and he says his boss is threatening to fire him. He says he can't afford to volunteer any more time."

"Scotty, you think he's jerking me around because he knows I need him?"

"No, sir, I don't think he has a clue how valuable he is. I think he and his wife are busting ass to get him through law school and he needs the money. Remember, they've got two kids."

"Oh, yeah, yeah. What does his wife do?"

"She cleans houses."

"Oh. And him? What does he do?"

"He works three or four late night shifts a week at the Speedy Gas convenience store on the corner of I-20 and Washington."

"That's not a real safe neighborhood."

"He says that's why he works there. They have a hard time finding people to fill the night shifts so they pay well and work around his classes and exams. . . up until now, anyway."

"What's he get a week?"

"Probably ninety to a hundred and twenty bucks, net."

Cummings broke out in a laugh. "Ninety to one hundred and twenty bucks!" he repeated. "You're kidding me."

Scott Houghton shook his head.

The Governor leaned back against his desk and ran a hand over the stubble on his chin. "You tracking Amos Webster lately?" he asked.

"Everyday."

"It's his time, plain and simple. The damn Republicans have been crippled since the '98 elections. They might still be able to hang on to the House but since Gore finally got out of the way, they ain't gonna get the White House back this time, either. Out in the streets, you can feel the racial tension already. Makes you wonder what's going on up in New York or out in Chicago and L.A. And it's like the whole damn world has been whipped into a frenzy over this change of millennia thing." He went back to rubbing his face. "It might be time to put Johnson on the payroll. Is he done with school yet?"

"One to go."

"I wonder if he could be talked into putting it off for a year," Cummings thought out loud.

Houghton shrugged his shoulders.

"Talk to Jeanna about my schedule and set up an appointment, ASAP, between me and the boy."

"Done."

Chapter 23

One afternoon as Anita was hurrying to put the groceries away so she could start dinner and get the girls to bed at a reasonable hour, a knock came on the side door. Hardly anyone used that door but Loretta, and Nita knew from the sound that it was her.

"Is he home, yet?" Anita's friend whispered through the cracked door.

"Joab? No. Why?"

"Good," said Loretta, "It's here!" she squeaked, handing Anita a box. Her son slipped in behind her.

The theme from "Barney and Friends" could be heard coming from the living room. "Go play with Mandy," his mother suggested and he ran off toward the sound of the TV.

"Oh, let's see." Anita took out a kitchen knife and slid it through the tape along the top edge of the box. Then, she reached in and pulled out the first item. "American History," she said, holding up a textbook.

"What else? What else?" Loretta asked, excitedly.

"Algebra II. Man, I hope I can do this. I had a hard enough time with the first algebra."

"English, Spanish II, and last, Advanced Biology. Here are the videotapes. Oh, Loretta, I hope we didn't waste all this money."

"Listen to you, girl! You'll do fine, and so will I. The teachers in the videos explain everything. If we get stuck, we'll help each other or find somebody at the high school. 'Sides, we ain't looking for As. All we gotta do is pass."

In this neighborhood as in countless others over the earth, many relationships are birthed in need. Things that the middle class can afford to pay for, like babysitters and auto mechanics, are provided through mutual empathy and pooled resources. Jumper cables, socket wrenches, lawn mowers, and rides to work when cars give out, are shared. The poor know how to lean on one another. It is a mixed blessing, but it is a blessing. From the start, the similarities between Loretta and Anita were hard to miss. Both were young, attractive, single moms with two children, though Loretta's second was a son born 'most a year sooner than Mandy. Both had gotten pregnant in high school and both had dropped out before graduating.

Loretta had moved in next door to Nicholas eight or nine months before Anita had come to Atlanta. By that time, Nicholas had already initiated and abandoned an affair with her. But it was the older daughters, Cinda and Shameeka, who first discovered each other and were soon rarely ever apart. Although both women had traveled many of the same paths, Anita was struck immediately by Loretta's lack of bitterness, then the hallmark of her own existence. Often, when comparing notes on the treacheries of men, Anita became appalled at the apparent ease with which Loretta accepted her misuse.

"How can you forgive that scumbag?" she had asked one day, exasperated by Loretta's lack of anger with her abusive ex.

Loretta had just smiled and shrugged her shoulders, "Jesus forgave the man nailing his feet to the cross, and Jesus didn't do nothing wrong. I just can't see how I can be holdin' no grudge."

Well, maybe her friend had a hole in her head where a perfectly well-justified hostility belonged, but at least Jesus hadn't instructed her to stay and get beaten to a bloody pulp, every weekend. And, anyway, it was Anita's good luck to have landed beside such a friend on a street where the odds were not in her favor. And Ruth seemed to love Loretta almost as much as Anita did.

"You think you'll really be able to keep it from Joab for a whole year?" Loretta asked doubtfully.

"I will if you and Cinda can keep your mouths shut. Between his classes and his work, I should have enough time to do this stuff while he's out of the house."

Like battle buddies in wartime, both women had taken turns carrying one another through dark, dangerous places. When Loretta's former husband came to vent his rage upon property he still considered his own, Anita threw open the side door to receive Loretta and her children. Together the single mothers huddled in prayer as the man banged on the house, called down curses upon his family, and threw beer bottles at the windows until the police finally arrived. Likewise, Loretta's arms were open to receive Cinda or Mandy whenever Anita was on the spot. Loretta arrived at the hospital moments after her best friend's voice crackled over the answering machine informing her of Cinda's rape. Now both women were fixing to help each other correct a youthful error in judgment.

In their hopes for their children, they could feel the day coming when one of them would say, "You didn't graduate. Why should I?" Today, they were preparing an answer.

Giddy at the prospect of acquiring some small measure of intellectual credibility, Loretta and Anita giggled at their conspiracy.

All traces of high school studies were well hidden by the time Joab got home from his day of classes and one meeting with the governor. Three little girls jumped up from the TV and ran at him to deliver the greeting. Cinda and Shameeka (spending the night) ran at him with the usual enthusiasm. Mandy waited for him to pick her up and receive his tender kiss on the cheek.

It was obvious that it was Mandy's turn for the video as shrill little mice voices sang "Blue Moon" for the eighth time that week. Mandy went back and sat two feet from the screen while the older children searched the toy box for horses. The Barbies were apparently desirous of a ride before bed.

"Wasn't *'Babe'* playing when I left this morning?" he asked Anita, entering the kitchen.

"I don't know. It's all running together." She was just finishing post-dinner clean-up. He walked up behind her and gave her a kiss on the neck.

"What'd the governor want?" she asked, preparing a plate for him.

"He wanted me to take next year off from school so I could come work for him full time."

"Oh," she stood still, "What did you tell him?"

"You know how I love politics, Neet. This is kind of a cross road opportunity." Anita felt herself wanting to cry. "But I told him that my wife had her heart set on Savannah by the fall of 2000, and I wasn't going to make her wait any longer." Anita did not respond, but stood silent in front of the stove. "Nita, you okay?" he asked.

"This is a big chance for you, Joab," she said. "You sure you don't want to take it?"

"No. I've already accepted a job in Savannah. Mr. Keylar's a good man and I want to raise my girls near family. Besides, my wife misses home."

Anita put the plate down, spun around and hugged her husband's neck like she'd never let go. "Thank you, Joab," she wept.

"I know you want to go home," he said, putting his arms around her and lifting her up off the floor. "But listen up," he continued, putting her down again. "Cummings hired me anyway! Part time. And he's willing to work around my class schedule and everything, except I have to stay through the Democratic National Convention that July. I probably couldn't take the bar by then anyway. I'm going to the National Convention! Is that some kind of crazy?"

"Why you?"

"I help him remember names and stuff. But listen, I get $16,500.00 a year and he's gonna fix it so I can get government health insurance for the whole family, and he's gonna give me a $1,000.00 bonus so I can buy some business suits for work!"

"Well, praise the Lord!" Anita shouted, and the Johnsons laughed so hard the children came running to the kitchen.

"Oh, Joab, can I buy a minivan?" Anita asked as though it was the top item on a fairy tale wish list.

"Sure, whatever you want," he said, delighted with the sound of it.

Joab quit his job at Speedy Gas, finished his second year finals, and was immediately immersed in the governor's social and political calendar. Generally, Jeanna would get him a probable list of the important people planning to attend an upcoming event. The next day, a car would be sent to bring him to the governor's mansion where he would wait for Theo Cummings to finish getting dressed and the two would be chauffeured to the event, Joab briefing the governor on correct name pronunciations, professional backgrounds, network connections, personal details, wives, children, divorces, weddings, illnesses, etc. Joab understood his function and became more entrenched in the governor's political machine with each passing day.

Joab found that most powerful men were vain and were all too pleased to talk about themselves. The more cagy ones preferred to listen, but they were the exception. Hiding behind the innocent humility of a law student hanging on the words of those who had already *made it*, Joab could lead men into relaxed conversations of business. With the mention of a daughter's name, vaults of parental experience popped open. Joab also kept up with sports enough to keep pace with big fans. Realistically aware of his striking appearance in tailored Brooks Brothers suits, Joab observed a personal rule never to talk to wives one on one, but only mingled with them in groups. Professional women were a bit more dicy. To them, personal revelation was more closely associated with intimacy. Then, too, he found that a good percentage preferred to be in control of their relationships and an attractive, younger subordinate was an obvious target for recreational sex. A clear line had to be drawn and maintained. Soon, Joab could be seen at the governor's elbow at almost every function, discreetly leaning close to his ear, as needed, to lubricate the mechanics of socio-political intercourse. Jules Shemisaki might well have been impressed.

Neither Joab nor the governor (rumored to have conquered a drinking problem early in his career) ever sipped anything stronger than ginger ale.

Clearly, Joab had lucked into a prestigious plumb of a government job. In truth, however, the social side of politics bored him; the small talk, the pretense, the necessary stroking of each inflated ego. What intrigued Joab was Scott Houghton's job. Scott's official title was press secretary, but that was not the half of it. Scott was a political strategist. Where Cummings understood the secret motivations of individuals, Houghton understood them collectively and geographically. He meticulously tracked national trends and global forces and crunched vast stores of information in a mind possessing a miraculous ability to read the future and use it to his employer's advantage. His office was a clutter of magazines (liberal and conservative alike), newspapers, political biographies, auto- biographies and fiction. Two TV's and a computer kept a steady flow of cutting edge news and commentary gushing into his office. Thanks to portable computers and the World Wide Web, Houghton could, and often did, stay in touch even while going to the bathroom. Joab wondered how many TVs he kept in his bedroom and what methods his wife may have used to distract him long enough to produce three sons. In any case, Joab greatly enjoyed picking his brain.

"How did you learn all this stuff?" Joab asked one day.

"Oh, man, I've always loved it. It's just about power. Hell, I knew everything about Watergate almost before I could read. A lot of it is just plain old common sense, really. Here, read this article."

Scott grabbed a newspaper clipping entitled "Tax Money for Churches" from the pile of literature on his desk and threw it across to Joab.

"What's it say?" he asked.

"It says some Republican congressmen are trying to resurrect a bill that would enable substance abusers to choose church rehabilitation programs and pay by government vouchers, and (Joab's stomach turned as he read on) if passed, former substance abusers would be given government scholarships which could be used for private secondary education without excluding religious institutions and that those institutions would be free from federal supervision. There are strong concerns over separation of church and state violations. Proponents claim tax money is defederalized once it has been given to the citizen or parent—"

"Yeah, yeah. Skip down to the opposition paragraph," Scott interrupted, "Who's against it?"

"Um, American Psychological Association, National Association of Alcoholism and Drug Abuse Counselors, National Association of Psychiatric Health Systems, International Reading Association, National Association of State Boards of Education, the National Parent-Teachers Association,—"

"Here's the question," Scott interrupted again, "Who loses if the bill passes?"

There was a silence as Joab tried to imagine what Houghton was looking for.

"I'll give you a hint, look for the money," Scott offered, sarcastically.

"Well, I guess," Joab stammered, "most of those associations would find themselves with more competition for government funding."

"Hell-o. See, Joab, I knew you were smarter than you looked. The majority of people reading that article would just assume that all those dedicated associations are motivated by a simple desire to serve their fellow man and improve the human condition for reformed drug addicts. And I'm sure this is true to some degree, but still a lot of money is at stake. Always ask yourself who loses and who wins and you'll discover the source and direction of spin. All news stories are editorials. Don't let anyone tell you differently and don't take any news presentation at face value. In this particular case, the biggest loser would be the general public. Separation of church and state is too critical to mess with."

In that moment, Joab felt another layer of boyish naiveté fall away from his character. It was instantly replaced with a fresh layer of cynicism. And also in that moment, Joab began to grasp the extent to which his secret lawsuit put him at odds with his employer. All he wanted to do was be able to send his kid to a safe school where they still kept standards. Joab felt a stab of gratitude for Charlie's strategies to preserve anonymity. Joab would never have guessed that the decision to file under an assumed name would wind up protecting his job as well as his daughter.

On that front, there had only been minor skirmishes. One resulted in the local school board being let out of the case. This elevated <u>Doe vs. School Board</u> to a state level. Charlie Keylar didn't seem to be concerned, so Joab didn't worry either.

✦ ✦ ✦

The week before his final year of formal education began; Joab moved his family to a safer neighborhood amid great rivers of tears between Cinda and Shameeka, and not a few between Anita and Loretta.

"It's not like we're moving to China," Joab commented at the elaborate display of rampant feminine emotion. And, indeed, the second graders generally spent Friday night together at one house or the other.

Within the scope of American history, it was a great time to be a Democrat. For Joab, it was a great time to be a *black* Democrat. On the eve of the new millennia, there was a mystic optimism for the nation and a growing faith in the basic goodness of the American heart. In spite of President Clinton's second term and the relentless proliferation of Monica Lewinski jokes, Republicans did manage to curb the growth of government producing weak, but steady, economic growth. Still, the press continued to report any proposal to lower taxes as "deep cuts in social programs" and the Democrats wept loud and long over the would-be victims of "Republican tax cuts for the rich." None, however, wept as loud and as long, or was given as much airtime and news copy, as Amos Webster.

A self-proclaimed prodigy of affirmative action and a former ward of the welfare state, Webster was living proof that faith in the Great Society was yet justified. Webster became the embodiment of the ultimate American Dream in a country where, unrecognized by most of its underclass, the demands of socialism in the form of a forty to fifty percent tax drag on income had largely swallowed up their own chances to achieve it. But no matter, instead of economic compensation, they enjoyed the social currency of victim status while the financially independent were shamed into self-effacing silence by a relentlessly hostile press. The king of emotionally charged rhetoric, Webster's keen partisan ears heard America's New Year's resolution to purge itself of the hideous guilt of slavery. His political nose sniffed out and exploited their urgent need to wrap up 300 years of guilt and deposit it, once for all time, within the parcel of sin allotted to the last thousand years. The public sanitation department of history was sure to extract a steep fee for hauling off the rotting left-overs of involuntary servitude. Webster, himself, might even be persuaded to drive the garbage truck. Even so, the stinking cargo would only be driven once around the block and white America would awaken to find it again drawing flies from their front doors. After all, it was still good for another fee or two. What Webster saw when he looked upon his great nation was a people desperate for a clean start; a generation which placed its hope in the good will and keen intellect of man. And good will could be easily purchased, as long as your neighbor was compelled to pay for it—or at least buy it on credit. So, even as the stampeding bulls of Wall Street were being pursued by growling bears, Americans closed their eyes and continued to leverage the heritage of their children and their children's children.

Also contributing to Webster's soon-to-be, slam-dunk victory, was the blackmail of the majority. Many whites could be counted on to pull the lever for Webster simply to avoid the ravages of racial rioting sure to follow a Republican victory. They wouldn't enjoy it, but they would do it. This made little difference to Amos Webster.

Joab loved Sen. Webster, D-CA. He loved catching him on C-span or CNN. It made him feel good just to listen to the man, knowing that, through the governor, he was an active member of the Democratic team, the team that cared about the down-trodden. A man in his early fifties, tall, dignified, articulate, and passionate, Webster was an inspiring figure. Once or twice, Joab let himself play his old game, wondering if Senator Webster had ever visited Savannah, Georgia, maybe a quarter of a century earlier, and had indulged in a brief encounter with a shy sixteen-year-old girl.

Unlike many of her competitors, Anita's employer offered nothing under the table as a kind of welfare supplement, and it had cost her. Over the years, she'd lost some good workers. But though the IRS generally turned a blind eye to urban businesses, they could never be fully trusted. Should the luck of the draw make her business the one audited and then prosecuted, there was precious little money for attorney's fees and no one else to raise her kids.

Week after week, Joab and Anita took note of the State, Federal, Medicare and FICA deductions printed on their paychecks. Sometimes it was difficult to remember Webster's precise words when speculating on which household bill might have been covered by the missing income. Then, too, Joab had a vague sense that the $500.00 per child tax credit was in danger of being repealed under a Webster administration. At a combined income of $31,500.00 gross, a thousand dollars brought home a lot of bacon. Still, taxes were a necessary hardship and Joab could not turn a cold heart toward the less fortunate people he saw, every day . . . . even if he was beginning to recognize them as direct competitors with his own daughters for the food on his table, the clothes on their backs, the roof over their heads, and the education he longed to afford them.

✦ ✦ ✦

Theo Cummings had accepted an invitation to a large, very private party with his closest supporters for the New Year's celebration of the millennium. That left Joab free for the weekend. He and Anita decided to spend it in Savannah. When Miss Lucy heard that one of Anita's high school classmates had invited them to a big party, she insisted they attend.

"You two go on out and have yourse'fs some fun. Grandmama Lucy will watch the babies," she said with a wink. "Y'all work so hard. You deserve a little bit of a good time."

Joab hesitated. "I hate to leave Grandma Ruth all alone."

"Who said she was gonna be alone? I was gonna invite her over to spend the night and the four of us can have a party of our own."

So it was settled. Joab and Anita headed out to a beach party on Tybee Island, leaving Cinda, Mandy and the two grannies poised to ring in the next thousand years. Miss Lucy had been to the Dollar Store to pick up party streamers, silly hats, noise makers, confetti and the like. Ruth showed up with the camcorder, three miniature video cassettes, cake, ice cream and a bottle of ginger ale (make-believe champagne) to toast to the future with the cherished young to whom it belonged. Cinda and Mandy were greatly excited. But in spite of their best efforts, their limp bodies finally lost the great battle against slumber at around 11:15PM. One half hour later, they were roused, bleary eyed, to dance around the living room with a pair of mature women who had not acted quite so immature in decades. It was great fun and would remain, for little Mandy, one of her earliest and most wonderful memories.

Anita and Joab never made it to their beach party. After driving most of the day, both of them were pretty tired but neither had mentioned it, not wishing to dampen the festive atmosphere of such a rare and auspicious occasion. Joab's mind drifted.

"You know, Nita," he said at length, "a year from now, I will have graduated, passed the bar, and be all settled in at Mr. Keylar's firm, and YOU will be officially retired."

"Oh, thank the Lord!" she hollered, throwing her head back. "I can't believe it's really gonna happen."

Joab's eyes darted from the road to the smooth arch of Nita's neck and the rounded angle of her chin in the moonlight. He had to pull his eyes back to the road. She was so beautiful. He felt an old possessiveness wash over him.

"You know," she said at length, "it's gonna be a long, dangerous drive home, tonight."

"Yeah," he agreed. "You know, my mama's planning on spending the night at your mama's house, tonight." Then, about a half-mile later he added, "'Course my mama's expecting us to sleep at her house."

"You know, Joab," Nita responded, casually, "It just might be time to start on that son you always wanted."

A wide grin spread across Joab's face and Anita's prized, previously-owned Ford Aerostar abruptly pulled a U-turn.

✦ ✦ ✦

Next morning, January 1, 2000, Joab and Anita lingered in bed, luxuriantly perusing the channels for reruns of last night's celebrations. Apparently it had been nothing for law enforcement officials to celebrate. Minor riots had erupted in the major cities, auto fatality statistics were still coming in, and a total of nine churches had been set ablaze. Y2K computer glitches failed to provide the greatly anticipated catastrophe. All in all, it looked like the Republic would survive. It was hard for news anchors to hide their disappointment.

At 10:00 Mandy and Cinda came exploding into Grandma Ruthie's double-wide to discover their parents still in bed. Cinda led the charge, as usual.

"Happy New Year!" she shouted over the TV as she leapt on the bed.

"Happy New Year!" Mandy chimed in. And the two wriggled all over their parents like puppies.

"Now, c'mon little girls. Leave Mommy and Daddy alone to get dressed." Ruth suggested from the doorway. "Miss Lucy and I fixed them a great, big, pancake breakfast."

"With whipped cream on top!" Cinda enthused as she and her sister jumped heavily off the bed.

Smiling, Ruth closed the door behind them.

✦ ✦ ✦

In May of 2000, things began happening at such an accelerated pace, that the Johnsons barely had time to keep up. The first week, Anita took a kit test and her dipstick came up a pink-for-positive. She had a hard time keeping a straight face, that evening, when her husband walked in the door. She thought she might burst with the news by the time the girls had finished supper and begged to be excused to finish watching a rerun of "Jumanji".

"Guess what?" she asked, trying to make it sound casual.

"Oh, yeah?!" he answered.

"Yeah," she said, bobbing her head and giggling. Then their laughter filled the house. In moments, the phone rang at Miss Lucy's, next at Grandma Ruth's, then Joab and Anita headed for the living room to inform the expectant big sisters. Cinda and Mandy were sure they were in trouble when their Daddy turned off the movie right before the end (which, incidentally, they had already seen at least seventeen times before).

"Your Daddy and me have something to tell you. It's very important so you better listen up," Anita started. Both children stared wide-eyed up at their mother.

"Go on, Babe, you tell them," Anita urged.

Joab knelt down. "Cinda," he said, "do you think you could teach Mandy how to be a wonderful big sister, just like you?"

Cinda nodded obediently.

"'Cause I think there's going to be another baby around here soon."

Finally, her face broke out in a wide grin. "Really?" she squealed. "All right!" And popped up to hug her mother. Mandy needed a bit more information. Anita picked her up and threw her weight over one hip. At four and a half, this was beginning to take some effort.

"Mommy and Daddy asked Jesus to give us another baby and He put one inside of Mommy's tummy. Oh, it's very tiny now, but it will grow a little bit every day, just like you do, and then one day, it will come out to meet his wonderful big sisters, Mandy and Cinda."

"You have a baby in your tummy?" she asked.

Anita nodded.

"Does it hurt?"

"No. But it makes my body kind of tired."

Mandy took her mother's face in her hands and kissed her lips.

"Go to bed, Mama," she said, "Can I stay up and watch the end of Jumanji?"

◆ ◆ ◆

Charlie Keylar notified Joab that the case was likely to be tried the first week in August. He had decided that anonymity would be lost if Joab and his family attended, but he was planning to have Ruth by his side. Joab was disappointed. As a soon-to-be lawyer, he was most anxious to witness a trial, especially under a Federal judge in the capital city of Georgia.

◆ ◆ ◆

Soon, the last round of finals was over and it was the big day. Most of the family traveled up to Atlanta for the graduation. Jethro came up with his clan. John and Lyndon, still in the Navy, were out at sea, as usual. Aunt Sarah could not afford passage back from New Mexico but sent a card and a fifty dollar check. Aunt Annie, Aunt Maybell (leaving her two kids with their father), and Miss Lucy all drove up together and JC drove with Ruth. Abe, well into his 30s, attended with his new wife, Cathy, and their daughter. Cathy was a leggy, young white girl with strawberry blonde hair and a shy smile. Abe had waited long to marry, and family speculation was that he probably never would have, had divine providence not intermingled his genes with those of a pro-life Irish Catholic. Their daughter's soft skin appeared to be an equal mix and her features had clearly drawn from only the best of both parents. Their pride in her was obvious. Joab's girls couldn't stay away from her.

Abe had been seven years old when Joab was born, and so, had been the closest male to his age. As such, he had spent the most time with him growing up. He had taught Joab how to swim, do a cannon ball off a pier, throw a casting net, gig for flounder, mow the yard, make a basket, smoke a cigarette and drink a beer. Shy, his own self, Abe overcame his desire to put off the inevitable first introduction of his new wife, and drove up from Port Royal, SC, for Joab's day. He was glad that he did. Joab's girls couldn't stay away from his baby and the prospect of a new generation bound by the crazy glue of blood was deeply satisfying.

After the commencement ceremony was over, all Joab's kin encircled him with much fussing. When the buzz died down, all the hugs and back pats were received, and the fancy diploma was passed around, Anita stepped up to congratulate her husband. She slipped a card in his hand that had "personal" hand-written on the envelope.

"Can I open it now?" he whispered.

"If you don't show nobody," she whispered back.

When he opened the graduation card, Anita's equivalency diploma slipped out. Anita watched as he picked it up and unfolded it.

"It ain't much compared to yours, but it's a start," she said. She hadn't expected him to cry.

He put his arms around her and lifted her off the floor aware of the slight bulge of her belly against his.

"I love you, Nita," he spoke in her ear, "and I'm so proud that you're mine and that you're the mother of my children. That makes three diplomas you've earned since I've known you."

Anita cried, too.

"Hey, hey! None of this. Put that woman down," Annie broke in. "We're all starved! Let's go eat!"

Reservations had been made for a back room at a *Golden Corral* restaurant. JC led a short, quiet prayer, thanking God for Joab and the food. After the "amen," the Johnsons headed for the buffet, children first. Anita fixed Cinda's plate and Joab took care of Mandy. Aunt Annie had made sure she got the seat next to Joab.

"So, Joab," she said after settling in with her second helping, "when y'all fixin' to c'mon back home?"

"Sometime after the convention, probably, early to mid-August. Mr. Keylar's going to let me clerk until I pass the bar."

"That's right! Ruthie tol' me you was goin' to the National Convention this year! Hoowee, ain't you jus' somethin'! You think you'll get to meet Mr. Webster? Looks like we finally gonna get us a black man in the White House (she chuckled at her play on words). I'm glad I'm living to see it."

Joab just smiled and nodded, cutting a piece of chicken for Mandy. It was embarrassing to be the celebrity of the family.

"If you do, you tell him your Aunt Annie would crawl over asphalt in August to vote for him. I would, too. And I'd bring along some friends."

"I'll tell him," Joab said.

"You, um, find you a place to live, yet? I mean back home."

"No, ma'am, not yet."

"Well, you know I got me a pretty good job out towards the new mall."

"Yeah, I think Mama said something about that."

"Well, it's a long drive and I've been thinking it's time to get me an apartment closer to work. That would leave Big Mama's house empty and I know Ruth and Miss Lucy would love to have the kids close by. No rent, and Anita might could use some extra hands once the new one comes along. Jethro's been pretty good about keeping it up. . . . Unless you wanted somethin' bigger or somethin'."

"I don't know, Aunt Annie, you've been in that house for a long time now . . ."

Annie read his hesitation like a billboard. "Well, I already put me a deposit down on one of them fancy new apartments on the south side," she lied. "'Sides, I'm 'bout sick of mowing that damn lawn."

"Well, between Nita, Miss Lucy, Mama and the girls, I believe I'll be living by myself if I live anywhere else."

"You know, Joab," she said, "I ain't never had kids. I made my choices and I ain't about to whine about them now, but I 'member the day you was born like it was yesterday. Ruthie was so scared and young, her own self, and you come out kicking and screaming and strong as a bull. I just knew you'd grow up to be somebody. We're all real proud of you."

Joab felt powerfully awkward accepting such a compliment. Finally he just put his arm around the wide shoulders of this beloved woman and gave a squeeze. He was looking forward to being back home more than he had realized.

Most of the next four weeks were occupied by an intensive law review course designed to prepare him to pass the bar exam. At Emory, "the Bar" was respectfully referred to as "the Bitch Mother of Exams." She lived up to her reputation. It would be two to three months before he would know if he had passed. He gave instructions for the results to be forwarded to Big Mama's address, wondering if such a long wait was an intentional part of the Bitch Mother's torture.

Abruptly, Joab broke through into a wealth of spare time he had not known. He had half expected the governor to gobble up the bulk of his newly-freed hours, but his job responsibilities continued to be met mostly at social functions in the evenings or on the weekends. This left him with luxuriously long summer days to enjoy with his daughters.

One afternoon in July, Judge Dowling sat in his study pouring over the extensive briefs of _Doe vs. School Board_. There were boxes of deposition testimony and stacks of public school textbooks to scrutinize. Dowling was well aware of the far-reaching implications of this case. It took aim at the heart of the "establishment clause" of the First Amendment. A man of extraordinary mental acuity, Dowling had long ago memorized the entire _Constitution_ as well as _The Declaration of Independence._ The first words of America's Bill of Rights were as clear as ever in his mind: _"Congress shall make no law respecting an establishment of religion, or prohibiting the free exercise thereof;"_

The Judge had more than a casual grasp of the legal precedents Keylar was challenging: two landmark Supreme Court decisions regarding public education: _Engel v. Vitale (1962)_ which forbid prayer and _Abington School District V. Schempp (1963)_ which forbid Bible reading. In two decisions, eight men effectively cut the tie that anchored America to her religious moorings since the Mayflower Compact. Kelar's gutsy assertion was that these decisions had been used to implement a state religion in violation of the clause those decisions claimed to uphold.

Dowlings ears registered a piercing scream for help and instinctively looked up. Beyond the sliding glass doors of his book-lined room, his grandchildren played joyously in the pool. The scream was a harmless part of their horseplay. He watched them squeal and tease, splashing and chasing one another. His wife, still lovely after so many years, urged them to slow down and be careful. But their exuberance simply defied restraint.

Eyes adjusting to the brightness of the pool deck, Dowling permitted himself a moment of mental respite while he observed his beloved brood. There were six of them; four from his daughter and two from his son, each one more beautiful and precious than the next. He loved them—perhaps as much as he had loved their parents, but with more wisdom. His money had sheltered them from much of the violence and ugliness of contemporary America. Each of them attended a good, private, school. He had always been happy to write a check for a tuition shortfall if his son or daughter couldn't scrape it together. What was his money for, if not to invest in their future—to prepare them to succeed when he was no longer there to protect them?

At length, the judge returned his attention to the stacks of paper covering his desk; thinking, digesting. He had never met Joab S. Johnson, but he respected him. In one of his briefs, Keylar made reference to Cinda's rape. Dowling's heart went out to Johnson as he tried to imagine himself in the younger man's shoes. The trademark questions of a good judge churned in his soul: *How would **my** children have turned out if poverty had prevented **me** from raising them in a safe neighborhood? What would I have done if forced to stand by and watch my children denied the tools necessary to elevate themselves in American culture? What would **I** have done if forced to send my children to a school that actively tore down the morality my wife and I labored so hard to build up in them?*

The Honorable Judge and Mrs. Dowling were Southern Baptists. After skimming through a stack of textbooks from Johnson's daughter's class, he was appalled at content that should have been considered inappropriate for any class, but especially for such little ones. *Sex outside of marriage isn't promoted in our religion, but it is in public schools. Homosexuality isn't promoted in our religion, but it is in public schools. On the other hand, ancient standards of right and wrong **are** taught in our religion, but they **are denied** in public schools. Belief in a Supreme Being **is** taught in our religion, but **it is denied** in public schools. The very language of the Declaration of Independence and the Constitution recognize rights as gifts bestowed **by the Creator**, not by the government.* His blood pressure began to rise with the ironic realization that *Public school children are being taught that the provider of their rights does not exist. And not because the vast majority of their parents had no faith in God, but because a tiny handful of militant parents had exploited a flawed law to deny all children what they themselves had rejected. What a disastrous mess! Of course, Keylar is right!* Dowling concluded, *largely anti-Christian values **are** being impressed upon children subjected to public education. Undeniable. But could one bundle those values into a package that defines them as a religion? This is the only issue upon which <u>Doe vs. School Board</u> will turn.*

The Judge scanned Keylar's citations and case laws, riffling through page after page... and then, *Ha!* The Judge slammed his palms on his desk. *There it is! <u>United States v. Seeger, 380 U.S. 163</u> (1965).* He leaned back in his chair and chuckled. *Apparently,* he mused, *in their usual effort to let as many men out of the draft as possible, the liberal judiciary of the sixties defined religion so broadly as to include almost any set of loosely-held convictions; even without belief in a Supreme Being. In light of "Seeger," the philosophies set forth in this educational material absolutely fall under the Supreme Court's definition of religion!* He chuckled more deeply as he considered the surprise of liberal judges when they discovered that their own inclusive definition of religion would ultimately force them to release the grip they had maintained on the minds of American children for almost a half century.

Judge Dowling's resolve became more set as he studied the marked pages of textbooks and each deposition exhibit. As the sun began to slant through his glass door, Mrs. Dowling came in urging him to join his family for dinner. Only then did he set the files aside. Mentally exhausted, but spiritually refreshed, he joined her to be blessed by an evening with their rich harvest of children and grandchildren.

✦ ✦ ✦

Judge Dowling had read every document twice and was thoroughly familiar with all the evidence by the day of the trial.

If Charlie had resisted intimidation before, he had to mentally beat it back the moment he stepped into the courtroom. To Keylar, federal courtrooms were the cathedrals of democracy, and he never entered one without a sense of awe. But upon seeing the legion of lawyers in opposition, he was positively quaking in his wing-tips. Only a couple of attorneys had shown up for depositions, but now there had to be well over a dozen in the room! With the straight face of a hired gun from a simpler day, Keylar carried his wide briefcase to the right-hand table in front of the bar and began laying out his weapons. Ruth followed close behind, pulling two file boxes stacked on a small, folding dolly. Her stomach was a hive of hornets but she followed Charlie's lead and appeared calm and confident. At their entrance, all activity on the left side of the courtroom ceased.

"Good morning," Charlie said, smiling at all their serious faces, "I'm Charlie Keylar." He extended his hand. The first one to shake it was a Washington attorney who identified himself as a specialist in Constitutional law. There was an in-house lawyer for the National Education Association and one from the American Teachers Federation. There were also outside attorneys retained by both unions. There were lawyers from Pickens County, lawyers from the State Education Association, lawyers from the State Attorney General's Office and lawyers from the Federal Department of Education. There were assistant lawyers, observing lawyers, associate lawyers and paralegals. In their ranks they had black lawyers, white lawyers, female lawyers and one Hispanic lawyer. They occupied two rows of tables behind the counsel table. They clicked away on six laptops and passed notes via networked email—very slick. Behind the bar on the left side sat much of Atlanta's public education power structure, as well as several attorneys and a paralegal from the American Civil Liberties Union. Charlie quickly decided there were far too many names to remember. Only Joab would have retained all of them—if he were here.

Next, Charlie introduced himself to the small group of people gathering behind the bar on the right. There were several headmasters from private local schools, two priests from the local Catholic diocese, a couple of folks from the State Association of Private Schools, one representative from the Home School Legal Defense Fund, one observer from the Eagle Forum and one attorney from the American Center for Law and Justice.

In the very back of the room, three members of the press were cautioned not to enter Judge Dowling's court with cameras.

Ruth prayed silently as she helped Charlie organize his papers.

Suddenly a bailiff appeared from a door behind the judge's desk.

"All rise for The Honorable United States District Court Judge, Ernest M. Dowling, III," he bellowed. But it was too late. Everyone had jumped to their feet the second they had seen the door crack open. The judge entered in his long robe and stepped up to a raised platform where he took his place upon the huge, throne-like chair, behind a desk much larger than the one in Charlie's office.

For two hours he listened patiently and attentively as both sides presented their arguments. From his polite manner and meticulous adherence to formal decorum, it was hard for either side to know which way he was leaning.

At last the judge spoke, "There seems to be no genuine dispute as to the material facts here today. I realize you lawyers are at odds about the inferences to be reasonably drawn from those facts and the law applicable. However, I see only one reasonable group of conclusions to be drawn from those facts, and the applicable law is also clear. (There was a riveting silence in the room.)   Based on the evidence presented here today, it is my opinion that public schools, in truth, are no less religious than parochial schools. . . that is if one is to accept the United State Supreme Court's definition of religion as cited in Mr. Keylar's brief.

At this point, there was much sputtering from the left side of the courtroom.

"Excuse me," said the Judge, "I'm not finished. –Therefore, since our government has failed in its attempts to uphold the establishment clause, it has two choices under our Constitution. It can either abandon public funding of education altogether, or it can make public funding available to all schools without interference or discrimination against any institution whether public or private.

One of the lawyers for the NEA launched, "But, Judge, don't you think you are taking a rather skewed view of the law, for example—"

"Excuse me," The Judge interrupted, "but I am still speaking. Kindly refrain from any further interruption until I am finished. –Also, in a pluralistic society such as ours, it is the right of the parents to choose the school they wish their child to attend. That will be the basis of my written order, which I will soon file."

There was a dead silence as the education lawyers bit their tongues almost to the point of bleeding.

"Now, I am finished," he announced.

Several attorneys stood at once. The Judge listened politely as they took turns trying to convince him that he was mistaken without actually accusing him of being an ignorant fool and dead wrong. Charlie knew when to keep his mouth shut. Finally, when he had had enough, the judge lifted his hands and announced, "You know what my thinking is. I've got your briefs. I've heard your arguments. This hearing is adjourned." With that, his gavel fell.

Charlie and Ruth exchanged a glance which betrayed the frailty of their composure. Swiftly and wordlessly, they packed up their papers.

On the way out, Charlie nodded respectfully to the other lawyers and blew off a couple of reporters with a "no comment" comment. Ruth followed, file boxes trailing on wheels behind her. The defense team was still muttering in disbelief when the doors swung closed. Neither Charlie nor Ruth looked at each other until they were alone in the elevator of the parking garage when Charlie shouted, "We did it!" throwing his arms around his secretary. They danced to the car.

That night, Loretta watched the girls while Charlie took his clients and his secretary out to a celebration dinner. There was much to talk about.

Not far away, in another Atlanta restaurant, Ernie Dowling met Cliff Ionesco, a close friend from his old firm, for cocktails. After discussing _Doe vs. School Board_ for a while, Dowling asked his old buddy what he thought Theo Cummings would do if he knew his black protégé had just given his strongest constituents a black eye.

Ionesco's mouth curved into a wicked smile. "I don't know," he said, "but it sure would be fun to find out."

"Course, I guess it'll never happen, because no one is supposed to know that John Doe is really the governor's very own Joab Johnson."

"Right," Ionesco said.

By 10:00PM Ionesco's leak had made its way back to Scott Houghton.

Chapter 24

The next morning, Joab was called into an emergency meeting with the governor. Cummings was sitting behind the desk of his imposing office when Jeanna let Joab in. Scott Houghton stood leaning against a bookcase.

"Close the door, please, Jeanna," the governor asked as his secretary left the room.

Joab's mouth went dry, his intestines constricted and he remembered, with crystal clarity, how it had felt to be called to the principal's office back at St. Paul's.

Cummings threw a portion of this morning's edition of *The Atlanta Chronicle* down on the leather top of his desk.

"'*John Doe Wins Victory Against NEA,*'" he quoted a headline. "Do you know anything about that?"

Joab's tongue stuck to the roof of his mouth.

"Why didn't you tell me you were the 'Doe' in 'Doe vs. School Board'?" Scott asked from the corner.

"How - who told you?" Joab stammered.

"You work for the governor, Joab. The incredible thing is that we didn't know two years ago," Scott asserted, flatly.

"My attorney advised me not to discuss it with anyone. Besides, the judge put us all under a gag order to protect my daughter."

Protect your daughter, my ass, Theo thought. *That old buzzard was just setting the fuse on a bomb.* For a second, the Governor's thoughts digressed into speculation on possible means of retaliation. After twenty years of looking, he still couldn't find a way. *Those damned Federal Court Judges with their cursed lifetime appointments,* Theo lamented bitterly. *Loose cannons every damn one of them!*" And Theo's mind arrived again, kicking and screaming, at the detestable truth;

even a governor can't *make* a U.S. District Judge do diddily. Theo Cummings hated Ernie Dowling with a hatred that hadn't aged a day since college. *Helen, God rest her soul, should have blessed the day I rescued her from that snake!*

"We had a right to know." Houghton filled the momentary void left by Theo's silent rantings.

"I guess I just didn't think it was that important," Joab stated weakly.

"Didn't think it was important!" Cummings repeated incredulously. "Joab, you know my constituents better than I do. You know how closely I work with the National Education Association trying to improve our schools."

"I ought to kick your ass," Houghton interjected, taking a step toward him.

Joab didn't like feeling cornered, but chose to ignore Houghton.

"Respectfully, Sir, the NEA is no one's friend but their own. They're scamming you and everybody in this country. The more money you give 'em the worse our kids do on standardized tests! So what's their response when we try to hold them accountable? They ram outcome-based education down our throats to get rid of the tests! They fill our kids up with circumstantial morality and wonder why they gun each other down in the halls. I just wanted Cinda out of there is all. And you," he said turning to Houghton, "where do *your* kids go? Atlanta Christian, is it?"

"My kids got a fine education in public schools and I'm proud of that." Cummings offered.

"With all due respect, Sir, that was thirty-five years ago. Where do your grandkids go? . . . You see?" Joab answered when the Governor failed to respond.

Cummings' face softened. "Now there's no reason to get all upset about this. Go on and have a seat, Joab." He indicated one of a pair of chairs on the far side of his desk. Joab sat. Houghton went back to leaning against the bookcase. "Now, Joab, you're a bright young man. You'll start making good money once you pass the bar. You'll be able to afford private schools, if that's what you want. It seems to me what you need is a little patience."

"And while I'm being patient, Cinda's getting older. She'll be going into third grade next year, and the only reason she can read is because *I* taught her. Since she's been at MLK Elementary, she's been mugged by older students three times, once at knife point. No, governor, if you really want to improve the school system, I'm convinced that the only way is through the free market. Parents are fed up and so is business. The NEA and the ATF are flat out of chances. You should look into it. It's a winning campaign issue, governor. I just know it is. I can feel it."

"You know, Joab, maybe you're right," Cummings agreed. "I'll tell you what. I'll look into it. There have been a number of experimental voucher programs in other states. Scott, do you think you could launch a study?"

Scott nodded, "Sure, I'll get my staff working on it today, if you want."

"Maybe I could get my attorney to send you some of the briefs," Joab offered. "The teaching establishment, within clear view of the government, started indoctrinating our children decades ago, often at the expense of teaching them. It's scary. Wait 'till you read some of this stuff!"

"Good. In the meantime, Joab," Cummings continued, "we've got the convention coming up in less than a week. I need your word that you'll keep this very quiet until it's over. If the press should find out that you're John Doe, I want you to promise me no interviews."

This sounded reasonable. Joab had no desire to embarrass the Governor in an election year, and he had every hope that the man would come around to considering the voucher, once he was made aware of the facts.

"Absolutely," he said.

"Good. I'll see you tomorrow afternoon for the Southern Heritage rally."

"You're not *seriously* thinking about the voucher," Scott asked, once Joab had left the room.

"Hell, no!" Cummings answered, "You know Teachers Unions are my biggest donors. Besides being loose with the checkbook, they can get their people out to man phone banks, stuff envelopes, and every other damn thing. Nah, I ain't about to piss off the NEA, but that black boy's right about one thing, they had better start making me look better on these national scores, or the people are gonna get mad, and there won't be a damn thing I can do about it . . . You found me a replacement for that kid, yet?"

"No, sir, we're looking. I've had a couple of prospects but not in the right color."

"Well, keep looking. This one's out of here the day after the convention and we'll only have three and a half months until elections. Crying shame Johnson turned out to be such a pain in the butt. I believe he'd have stayed if his wife could have been talked out of Savannah."

"From what I've seen, she's not real bright. She'll keep holding him back until he wises up and gets rid of her. Too bad."

"Ah, maybe it's for the best," Theo reflected, "Can you imagine explaining him to the NEA if he happens to win this thing in the Big Court?"

"It'll never happen," Scott said, confidently. But even he wasn't so sure any more.

✦ ✦ ✦

By the time Joab got home, the leak had reached the press, and they had his number. The phone was ringing as he walked in the door.

"Hey, Babe, it's someone from The *Chronicle*," Anita said, giving him a kiss and handing him the receiver.

"Yes, this is Joab Johnson," she heard him say. "No comment. . . No. No comment. Don't call here again." He hung up.

"What's up?" Nita asked.

"They want to know about the School Voucher case. We can't say a word. Just tell them they have the wrong number and hang up. I had better call Mr. Keylar and tell him what's going on."

Joab gave Charlie the long version of everything that had happened. Call waiting clicked every few seconds and a news car was parked out in front of the house by the time he had finished the conversation.

"It's probably a good idea to keep quiet about this, anyway. If you gave Cummings your word, you gave him your word. Go on and keep quiet 'till after the Convention. It'll give me time to think," Charlie had ordered, "But don't you give Cummings any specifics of the case. They can look it up themselves. Just speak in generalities, okay?"

"He told me he was going to do a study on the voucher and look into it."

"Fine, but he's very thick with the NEA and the ATF."

"Yes, sir," Joab had said, resolved to follow his attorney's advice.

It was hard not to be impressed by The Convention. In spite of a well-executed appearance of indifference, Joab ached to give Anita every detail of his elbow-rubbing with such giants as Barbara Streisand, Hillary Clinton, Whoopie Goldberg, Ted Kennedy, Jessie Jackson *and* his personal encounter with Amos Webster, himself! *Wouldn't Aunt Annie just drop her jaw!* There were cameras and microphones everywhere, banners, balloons and confetti, spirited songs and passionate speeches and more nightly parties than any one person could ever hope to attend in a month of conventions. Though the event was grand in scope, Joab was struck by how small the power structure really was. It was, in fact, quite possible for one person to know almost all of the major players, personally. Consequently, he wondered why he had been surprised to discover that Theo Cummings was already well acquainted with Liz Straddlethorp. She had apparently kept up with Lesa and was pleased to inform him that his old lover had been elected as a state delegate from Hawaii. Joab told her to give Lesa his regards, smug in the knowledge that such a greeting would carry with it the knowledge that he had made it to the National Convention before she did.

Though Victor Mason, vice-presidential running mate, yanked at the heartstrings, the undeniable climax of this four-day, progressive pep-rally was clearly and predictably Senator

Webster's address. He started off with a personal history during which all who had labored to minister mass-healing through the far-reaching embrace of a vast government were, finally, vindicated. The recent years of anxious uncertainty could almost be felt melting away. Webster ended with, *"I have a dream."* There was a long, rich, pause during which African-Americans and misty-eyed ex-immigrants alike, riveted to a single, simultaneous signal, received in tens of millions of family rooms, bedrooms and bar rooms, considered the very nearness of that ancient and awesome dream - prominence in the land of captivity.

After the pause, Amos repeated one word, "November… November!"

For Joab and the governor, the official close of the main event was followed by a giant bash, honoring Bill Bradley. On the way home, Theo Cummings detoured the limo.

"I'm still too wound up to go to bed," he told Joab, "Let's get us a little nightcap. What do you say?"

This was a most unusual question coming from the governor. Joab had never seen him so much as sniff alcohol.

"Sure," he said, "Fine with me." Joab thought he could use a beer, himself. It had been an exciting four days and he wasn't looking forward to the let-down either.

The limo stopped outside a glass tower in downtown Detroit. Joab had never been this far north before. Even in August, a gust of wind blew dust into his eyes as a valet held the car door.

In moments, the elevator operator let Joab, Gov. Cummings and his two bodyguards off in the lounge of *The First City Club,* high above the glittering landscape. Two walls of the room were panes of glass, floor to ceiling, which afforded a spectacular view. Theo found a table next to what felt like the edge of the earth. Joab couldn't resist a childish urge to lean close to the glass and peek down into the straight canyon below. Several limos were dropping off passengers, way down there. Apparently other dignitaries shared a similar desire to avoid their hotel rooms a while longer. The bodyguards took a table at a respectable, but close, distance.

"What'll ya have?" Theo asked.

"Um," an attractive bleach-blonde in her mid-thirties was leaning over their table. She wore a black skirt, very short. "Uh, what kind of beer you got?"

"Now, Joab," Cummings interrupted, "It's high time you started cultivating a pallet for a good scotch whiskey. Y'all don't happen to have Lagavulin," (He was speaking to the cocktail waitress now.) She nodded. "Good girl," he said.

Joab shrugged, "Okay."

"Two." Theo's eyes enjoyed the sheer, black stockings as she walked to the bar. "A single malt from the Isle of Inlay, Scotland - very smooth."

Joab knew the governor would not be seriously interested in the waitress. He had long observed Theo's general romantic aversion to fellow politicians and bar maids, alike. Barmaids had a tacky penchant for sticky break-ups and tabloid headlines—and female politicians? Theo's was part of a generation that would never welcome direct, professional competition from a member of the weaker sex. No, if Joab knew Cummings, which he did, he would find a secretary type; mildly reserved with just a dash of bimbo, witnessed by a blouse unbuttoned low enough to offer a glimpse of cleavage, from the right angle, of course - no severe haircuts, no one under thirty-five. Both men casually searched the room for her. There were a couple of prospects, but both seemed engaged, at the moment. Worth monitoring, though.

Joab thoroughly enjoyed his scotch but switched to ginger ale after his first. The Gov's second round was a Rusty Nail. Joab started the conversation with enthusiastic reflections on the convention. His companion seemed not to be much interested.

"How many National Conventions have you attended, over the years?" Joab finally asked.

"Oh, gees, let's see . . . I don't know. The first one was for Hubert Humphrey back in 1968. Helen came with me. Hm, we had a ball. I was a brand new Georgia senator out to change the world; all ambition and aspiration. Helen was five months pregnant with Lynley, and the most beautiful woman at the damn thing, the smartest, too. She'd have made a fine politician herself—kept me out of the ditches more than once. But she preferred just staying home to raise our girls."

The governor swirled the ice at the bottom of his glass. Joab had never really heard him talk about his wife before. Word was that he missed her. Word was true, from the sound of it.

"She'd have liked my wife. Anita loves being a mom."

Cummings nodded to the waitress and another round appeared at the table.

"Well, it looks like Webster's in," Joab observed.

"Oh, he's in. I don't know what could stop him at this point. He'd have to screw up pretty badly to get beat, now."

"Man, he made some pretty big promises about education. I just hope he keeps them."

"Hell, I made better speeches than those twenty years ago. It won't change. Public education will never change, 'cept to get worse, maybe."

Joab was shocked to hear such talk coming from the mouth of "The Education Governor."

"What makes you say that?" he asked.

Cummings took a sip of his third drink. The corners of his mouth turned down as he swallowed. "I say it because it's true. Hell, man, I've been there. I've been up to D.C., pounded on all the doors; Secretaries of Education, Presidents, Vice Presidents. Oh, they talk a good talk; we all do, but at the top, they don't want it to change. All governments like to keep the people stupid. Ain't you ever studied history, Joab? Never mind, you probably got the revised version anyway. Government is good and kind and takes care of all its people like a loving parent. We'll feed you. We'll clothe you. We'll educate your darling children. Just ask the Russians. Ask the Chinese, or even the Cubans, for that matter. Ask Imelda Marcos with her 9,000 pairs of shoes or whatever the hell the number is."

Joab stared across the table at Theodore Cummings, dumbfounded, struggling to digest what his ears were hearing.

"Now, Joab, listen up," he said, "You're going to hear some truth. I know you're not used to the sound of it, so you might not recognize it, but try. In every society, there are two kinds of people: sheep and wolves. In medieval times, this was clearly understood and accepted. The sheep knew who they were and kept their place. In modern times, it's a bit more tricky, especially in a country which considers itself free, like America. You see, here, the sheep dress up like wolves, and the wolves must dress like sheep. The sheep must never discover what they really are; merely livestock, a food supply maintained by and for the wolves—who look like sheep, of course.

"Public education, in this great nation, is well-paid to raise up good little sheep. Billions of dollars to turn out millions of sheep. Millions of them can barely read, most of them, bless their hearts, can't even connect cause and effect anymore."

Joab stared at his companion with something approaching disbelief. Cummings decided to offer an example. "Take trickle-down economics: It doesn't take a genius to see that when your neighbors are making more money, so are you. But our wonderful press sheep, enlightened promoters of the sheep mentality, relentlessly poke fun at anyone who suggests such a thing and the mass flock soon accepts that it *doesn't* know what it knows. Thoroughly well-trained sheep can be easily turned. All it takes is one emotionally charged video clip and a sound bite nipping at their heels. Or fear."

"Wait a minute," Joab finally broke in, "You're telling me that the state of our public education system is premeditated and intentional?"

"Ask yourself this, Joab," the governor said, instantly sober, "With all the money and accumulated knowledge we have at our disposal, how, in God's name, could it be otherwise?"

Joab made no response.

"Don't look so startled, boy. You're about to leave the flock and join the pack. You'll be able to send your girls to *real* schools pretty soon. Only you had better stop fighting the system. You'll never change it. I couldn't, and you won't. You have a future in politics, if you want it, Joab. Webster will open a lot of doors for the Negro. Only you had better drop the suit. . . . Well, I think I'll go over there and talk to that sweet thing in the open blouse. You just sit here, awhile, and think about what I told you," he said, rising, "And consider the sheep costume a gift."

Joab did sit there and think. He stared out at the dark skyline of the Windy City, his brain swimming, trying to recall his high school history classes. *Stalin, Mao, Castro and many other Marxixt tyrants of the previous century, all promised fairness in a seemingly unfair world through economic redistribution. Estimates on Joseph Stalin were that he had slaughtered over 40 million of his own citizens and sent untold millions more to prison; anyone who could be perceived as a challenge to his dominion. Even the entire upper ranks of his military had not been safe from Stalin's quest for absolute power; they, too, were purged. The consolidation of Mao Tse-tung's power cost his countrymen at least as many lives. Staggering numbers - impossible numbers to grasp in individual terms. Yet the estimates were correct. Inconceivable slaughter accomplished while the rest of the herd stood by bleating the chant begun by the wolves, "For the common good. For the common good."*

Joab reached back in his mind to what the nuns had taught him. *There were Pol Pot's killing fields and Hitler's gas chambers. . . And what were the first institutions they had seized? The schools. The sheep had to be trained. How else could the lasting supremacy of the regime be assured? But America is a Constitutional Republic!* Joab reasoned. *Not susceptible to the excesses of a dictatorship. Yet, what is the guardian of a free people? Education—the ability to discover the truth and make informed decisions in the face of relentless propaganda. Were the children of America being intentionally denied the ability to make informed decisions?* Joab didn't know if it was intentional. In a sense, that didn't matter. *The consolidation of power in Washington, DC is running parallel to the plummeting literacy. The lesson is written in human blood, over countless generations;* **an all- powerful government is no friend of the people**. *Our Founders knew it and took great care to create safety mechanisms that would disburse the power among the people. Now, federally enforced ignorance was causing those safety mechanisms to fail. Corrupt politicians in concert with* *gluttonous teacher's unions had proven themselves social cannibals who devoured the potential of the young to empower and enrich themselves, exploiting the love of the parent and producing ever more ignorance for ever more money. Unworthy stewards, at best.*

"Not *my* children," Joab said, out loud. Then he uttered the words that would change the course of his life, "and not anybody else's, if I can help it."

The next time Governor Cummings looked over at his table, Joab was gone. No matter, Houghton would have the boy's letter of dismissal waiting by the time his private, chartered jet landed on Georgian soil. Besides, the Governor was greatly enjoying his fall from the wagon and there was a good chance that his charming companion could be talked into coming back to his hotel room. In such a case, a limo ride for two was infinitely preferable to one with three. He'd let the guards off early.

As soon as Joab set foot in his hotel room, he got on the phone with Delta and booked himself a flight to Atlanta. Next, the sound of the phone woke Anita with instructions of when and where to meet him. By the time Cummings got around to checking his messages, the next day, and wondering if the alcohol hadn't given his tongue a little too much liberty, Joab was already home. On the way from the airport, Joab had given his wife the gist of his conversation with Cummings.

"Now, Joab, listen to yourself. Are you actually telling me that you think the government is trying to keep our kids stupid?" she asked in a tone which implied he might be out of his mind.

"I know it sounds unlikely. But this is the question Cummings asked: With all the knowledge and money our schools have, how else could they be failing so?"

"C'mon, Joab," Nita began, but he cut her off.

"Now, Babe, just try and forget everything you've heard from the people on our TV and all the things we read in the paper and look at what you know, first hand. There has never been a nation smarter or richer than we are. No country spends as much on education as we do. Why do our kids do worse every year? I'll tell you, Anita, I keep asking that question and asking it. I think Cummings was telling the truth. He was drunk, but he was telling the truth. And I'll tell you what else, malice or incompetence, the poorer children of this nation are sinking in ignorance and the government is either unwilling or unable to pull them out. It's time for parents to take it back."

Anita wasn't sure whether it was malice or incompetence, but she did agree with her husband that, in the final analysis, it didn't matter. School clinics were taking more liberty with their daughter and sex education classes were becoming impossible to opt out of, even for the very young. After Cinda's rape, Joab and Anita were united in their determination to preserve what was left of their daughter's innocence and childhood. If it took an educational revolution to get Cinda to the physical and emotional safety of St. Paul's, Anita was prepared to ride beside her husband as he led the charge.

Once home, Joab handed out Webster buttons, t-shirts, and souvenirs to his daughters, with much less enthusiasm than he would have imagined twenty-four hours earlier. Anita had the house mostly boxed up and a U-haul on standby for the following Monday. Grandma Ruth was coming to pick up the girls on Sunday so Anita could make the drive home to Savannah in the truck with her husband.

After a family dinner that evening, Joab called Charlie Keylar.

"Hey, Mrs. Keylar," he said. "This is Joab. I'm sorry to call you at home, but can I speak to your husband... if he's not busy?"

"Sure, sure," came her cordial response, "I can tell you, he's looking forward to having some help in the office. We can't wait until y'all get back here."

"You and Nita both," he laughed.

There was a brief silence after Joab told Charlie about his cocktails with Cummings.

"Well, Joab," Charlie finally said, "I think it's time to start talking to the press.

"I think it's time to change parties."

"That might be true, too," Charlie laughed, "but if you start sounding like a conservative, and you've been sounding more like one every day, don't expect a positive spin from the press. Give an interview to anyone who will listen and spell your name right. Stick to the foundational issues that won the case for us. Go on and call *The Chronicle* first thing in the morning. Let's get this case out in front of the public."

"Yes, sir," Joab said, "It'll be my pleasure!"

"You know, Neet," Joab observed, that night in the dark, "I thought Mr. Keylar was being over-dramatic when he told me this might be a wild ride. Now, I'm not so sure. We might be in for a lot of attention. It won't all be good. You gonna be okay?"

"Yeah," she answered, her voice clear and confident, "You just go on and do whatever it takes. Don't worry about me."

"Good for him!" Judge Dowling commented while reading the Sunday paper over breakfast.

"What, Dear?" his wife enquired, pouring him a second cup of decaf.

"Ah, this kid, Joab—school voucher case—"

"I remember."

"He finally gave an interview. Listen to this, quote,

'The core of our case is this; Secular Humanism is as much a religion as Buddhism or Islam. Our government has been using public education to indoctrinate our children into Secular Humanism and that's a clear violation of our constitutional rights. It's also an assault on the separation of church and state.

Religion-free education is unattainable. We've tried. We've failed. It can't be done. All I want to do is exercise my right as a parent, to choose what religion my girls will be raised in and what code of morality they will be expected to adhere to.'

Mrs. Dowling stood behind her husband, reading over his shoulder. "He sounds very articulate."

"Just graduated from law school. He's good. And he's right. Got the NEA mad as hornets. He's triggered their self-preservation instinct. They'll come at him with everything they've got and make the Democrats earn every nickel of union donations ever made to the National Committee. I wish there was more I could do. It's out of my hands now."

His wife kissed the top of his bald head before setting down the coffee pot.

◆ ◆ ◆

Predictably, Joab's letter of termination was waiting when he got home. He didn't care. His government contract provided that his family's health coverage would remain up to a full year after he left the governor's employment. The clause had been Mr. Keylar's suggestion and Anita remained assured of fine care for the birth of their third child.

Shameeka spent the night visiting with Cinda and the following day, the little girls parted amid gushing tears when Ruth appeared to drive her grand-daughters back to their family home on the outskirts of Savannah. After the departure, Loretta and her son arrived to help finish up the packing.

While wrapping newspaper around a picture frame, Loretta asked, "You think I could find a good job in Savannah?"

"Sure!" Anita answered enthusiastically.

"Well, there's not much to keep me here, and I think it might be good to put a little distance between my kids and their father."

"I'll keep an eye on the want ads, and Joab will keep his ears open. I'm sure we can find something. You really think you would?"

Loretta nodded and Anita squealed as she gave her a hug.

The phone and electricity were not due to be disconnected until the following Monday. That evening, over pizza, Joab received a call from a local radio talk show and a local TV show. The U-haul remained parked in the driveway for an extra 24 hours while Joab made the time to do the interviews.

Anita's heart raced as a tape slowly recorded her husband's voice coming through the radio.

"Good morning, Atlanta!" said the host over the familiar notes of his lead-in music. "You're tuned in to the *Neal Boortz Radio Show*, and this is Neal Boortz. We've got a great show coming at y'all today. Our guest, this morning, is involved in a lawsuit which just might impact a great number of our young Americans. Stay tuned for an interview with Joab Johnson." There were a series of commercials, and then he was back. Anita lay on the living room floor beside the large, portable stereo. They were the only two objects in the room.

Boortz: Now, Joab, you're currently involved in a lawsuit that you're hoping will compel the government to pay for your children's private education—the voucher."

Joab: That's correct.

Boortz: What are your chances of winning?

Joab: We've already won on the trial court level. Of course, the National Education Association and the American Teachers Federation filed their appeal before the ink was dry on our ruling. They're only stalling the inevitable. Public education, as it exists, is in violation of the constitutional rights of every parent, but nothing's been done because it's only the children of the poor who are trapped in it. Affluent parents have always been able to escape public education. And the free market has let *them* hold private institutions accountable for genuine results. But the children of the poor are herded into public schools for social experiments that continue to fail.

Boortz: Those are pretty strong words.

Joab: Look, I'm not against the teachers. There are plenty of good teachers and they all have a tough job. I'm not talking about them. It's the federal, state, and union control of education that my suit addresses. Education should be accountable to parents, not the government. After all, we're the ones that love the kids. We see them every day, and know what's best for them.

Boortz: I understand you would choose a parochial school for your children. What's your response to the separation-of-church-and-state crowd?

Joab: They're actually on our side, only they don't know it yet. Look. Learning is work, right? All normal kids would rather play. So, in order to make them work, principles of discipline need to be employed and enforced.

Boortz: Normal *adults* would rather play.

Joab: The problem is that all discipline goes back to a moral code and all moral codes have their roots in religion. The disciplinary codes now being imposed on the vast majority of public school kids are rooted in the religion of Secular Humanism. Does that sound like the separation of church and state to you? It sounds like state-sponsored religious indoctrination to me, to my lawyer, Charles Keylar, and to one federal judge, so far.

Boortz: C'mon, humanism is a philosophy, not a religion.

Joab: According to the U.S. Supreme Court Secular Humanism is a religion. And here's the point. Religion-free education is a myth. It always has been. Somewhere around 95 percent of all Americans consider themselves "spiritual." So, someone's convictions are always going to be imposed on our kids because all people have them. Money made it possible for my mother to send me to a school that agreed with her convictions. I don't have that option. As a parent who pays taxes, I should.

Boortz: Okay, stay right there. We'll be back after this commercial break, with Joab Johnson, school choice advocate. . . (six commercials). . . Okay, this is Neal Boortz and we're back with school choice advocate, Joab Johnson. For the sake of argument, Joab, we've invested billions in education; why not just fix what's broke?

Joab: Exactly! And that's what the free market does. Right now, there's no accountability because education exists as a government monopoly. The free market is ruthless but efficient. It's really just natural selection in the marketplace - survival of the fittest. Companies that produce, thrive. Those that don't, fail. That's why I can say that I'm all for the teacher. The ones who are good at what they do should welcome the free-market. They stand to benefit greatly. They'll always enjoy job security, just like lawyers who win cases, and talk-show hosts who pull in listeners. That's the genius of the free market; it nurtures results, while it weeds out failure. The only people fighting this are government and educational bureaucrats who have sold our kids out for benefits and job security. And teachers who can't teach? They need to find something else to do, anyway.

Boortz: You're never gonna win the bleeding hearts with rhetoric like that.

Joab: (laughing) Look, I'm a compassionate guy. I'm full of compassion. I really am. Only my compassion is for the kids. The system has sold them out. If I don't fight for my kids, who will?

Boortz: Well, that's about it for our time. Is there anything else you'd like to say before the break?

Joab: I'd just like to say that accountability is the key to education. But accountability is essential *on both sides*. When private schools can finally receive tax vouchers, Those schools must retain the right to reject students who refuse to meet their disciplinary or scholastic standards. Otherwise, the government will use the voucher as an excuse to dictate policy to the private sector, and we'll be worse off than we are today. Parents must win *full* control. Government has challenged parents for our own kids! It's time to make 'em back away from our children.

Boortz: So, what happens to kids who are troublemakers or not as smart? How does the voucher address them?

Joab: That's the beauty of the free market! As needs arise, so will the institutions that address those needs. Military schools or institutions set up to handle discipline problems will be supported. Schools or programs specially tailored for ADD or ADHD students will fill the void. Believe me; the market will not leave those vouchers, uncashed, in the pockets of the parents. As a result standards will rise as schools compete for that money. It's not like this is some mystical theory. It's the economic machine that produced America's wealth in the first place.

Boortz: I agree, but it's still gonna be a tough sell.

Joab: Look, man, I'm not saying it's going to be easy. It's going to require a heck of a lot more effort from parents. They'll need to seek out or even create schools to meet the needs of their kids. Then, they're going to have to pay attention and hold those schools accountable for results. But, you know, as a dad, that's my job. We've been leaving it up to the government too long and our kids are paying the price. Parents who are unwilling to put in the effort to make sure their kids are well-educated need to ask themselves why they had kids in the first place.

Boortz: You don't mince words, do ya? Well, I'm way over time for the break. We've been talking to the outspoken Joab Johnson, school choice advocate, headed for the United States Supreme Court. Thanks for being with us today and good luck.

Joab: Any time. Thanks for having me.

Boortz: Next on Atlanta Sunrise, your calls and suggestions on how to improve public transit in our great city. Right after this . . .

Anita pressed the button and stopped recording, rewound and played it back. For the first time, she began to understand why she had to reject welfare. Her husband could never have gone before the public, could never have engaged in this battle, if his children had remained dependents of the government.

Joab's interview with Boortz was followed by one for a local news show. By the time Joab's key got to the front door, Anita had listened to his radio interview seven times. Joab said he didn't know when they would air the TV show, but expected they would let him know and send him a videotape.

The couple ordered Chinese take-out for dinner which they ate while sitting on the floor. Afterwards, Anita spread out pillows and blankets and they made love to the sound of classic Motown in an almost empty house.

The U-haul pulled out of the driveway, and by 8:00AM. Atlanta, Emory, Martin Luther King, Jr. Elementary, Domestic Cleaning Services, and The Education Governor were soon shrinking away in the rear-view mirrors.

Chapter 25

Joab felt an inexplicable joy as his U-haul approached his boyhood home. Anita felt it, too. She slid across the bench seat, and pressed close to her husband, placing her left hand on his thigh. Her back was straight, her head high, and her lips drawn into the crescent of a smile as her eyes took in the welcomed sights of childhood. The Johnsons were returning after what seemed like many hard miles. Gone were the youthful delusions of cheap glory. The couple who returned had known defeat, as well as the quiet pride of a costly victory.

Bright anticipation gripped Joab and Anita as they turned onto the dirt road that led to Big Mama's—*their* house. Dust rose up behind the truck. Long clumps of Spanish moss swished once as it passed by. A doe, startled from her daylight rest, jumped to her feet, hoisted the warning of her white tail, and bounded into the underbrush from which she watched them go by. Joab slowed at the inlet. As ever, a shrimp boat bobbed across the blue green waters with all the urgency of a snail.

All at once, the wax myrtles came to an end and there was the Ancient Johnson Oak, gnarled, stately, deeply rooted and presiding over another generation. It covered the barefooted daughters with shade and protected their play from the mighty summer sun. They swung on its tire; Cinda sitting on top and Mandy curled through the middle with her feet pulled up. Both ran for the truck as it came to a stop. Ruth stood up from her chair on the porch where she had been watching her babies while waiting for their parents. The screen door slammed when Miss Lucy appeared. She nearly shrieked as she descended the porch steps, ignoring the thick heat. The next moment Anita was enveloped in an exuberant and sticky bear hug.

"My baby's home! My baby's home!" she exclaimed.

Then she backed up a step and placed a hand on the swell of Nita's belly.

"Ya feelin' any kickin' yet?" she asked.

"Started a few days ago," Anita smiled.

Miss Lucy's eyes were still streaming when she ran around the car to greet her son-in-law; he with the grinning Cinda astride his wide shoulders.

"Thanks for bringing her back to me," she said, "for bringing them all back."

Joab considered the possibility that this woman really had forgiven his transgressions against her daughter.

Ruth was last in line. "Welcome home, son," she said, "Welcome home."

"Your Mama's got some big news, Joab!" Lucy blurted out. "Go on, look at her left hand," she whispered to Anita.

"C'mon, Mom, let's see," Anita coaxed.

Almost embarrassed, Ruth displayed the diamond solitaire.

"JC?" Anita asked.

Ruth nodded and exploded in a rare burst of laughter. "Can you believe it? Me, a bride—after all these years!"

"Congratulations, Mama!" Joab said, genuinely pleased. "JC's a fine man."

"Thank you."

"What? What?" Cinda urged, still on her father's shoulders.

"You remember Mr. JC?" Anita asked. "Well, him and Grandma Ruth will be getting married, and he's gonna be your grandpa."

"All right!" the child responded. "Can I be the flower girl this time?"

✦ ✦ ✦

The days ahead were pleasant for the Johnsons. While Anita nested Big Mama's house, the little girls enjoyed the freedom of wide-open outdoor play and the discovery of neighbors and kin alike. At his office, Joab was learning the difference between theory and practice from his mother and his boss.

Occasionally, a local newspaper or magazine called for an interview. In compliance with ethics rules, Charlie refused any comment on the pending suit but strongly encouraged Joab to agree to every one of them.

"And don't forget, that's K-E-Y-L-A-R," he would tease Joab before each interview.

Joab was a little surprised by the pervasiveness of bias in print media. Conservatives tended to support his cause while liberals opposed it vehemently. Joab also learned the difference between the meaning of the words "editing" and "censorship." Basically, there was no difference except that of conviction. "Editing" was when your publication refused to print material which would strengthen an opposing position. "Censorship" was when *another* publication refused to print material which would strengthen *your* position. Joab was outraged, at first, but Charlie showed little surprise.

"Shake it off, Joab," he admonished, "Just take 'em as they come."

Still, Joab found it hard to get past the sting of a particularly personal attack by a Savannah-based magazine published by and for African-Americans living in the Lowcountry.

"If won," the article had stated, "Johnson's misguided crusade would nullify many of the hard earned victories born of the Civil Rights Movement. With one Supreme Court decision, the gates to re-segregation and white-flight could be thrown wide open and the path to equal access to education destroyed. As the greed of the free market inflates the cost of education, children of parents with the deepest pockets would still go to the best schools while the condition of the poorer institutions would erode completely. Only under the strictest codes of affirmative action and the tightest possible federal controls could such a system spell anything but disaster for our community. Johnson opposes both. Let us pray that the next president of the United States, Amos Webster, will continue to oppose such divisive and regressive schemes and that the voices of those like 'Brother' Joab Johnson will remain on the fringe of our culture. Joab had read the words with a heavy heart.

Joab was stunned. The man who had done the interview had given no indication of such venom. *How could he fail to recognize that "the tightest possible federal control" and "free market" are, in fact, mutually exclusive? The suggestion was like saying; let's fix the problem by applying the problem to the private sector, too.*

And something about "affirmative action" didn't pass the gut check, either. As Joab churned inwardly the reasons came to him: *Affirmative action sends the same message as welfare, only worse. Welfare presupposes the failure of fathers as providers for their offspring and the endorsement of a welfare check constitutes a personal declaration, by the mother, that the father of their child is, in fact, non-essential to her family—expendable. How can any American man seek respect in the face of such potent and justifiable undercurrents of social condemnation?*

Affirmative action carries that same condemnation out of the home and into the workplace. No matter how carefully the words are chosen, or how passionately the talking heads try to pin it on an omnipresent bigotry – a bigotry whose roots had been severed by the judiciary and denied regrowth by the legal system – the real message of affirmative action always comes through: people of "certain ethnic races" can not compete on an equal footing with white men. Standards have to be lowered, exceptions made, in order to compensate for their inherent inferiority on college campuses and in the workplace. It is here that the dying roots of racial tensions are nurtured to new life by leaders like Jesse Jackson who cram quotas down the throats of American universities and businesses until the God-given abilities of every non-white are called into question. In the end, the wholesome pride of achievement is swindled from the individual in the condescending assumption that skin color, not competence, got the scholarship; got the job... Joab was finding his message.

It was after the publication of this article that Anita first sensed a social chill and Joab's first piece of hate-mail arrived, unsigned. Even at church, where Ruth was so loved and respected, there was a subtle tension. Miss Lucy was the obvious choice for those who wished to air their disappointment at Joab's flagrant affront to black unity—"and at such a critical point in American history." No one was bold enough to approach Ruth—or JC, for that matter.

Miss Lucy would immediately turn around and complain to her daughter, "I know it's nobody's business if Joab is a Republican (she spoke the word with obvious disdain) and is gonna vote against Webster. That's his right. But why, in the world, does he have to tell everybody about it?!"

"I don't know, Mama;" Anita would answer, "it's just in him." It was the only way she could think to explain it in a way her mother might understand.

"Ya know, it ain't gonna be long 'fo the kids at school are gonna say somethin' to the girls," Miss Lucy would continue. Anita worried more about her mother.

One day Susan Keylar put in an excited call to her husband. "Turn on your radio, Charlie, to A.M. 630! He's talking about our case!"

Computer screens froze and Dictaphones fell silent as everyone in the office gathered 'round Ruth's radio to hear the king of Conservative Talk Radio give a full five-minute commentary on *Doe vs. School Board* – with half his brain tied behind his back.

"This case makes a very interesting point," he said, "Look, we all know that something like ninety-eight percent of all humanity, everywhere, consider themselves spiritual or religious on some level. We know there's media bias. There's bias in everything. Why can't we just acknowledge that all people have convictions and that those convictions are going to filter out in one form or another? No big deal. If worldview bias is inevitable in the media culture, why can't we just admit that worldview bias is just as inevitable in education? Look, someone's worldview is getting crammed into those little skulls full of mush. Most of the time it's not the worldview of

the parent. It should be, though, my friends, it *should* be. . .
Back after this with a feminist update. Wait till you hear this
one, folks. You won't believe it. Don't go away."

"Well, he nailed it," Joab observed.

"You know, I always thought that man was too arrogant to
abide, but I've got to admit, he's got a knack for getting down
to the core issues," Charlie said, smiling. "It's getting out
there."

✦ ✦ ✦

Seemingly overnight, Joab became the toast of the talk
radio circuit. Anita recorded every interview, and the audio
cassettes began to pile up. It was in the safety and shelter of
like-minded radio hosts that Joab's message began to expand.
It was here, too, fielding phone calls, that Joab learned to think
on his feet. . .

Host: Hello? Brian from New Bedford, you're on the air
with Joab Johnson, school voucher advocate.

Caller: Hello, Mr. Johnson?

Joab: Yes, Brian. What's on your mind?

Caller: My wife's a sixth grade teacher, and I can tell you
she's very dedicated. I think public education is just getting a
bad rap. There's a lot our school system here, in New Bedford,
does right.

Joab: I'll say it again, I have nothing against teachers. I have
the utmost respect for most of them and if your wife is as
competent as you say she is, she should welcome the free
market. So should her school! Any institution that delivers a
stellar education should have nothing to fear from a little
competition. The good ones will do fine. I do take issue with
union bureaucrats turning American education into
something approaching an entitlement program or politicians
who make great speeches about fixing the system while
sending their kids to private schools. Enough is enough, man.
It's time to demand the same choice and opportunities their
kids have. Heck, it's our tax money. Why is it such an
outrageous concept for us to decide where to spend it? After
all, they are our kids, aren't they? . . Hey, Joan in Houston.

Caller: Hey, Mr. Johnson. Thanks for taking my call. My question to you is: What about the parents who don't have the time to be as involved as you? I'm a single mom with no support from my children's father. There are a lot of us out here and there is no time!

Joab: How many kids do you have, Joan?

Caller: Three.

Joab: Wow. I still marvel at the guts and dedication of the single parent. My wife was a single parent for almost two years, and I have a good idea of what an incredibly difficult and relentless job it is. But at the risk of sounding insensitive, I still have to say that I have to do what I think is best for *my* kids. I'm just an ordinary guy trying to take my family back from the government. They're *my* kids. In order for the free market to work well, parents are just going to have to pay closer attention. Our kids can't afford the luxury of our apathy anymore. Kids that have the best odds of growing up to be healthy and productive adults, who stay out of the ditches, are kids with two parents. That's not my opinion. It's not my fault. It's just a fact. That tells me that the real safety net for children is the family. Today, more kids of African-American heritage will be born in a fatherless household than those who won't. And the white community is catching up with us. Why? Because our government has adopted policies to bankroll the break-up of the family.

"They were giving my daughter self-esteem classes in the first grade. My daughter had low self-esteem. Do you know why? Because she thought her daddy had abandoned her. Now, if she knew, in her heart, that she held no value to her own father, what kind of class is going to be able to make her whole? Well, her Daddy's back and her Daddy's staying. I know which school is the best one to meet her needs. If I have to fight the government to let me send her there, then that's in my job description, too. A government that prevents fathers from doing right by their kids because of the fathers who won't, is a government in need of correction. They need a better plan.

Host: Donna, in St. Paul. . . Donna, are you there?

Caller: Yes. Hello. I have a comment for Mr. Johnson.

Joab: Fine. Go ahead.

Caller: I'm a single mother of an eight-year-old son. His father was physically and verbally abusive, and I bless the day he walked out of our lives. I work about sixty hours a week just to get us by. Now just where do you think I'm going to find the time for "accountability sessions" at school? I can barely get the time off for quarterly teacher's conferences as it is.

Joab: Look, Donna, I'm truly sorry you and your son had such an unfortunate experience. I believe there is no tougher job than raising kids by yourself, because it's a job that was designed for two. But the fact remains that parents have a tough decision to make: do we want our schools to warehouse our kids, or are we going to demand an education that equips them to succeed in a competitive world and provide them with some parameters of acceptable behavior?

It was at this point that the social temperatures surrounding the Johnsons plummeted into a deep frost. Joab was rapidly realizing how real the culture war was. He thought the term an understatement and was increasingly thankful for the safe haven of extended family and the strength of his wife under increasing community ostracism. The Keylars, too, formerly considered enlightened liberals, were experiencing their own degrees of frostbite from neighbors and friends.

Charlie kept a steady paycheck coming to the Johnsons in spite of the expanding amount of time Joab spent away from the office. "Publicity expense," he teased.

Inevitably, Joab attracted the attention of TV talk shows where he discovered the third dimension of media bias.

On one occasion a perky, little reporter-type finished up a pretty routine interview with a detour: "Setting the voucher issue aside for a moment, I'd like to touch on another subject." Joab sensed an ambush. "I understand that you divorced your wife during which time she was forced to go on welfare, yet some of your statements, here and elsewhere, imply a disdain for government entitlement. What would you tell our viewers who may be asking what alternative she had?" The woman maintained a cordial and expectant expression, as though she were genuinely interested in his answer and was oblivious to the trap she had just set. The real question was this: *After you abandoned your family, would you have had them starve as well?*

Joab shifted on his stool. He did not wish to set blame on Anita. The perky, little reporter-type thought she smelled blood.

"Uh, well, my wife and I got married while we were in high school and we had our first daughter right away. We were under tremendous financial pressure and my wife was courageous in her efforts to support our family while I attended college. But looking back, I think we could have made it without a welfare check and, in fact, would probably never have divorced."

At this the reporter-type furrowed her eyebrows and consulted her notes. "But weren't you having an affair at the time your wife left you?" She tilted her head to receive his answer out of the side of her eyes. Snap! Set and sprung. The question the curious viewers heard was this: *Isn't welfare wonderful for enabling such a selfless woman as your wife to rid herself of such a slimy, low-life, scumbag of a typical male like you?*

Joab never liked being cornered. "Look, Ms. Sturgeon, I will not be drawn into a defense which pits me against my wife. I will say that we were both young, and we both made mistakes. But the test of wisdom is not whether we make mistakes, but whether or not we learn from them. What I have learned is this; my kids need their Dad and welfare pays for Dad's to walk."

Anita watched in her living room with her stomach in knots, relieved that she had put her daughters to bed early and apprehensive that their schoolmates would discover the nationally televised ammunition against their father. For the Johnsons, the culture war had drawn blood.

That night, on the phone from Atlanta, Joab promised Anita that he would not accept any more TV engagements where they did not commit to stick to the subject of school choice and the pending lawsuit.

The next morning, Anita's mother dropped by for a cup of coffee.

"Did you see Joab on TV last night?" Anita asked.

"Yeah, I sho' did," Miss Lucy lamented. "And yesterday Miss Agnes a'ksed me if I was gonna vote against Amos Webster like my son-in-law."

"What'd ya tell her?"

"I told her I'd vote for him as soon as he put *his* kids in public school."

"Get out," Nita laughed.

"No. I did. I swear."

"Yeah?"

"And I will, too. I've been thinkin', Nita, and I've been thinkin' maybe Joab's right. . . And maybe things would have turned out different for Nicky if he'd had a daddy to stay around. Maybe he wouldn't a been so mad all the time. . ."

"Ya did the best you could, Mama."

"Yeah." There was a long pause. It was pushing two years since anyone had heard from Nicholas.

"Hey, Mama! They're doing the ultrasound next Friday. Joab's comin', and we're takin' the girls out of school early. Ya wanna come? They might be able to tell us if it's a boy or a girl."

"Sure. Sure. They didn't have those things when I was big with you. It's a strange thing to peek in on a baby's secrets."

✦ ✦ ✦

On Friday, Joab placed his usual call from the office to see if his notification had arrived from the bar.

"Not yet, Babe," Nita lied, "Just the usual bills and the normal love/hate mail. How do these people get our address?"

"I don't know," Joab responded, "but they got the one at the office, too. . . I guess I'll be home around 7:00. See ya later."

"Joab Samuel Johnson!" Anita reprimanded, "This is the day of my ultrasound! Have you forgotten?"

"Oh yeah, yeah." Joab jumped in, "I can go. I can go. What time are you coming?"

"The girls and I will be there at about 3:00 and we can't be late now."

As soon as Anita hung up with her husband, she put in a call to Charlie.

✦ ✦ ✦

Around 2:30 Charlie's secretary buzzed Joab's desk. "Joab, Charlie would like to see you in the large conference room."

When Joab opened the door, there stood Charlie, Ruth, Anita, Cinda, Mandy, Miss Lucy, and the rest of the office staff.

"Daddy!" Mandy said, and ran to beat Cinda to the hug.

"Hey girls!" he said, patting their backs, "Anita, aren't you early?" he asked, checking his watch awkwardly. There was a single piece of paper lying on the end of the long table before him. Joab followed Anita's eyes to it.

"Is that it?" he asked.

She nodded.

"Did I make it?" he asked.

She nodded and the whole room broke out with shouts of laughter and congratulations. Anita had brought a bottle of champagne, and everyone toasted to the new associate in coffee mugs. Cinda, Mandy, and their mother, had Sprite

An hour and a half later, Anita lay on a table in a small room with her personal entourage all around. Everyone faced a TV on a high shelf in one corner of the room. Anita's shirt was pulled up above the swell of her belly and she tried not to think of the fullness of her bladder which pushed the baby into a better position for picture-taking, but which made it hard to concentrate. The technician explained the procedure to the children, popped the video cassette into the slot under the TV screen and pressed "record." Then she squeezed some clear goop onto Nita's tummy and placed the scanner in the goop. At once, a grainy, indiscernible, black and white image appeared on the screen.

"The picture comes from sound waves, not radiation," The technician explained. "It is harmless to the baby." Then she turned the light out. All stared at the rolling shadows passing on the screen as the scanner slid across Anita's belly.

What picture? Cinda thought.

"Oops. There we go," The technician commented.

All at once, the baby appeared. Approaching the end of the second trimester, it was very well-formed.

"See?" the technician continued, "There's the head." A drawn circle appeared around the head like a football commentator's notes. "And there's the heart." A heart appeared around a small area that was steadily pulsating.

"It's sucking its thumb!" Cinda exclaimed.

"That's right!" The technician agreed.

The image was surprisingly clear. The baby was extremely animated. It pulled its hand away from its mouth, kicked its legs, and opened its jaws wide.

"What's it doing?" Joab asked.

"They like to gulp amniotic fluid," the technician explained, obviously enjoying her work. "Would you like to know what it is?"

"Only if you're sure," Anita said.

"Well, you're never really sure until they arrive."

"How long have you been doing this?" Joab enquired.

"About nine years."

"Nine years, huh? How many times have you been wrong?"

"Three times, I think."

"Okay, go on and tell us," Anita said. Joab took her hand and started administering "the grip".

"Well . . . he's got all the right parts to be a boy."

"A boy!" the couple repeated. Joab kissed Anita's forehead.

"I wanted a girl," Mandy whined.

"Oh, now, a baby brother is just as good as a baby sister," Miss Lucy assured. "The important thing is, he gets here safe."

Mandy would need more convincing but Cinda was sure Grandma Lucy was right.

"A son." Joab said in awe.

"Babe. . . Babe, you're breaking my fingers." Anita whispered. Joab released them.

"How does he look?" Joab asked, while the technician clicked off all kinds of measurements.

"He looks great! Right on track. Late December, right?"

"That's right," Anita answered.

✦ ✦ ✦

In the next month, Joab did several public speaking engagements which he enjoyed greatly. He liked the connection with the public. His favorite had been as one of a host of conservative speakers at a "Road to Victory Rally" in Washington, DC sponsored by the Christian Coalition. Not being a religious zealot, Joab was a bit surprised at the invitation and the warm welcome he'd received.

His last engagement, before the November elections, was at his college alma mater, and he was looking forward to it with great anticipation.

"Come with me, Neet," Joab asked on a whim, "It will be fun to go back."

"Oh, Joab, I don't know."

"C'mon. Your mother can watch the girls. Duke's putting me up in a nice hotel and it will be one of our last chances to relax together before the baby comes."

"I don't know, Babe. . . I kind of hate to be away from the hospital this far along."

"A hospital? Duke's got one of the finest hospitals in the country."

Anita rolled her eyes. "I'll call Mama in the morning."

As an alumnus of Duke, Joab had refused any fee for his time; however, he was not shy about asking for a second plane ticket for his wife. The university was delighted to provide one.

Anita had never flown before and she was visibly nervous during take-off. The sky was overcast and drizzling as she leaned close to the tiny window. She watched beads of rain turn into thin, horizontal streaks as the aircraft gained speed. The baby squirmed within and she released one arm rest to lay a hand on her belly. Then the earth fell away. The city diminished and disappeared in fog. Like magical special effects in a Spielberg movie, the plane ascended into a sunny day.

"Wow," Anita whispered, "We're looking down at the clouds."

Eventually, they broke up into gigantic, puffy formations, flat on the bottom, as though they all sat on the same glass shelf. They appeared so dense and tangible, on the way down it seemed strange to fly through them rather than around them. Anita began holding her breath at about a thousand feet and did not stop until the craft surrendered its rebellion to gravity.

The Johnsons made a connection in the vast Atlanta airport and hopped a 737 to Raleigh/Durham where the University had a rental car waiting. There was no hurry. Joab wasn't speaking until 7:00PM.

"How about a drive past Shady Oaks?" Joab suggested.

"Okay," Nita agreed, brightly.

It was a beautiful day for a drive, cold and crisp. The roll and twist of the road gave Joab a brief pang of longing for his old bike. Bubba had expanded the trailers into a second field. Other than that, the place looked the same. Anita was a little disappointed to see that her shrubs were unattended and grown up in weeds, but not surprised. An unfamiliar Toyota pick-up was parked outside of Tiesha's.

Joab was careful to avoid Lesa's old neighborhood on his way to the hotel. Once checked-in, a bellboy carried Nita's over-night case as he led them to their suite. Nita felt pampered and rich. The couple had a quick shower, changed into more formal clothes, and enjoyed an early dinner in the hotel restaurant, compliments of Duke. Then it was on to the campus.

Joab's itinerary indicated that he was to report to the Dean's reception room, in the main administrative hall, where he would be greeted by a faculty member from the Political Science Department. It was early evening. The building was mostly deserted. A secretary apologized for Dean Lawrick's absence but said he hoped to meet Joab later. In his four years at Duke, Joab had never been to the Dean's office. He was impressed. Mahogany paneling, Persian carpets over marble floors, and many old, leather-bound books. It had the classic appeal of intellect and success. Joab and Anita stood before the window to take in a stunning view of the campus. Joab's heart sank when he turned around to discover Professor Glenda Blackwell.

"Hey, Ms. Blackwell," he said, extending a hand and forcing a smile.

"Well, well, Mr. Johnson, Governor Cummings must have put the polish on you! I hear you were quite an asset to his administration."

Did Joab detect the raw edge of sarcasm? "Ms, Blackwell, this is my wife, Anita," he said.

"So nice to meet you – finally." Blackwell responded, "When is your baby due?"

"Late December. It's a boy," Anita offered nervously.

"A son. Isn't that nice. Congratulations, Joab. What does that make, four or five now?

"Three. Only three."

"Well, Joab, I hear you've become conservative in your old age," Blackwell teased pointedly. "I'd have thought Liz and I would have trained you better than that."

Joab forced a laugh. He didn't like talking about Liz Straddlethorp. His connection to her was too close to his connection to Lesa. Maybe it hadn't been such a good idea to bring Anita. He wondered if Blackwell was malicious enough to bring up Lesa in front of his pregnant wife. She took her politics very seriously and he was suddenly facing her from the enemy camp. She had been intimidating enough from the same side. He wondered if Blackwell was aware of the tiny beads of sweat appearing around his temples. He half-suspected she got a strange satisfaction from making people sweat.

"Oh, how is Sen. Straddlethorp these days?" he asked. There was no way around the question.

"Great! Great. I had lunch with her the other day. She's working hard on the Webster campaign. You know how that goes. You know, Joab, she often talks about that first campaign. She said you have a natural way with people."

Enough of that. Joab cut her off. "How's Professor Morse doing? I was hoping to see him on this trip."

"Oh, he's fine, far as I know. He's on sabbatical. I'm sure he'll be sorry he missed you."

"Oh." That was disappointing. "I hope you'll give him my warmest regards when he returns."

"Well, Joab, I have been given the proud honor of introducing you tonight. Just let me fill in your bio and then we'll walk over and do a sound check, okay? We have arranged for a faculty reception following final questions this evening. The Dean is most anxious to meet you. "

Just before they opened the doors, Joab got Anita a Sprite and she took a seat on the front row. Joab was given a podium but he carried a wireless mike and was free to move about the stage. There was a standing microphone at the front of the center aisle for student questions at the end. Media sent over a film crew.

Soon, Joab and Glenda Blackwell stood in the wings of the stage, listening to the hum and shuffle of people finding their seats.

"You know, Joab," Ms. Blackwell whispered, "I find your condemnation of affirmative action a little surprising since you yourself were one of its beneficiaries."

Joab had brought no notes and all the words he intended to say evaporated in his mind. *No!* his brain protested, every thought defensive, *If I ever **earned** anything in my life, I earned my degree!* Sweat broke out on his forehead as memories sped through his brain and he struggled not to appear like a wounded puppy. His years at Duke had been the toughest in his life. His diploma had been no gift. A younger man, a student, may have been crushed. But a younger man would not have been trained in political manipulation by Scott Houghton. Joab went back to what he **knew** that he knew.

"And tell me, Glenda," Joab's words were hushed but clear, "What was your SAT cut-off for *non*-minority students back when I got accepted? Fourteen? Fourteen-five? You might need to check the records. I think they may have had to lower the standards for *white boys* the year I got in."

Joab's old mentor wished she *had* broached the subject of Lesa in front of his wife. There was no explanation for the contempt she felt for this man. Glenda Blackwell had no respect for men she could intimidate, but she despised those she could not.

Joab's introduction was nice enough, but with little flourish. Anita thought she would die when Blackwell asked her to stand. Her palms were moist as her husband entered the stage. Anita had never actually seen him speak, live, before. He was extremely handsome in his lawyer's uniform and she was very proud to be his wife, though she could have done without the public acknowledgment.

Joab started by recounting a few fond and amusing memories of his time at the university. Then, he gave an overview of *Doe vs School Board* and the reasons for the trial victory. He did not mince words, but gave a blistering indictment of the NEA and the wretched state of public education. To his surprise his remarks were well-received and affirmed by applause.

"I believe we'll win the appellate court battles, too." he said, "because the system still works and the intellectual and moral upbringing of children is the rightful responsibility of parents, not government. It has clearly overstepped the boundaries of a free society and it will be corrected. But that's not really what I wanted to say to you today. Through this suit, I have discovered a broader message and one whose time has come.

"I'm not much older than y'all. Maybe a few years. We were raised in a time when it is assumed that women will compete with men and can expect equal pay for equal work. And that's a good thing. Every American deserves to live up to their potential. I have two daughters and, in fact, that's why I'm fighting this lawsuit. But it still takes a man and a woman to make a baby, and at the risk of sounding politically incorrect and causing a riot, it still takes a man and a woman to raise one right. My Mama did a pretty good job with me. She worked hard at it, but I still would have liked to have had a dad. Those of you who were raised by a single parent, when you were alone in the dark, in your bed at night, didn't you wish for two parents? I did.

"You know, lately you hear a lot about respect. In my old neighborhood in Atlanta, you can get shot for disrespecting somebody, 'cause they think they can demand it like they have a right to it, or something. But you can't demand respect. You can't take it by violence. Because it doesn't come from others. Respect is something a man or woman earns. It's something you walk out day by day. And it's HARD. It means putting up with a boss you hate because you need to feed your kids. It means going home when you deserve a drink with the guys. It means staying faithful to your spouse when opportunity is all around you. It means laying your life down for your family, day in and day out for a lifetime, and it's *hard*. But that's how a person earns respect, and if he does any less, he doesn't deserve it.

"Those are harsh words. Do I say them out of an inflated ego and an overdeveloped sense of self-righteousness? No. I say those words out of humility and conviction because I messed up and I messed up bad. I believed a lie that's been impressed upon our generation. I believed that it takes a village to raise my kids and that my family'd get along fine without me. Only they didn't. In spite of the heroic efforts of my wife. And I want to tell you men something out there: you are not expendable. Your family won't get along fine without you. They will be damaged. They will be exploited and your children will probably grow up to be less than they might have been.

"See? (Joab left the podium and came to the front of the stage.) I'd lost sight of something my Mama knew; your kids are your treasure. And a treasure that's not guarded gets stolen."

Anita could hear the passion in her husband's voice and a lump formed in her throat.

"I know this might sound premature to you and irrelevant to where you are, but what are you doing here if not preparing to give back to the society that gave to you? And isn't the most important part of that equation giving back emotionally whole and healthy children to take your place one day?

"So decide right now to do better than I did; better than most of our parents did. Decide, right now, to be careful where you scatter seed. Commit to plant your seeds in fertile soil—and stay around to help them grow. Because the measure of a man is not in how many seeds he scatters, but how well he nurtures them. Because manhood is not measured by virility, but by fidelity—." Suddenly, there were two startling POPs and Joab wasn't standing anymore.

There were screams, but Anita didn't hear them. She stood to see her husband lying near the edge of the stage. She saw a red patch on the right side of his starched, white shirt and watched in disbelief as a red puddle formed under his navy jacket.

"Joab?" she shouted, panic in her voice.

From behind her, a young woman shouted hysterically, "He'll set us back a hundred years!"

Ms. Blackwell was horrified to recognize the young woman as one of her own students from her Studies in Black Feminism class. She was even more horrified to recognize the student's words as her own. Someone had grabbed the gun out of the student's hand and a large male student held her elbows behind her back. Ms. Blackwell ran for the telephone while Anita tried, pathetically, to climb up on the stage beside her husband, her large belly making it impossible.

"Someone call an ambulance! Someone call an ambulance!" Anita shrieked as she ran across the front of the stage to the stairs.

There were several people around Joab by the time she got there. She knelt beside her husband and pulled his jacket tight around the wound in a futile effort to stop the blood from pouring out of his body. He was not conscious.

"I know CPR," someone said.

"Oh, God. Oh, God. Oh, God," she kept repeating until she heard the sound of an ambulance. Someone pulled her away from him and the paramedics took over.

Anita would not remember the trip to the hospital. Some nurses asked her questions about allergies and medical history. Then the flurry of activity was over as instantly as it had begun and Joab was rolled away. Ms. Blackwell appeared at Anita's elbow, moving her toward a bank of chairs.

"Anita," she said softly, "Is there anyone I can call for you?"

"Um . . ." Anita stared at the floor.

"Is there anyone you would like to call?"

"Um, my mother-in-law."

"Good. Let's go find a phone."

Ms. Blackwell punched in her credit card number and, mechanically, Nita punched in Ruth's number.

"Hello, Mom?" she said. "Yes, something is wrong. Someone shot Joab . . . with a gun. A student, I think. Just shot him . . . No. No word. He's in surgery now . . . No. He wasn't conscious when they took him away, but he was alive. Please come. I need you. Don't tell my mother, yet. Just come."

"Where are you?"

"Duke University Hospital."

"I'll be there very soon."

✦ ✦ ✦

Ruth dialed Charlie's number immediately. He had a business acquaintance with a small plane. In a few moments Charlie called back and said a pilot would be waiting for her at a small airport nearby. Next, Ruth called JC, who insisted on going with her.

Ruth prayed as she packed.

On the way to the airport, J.C. turned on the radio. He had hoped to find some soothing music, but it was 10:00PM and news was on almost every station. "More fighting in Serbia . . . A controversial school choice advocate was shot by a student at Duke University earlier this evening. Joab Johnson was giving a speech when a young woman opened fire." Ruth stared at the radio as she heard her son's voice, " . . . Because manhood is not measured by virility, but by fidelity." Then there were the sounds of two successive shots and screaming. The news reporter finished, "No word yet on the motive for the shooting or Johnson's condition."

"Good God in heaven, Ruth, I'm sorry." JC stammered.

"Pray with me JC." He reached out and took her hand.

Watching Joab's speech in front of a closed circuit TV at his home, Dean Lawrick saw the shooting in real time. He appeared at the hospital, soon after Anita hung up with Ruth.

"Mrs. Johnson," he said, rushing up to Anita after a nurse pointed her out, "I'm Dean Lawrick and I'm terribly sorry. We had no way of knowing— Everything possible is being done for your husband. This is a world-renowned hospital and I can assure you he will receive the finest care. Is there anything I can do?"

Anita shook her head. She turned her eyes inward. The baby was still, probably sleeping. She thought it strange that he could sleep in such turmoil.

"Her mother-in-law is flying up from Savannah," Ms. Blackwell offered.

"Good. Good. Have you been with her the whole time?"

Glenda Blackwell nodded.

"Has anyone offered her a sedative?"

"She won't take anything with the baby."

"The O.R. waiting room is just down the hall. She might be more comfortable down there," he suggested.

"No," Anita protested, weakly, "I want to wait for the doctors and Mom."

"I'll make sure they know where to find you," Lawrick promised.

There was one other family in the waiting room. Headline news droned on in the background, though no one paid any attention. Lawrick sat Anita in a comfortable chair, pulled up another for her feet and got her a Sprite and a blanket. Then there was nothing to do but wait. Anita stared, unblinking, at the carpet. Finally, Ruth and JC arrived. It had been less than two and a half hours since Anita had put in the call.

"Oh, Mom," Anita said, "Thank God you're here."

"Don't get up," Ruth insisted, taking her hands. "Any word?"

Anita shook her head. "He's still in surgery."

"Mrs. Johnson? I'm Vic Lawrick, Dean of the University and this is Glenda Blackwell. She's a former professor of Joab's."

"Pleased to meet you. This is my fiancé, Mr. JC Pinckney."

Vic Lawrick was assuring Ruth of the competence of the medical staff when her ear picked up Joab's voice—"Because manhood is not measured by virility, but by fidelity…"JC, Ruth and Anita looked up at the screen. JC knew what was coming but could not get to the on/off switch in time. Both women watched in horror as Joab went down again. Anita jumped to her feet.

"Oh, God, no!" Ruth held her as the tears finally came. "The children! I can't let our children see this. I have to call my mother."

Lawrick produced a cell phone, and Anita told her mother what had happened and gave her strict orders that the children were not to go to school tomorrow or go near a TV. Miss. Lucy promised.

In Charlie Keylar's study, Headline News replayed Joab's shooting and his final words every half hour. By morning, Charlie knew it would be on every major network as the most emotionally jarring footage since the Rodney King beating. And by noon, roughly half of all Americans would have seen it and news ratings would have taken a little leap. By evening there would be opinions and commentary and hype as the media relished another feeding frenzy.

After three hours, the doctors entered the waiting room to deliver the prognosis. They felt as though they had repaired most of the damage and his chances were fair, but they wouldn't really know until he woke from the coma. The family would be able to see him in the ICU in a few moments.

After the doctors left, Ruth extended her hands to Anita and JC. Anita reached out to Glenda Blackwell, but Glenda backed away.

"I am not a praying woman," she said.

Vic Lawrick bowed his head from where he stood.

"Sweet Jesus," Ruth began, "I gave Joab back to you when he was three years old. I remember the day so clearly . . . So I've always known he belonged to you. But if I've found any favor in your sight, please, don't take him yet, Jesus. Not yet. Give him more time. 'Cause he doesn't know you, yet. And how could we face eternity without him?"

At 4:00 a.m., Susan Keylar coaxed her husband into bed where he would stare at the ceiling until dawn.

"It's not your fault," she told him, "It's just the times we live in."

Outside the main entrance to the hospital, the students and people of Durham gathered to stand vigil.

Chapter 26

Christmas morning, Ruth stood on her porch as the gold and pink clouds of dawn faded into white against a deepening blue sky. It had been a mild winter so far. She heard her husband start the car and rev the engine, warming it up.

It had been full dark when the call came from Miss Lucy. Anita had just arrived at the hospital and the baby would be coming fast.

In warmer months, Ruth often took her coffee on the porch as the sun came up. She wondered if JC would join her this spring. She liked to hear the birds. This morning there was a new sound—a chattering, almost. Ruth looked up to see a half dozen birds settle on a young Sweet Gum nearby. Bright green, they were, with curved-over beaks. The taillights of Ruth's Buick brightened as JC backed out of the carport and waited for her to descend the stairs. As she watched, the small flock took flight and was gone.

Carolina Parakeets? Ruth mused. *Probably some escapees from an exotic bird breeder.* Yet, she wondered . . . *some days, all things seemed possible.*

At 8:03, Joab Samuel Johnson, Jr., was pushed into the light of day. He would become the first son, in four generations of Johnsons, to be raised in a home with his mother *and* his father.

Joab, Sr. cut the cord.

The End

Epilogue

It is said:

The wheels of justice grind slowly, but they grind exceedingly fine.

... And so the wheels turned as <u>*Doe vs. School Board*</u> made its way to the United States Supreme Court. Finally, one bright August day, Lucinda Ruth Johnson, Amanda Nicole Johnson, and Joab Samuel Johnson, Jr. attended their first day of classes at Savannah Christian Academy. With them, the free market re-entered American Education. Their tuition was covered by vouchers. Even so, government's ability to exploit public education as a means to establish a state religion was finally in check.

Authority had returned to its rightful place - the parents.